Praise for *The Earthquake Child*

"A riveting familial rollercoaster, *The Earthquake Child* portrays one mother's determination to raise a child. Bravo to Elayne Klasson for so honestly describing the ripple effects of adoption, for child, birth parents, and adoptive parents. This is a gripping story wrought with emotion and truth."

—JEANNE MCWILLIAMS BLASBERG,
author of *Eden* and *The Nine*

"In Elayne Klasson's new novel, the mother-child relationship takes center stage, but is amplified by the adoption equation. This well-crafted and true-to-life plot involves two mothers and the son they both cherish. It is about love, loss, longing, and the road to becoming whole. *The Earthquake Child* shows the fierceness of a mother's love, the angst of adoption, and the secrets that set individual wants and needs colliding. Whether you are inside the adoption experience or on the outside looking in, Klasson's well-informed novel will leave you thinking. And isn't that what a really good book should do?"

—JULIE RYAN MCGUE, author of *Twice a Daughter:
A Search of Identity, Family, and Belonging*

"This fine novel provides the reader with many pleasures. You'll find well-drawn characters to care about, a suspenseful story, an emotionally-resonant depiction of the psychological stresses related to adoption, and a prose style that is clear and enjoyable to read."

—MONICA STARKMAN, MD, author of *The End of Miracles*,
Professor emerita of Psychiatry,
University of Michigan Medical School

T0043067

Praise for *Love is a Rebellious Bird*
2019 National Jewish Book Awards Finalist

"From first love to last love, *Love Is a Rebellious Bird* by Elayne Klasson explores the manner in which some one special always holds a place in our heart. This book illustrates that our connections help us deal with the obstacles we all encounter . . . its message will resonate with readers who maybe facing challenging life decisions now; realizing we will all experience the vicissitudes of life sooner or later. This poignant novel addresses the nature of love and commitment (through a Jewish lens) and is a remarkable depiction of such."

—JEWISH BOOK AWARDS

"Klasson fills every scene she can with thought-provoking reflections on the nature of love, family, and romance. A surprisingly complex and realistic love story delicately narrated by an endearing protagonist."

—KIRKUS REVIEWS

"Elayne Klasson's artistic and compassionate novel *Love is a Rebellious Bird* focuses on a lifelong love affair . . . an operatic, enduring, and subtle romance."

—FOREWORD CLARION REVIEWS 5/5

"*Love is a Rebellious Bird* vividly evokes the worlds of Judith Sherman and Elliott Pine: 1950's Chicago in the Jewish neighborhood of West Rogers Park, the subsequent whiplash of the liberated '60s, marriages that fail and marriages that thrive, losses from illness and ambitions denied. Klasson shows us the seismic repercussions of a love, more unequal than unrequited, that vibrate over a lifetime. While Elliott may never fully love Judith the way she deserves, the reader certainly will."

—STACEY SWANN, author of a
Good Morning America Book Club pick *Olympus, Texas*

THE EARTHQUAKE CHILD

THE EARTHQUAKE CHILD

A NOVEL

Elayne Klasson

SHE WRITES PRESS

Published 2023
Printed in the United States of America

Print ISBN: 978-1-64742-446-6
E-ISBN: 978-1-64742-447-3
Library of Congress Control Number: 2023902859

For information, address:
She Writes Press
1569 Solano Ave #546
Berkeley, CA 94707

Interior design by Katherine Lloyd, The DESK

She Writes Press is a division of SparkPoint Studio, LLC.

Permission for unprinted "Elegy for a Sweet Family Man" on page 154 by Hank Lazer.
Permission for quote on page vii given by author, A.M. Homes.

To D.K.

And to Wendy

"To be adopted is to be amputated and sewn back together. Whether or not you regain full function, there will always be scar tissue."

—A.M. Homes

Chapter 1

THE RUNAWAYS

2006

Nick and two other kids slipped away from Mount Richmond Academy late on a moonless night. Using headlamps, they traveled west, hoping to reach Wilcox, the town closest to the school. At daybreak on the fifth morning, they discovered a small cave and collapsed into exhausted sleep. The weather was mild that summer in the Oregon high desert, and they slept deeply until nearly noon, when the whirring noise of a helicopter overhead woke them.

Nick slowly sat up, rubbing his shoulders. The nights of walking, sometimes stumbling, through the rough terrain had made his muscles ache. Sleeping nearby were his traveling companions, Noa and Jacob. *A sorry duo*, Nick thought. They weren't kids he might have deliberately chosen for this getaway and long hike, but they were the only two who remained from the original group. Noa, in Nick's opinion, was the school's most disagreeable girl, and her boyfriend, Jacob, a skinny, pathetic kid, had no mind of his own. The stench in the filthy cave was made worse by the smell of their unwashed bodies. Energy bar wrappers and who knew what else littered the cave's floor. Nick stared longingly toward the entrance, at the fresh air and clear blue sky beyond. He didn't move, though. The sound of the chopper froze him in place.

Jacob woke and rubbed his eyes. In his puny voice he asked, "A helicopter?"

"They're fucking pigs," Noa said. She walked to the cave's opening and looked out. Her hair, with its wild red curls, would be visible to anyone watching them.

"Military. Probably practicing to kill babies in Iraq." Without turning back to the boys, she stomped forward and raised both middle fingers to the helicopter above.

Nick quickly ran to the opening. He grabbed Noa by her sweatshirt and forcefully yanked her back into the cave. "Don't be an asshole, Noa. They're searching for us. I keep telling you, we've got to stay out of sight during the day."

Only sixteen, Nick was already an accomplished survivalist. Under his guidance, the three had hiked almost forty miles off-road from the school. Although their food and water supply was nearly exhausted, Nick remained confident his skills would get them to Wilcox. He just needed to impress on the other two, especially Noa with that wild red hair, that they must stay hidden during the day. They must not, under any circumstance, get picked up and dragged back to Mount Richmond, their piss-assed school. He'd run away from home in California several times and always landed on his feet, but now the stakes were higher.

Noa slapped at Nick's hand. "Hey, you're the asshole. Don't touch me." She fixed the boy, a good foot taller than she, with a deadly stare, then reached into her pocket for another energy bar—her last.

They were running from Mount Richmond Academy, a therapeutic boarding school with 120 teenaged students, most there against their will. Nick had arrived at the program less than a month before.

"Fake it until you make it," older students told him.

They meant for him to follow the rules until he turned eighteen.

After that, he could sign himself out and do as he liked. But the prospect of staying at the school for almost another two interminable years was not one he entertained. Nick knew he didn't belong at the school. He'd been taken there, snatched off the street by goons hired by his mother, and he was not going to stay and fake anything.

At night in the dorms, the kids talked. They told stories of how, before being delivered to the school by their parents (or in some cases, like Nick, by bonded and licensed escort services), most had wreaked havoc on their families. Drinking, drugs, and not coming home at night were typical reasons kids were at Mount Richmond. With the boys, the anger was directed outward. In most of their homes, as in Nick's own, there were holes punched through Sheetrock. With the girls, more typically, there was cutting or an eating disorder, something inflicting pain upon themselves. The kids at Mount Richmond, sometimes ashamed, sometimes defiant, recounted stories to each other: the violence, trouble with the law, self-harm.

From the time he was brought to the school, Nick was cautioned that no one made it more than twenty-four hours after running away before being picked up. Water was scarce in that isolated region. There were irrigation ditches, but the water in them was likely contaminated from grazing cows. Someone could get a bad case of E. coli, maybe even die, from that polluted water. Running from the school meant risking dehydration, sickness, or worse. The steep, uneven terrain also meant the chance of injury. A broken ankle might be fatal in these mountains, a person not discovered until it was too late. Mount Richmond's isolation was intentional, the staff told him. It was for his own good he'd been removed from the temptations that got him into trouble.

His own good. Nick narrowed his eyes when he heard those words. There was no way the school would contain him. His plan to escape was fueled by fury.

3

Led by Nick, the trio had slowly made their way by night toward Wilcox, where civilization waited. All three still wore the dark polo shirts, navy sweatshirts, and khaki pants, now filthy, that was the uniform of Mount Richmond. The evening before, they'd covered nearly ten miles. Their feet were blistered and bloody, their food supplies almost depleted, and the jugs of water stashed into their backpacks were nearly empty, but none had gotten sick or hurt. Nick's confidence was unshaken.

Noa and Jacob did not share this confidence and were beginning to doubt Nick. They'd slept only a few hours at a time and were exhausted. They were sick of energy bars and trail mix and, more troublingly, there was little left to drink.

When the sound of the whirring blades finally grew faint, Nick strode from the cave. He shaded his eyes, carefully scanning the valley below. Suddenly he shouted triumphantly. "There it is!" he said and pointed east.

The eyes of the other two followed his raised arm and saw it as well: the outskirts of town. There were a few houses scattered on large parcels of land. Beyond these were regularly laid-out streets. Nick had been right. Yes, the terrain had been steep and rocky, and they were tired as well as hungry and thirsty, but they'd done it. They'd reached Wilcox. Nick had led them to freedom.

Nick would never forget being kidnapped by the two thugs his mother hired to bring him, against his will, to Oregon. He kept hearing the sound of the car doors' locks clicking shut, picturing how he'd been driven away in the ugly beige Nissan, as his friends watched. It was the most outrageous act inflicted upon him in his young life, and as soon as he'd been admitted to Mount Richmond, he knew he'd find a way out. Although confident of his survival skills, there was one problem. Nick hated being alone. He liked an audience—people to appreciate him. He also realized having good-looking girls along would be an asset, so he talked up his project to some of the braver female students. He was surprised at how difficult it had been to get any of them, either the boys or girls, to agree to the runaway. They were pussies, with no fight left in them. They hated Mount Richmond, yet running away seemed beyond their energy or imagination. Maybe Noa with her crazy conspiracy theories was correct— the school had brainwashed them.

Starting out, there had originally been six. But after that first chilly night in the woods, two boys and the other girl gave up. They left their supplies with the remaining three and promised to divulge nothing. Nick wasn't pleased to be left with only Noa and Jacob, but he was determined to keep moving. He might have been okay with only Jacob. He and the other boy had arrived at Mount Richmond the same week. Both liked the same kind of music: death metal. Both passionately hated the school. But Jacob and his hot girlfriend, Noa, were inseparable. And Noa increasingly was a problem.

The previous week, Nick had seen the two lovebirds get busted for having physical contact. Touching a member of the opposite sex was one of many infractions at Mount Richmond. At admission, they'd been given a set of rules stating they were to abstain from physical contact with other students until they'd earned certain privileges. Holding hands, hugging and, God-forbid, kissing were big deals. These had to be earned through good behavior.

"Bullshit," the kids said to one another.

There had been no privileges earned by Noa or Jacob. Neither was particularly good at following rules. Jacob was on the lazy side, easily distracted, never finishing his chores. Noa said "fuck you" to every staff member who spoke to her. She hated them all without exception. Both were put on restrictions after they'd been caught making out behind Jacob's dorm. The no-touching rule, among others, was unacceptable to Noa. In group therapy, she reported she'd been avidly sexually active since middle school. Who was this place to tell her what to do with her own body? Jacob had never before had a girlfriend. To his dorm mates, he shyly admitted his surprise that Noa, with her beautiful red hair and sexy body, had chosen him.

Nick couldn't figure it out either. He was much better looking than puny Jacob and had made some moves on Noa, which she quickly rejected. He supposed Noa liked that she could call the shots with Jacob and tell him what to do and not do. She could mold him to her will. Jacob may not have understood it, but with Noa, willing and gorgeous, crawling all over him, the little fucker just accepted his good luck.

As soon as Noa heard the escape plan through the underground student communication system, she passed Nick a note. Noa, and her boy toy, Jacob, would be at the designated meeting spot on the gravel road behind the boys' dormitory at midnight on the next moonless night.

"I'm getting laid and I'm getting a beer," she said to Nick when they met up at the spot.

Jacob nodded enthusiastically.

Tall, blond Nick was different than most of the kids. He didn't break rules, nor give the staff a hard time. But he wasn't buying into any of the crap at the school either. He listened at the endless group therapy sessions, quickly learning what was expected. He had real talent for mastering the psychological lingo of group therapy: speaking fluently about abandonment, loss, and grief. But when alone with the other kids, with no staff around to hear, he lost the obedient smile and charm he showed the adults. Group therapy was nothing but a pity party, he said to the other students. A waste of his time.

"I used to buy guns. On the internet," he casually told the boys in his dorm. "For the Bloods and Crips down south." He stretched his lanky body out on his bed, hands under his head.

"Right, Nick," said the boy in the next bunk. "And how exactly did a pretty white boy like you meet the Bloods and Crips?"

Nick narrowed his eyes. "Oh, I got my contacts," he told the kid menacingly. "In LA."

Nick did seem to know a lot about gang stuff; and the other kids began to be a little scared of him, which Nick liked very much.

Although Noa and Jacob were a year older, Nick knew they were the ones who needed to be taken care of. He'd been on the streets. The last time he ran away from home in Northern California, he'd hooked up with a cool hippie group at a music festival in San Francisco. They were called the Dream Catchers. The music was lame, but he stayed with the group for days, until his mother found him and brought him back. From the Dream Catchers, he'd learned some serious panhandling skills, even how to get gas from pumps when someone walked away for a few moments. Nick was confident that once they got some distance from Mount Richmond, they'd survive just fine. He was unafraid. With his good sense of direction and street smarts, he was sure he'd be free of the school and even his mother. He'd travel with the other two, Jacob and Noa, until he didn't need them any longer. Then he'd ditch them.

Nick wasn't his real name. When he'd been adopted, soon after he was born in Wisconsin, his parents named him Joshua. For as long as he could remember, Nick hated this Old Testament name. He wasn't anti-Semitic, but he felt his name was another example of how he was living the wrong life. His parents, both Jewish, had tried molding him into something he was not. When he was adopted, he had been dropped into a world he was not meant for. The Russells, his adoptive family, couldn't even get naming him right. Joshua. The name irritated him. It made him want to puke. When he was a little boy, he'd woken one morning and knew with certainty that his name was *not* Joshua. His name was Nick. He fantasized that his birth mother had actually given him the name Nick, but he had no evidence, as he'd never seen his original birth certificate from Wisconsin. As much as he knew anything, he knew he was more a Nick than a Joshua. (And that was what his mom always called him, "Josh-u-a," not Josh, all three syllables clearly pronounced, like straight from the Bible.)

So, at barely sixteen, when Joshua was admitted to Mount Richmond, he told everyone to call him Nick. And it worked. The staff went along with it, feeling a name change harmless. There were plenty of adopted kids at Mount Richmond. Most questioned how they fit into the family they lived with . . . the family they were not related to by blood. Some of these adopted kids were different racially or ethnically than their adoptive parents. There were Black kids or Asian kids adopted by white couples. Many did not look like their parents. Most were different temperamentally.

The staff said, "Sure, Nick, we'll call you by whatever name you'd like."

Nick/Joshua Russell thought there was a lot more besides his name that was wrong with his life in Northern California. The only things the Russell family cared about were money and prestige. They lived in a big, rambling house in Los Altos, a house uncomfortable to Nick in its size. When he ran away, which he'd been doing on a regular basis since he was fourteen, he saw how normal people lived. Before he'd been brought to Mount Richmond, shoved into that beige car, and forcibly taken to Oregon by the assholes his mother hired, his greatest pleasure had been listening to music. In the lyrics to the songs he loved, Nick heard about real life.

Like everything else his mother found for him, he couldn't believe what a wrong fit this school was. He wanted no more of the talking bullshit, the therapy, the rules. Noa was right. She said Mount Richmond was like a cult. He wasn't going to let it, or his mother, control him. He considered running away as keeping his integrity, being true to his authentic self. There was no choice but to get out of Mount Richmond.

He first started to get into trouble two years before and his mother shipped him off to a wilderness camp in Utah, a place some therapist friend of hers recommended. Wilderness camp had been okay; Joshua actually excelled there. He'd learned to start a bow-drill fire in mere seconds, rapidly twirling a spindle in a hole until a spark flew out. Leaning over a small pile of twigs, he blew and caressed it until a flame started from the single spark he'd created. He could cook decent meals over open fires, too. He once made a cheesecake, baking it inside an ordinary tin can, the wrapper peeled off, and then letting it cool in the chill of the evening. It'd tasted pretty damn good, but by then he and the other boys at the wilderness camp were so starved for sugar, the cake delighted their numbed palates.

Counselors at the camp talked nonstop crap about the curative powers of nature and how the great outdoors should inspire you to change your life. A bunch of bull, but still, Joshua *was* good at it. They were assigned to write in a journal every day about their goals. Instead, he wrote rap songs, with verses about pimps and whores. He drew daggers dripping with blood. And although he was one of the most able boys at the camp, he dreamed every day of getting back to California, about getting high again with his friends. His main fear was that his friends on the street would forget him.

When he returned from wilderness camp, the summer he turned fifteen, he searched for his friends, mainly kids from neighboring East Palo Alto. They had not forgotten him and welcomed him back. But his mother continued to make him feel like shit. He wasn't studying enough. He wasn't trying hard enough at school. He wasn't living up to his potential. She never stopped.

"Who are your friends?" she asked. "Have you met their parents?"

When he got sick of her nagging, he'd run away.

Always there were cars to sleep in and people to share food and drugs. He never had trouble attracting girls. Girls wanted to take care of him. Joshua would tell them he'd been kicked out at home, which he hadn't, of course, and they'd feel sorry for him and drive him to McDonald's, buying him whatever he wanted.

In the middle of tenth grade, after several runaways, his mother looked at Joshua's pathetic grades and tried to enroll him in a fancy private school in Los Altos. It was a school for kids with learning disabilities, but when he visited, he saw they were really just a bunch of pampered jerks, worse even than at his public school. The private school must have known he didn't belong there, either, because they didn't accept him. Joshua didn't belong in that private school, just like he didn't belong at Mount Richmond Academy. He belonged with his friends on the street, kids he hung with when he ran away. With them, not the fuckheads at school, and not with his family, the feeling he was a wrong fit lessened.

When Joshua was little, living in the big house in Los Altos, he used to watch *Sesame Street* every morning. Eating his bowl of Fruit Loops, he watched the small television set on the kitchen counter in front of him. Sometimes there was a segment where the screen was divided into four squares. A familiar song was sung with this divided screen: "One of these things is not like the other . . ." Of the four items, one was always different. Kids were supposed to figure out which one didn't belong.

One morning, the screen showed three dark-haired people, with a blond head in the fourth square. It was easy to see which one didn't belong with the others. Exactly like his own family, Joshua thought. His mother and his siblings were small, dark-haired people. By age twelve, Joshua was already the tallest. The others in his family had thick, wavy brunette hair. None of them had a big, round head like his. His mother regularly had his smooth, blond hair trimmed into a dumb-looking bowl cut that hung almost to his eyebrows. Ever since he could remember, people couldn't seem to stop running their hands over his silky, straight hair.

"What an angel he is. Where did he get this golden hair?" they'd ask his small, olive-skinned mother.

His mom would laugh nervously, one of the few times he ever heard her at a loss for words.

She'd mutter, "Oh, his grandfather was a blond," and try to change the subject.

Now, in the cave in the high desert of Oregon, he looked down at his filthy clothes and ran his fingers through his dirty hair. One of the first things Nick (for now he thought of himself as Nick all of the time) wanted to do when he got out of this shitty cave and could get his hands on some money was to ditch the preppie clothes the school ordered for them from Lands' End. Then, he'd get a haircut. A Mohawk. He wondered if Noa knew how to cut hair so it stood up in the front and was shaved at the sides. It'd be a great disguise. People wouldn't know to look for someone with a Mohawk. And a tattoo. He wanted to get a skull and crossbones tattoo with "Sam-a-el" written below it. It was his favorite group, a badass death metal band from Europe, which was totally hard core. He couldn't wait to see his mother's face when she saw her pretty little golden boy with a Mohawk and a skull and bones tattoo on his arm.

He knew he had to ditch Jacob and Noa eventually. They'd slow him down. He needed Noa for a while to get them rides. But after that, he'd find a car. He was sure he could make it back down to California in a day or two. That was his plan. There was a guy back home who knew someone who could teach him to manufacture ecstasy. He had another friend who had a place where they could make the stuff, an abandoned shack in the Santa Cruz Mountains. Ecstasy was supposed to be easy to make, not any harder than the experiments

11

they did in chemistry class. They'd have as much E as they wanted, and they'd live pretty on the money they got from selling it.

Nick had good buddies, buddies a whole lot cooler than the pussy-whipped Mount Richmond kids. His drug buddies were real friends, better than anyone he'd met at Mount Richmond. They were people he could trust, who loved him unconditionally. There'd be no staff listening over their shoulders. No groups where they were supposed to talk about their feelings. He and his buddies understood each other without group therapy. He wasn't afraid of living on the streets. He knew how to do it. When he had more cash, he'd go up to San Francisco, where there was real action.

The damn helicopter circling overhead was a concern, though. And so was crazy Noa jumping out of the cave and flipping it off. He hoped the helicopter pilot hadn't seen her, but Noa was hard to miss with her flaming red hair. Though tiny, the girl was really built. Nick hadn't told the others, but he thought he might have heard dogs barking in the early morning. He wondered if there were dogs searching the mountains.

"Noa, listen," Nick said. "I think they're looking for us. I'm sure Mount Richmond didn't like having to call our parents and tell them they'd misplaced us. So listen to me. Just shut up and chill until it gets dark again. Then we'll make it to the town down there."

Noa looked at Nick as if he were an insect. "Since when are *you* telling us what to do?" She chewed her energy bar and looked the two boys up and down, making them squirm. She stared at Nick, pointing her finger at him. "You act like you're the boss. Don't forget, pretty boy, you are nothing but a sixteen-year-old punk. Younger than me and Jacob. Quit talking like you're in a gang or something. You're full of shit; everyone knows that."

Nick bristled. Noa was such a bitch. He was going to get away from her and her pussy boyfriend as soon as possible. Those two losers deserved each other.

With the noise of the helicopter finally gone, Noa picked up her backpack and stepped out of the cave again. She scanned the sky, then glanced back at the boys. "I'm tired of this shithole," she said. "You both stink and this cave stinks. I want a drink. See that house, the one down the hill and to the right? I just know they've got some nice cold beer in the fridge." She started walking toward the house she'd pointed to.

"Good riddance, Noa," Nick called after her.

She didn't turn back.

Jacob stood up and, shrugging his shoulders, brushed off his pants and lifted his own backpack to his shoulders. He followed Noa down the hill and picked his way carefully among the boulders.

"Wait up," he said.

"Shit," Nick muttered to himself. He was alone in the cave. Left behind and thirsty. The thought of a cold beer fought with his concern about the helicopter and the dogs. He tried to convince himself the school couldn't be paying choppers to search for them. Hiring helicopters and search dogs cost serious money. Even his control-freak mother wouldn't go that far. She didn't have that kind of money. Of course, he never would have believed his mother would have him kidnapped, either. But a helicopter and search dogs would be too much.

Nick caught up with the other two. He argued with them for a few moments. But he was hungry and thirsty and never good at waiting around. His desire for action won out over his caution. Erasing the picture of his mother from his brain, he focused on the house they'd seen. Food, drink, and who knew what other luxuries would be waiting for them. Maybe even a car. No, probably not a car.

"Okay," Nick said. "Let's get going. Hopefully that 'copter doesn't make another pass this way. We're better off together, the three of us. At least until we get back to civilization."

"I suppose that means you need a girl to get you rides. Nick, you are such an obvious prick," Noa said.

Nick looked warily at her. It bothered him that she saw through him.

They stumbled through the dry scrub. It was July, and the sun beat down on them. Nick's fair skin burned easily and he flipped the visor of his black baseball cap from back to front. Noa, also fair, had no head covering. The sun was starting to burn the pale, freckled skin across her nose and cheeks. Up until now, they'd mostly stayed under cover during the days. Nick silently passed his baseball cap to her. She stared at him but took it and pulled it over her red curls.

They walked without speaking for an hour or more, their throats parched. Nick occasionally kicked at rocks, leading the way. Jacob, the least naturally athletic of the three, began to breathe heavily, lagging behind. By the time they got to the house, they were sweating and their water was gone. They stared at the house while catching their breaths. It was silent. The place was in bad repair, run-down with peeling paint and torn screens. There was also a boxlike mobile home parked behind it, which they hadn't noticed before, and a white Ford extended cab pickup in the driveway. The truck was fairly new, clean, and the two boys circled it appreciatively.

When Nick turned away from the truck, he saw Noa had yanked open the unlocked back door. As he watched, she casually walked into the kitchen.

Nick whistled though his teeth. "That girl is crazy. People could be right inside. What the fuck is she doing?"

In a moment or two, Noa appeared again. "Coast is clear," she said sweetly. Then she held up a can. "Mmmm. This sure is refreshing!"

Jacob hesitated. It was obvious he wanted to follow the girl inside, but he looked over to Nick, waiting to see what he would do.

Nick's throat was so parched, he could practically taste the beer Noa held. "All right," he said, and shouldered his backpack. "Let's do this."

They headed toward the open kitchen door, Jacob checking behind him to make sure Nick still followed. The boys crossed the threshold into the kitchen. Inside, they looked around cautiously. Nick grabbed another beer from the still open refrigerator and tossed a third to Jacob. Then he began to explore.

The house was small, on one level. It was carpeted throughout with a stained beige carpet, even in the kitchen. Nick sauntered through it, opening and closing drawers. As he walked through the house, his confidence grew. It was exactly how he dreamed it would be. There was a dining room and living room, with two bedrooms and a bathroom off the narrow hallway. He pocketed some change he found on top of a bureau in one of the bedrooms, then walked back toward the kitchen. The other two had opened a fresh pack of Oreo cookies and were scarfing them down.

"Anything interesting?" Jacob asked.

"Nope, just some old people's shit. The whole house smells of old people. What's to eat? Besides cookies?"

"There's some eggs and a package of ham. That'd taste good, but I'm not going to cook for you guys. Either one of you know how to make eggs?" Noa asked. Neither boy replied. She shrugged and pointed. "Some apples on the table."

Nick took a few and shoved them into his sweatshirt pockets.

Jacob said nervously, "I don't think it's a good idea to stick around here. I think we ought to get going. It feels really weird; they could come home any minute."

Nick ignored him and opened a kitchen drawer. "Will you look at what these helpful people so considerately left for us?" He held up a ring of keys, dangling them high in the air. "I love when people are careful and keep a set of spare keys in a drawer, don't you?" He spoke to Jacob, who had his back turned and was staring at a closet off the living room.

"Nice," Nick said. "Very, very nice." He pocketed the keys, then walked over to the closet Jacob was facing. Without hesitating, he opened its door, then said, "Holy shit! This *is* our lucky day."

The others walked behind him. Their eyes widened. Inside was a small arsenal. There were two rifles propped upright on the closet floor and several handguns on a shelf. There were boxes and boxes of ammunition.

Nick picked up a handgun. He caressed it reverently in his palm. The other two backed off.

"Hey, that's not a good idea, man," Jacob said, his voice rising almost to a squeak.

"You're a jerk, Nick," Noa said. Perspiration streamed down her face. "Put it away. You're going to hurt someone. You really are a weirdo."

Jacob backed farther into the kitchen. His head swiveled to the back door. "Come on, Nick, she's right—you're gonna hurt someone. Put the gun back. We don't need a gun. Let's get the hell out of here."

Nick grinned. "I'm not leaving this gun behind, dude. If you think I am, you're going to have to wrestle me for it. You'll have to take me down. This is exactly what I've been looking for." He opened the gun's chamber and saw that it wasn't loaded. Then he reached inside the closet and ran his hands over the boxes of ammunition, removing three.

"Okay, we did well here," Nick said and stuck the gun into the waist of his pants. "Now let's have a look at that truck."

He led the way out of the kitchen, but before he reached the truck, he stopped and said to Noa, "Keep a lookout. Let me know if anyone is coming. I want to check out that trailer."

Noa looked at Nick and then down at the gun tucked in the boy's waistband. She swallowed and nodded.

"Come on, Nick," Jacob said. He was sweating as well. "Let's just get out of here. These people might come home for lunch. What if somebody's asleep in that trailer?"

"Don't be such a pussy," Nick said. "Stay here if you want and keep watch with Noa."

Jacob glared at Nick but followed.

Nick climbed the two steps to the doorway of the mobile home and turned the handle. It, too, opened.

When the boys came back out, Nick still had the gun jammed into the top of his pants. Jacob had grabbed a plastic wrapped loaf of bread and a sealed package of lunch meat. He also had looped a pair of binoculars and a camera around his neck. Nick waved something triumphantly at Noa. It was a cell phone. "This gets better and better. Right? It was in a charger, just waiting for me," he said.

All three stared longingly at the phone.

Finally, Nick broke the silence. "Okay, let's try the truck. See if the thing starts."

Jacob and Noa hesitated. Then Jacob moved to the driver's side.

"Please, let's get out of here," he said, and glanced around nervously. "Let me have those keys, Nick."

"Who says you're driving?" Noa asked.

"I'm the only one with a license, right?" Sweat stained the back of his shirt. "Shit, guys, just get in. Please. They could come back any minute."

Noa went to the passenger side and climbed in beside Jacob. She slammed the door. Nick shrugged but got into the back seat and passed Jacob the keys.

Jacob, hands shaking, put the large Ford key into the ignition. It turned over immediately.

"Whoa," Nick said. "Will you listen to that? How much gas?"

"About half a tank," Jacob answered. "Let's get the hell out of here."

"All right, bro," Nick said. "Where are we off to?"

Jacob bit his lip and then slowly answered. "I know people in Salem. My aunt lives there. I think it's about four hours from here."

Nick nodded and picked up the cell phone. He couldn't wait to start making connections again. He'd hated being cut off from his friends, hated that he'd been forced into that car back in Los Altos without being able to tell anyone where he was going. More than food or drink, more even than the gun tucked into his waistband, he wanted to connect with the kids back on the street. To tell them that despite his mother having him kidnapped by a fat-assed bounty hunter in a car with childproof locks, he was coming back. And it was on his own terms.

Chapter 2

THE QUAKE

1989 and 1990

The earthquake hit shortly after five o'clock on the afternoon of October 17. When the trembling began, Eleanor was alone in the house, standing in front of a mirror in the upstairs bathroom. The weather in Los Altos had been still and warm all day, a bit of humidity in the air, unusual for Northern California in October.

In the years to come, she called this earthquake weather. The papers reported that the Loma Prieta earthquake was a violent collision of tectonic plates in a previously ignored section of the mighty San Andreas Fault. Located fifty miles to the south of San Francisco, it measured 7.1 on the Richter scale, lasting a mere fifteen seconds. However, time did strange things during those fifteen seconds, expanding and undulating. And during that brief time, Eleanor had a powerful and surprising thought. Even in the midst of her terror, Eleanor Russell realized how much she wanted another child.

As the shaking continued, Eleanor feared the whole house would come down, its wood beams and plaster walls collapsing on her. She feared she would be buried under the rubble with no one arriving in time to find her and she felt the frail, flesh-and-blood humanness of her own body. For the first time in her life, she thought she might be facing death. On that Tuesday afternoon, she put her hands to her belly and felt a longing that she could never adequately explain afterward. It didn't matter that she already had two teenaged children. They were from her first marriage, another lifetime ago. She wanted a baby, one that was hers and Ron's. She thought she had made peace with this urge for another child, but it was jostled loose by the shaking of the earth.

The teenagers were at practices: Max at soccer and Lara rowing on the reservoir. Ron had left for a medical convention in Atlanta the day before. He infrequently traveled without her. They liked traveling together since they hated spending nights apart. Both had been alone much of their lives and still marveled at the words, "my husband, my wife." But she taught at the local college, and it was impossible to leave this close to midterms, so Ron had gone to Atlanta without her.

She'd been fixing her hair and makeup, getting ready for the monthly school board meeting in half an hour. Eleanor was president of the Los Altos Union Elementary School Board. Each time she stepped up to the raised semicircular platform with its smooth, sweeping desk, a microphone placed in front of each comfortably padded chair, she was self-consciously aware of her appearance. She fussed in front of the mirror not for the other nine members of the school board but for the audience who would be sitting in front of her.

Los Altos was a community of concerned and involved parents. Even on an evening with a relatively short and innocuous agenda, fifty people might attend. The *Los Altos Weekly* usually sent its photographer, Alton, a man who took his job very seriously. He'd perch on his heels facing the raised dais, ready to snap shots for the paper. Although he couldn't have planned it, his pictures of her were often unflattering—perhaps eyes at half-mast looking as if she were sleepy or lips curled up on one side, appearing as an argumentative sneer.

As she got ready, she practiced an alert, interested expression in the mirror, her eyes open wide and mouth fixed in an encouraging smile. She'd been forewarned that, in addition to the town weekly, KRON, the local television station, was sending a reporter and film crew.

A fifth-grade teacher in their district was being investigated. He'd been accused of inappropriate behavior when he'd been alone with a boy he'd been tutoring after school. It was a nasty business. Eleanor knew worrying about her appearance was not what she should be focusing on. But she was Eleanor, a person exquisitely aware of how she appeared to others. So she carefully applied cover-up under her eyes, so they would appear distinct but not raccoon-like, if the meeting should make the ten o'clock news.

The school board meeting never took place. With eyeliner applicator poised in midair, she heard the first deep rumbling. It sounded as if a heavy truck were passing their house, but Eleanor and Ron lived in the hills where there was no truck traffic. The rumbling was immediately followed by a huge rocking. The entire house swayed from side to side. From the upstairs bathroom, she heard the joints twist and moan—a sickening sound. As she gazed into the mirror, she saw with horror that the heavy pine armoire directly behind where she stood was tipping forward, heading for her. She stepped to the right just in time to watch the wooden piece crash with such force that the burgundy tiles covering the countertop cracked, and the mirror above shattered. The doors flew open, the wood splintering. Towels and sheets flew off the shelves.

Eleanor stared at the fallen armoire for a second. Still hearing her house torquing and cracking, she ran from the bathroom, fearing she'd not make it outside before the roof collapsed. She wondered if this was the big one. Was this the one in which the world as she knew it would disappear? She began descending the stairs to utter quiet. However, when she reached the landing, the house began to groan and move again. At the landing, her favorite piece of artwork rested on its heavy marble pedestal. It was called *In the Evening*, a green patinaed bronze of an elegantly draped female figure, sculpted by a famous artist. She and Ron had bought the sculpture seven years earlier when they felt flush and romantic on their honeymoon, a time when all, including a baby, seemed possible. Now, the pedestal and the bronze atop it swayed at the instant she ran past. The heavy sculpture slid off its base, hitting her hard in the knee, opening a nasty gash.

When she reached the bottom of the stairway, blood flowing down her leg, she gasped at the sight of the first floor. The massive wood beam that supported the front entry of the house had collapsed, dragging the plaster ceiling down with it. She stood still for a fraction of a second, absorbing the sight of the entryway now open to the sky. Then, another huge aftershock hit. With this jolt, seemingly bigger than the previous one, the old upright piano that rested against one wall of the living room began to roll along the hardwood floor. As she watched, it crashed through the glass picture window, the one facing north, its views all the way to San Francisco. The piano dropped to the lawn with a thud, its strings reverberating crazily.

She moved fast. Everything in the downstairs was tipped over, china and crystal on the ground, all of it smashed and broken. The liquor cabinet was on its side, and she smelled a sickly, sweet stench from the mix of alcohols: sherry and vermouth and Scotch flowed together, soaking into the deep-red Persian carpet she loved.

She ran toward the back door to avoid the ruined living room with its smashed picture window and open ceiling. On her way to the kitchen, she caught a split-second sight of her son Max's room. Everything was on the floor as well, with drawers tipped out and bookshelves emptied. She had a pang as she saw his precious model airplane collection crushed on the ground, pieces of the painted metallic wood glinting in the debris. Those airplanes represented hours of Max's childhood, when he'd built every model of every airplane available at the hobby store.

As she went for the door, she spotted a pan of brownies, still miraculously on the counter where she'd placed it after taking it from the oven an hour earlier. She couldn't understand why the metal pan hadn't slipped to the floor, but after she retrieved her purse, the car keys inside, from under a counter stool, she grabbed the brownies as well. It was the single unbroken thing she could see. Food. Wherever they were going, they'd need food. She ran outside clutching the still-warm pan.

The house still swayed, although now less violently. It stopped for a few seconds, then started up again. She supposed these were all aftershocks, although she wasn't entirely sure these waves were actually happening or whether she was so jangled, she imagined the earth still moving. Her car was parked in the driveway. It was the Volvo convertible Ron had recently bought in a beautiful color of silver, tinged with a pinkish undercoating. Desert Rose. Eleanor loved the car and had persuaded Ron to splurge on it. A Volvo was as fancy as Ron would get. He said the doctors' parking lot at the hospital was already filled with conspicuous consumption: Mercedes, Jags, and Lexus. He'd agreed on the Volvo only when she showed him the safety statistics.

As she opened the car door, she saw movement underneath. It was their dog, a large, red vizsla who, on the best of days, was neurotically high-strung. He trembled violently. Eleanor's daughter, Lara, had rescued him years before from the shelter and named him Clifford. The dog had a strangely pointy head and a long tongue that didn't seem to fit into his mouth. Lara felt sorry for him when she'd spied him at the shelter, hanging his head. She thought no one would ever want to adopt such a pathetic-looking dog with a deformed head.

Now, whining pitifully, Clifford jumped into the car as soon as she opened the door. Eleanor couldn't imagine how the big dog had squeezed under the car. In the back seat, he tried to flatten himself. Eleanor never let Clifford ride in the beautiful, new car. Because of his propensity to throw up, he was only allowed to ride in the old van parked in the garage. But the lights had gone out with the first tremor and without electricity, there was no use trying to get the garage door opened.

"Shit," she said. She remembered she'd been warned to turn off the gas in a major earthquake. But she had no idea where the special wrench was or even which pipe, exactly, she was supposed to turn off. What an awful time for Ron to be away. But she had to find the kids. She put the brownies on the seat beside her and drove wildly through town looking for Max and Lara.

With no functioning traffic lights and her car weaving down the road, it was amazing she actually found her kids. Max was huddled with his soccer coach and a few other boys at the park where practice was held. At first, Max refused to get into the car because it smelled so disgusting. Clifford had, indeed, vomited.

"Get in. Now. Thank God I found you," she said. She clutched the wheel because she couldn't stop her hands from shaking.

"Mom, there's blood running down your leg," Max said, when he finally slid into the front seat and lifted the pan of brownies onto his lap.

She shuddered as she thought about the armoire almost crushing her and then the falling bronze sculpture. "Wow. You're right," she said, and reached for a napkin from the glove compartment. She pressed the paper hard against her bloody knee.

A few minutes later, she found Lara. Eleanor's ex-husband lived in the flat part of town, which was much less damaged than the hills. Lara had gone there after school. She hugged her daughter with relief and told her to stay where she was for the time being.

A few days later, when Ron finally boarded a flight from Atlanta and arrived home, he was maddeningly dismissive.

"I know what an earthquake feels like," he told her later that week at what must be her hundredth repetition of the story. "But you're all fine, thank goodness. Even Clifford. The other stuff is replaceable."

His calm infuriated her. They'd moved to a rented condominium because the house was uninhabitable. It was a two bedroom and the kids, for the first time in their lives, had to share a room. Eleanor and Ron were aware they had to keep their voices down; the walls were thin and the kids in the next room. They rarely argued since both were wary of fights. He didn't want to turn into his loud, bullying father, and she worried things would get out of control, where words would be said that couldn't be taken back. This had happened in her first marriage. She tried to explain.

"It wasn't like the other quakes. I thought I'd never see the kids again, never see you again. I don't want to live here anymore. I want to move. Somewhere where we aren't on top of a fault line."

"Oh, for Christ's sake, Eleanor. There are disasters everywhere. Floods, fires, tornadoes. We live in the most beautiful part of the most beautiful state in America. God's country. The weather is almost perfect. Do you want to start shoveling snow off your car every morning? And you're not even considering our jobs. I practice here. You teach here. The kids are in school here. You're being crazy and you know it." He picked up a newspaper and tried to start reading.

"Arizona. Let's look at Arizona. I can't think of a single disaster that happens in Arizona," she said.

After many repeated discussions with Eleanor, Ron sighed and finally scheduled a trip to Arizona. They stayed at a nice hotel in Scottsdale, with views of Camelback Mountain. As they drove around Scottsdale, Eleanor tried to find something positive to say.

"I love the dryness, don't you? And the rock formations in the desert. Red, brown, pink. The color changes are so subtle."

Ron turned toward her. "And it's hot and boring."

She pointed out a large community hospital they were passing. "Looks new," she said.

"Do you know how long it would take me to get a license to practice in Arizona?" he asked.

She shrugged her shoulders.

"Years," he said.

On Sunday, they took the flight home. She gave up Phoenix. The thought kept going through her head that it was not a move to Arizona she wanted, it was a child. But she wasn't ready to say that aloud to Ron . . . not yet.

Instead, she dragged Ron to couples therapy. Joyce, the pleasant therapist, listened with empathy as Eleanor described the fear she felt every night lying in bed, imagining she felt the shaking again. And how Ron lay in bed beside her, snoring.

"Eleanor," the therapist said, "perhaps you'd feel better if Ron at least acknowledged your feelings. Let you know that he understands how frightened you are."

Eleanor began to cry. "Maybe. Maybe he just needs to tell me that I'm not being crazy. I really thought I was going to get buried in the damn house. He can't imagine what a 7.1 earthquake felt like. Everyone says we got hit especially hard. The tremors radiated out, and our house was directly on one of those radiating lines."

Weeks later, Ron unrolled a set of blueprints, explaining to Eleanor the house's retrofit was state-of-the-art and could resist all but a cataclysmic quake. He showed her how the walls would be on rollers, allowing them to move *with* tremors, not against them. Ron spoke calmly, saying they had to go on. They must look forward, not back.

Ron had always loved their home. It was his dream house, high on a hill, with a commanding view of San Francisco Bay. Before the earthquake, he would sometimes sit beside the large windows of their bedroom in the evenings, his comfortable chair facing the glittering lights, and watch in silence for an hour or two. Eleanor would be in bed, reading. She would wonder what he was thinking as he gazed out at the city.

She realized she was never going to convince Ron to move, either from the house or California. So, she took his advice. She thought of the future. As he busily supervised the house's retrofit, she began to think more about a baby. They were over forty. Married in their mid-thirties, they had been unsuccessful, first in conceiving a child, and then in sustaining a pregnancy. With regret, a few years ago, they had decided a baby was not meant to be. They told each other they'd be content raising the two children from Eleanor's first marriage. However, after the earthquake, the idea of adopting, once a passing thought, lodged deep within her. She returned to it again and again. Part of it was an overpowering need to affirm life. She'd been so terrified. She thought she was going to die under the rubble and never see her family again. All the possessions she'd once thought were important—the crystal, china, and Persian rugs—now seemed silly. She wanted a baby with Ron.

At first, she didn't mention adoption. Although Ron had wanted a baby when they first married, he seemed, more than she, to accept that with their fertility problems, it wasn't going to happen. But in the weeks and months after the earthquake, while they were still in the rental and rebuilding the house, it became the single thought that gave Eleanor joy.

In the spring after the earthquake, she drove Max to his baseball practices. Waiting in the car, she watched mothers pushing strollers in the park, putting their little ones in baby swings. She'd heard the desire for a child after a trauma wasn't an unusual reaction. When people faced life-threatening situations, they sometimes reacted by craving a new life. Women got pregnant after they defeated cancer. Her own cousin Myrna had a baby after she recovered from breast cancer. Eleanor remembered reading somewhere that people in concentration camps, even facing the gas chambers, continued to have sex. Her rabbi once said in a sermon that when a funeral cortege meets a wedding parade, the funeral must give way to the bride and groom. The life force triumphs over death.

On her own, Eleanor investigated adoption. People she spoke to said they'd waited for a baby for a long time, sometimes years. She and Ron were too old; they didn't have years. Overseas adoptions could take even longer. Eleanor also heard every possible horror story: the pregnant girl who promised her baby to more than one family; the girl who hadn't disclosed her drinking and then the poor baby was born with signs of fetal alcohol syndrome; and the girl who wasn't really pregnant but had faked it with a foam insert in order to bilk a desperate couple out of thousands of dollars. Yet, against all the odds she heard about, she still had a good feeling about adopting. Her gut told her they'd be lucky. They wouldn't end up with a horror story.

She and Ron even knew an adoption attorney. Hal Mozart had been in their circle of friends for years. His wife, Donna, was in Eleanor's book group. Hal and Donna had adopted their own three kids. He had a small law practice, specializing in adoption, with just one part-time assistant. He rented space in a historic building in downtown Menlo Park, and his desk was piled with disorganized stacks of paper. But Eleanor trusted Hal. She knew Ron liked him, too. Hal was sincere about what he did and dedicated to helping couples find babies, and babies to find homes.

Twice a year, Hal ran adoption information seminars at the San Jose Airport Marriott. Slowly, as the house was being rebuilt, Eleanor introduced the idea of adoption. Ron was astonished, at first. He and Eleanor were too old, he said. They were busy enough raising Max and Lara. After the pain of several miscarriages and unsatisfying visits to infertility doctors, Ron thought she had put the baby business behind her.

"Ron, when we first met, you told me how much you wanted a baby. It was one of the first things you talked about. You asked if I was willing to have another child. *I* was the one who worried about starting over with a new family," Eleanor said. They were in the small bedroom of the rental. Their house would be ready to move back into within a few weeks.

"Yeah, but we were younger," he said. "We're over forty now. It's different."

Eventually Ron agreed to go to Hal's spring seminar. He warned he wasn't making any promises. They would just gather information.

When they first walked into the conference room at the hotel, it was May, seven months after the earthquake. Hal began in his soft, unassuming voice. There were about twenty people in the room. Those toward the back needed to lean forward to hear him. He was businesslike, explaining how "targeted marketing" could find them a baby. It was important to make an effective search.

He then added, "But along with a careful approach, you must have faith your baby is out there. Somewhere. Together, with faith and good advertising, you'll find your child."

"My recommended and proven method is simple," Hal explained in the seminar. "We advertise. Advertise in small-town papers, even throwaway penny-savers. Newspapers you'd find in a laundromat. We try to think about what a pregnant girl from a small town might be reading and where she'd be reading it. Then we start running those ads. There's no limit. I've had couples place five hundred ads. You'll use my phone number. Initially, when they call, I'm the one to talk to the girls, find out which ad they're responding to, and screen them. I make sure they're legit. Then, you'll take over. Ultimately, it's up to you and the girl to decide if you're a match."

The couples in the room seemed to hold their collective breath, busily taking notes, trying not to miss a word.

"How do we find the right newspapers?" asked a man with a neatly trimmed graying beard.

"When you sign on with me, you'll receive this," Hal said. He held up a thick, bound book, the size of the San Francisco telephone directory. "These are names and addresses of thousands of small-town newspapers. I focus only on states with laws favorable to adoption. Places where the birth mother has a relatively short time to change her mind. I don't do California adoptions; California is *not* a good state for adoption. Girls have six months to change their minds here. You don't want to fall in love with your baby and then, six months later, have the birth mom demand the baby back. She could change her mind if she finds herself a new boyfriend."

People groaned. This was everyone's worst nightmare.

"What do we say in the ads? Do you have examples for us to read?" asked a woman with a fashionable spiky haircut.

"Of course. I'll help you. But the important thing is, write from your hearts. Be honest. Say how much you want a child. Talk about what a baby would mean in your lives."

Eleanor was a college professor. She taught child development at the Cal State campus in San Jose. The people in this room reminded her of students who were asking what to study for the final. This was a room of overachievers, successful people who worked hard and believed determination was the key to getting what they wanted. They just needed a plan. The problem of infertility, for most of them, was the first one they couldn't solve with diligence.

There was a remarkable sameness to the couples, including the gay ones. All were nicely dressed, with a studied casualness. Most wore jeans, expensive ones. None were young. The women had subjected themselves to expensive mood- and body-altering fertility treatments. Infertility cost money, lots of it. Clomid, laparoscopic surgery, in vitro fertilization, artificial insemination, and even egg donors. These couples had stressed their bodies, relationships, and bank accounts. It had been tiring. Most seemed tense, even with each other. They ached for a baby, and nature had not taken its course.

As Eleanor and Ron well knew, sex on a strict ovulation schedule certainly leached joy from the act. Although the gay couples hadn't all gone the route of infertility treatments, they'd undoubtedly had their own struggles. Finding a partner who wanted a baby as much as you did, and was willing to undergo the scrutiny, expense, and uncertainties of adoption, was its own kind of stress.

Eleanor and Ron were different from most of the others in one important way, however. They weren't childless. She didn't mention this to the other couples, feeling she would appear greedy or less worthy of finding a child to adopt. But now, with Ron, her body was finished making babies.

In the first two years of their marriage, she'd had two miscarriages, one after the other. They had been painful and she'd grieved. After both, it seemed everyone she knew or passed on the street was pregnant. When Ron's sister, who she loved, had a baby the same day Eleanor was lying in bed recovering from her second miscarriage, she could barely muster congratulations. She blamed herself for the second miscarriage. Perhaps she'd tried to get pregnant too soon after the first miscarriage. Perhaps she'd been working too hard. She was ambitious, taking on too many committee assignments at the university. After the miscarriages, there was a complete failure to conceive. Finally, Dr. Baden, her fertility doctor, said he had little hope she could have a baby without complicated interventions. He'd determined she was already approaching menopause. At forty-one, this was young, but early menopause ran in Eleanor's family.

"Think of it like a fruit stand," Dr. Baden said when she was trying to conceive. "In the morning, the apples and pears are out in front, displayed in rows, each one shiny and juicy. But, by the end of the day, when the fruit seller is ready to close up shop, there are only a few pieces remaining. The ones that are left are a bit bruised and shriveled. That's the way your eggs are. There aren't many remaining. And those few aren't particularly viable."

What a depressing image, thought Eleanor: her eggs all shriveled and nonviable. The day they'd left Dr. Baden's office, Ron had put his arm around her and said gently that it was okay. He loved his stepchildren, Max and Lara, and he didn't want her to undergo the radical treatments—surgery and massive amounts of hormones—that getting pregnant would involve. He didn't think Eleanor could bear another miscarriage, either. The odds were bad, and it wasn't worth it. He'd been in Max and Lara's lives since they were seven and ten. Now they were fourteen and seventeen. They were terrific kids, and they were enough.

But Eleanor didn't believe him. Even before the earthquake, it grieved her that they hadn't had a baby together. Although she'd said yes to having more children because she wanted to marry Ron, she hadn't been completely sure at first. Yet she watched as Ron became a warm and generous stepfather. He deserved to have a child . . . a baby they could raise together. It was just like him to say it wasn't a loss. He asked so little for himself.

There was something else. Eleanor hated that she had to share Max and Lara with her ex-husband. Every other weekend, and Wednesdays for dinner, plus alternate holidays, the children went to Art's house. Eleanor longed for a real family, one where they didn't have to shuffle children back and forth. She dreamed of a child who was completely theirs. Max had been a baby, not even a year old, when she and Art split up. The complicated arrangements that went with divorce were painful to her and her idea of family.

With Ron, she knew she'd found someone who was going to stay around. He was steady, loyal, and committed to her and the kids. They were going to grow old together. Her theory about relationships was one she shared only with her closest girlfriends.

"Marry a man who loves you more than you love him, at least a little bit," Eleanor said. "Never marry a man you have to chase after. You'll always be chasing."

All during her first marriage, she'd felt like she was on the inside of a washing machine, tossed around with no stability. Eleanor was through with that particular kind of terror. Never again would she spend an evening watching the clock, wondering if her husband was late because he really was tied up at work or because he was screwing the aerobics instructor at the gym, a girl twenty pounds lighter and ten years younger than she.

Ron was a man who thought every pound on her was delicious. Although he often worked late, he was always where he said he'd be. Eleanor had found the comfort of a good marriage.

Art's house was bigger and his gifts to the kids grander. The children thought Art was so much fun . . . a kid at heart. As steady and sweet as Ron was, the kids never described him as fun. And she, Eleanor, couldn't really be described as a fun-loving type, either. She was the parent with rules. Since the divorce, she and Lara clashed a lot. Lara blamed Eleanor for the divorce. There was no way Eleanor could tell her daughter what it had been like when she caught Art in his lies about other women. To Lara, her father was perfect. He must have had his reasons for cheating. So, Eleanor kept quiet, but she was hurt by Lara's obvious preference for her father.

Lately, Lara's arguments with Eleanor had escalated. Neither mother nor daughter seemed to be able to control the harsh, spiteful things they said to each other.

In spring, after the earthquake, Lara stepped up her campaign for a car. "I have to get to the reservoir early for crew practice. I'm always having to ask for a ride. I hate it."

"You know the agreement. When you bring up your grades,

we'll buy you a car," Eleanor said. She, Ron, and Art had decided this together, and Eleanor thought it was settled.

One day, Eleanor heard her daughter on the phone with her father. "That's all she cares about. Grades, grades, grades. I can do everything else right, but if I don't have the grades to get into some college she can brag about to her friends, nothing matters."

Art phoned her soon after. "Lara tells me you're thinking of adopting a baby," he said.

"Did she?" Eleanor fought to keep her voice pleasant.

"Yeah, she says it embarrasses her," Art said.

"Embarrasses her? Why would our adopting a baby embarrass her?"

"I don't know. She says no one else who's seventeen has a mother pushing a baby carriage."

"Really? Well, we're just beginning to discuss it. What else did she say?"

"She says you're pretty tough on her about her grades."

Always, Art took Lara's side. A closet dyslexic himself, he had struggled with school his whole life. Now he was rich as Croesus and president of his own investment business. One Sunday, soon before high school was over for the year but before finals week, without discussing it with Eleanor and Ron, Art presented Lara with a new Mustang, a car any teenager would swoon over. When Lara drove up to the house in the baby-blue car and saw Eleanor's shocked reaction, her face changed from triumph to guilt. Then it set into anger.

"A car? Your dad bought you that?"

Lara slammed the door to the car, shouting furiously that her mother was trying to ruin even the Mustang for her.

Soon after Lara received the car, Eleanor and Ron attended Hal's adoption seminar. As they walked out of the conference room at the Marriott, Eleanor waited for her husband's reaction. He didn't speak until they reached the parking lot.

"I don't know, hon. It seems like such a long shot that we'd find a baby before we're too old. It feels like we're *already* too old."

"But we're healthy. We could at least try. We could set a limit, and if we don't find a baby in that time period, we give up on the idea," she said.

"It never happens quickly. You heard Hal," Ron said, and shook his head. "I work in a hospital, don't forget. I've seen adoptions go terribly wrong."

"Let's just give it until the end of the year," she said. "I promise that if we don't have a baby by the end of 1990, I'll let it go. But, please, let's try. Let's see if there is a baby out there for us. I feel it will happen."

Ron put his arm around his wife. "Sweetheart, you look so excited. Of course I want to have a baby with you. I always did. I just hope we're not in for heartache."

Under Hal Mozart's guidance, they ran an advertisement that appeared in classified sections of small-town newspapers throughout Kansas, Wisconsin, and Nebraska. Hal said these were states he'd had success in. She and Ron spent hundreds of dollars on the ad, which Eleanor composed and rewrote. Ultimately, their simple advertisement in the *Hartland Weekly Sentinel* in central Wisconsin caught a girl's eye. Less than six weeks after the seminar, in early July, they got the call.

Eleanor answered the phone, and a young female voice said, "Mrs. Russell? My name is Kelly. I saw your ad. I'm going to have a baby. Soon. In a month or so."

From that first conversation, Eleanor had known with certainty Kelly's baby was meant for them. She tried to make Kelly comfortable, so the girl didn't feel as if Eleanor were grasping, insensitively trying to snatch her baby away. They spoke every few days. Eleanor listened and murmured supportive things. Kelly was just a kid, almost the same age as Lara. It was apparent Kelly needed someone to talk to. She spoke about high school, before she'd dropped out, and about the pregnancy. She shyly confided in Eleanor. After a few conversations, she confessed she had another child, Sean. He was a bit over a year old. Kelly doted on Sean. Eleanor listened and let Kelly talk about Sean. The father of both babies was a boy named Esa. But Kelly said little about Esa, or their relationship, so Eleanor didn't push or ask many questions about the father.

"It's a boy," Kelly said. "I'm sure I'm having another boy. It feels just the same as it did with Sean."

Eleanor tried to think how it would have been if one of Lara's friends were pregnant or even Lara herself. All the girls liked talking to Eleanor, except Lara. They thought she was one of the cool mothers and spoke to her comfortably, even about sex. Eleanor could tell Kelly was trying hard to be brave. She told Eleanor she couldn't confide in her own mother, who was humiliated that she'd gotten pregnant again so soon after the first baby. Although Kelly was really just a child, Eleanor knew she had to find the right mix of treating her as a grown woman making a responsible choice, yet still a vulnerable girl needing love and comfort. She listened and tried to give Kelly the information she needed. Privately, Eleanor knew there was only one correct choice for Kelly: allow the Russells to adopt her baby. But Eleanor did not want to appear to be selling. She just had to help Kelly realize she'd found a perfect home for her baby. This was important, because after a while, Eleanor learned Kelly was speaking to three other families—three families *besides* the Russells. In the domestic adoption market, a healthy Caucasian newborn was sought after.

Even though there were other families under consideration, Hal was optimistic about the Wisconsin adoption from the start. He said they were lucky to have had Kelly call them so early in their search and so late in her pregnancy. It was highly unusual to find a birth mother so far along in her pregnancy. Girls rarely changed their minds so close to their due dates. He showed them the paperwork Kelly had completed. The girl stated she had no health problems, and she'd had prenatal care. There were no apparent medical issues anywhere in the family history. It was good the baby's father was also the father of Kelly's first child. This showed some stability. Kelly was raising Sean with help from her parents. He was developing normally. Because she'd contacted the Russells so late in her pregnancy, Hal felt she'd probably done all her thinking already, weighed her options, and decided on adoption.

"It looks like the real deal," he said when they met in his crowded office. Raising his eyes from his paper-strewn desk, he added, "But we have to remember she's speaking to four families. So, we can't be 100 percent sure."

Ron gave Eleanor a long look. "*Four* families?"

Eleanor hadn't told him this.

"Yeah, you're one of four. But she likes you and likes that you're Californians. It's a dream of hers for the baby to grow up in California. The other families are back East. She's definitely favoring you. She said she liked your ad, too."

"Four families?" Ron repeated. "What kind of song and dance are we supposed to do? Are we auditioning for this girl?"

"No, no," Hal said. "It's pretty typical. There are so many families looking to adopt newborns, she has her choice."

"I don't know. And what about our being Jewish? Aren't most of these girls Christians—opposed to abortion? Isn't that why they put their babies up for adoption?" Ron asked.

"No, I don't think your being Jewish is a problem," Hal said. "She actually likes that you have some religion in the home. She's doesn't seem concerned about the Jewish part. She likes that you're a doctor, Ron, and that Eleanor teaches college. Just keep telling her about yourselves honestly. If it's meant to be, it will happen; that's what I believe in this business."

"I still don't like it," Ron repeated later that night in their bedroom as he took off his shoes. "It feels like we're giving way too much power to a teenager. What does she want from us? Is she bilking all of us—trying to get money from us all? Is that why she's talking to four couples?"

"No, I don't think she's doing that," Eleanor said. It was strange how calm she felt. Usually she was the worrier. "I think Kelly's trying to make the right choice. That's all. I'm talking to her tomorrow morning. I'll ask about the other families again." She kissed his eyes before he fell asleep. "I know this is our baby," she whispered.

On August 11, 1990, Kelly phoned to say she was in labor. It was real, she assured Eleanor, not false labor. She knew the difference. They should get on a plane right away and come to Wisconsin. The girl's voice had some decisiveness in it, not her usual sleepy tone. It was only ten months after the Loma Prieta earthquake, and Eleanor couldn't believe it was happening for them. She took a quick breath in.

"Okay," she said. "I'll get there as quick as I can." Her heart was pounding. "But, Kelly, you're sure? I don't think I ought to come now if you aren't ready. You don't need more time?"

"I'm sure," the girl said. "Just come. I've got to get off now. I'm having a contraction."

As soon as she hung up with Kelly, Eleanor called Ron. He told her he was on call at the hospital the next day. She should make a reservation and go ahead without him. He'd join her in a day or two, just as soon as he got coverage. Next, Eleanor called her widowed mother-in-law, Jean, and asked her if she could come from Denver and stay with Max and Lara. She didn't know how long she and Ron would be in Wisconsin.

Ron's mother met Eleanor's excitement with silence. She heartily disapproved of the adoption. She had made it clear she thought they were making a mistake. Finally, she sighed and said okay. She'd get to San Jose and be there that evening. Her voice implied she would indulge Eleanor, even though she thought her daughter-in-law was crazy.

Eleanor then booked her flight to Madison, paying the astronomical full fare for her ticket. She retrieved the suitcase she'd kept ready in their bedroom, just as if she herself were the one going into labor. She'd packed only for herself—it felt like bad luck to pack for the baby. She could buy everything she needed later; there were stores in Wisconsin. Just before she boarded the plane, Eleanor called Kelly's house. She needed reassurance this was really happening, not just a distraught teenager's whim. The girl's mother, Ruth, answered.

"Yes," Ruth said. "I just returned from the hospital. Kelly had the baby. And it's a boy, just as she predicted."

A boy!

"So you ought to come," Ruth said. "We're waiting for you."

Eleanor tried to read Kelly's mother's voice. Ruth was emotionless, even when she said it was a boy. Eleanor couldn't blame Ruth for wanting to get the adoption over with. A grandma wasn't supposed to fall in love with a baby the family was giving up. It was understandable she needed to distance herself from emotion.

Eleanor was relieved it was a boy. She and Ron would have been thrilled with either a boy or a girl. But Kelly already had a son. Eleanor feared Kelly wouldn't go through with it if this new baby had been a girl.

She took the red-eye to Chicago and then a puddle jumper to Madison. When she got off the plane and walked across the tarmac, she felt flattened by the unfamiliar humidity of Wisconsin. She picked up her suitcase, got a rental car, and headed directly to the hospital.

It was only when Eleanor stood inside the entrance to University Children's Hospital, a nice, modern place, with a helpful woman in a pink smock at the desk, that she felt her first wave of trepidation. She'd experienced this before—buyer's remorse. She would wade through the most difficult of obstacles, work tirelessly to achieve her goal, and then, when the goal was in sight, she'd panic.

She wondered how she was supposed to behave in this situation. A girl was giving up her baby—giving to Eleanor the child she'd had inside her body for nine months. Eleanor couldn't fathom the enormity of transferring a human life from one woman to another. *How can Kelly give away a baby? Or Ruth give up a grandbaby?* She herself couldn't understand allowing a baby to be yanked from his flesh-and-blood family. Sudden sadness for Kelly nearly squeezed the joy from her heart. But it wasn't her choice to make. So she squared her shoulders, picked up her suitcase, and walked to the pink-smocked volunteer.

"I'm looking for Kelly DeGrasse's room. She's just delivered a baby."

"Third floor. Elevator at the end of the hall."

She asked if she could stow her small suitcase at the desk, and the woman nodded. As she passed the hospital gift shop, Eleanor considered flowers. Perhaps she should have brought Kelly a pretty robe. Maybe no flowers. Not yet. She didn't want to appear as if she were pushing the girl. Ron had warned Eleanor not to get too excited. She mustn't get her hopes up; there might be complications. But without seeing the child, Eleanor knew this was her baby, as much as she'd known anything in her entire life. She just needed to help Kelly say goodbye.

She checked the watch she always wore, adding two hours for the time difference from California to Wisconsin. The baby had been born eight and a half hours earlier. Baby DeGrasse was just over one-third a day old. It was time to meet him. It was time to meet the girl who had brought him into the world.

Kelly was in a private room. The door was open, so Eleanor walked in. Kelly's pictures didn't do her justice. Eight hours after giving birth, there was still a fresh prettiness to her large-boned face. Her dark-blond hair fell in natural waves, and she had clear, hazel eyes, widely set apart. During their phone conversations, Eleanor had noted Kelly's seriousness, apparent now. Eleanor went to the girl and tried to hug her, but this was awkward because Kelly was propped up on several pillows and didn't lean toward her. There were so many conflicting emotions crammed into this tiny room.

"How did it go?" Eleanor asked. "The delivery, I mean. Tell me about it."

Kelly shrugged. "Easy. Easier than the first time. Labor was much shorter."

The first time. It was amazing to realize that this girl with the round, childish face had already given birth twice.

Kelly's parents were there. Ruth was a thin, dark-haired woman, her father broader, with eyes set apart like Kelly's. Eleanor realized she was probably older than Kelly's parents. She wondered how she appeared to them, a middle-aged woman with some gray already in her dark wavy hair, makeup rubbed off, her slacks tight at the waist, and wrinkled from the flight.

There were others in the room. Two thin, dark-haired boys were in the corner, staring down at their hands. She didn't know if they were Kelly's brothers or if one could be the baby's father. She wished she knew, but she couldn't take them all in; she wanted to focus only on Kelly. She nervously wondered how firm Kelly was in her decision. Now that she'd met Eleanor and seen how old she was, would she still want to give her baby to Eleanor and Ron? Eleanor studied Kelly as they spoke. She wanted to remember every detail. Maybe someday her son would ask, and she could tell the boy all about this day, about the girl who had given birth to him. She tried to memorize Kelly's face.

"I'm making something for him," Kelly said softly. "It's nearly finished. I'm crocheting a blanket. Could I send it to him when it's done?"

"Oh, Kelly, of course you can. He'll treasure it, I'm sure. What a beautiful thing for you to do." She felt her eyes tear up but didn't want to be the only one in the room to cry, so she swallowed hard and took Kelly's hand. This contact seemed to embarrass the girl, so she moved her hand away.

"I suppose you'd like to see him," Kelly said. "You can, you know. The nursery is down the hall." The girl motioned with her chin. "I told them you'd be coming."

Eleanor's heart began to pound. It was hard to breathe. "I'd like that a lot," she replied. "But only if you're okay with it. I don't have to go see him yet. I don't know how you can be so brave about this."

The girl shrugged. "I can tell how much you want the baby. I guess I like to make people happy."

Eleanor thought she heard Kelly's mother sniff at what her daughter said, a tiny, yet unpleasant sound. Eleanor smiled at them and forced herself to walk slowly from the room. She tried to maintain control of herself, but was hardly able to keep from running down the hall. When she reached the nursery, she searched all the bundles—the sleeping ones and the crying ones. She tapped on the glass door. A nurse with a head of blond curls opened it, and Eleanor explained who she was. The nursery staff had been informed. The blond nurse said they were aware Baby DeGrasse was "to be relinquished." Another nurse, one wearing teddy bear printed scrubs, asked if she'd like to hold the baby.

Eleanor swooned. This was exactly like falling in love. She was shocked by her feelings and her pounding heart. She hadn't known she'd be allowed to hold the baby in the hospital. She thought she wouldn't get to touch him until they took him away. She'd expected she'd have to sit patiently, watching Kelly hold him, bottling up her feelings until she and Ron could take the baby home.

"You can wash your hands in the sink there and tie a gown over your clothes," the nurse said, and pointed to a bin of laundered hospital gowns.

Eleanor slipped a gown over her rumpled khaki slacks and shirt and scrubbed her hands. She was directed to one of the bassinets with a blue bundle in it. BABY DEGRASSE was written on the tag. She watched the sleeping infant for a long time, her heart still beating fast. When he began to stir, the curly-haired nurse suggested she pick him up and bring him to a white rocking chair at the back of the nursery. Eleanor could give him his bottle.

"I can feed him? Here?" Gift after gift, she was being given. She never forgot those moments holding him for the first time, feeding and examining every feature. She and Ron had said they'd give their son, if they ever had a son, the name Joshua. They both loved the name. It was Ron's father's Hebrew name. Since she had first gotten on the plane, the baby had been Joshua in her mind. She wished she could freeze those moments when she rocked Joshua and first looked into his face. With Kelly's widely set-apart eyes, he stared into hers. And, as with any great love, her heart was gripped with fear at the thought of losing him. She held and rocked him and sang to him in her off-key voice until it was time to put the baby back into his bassinet and return to Kelly's room.

Ron arrived in Madison toward evening the next day. He went directly to University Children's Hospital from the airport, as Eleanor instructed. When he walked into Kelly's hospital room, Eleanor felt relief wash over her. She had been sitting next to Kelly's mother and they had run out of things to say. Ron would make everything right. Ron didn't talk much, but he had complete calmness about him. At his own hospital, the oldest and sickest patients were comforted when meeting Dr. Russell.

"I'll take good care of you," he'd say to people on the phone on the eve of their surgeries. Eleanor would be reading in bed next to him and overhear. "I'll take good care of you [or your father, or your sister, or your daughter]." And, even though Eleanor knew that he'd already had a long, grueling day, and had to be up the next morning before the sun rose, she never heard impatience in his voice. He would take care of this new baby, too. Kelly would see this about Ron.

"Am I in the right place?" Ron asked politely. He spoke to Kelly in his best bedside manner, ignoring Eleanor. "Are you Miss DeGrasse?"

Kelly pulled her sheet higher and nodded. She probably thought he was yet another doctor to probe her.

Eleanor went to her husband, and introduced him to Kelly and Kelly's mother and father. Earlier in the day, Kelly said she'd sign the adoption papers after she met Ron. She needed to make sure first that her son would have a good father.

"Did you have anesthesia?" Ron asked. "That's my field, you know."

"I tried to do it naturally," she answered. "But it got bad at the end. So I asked for something. But by that time, the baby was too low, so they said I couldn't get the medicine anymore."

"Well. You were very brave," he said. "A real trooper."

"I guess. I just wanted him to be healthy," Kelly said.

"You've had a long day. And night. Would it be okay if we left now, maybe let you get some rest?"

The girl nodded gratefully. "Okay, yeah, I am a little tired," Kelly said. "But I wanted to tell you both something."

"Of course, but then you should get some sleep," Ron said.

Ruth had the newspaper in front of her, but she wasn't reading it. She was listening to Kelly, watching the girl intently, her forehead wrinkled. Eleanor felt Ruth was worried her daughter would say or do something wrong. She tensed whenever Kelly spoke.

Eleanor was struck then with great sadness. The exchange suddenly felt like merchandising. Each family was trying to sell themselves to the other, with the baby in the middle. He was the goods being traded. She wished this was over and she could take Joshua home to begin their life together.

"I filled out his birth certificate today," Kelly said. "The people from the Bureau of Records came by and asked me to complete it. I told them he was going to be adopted. But they told me I had to complete it anyway. The copy is on the table there." She pointed to the bedside stand. "They said that later on, after the, you know, adoption is complete, you and Mrs. Russell are supposed to file for a new birth certificate. With your names on it and everything."

"Sure, Kelly. We understand," Ron said.

She hesitated. Eleanor sensed something else was on the girl's mind.

"I gave him a name," Kelly said.

"You named him?" Eleanor asked.

"Yes," Kelly said. "I filled in a name on the form. But I bet you won't keep it. I wrote Christopher on the paper. Esa named our first baby Sean. Same as John Lennon named his son. He has a thing for John Lennon. But I love the name Chris. That's what I'd have called him." She paused. "My mother said that you wouldn't like it, though. It's not a Jewish name and you'll change it. Anyway, the man from the records department said it was only temporary, until you file for a new birth certificate."

Kelly turned away. Ruth put down her newspaper and glared at her daughter.

Eleanor was sorry to have asked. Her baby was Joshua. The name she and Ron loved.

When Eleanor and Ron left the hospital that night, they went to the Residence Inn where Eleanor had checked in the day before. They ate dinner in their room, then found a mall that was still open and bought a porta-crib. They left it in its box and propped the box against the wall. Ron carefully put the receipt into his wallet.

The next morning, Mike Lustig, a lawyer in Madison, called.

He said he'd been contacted by Hal Mozart. A local lawyer was required in addition to their California lawyer. If they retained him, he would give Kelly the paperwork needed to move forward. Kelly and her boyfriend, Esa, were to sign away their parental rights. After they did that, the birth parents were to physically hand over the baby to him. According to Wisconsin adoption law, the lawyer brings the baby to the new parents, acting as the intermediary between the adoptive and birth parents.

Mike was slick and smooth, everything Hal Mozart was not. He told them he'd go the hospital before Kelly was discharged. As soon as Kelly and Esa signed the papers, she'd give the baby to him, and then they would leave the hospital separately. Mike would bring the baby to Eleanor and Ron at the Residence Inn.

"So get the crib and all your stuff ready. What else do newborns need? Lots of diapers, I suppose. Tomorrow is the day!" he said to Eleanor on the phone. He was jovial and confident.

"Tomorrow is Saturday. You work Saturdays?" Eleanor asked.

Mike laughed, a short staccato that startled Eleanor. "Hey, the stork works seven days a week, right? But this stork does tend to bill a tad bit more for weekend deliveries. Also, if you don't mind, I'm gonna bring my girlfriend with me. I'm not too great handling babies. She's really excited about this."

"Sure," Eleanor said. "Okay. You'll get a car seat?"

"I hope you realize what this'll cost me. My girlfriend is going to take one look at that beautiful baby of yours and my bachelor days are numbered." Mike laughed again. "This baby is all my girlfriend has been talking about since I told her I needed her help on Saturday. You watch, by this time next year, I'll be having my own stork visit. Oh, and don't worry, we keep a car seat at the office. Our firm has handled a few adoptions before this one."

On Saturday morning, Eleanor and Ron sat on the edge of the bed, checking their watches. Eleanor felt sick with worry that Kelly would change her mind and wouldn't actually relinquish the baby. She worried Mike would appear empty-handed. Ron kept thinking of other things they should have picked up for the baby, but Eleanor didn't want him to leave. As it was, they'd filled the room with diapers, cans of formula, and stuffed animals. They'd built the collapsible porta-crib and bought a car seat of their own. Friends had sent flowers and balloon bouquets, too. Finally, there was nothing else to do or say, so they sat still and waited, holding hands and staring at the door.

At noon, there was a knock. Mike and his pretty, blond girlfriend, Yvonne, were there. Yvonne held the baby. They were both dressed casually in jeans and University of Wisconsin sweatshirts. Mike's girlfriend handed the little blue bundle to Eleanor.

"He never made a peep all the way over here," Yvonne said. "He's absolutely precious."

"Wait, wait," Ron said. "Let me get a picture."

Eleanor stood between Mike and Yvonne. Tears streamed down Eleanor's face, and Ron had to wipe his eyes before he focused the camera. Everyone in the picture had enormous smiles on their faces. It was Joshua's first photo and she planned to place it in his baby album.

"The stork delivers Joshua," Eleanor later wrote in the album.

Mike and Yvonne stayed only a short while. But before they left, Mike said he had a request from Kelly. He knew this was unexpected, but they shouldn't worry. Kelly was hoping she could see them again one last time, all of them together. She wanted Ron and Eleanor to bring the baby and come to her parents' condominium.

"Go to their house?" Eleanor asked, hugging Joshua to her. "Are they having second thoughts? Do we have to go?"

Mike shrugged. "I don't think she's changing her mind. Although, you do know she has seventy-two hours to do that. That's a reality here."

"Is it about money?" Ron asked. He put down his camera.

"Well, sure, there may be medical bills. You'll get those. Hospital bills, doctors' fees, et cetera. But I don't sense Kelly is negotiating. It's something else. I think she just wants to see you before you leave town to get the image of you all together in her mind. Closure or something. It all went so quickly yesterday. I tried to talk her out of it, but Kelly hung tough. I don't think you have any choice. I think you've got to do this."

Eleanor groaned.

"It'll be okay," Mike said. He looked down at the baby, asleep now in Eleanor's arms. "Just keep it positive. Here's the address. It's only about ten minutes from here. They're expecting you around eleven tomorrow. Call me if there's a problem."

Eleanor's stomach clenched, but she smiled weakly and walked Mike and Yvonne to the door, Mike making stork jokes the whole time. She was thinking dark thoughts. It would all be taken away tomorrow.

Somehow they got through the night and the next morning they packed up an enormous amount into the baby's diaper bag. As she strapped Joshua into his car seat, Eleanor suddenly straightened and said, "You know, I never brought Kelly anything at the hospital. We need to stop for flowers."

"That's going to make us late. It's not necessary. Let's just go and get this over with."

Eleanor was insistent. "It is necessary. I've got to bring them something. I can't waltz in and out with her baby and not bring anything. Come on, I'm sure we'll find a florist around here."

But they couldn't find one. They drove around Madison in circles. Joshua was starting to get fussy. It was almost time for him to eat, but Eleanor wouldn't give up. She told Ron he had to keep looking. Eventually, with all three of them in a bad mood, Ron pulled into a supermarket parking lot.

"You know I hate supermarket flowers," Eleanor said grumpily.

48

"It's this or nothing. Find something and let's get going."

She went into the market and all the flowers were sad and wilted. She settled on a gold foil-wrapped plant, undistinguished and lacking the cheer she desperately wanted to bring to Kelly.

They arrived fifteen minutes late to the DeGrasse house. They were hit by a blast of hot air when they opened the car door. Ron unhooked the car seat and Eleanor carried the baby in, still in his little chair. Eleanor had fed Joshua in the car. He was full and content.

Kelly's family lived in a townhouse, in a row of identical units. Ruth opened the door, not exactly welcoming them, but stepping aside so they could enter. She never glanced at Joshua.

The house resembled Ron and Eleanor's motel room. Everything was beige and blond wood and immaculately clean. Eleanor wondered again why they couldn't care for this beautiful new baby. It was a respectable townhouse, like thousands of others across America. It was clean and quiet. Too quiet, Eleanor realized.

"Is your little boy here? Sean?" she asked Kelly.

"No, Esa took him out for a few hours. To see his other grandma. Mom thought it was better if Sean didn't see the baby."

Eleanor nodded. Ron placed the plant on the light wood coffee table. Eleanor put Joshua in his seat next to the plant. They sat in a circle around the room, all staring at the infant. He was awake, solemnly blinking his enormous hazel-colored eyes and long eyelashes. Eleanor had dressed him in a pale blue sailor suit. Every part of him was round and sweet. Eleanor studied Kelly, slumped on the couch next to her father. She wished she could take the girl in her arms.

"I can't believe you're back in your jeans. Look at you—you don't seem like you gave birth three days ago." Eleanor immediately regretted her fake cheerful tone.

Kelly nodded. "Yeah. They're tight, but I got back into them." She stole little glances at the baby.

"Are you feeling okay?" Ron asked.

"Oh, sure. I'm fine," Kelly answered.

They sat a while more.

Kelly finally spoke. "Dad, doesn't he resemble Sean when he was just born? He has those same long eyelashes. He should have been a girl, with those eyelashes."

Her father barely nodded. He seemed not to know if the two boys resembling each other was a good thing or not.

Ruth didn't offer them anything to eat or drink. She sat stiffly with her arms folded. Finally, Eleanor commented on the drawings hanging on the living room walls. There were watercolors and pastel sketches of lakes and sailboats.

Kelly's dad slowly stood up. "Yeah, those are mine. I like to draw." He walked around the room and pointed to each, naming which of the Wisconsin lakes were depicted. The lakes had long, Native American names like Oconomowoc and Waupaca. "I like water. I'd have a little boat myself, if we had the money. I draw them instead."

As he talked about his pictures, Eleanor thought Kelly's father was the happiest she'd seen him. And even though, as usual, she went overboard in her compliments, the sketches really were lovely.

"Maybe the baby will have his grandfather's artistic ability," Ron said. "Inherit your skill."

Mr. DeGrasse looked down at his hands but didn't answer.

Joshua was beginning to fuss. Kelly's mother said, "I suppose you'll have to be getting back to your hotel now. The baby is getting restless."

In the half hour they'd been in the townhouse, no one had picked him up. Eleanor wanted to tell Kelly it was okay for her to hold the baby and say goodbye, but she didn't know whether holding the baby would make things worse. She didn't want to hold Joshua herself, fearing it would cause Kelly even more pain. So

Joshua remained in his infant carrier, balanced on the low coffee table, surrounded by his birth and adoptive families this one last time.

When they stood to leave, Kelly turned away from the baby seat. Eleanor noticed a small stain on Kelly's shirt. The girl's milk was leaking. Seeing the milk on Kelly's blouse made her unutterably sad. Before they even reached the street, the door behind them closed. Ron bent and carefully buckled the baby seat back into the car.

On the drive back to the motel, they said nothing. Eleanor felt weak with relief. She kept turning to Joshua. She'd expected Kelly to tell them she'd changed her mind. She was filled with dread thinking they'd be leaving without the baby. She hadn't even realized how frightened she had been. Now that it was over, she never wanted to put her baby down again. She thought of that poor bereft teenager back in the townhouse and vowed she would give this baby all the love she had to give.

They spent the next two heavenly days, before Ron had to return to California, getting to know their son. She couldn't remember a more distraction-free time in their marriage. They had only each other and the baby in the little motel room. They spent long periods of time just staring at him. Each day, a maid arrived, tidied the bed, cleaned the bathroom, and took the dirty diapers away. There was not even the most minimal housekeeping to do. Their whole world was Joshua, each other, and this fifteen-by-twenty-foot motel room.

Chapter 3

KELLY PREGNANT

1989 and 1990

When Sean, her first baby, was born and the nurse handed him to Kelly, cleaned up and surprisingly alert for a newborn, he'd only briefly rooted around, then quickly found her nipple, feeding that first time as naturally as if he'd been at it for months. The public health nurse visited her the next day and recited the advantages of breastfeeding.

"Breastfeeding also reduces fertility, a nice benefit," the friendly middle-aged woman explained and smiled.

Kelly sat up in bed, listening politely, especially to the part about it helping with birth control, but she needed no convincing. Breastfeeding Sean felt as if she was always meant to do it; she was a natural. The best part was she alone could do it for her child.

Her mother's lips pursed when she'd come into the room after Sean's birth. Kelly was a large girl, and her mother's eyes widened as she watched her daughter. Kelly's nipples were a deep, dark brown and her breasts so engorged, she had to use two fingers to make a space above Sean's mouth so he could breathe and not be smothered by her fullness. Kelly tried to ignore her mother's gaze and to focus on feeding Sean. But she couldn't help seeing her mother's look of disgust as she took in Kelly's large, pale thighs, exposed when the short hospital gown rode up.

Kelly had matured early. Ever since she was in fifth grade, her mother had told her that her shirts were too small and the buttons were pulling apart. Whenever Kelly left the house, especially in warm weather, Ruth had something critical to say about what the girl was wearing.

"I can see your bra straps plain as day, Kelly. Do you know what we thought of girls who went around with their underwear showing? The way you hang out of your clothes is disgraceful. And messy."

Ruth kept herself neat and tidy at all times. Even in the heat of summer, she rarely left the house without stockings. Kelly was not sure what it was about herself that so annoyed the woman, but she'd always felt she displeased her tall, slender mother. She thought it might be her plumpness, the round heaviness of her body, and the slowness with which she moved that most exasperated her mother. Her father, however, had the same roundness as Kelly and the same slow, studied motions. He never got out of the car quickly, as her mother did, but always sat behind the wheel for a moment or two before he opened the door and unfolded his bulky frame. Ruth remained standing beside the car, tapping her fingers on the hood with impatience, waiting for him. Growing up, Kelly had watched this scene countless times, always wondering why her mother was in such a rush and why she hurried her father along so much.

"Take this," her mother now said to Kelly in the hospital after Sean was born. She snatched up a receiving blanket she found at the bottom of the baby's bassinet. "Cover yourself. Your father's on his way up from the parking lot. Look at you, Kelly. Cover up and make yourself look decent." Just as she said this, Kelly's father came into the room carrying a large bouquet of balloons.

Kelly knew her mother had not breastfed either Kelly or her older brother. Her mother had mentioned to Kelly several times that she thought the whole thing seemed animal-like. Ruth had small, compact breasts, which she kept well covered under neatly pressed blouses and jackets. Kelly didn't think she had ever seen her mother's breasts, bare and exposed, as her own were that day in the hospital. She didn't care about herself, but she sadly wished she could see some sign of warmth from her mother toward the baby. Sean was her first grandchild. But Kelly was also prepared for her mother's disapproval. She had made her feelings known throughout her daughter's pregnancy.

Kelly had overheard her mother talking to her father, spitting out the words.

"I'm supposed to be happy about a fifteen-year-old having a baby with that useless kid? What can he do? Tinker with bicycles, that's about it. Oh, yeah, and get my only daughter pregnant."

"Ruth, honey, it's not the end of the world. Plenty of girls get pregnant these days. They grow up quicker."

Kelly's dad tried, as usual, to placate his wife. He reminded her how Kelly had always been good with children.

"She's going to be a fine mother, young as she is," he said. "She's so patient with kids. The neighbors always call her to babysit."

But Ruth continued rinsing the dishes, roughly clanking together the silverware, and didn't even bother to answer. Ruth seemed angry with him as well as with her daughter.

The night after Sean was born, Esa's mother had come to the hospital with her son. She was a sad, stringy-haired widow who was forever apologizing, and Kelly thought she could smell wine on her breath when she leaned over to kiss the baby's head.

"Oh, he's beautiful, Kelly. What a perfect little boy." The woman stepped back and stared at the baby. "I swear, he looks just like you. Look at that sweet round head and his light-colored hair." She'd brought a package for Sean. They were beaded moccasins. "These belonged to Esa when he was a baby," she said. "It's not much, but I thought you might like to have them."

After Esa left the hospital to take his mom home, Ruth continually talked about the woman and her moccasins. The moccasins really set her off.

"Don't think about bringing those things into the house, Kelly. They smell of bacon fat. You know they cure the leather in bacon grease? Or worse. The dog'll probably try to eat them."

Kelly thought the little shoes were cute, but she left them on the bedside table when she checked out of the hospital. Things were going to be hard enough at home without fighting about the beaded moccasins.

After she had Sean, Kelly dropped out of school. She'd never liked studying. All she wanted to do was to stay home and take care of her baby. The hours of the day floated by and she was perfectly content, not at all lonely, just relieved when her parents left for work and she could have the house all to herself with the baby. She was supposed to do homeschooling, but no one, including the school, seemed interested in making that happen.

Occasionally, Esa would come by during the day. She'd fix him a sandwich, making sure the kitchen was perfectly clean afterward, sponging off the counters so there wasn't a crumb anywhere it wasn't supposed to be. She devoted herself to taking care of Sean. She fed him, changed him, and played with him. It was like a pleasant dream holding him those early months, sniffing the intoxicating smell of his head. Sean wasn't an easy baby, but she thought she had never been so good at anything else in her life, even softball.

Back in junior high, she'd had the best pitching arm on her team. She'd even won an award from her softball league when they'd gone to the state championships in Larchfield. Sometimes in Target or at the supermarket, she saw people from her team, one of the coaches, or a parent, and they'd say something nice to her about her pitching. One coach even told her that her strikeout record from 1986 was still undefeated, three years later. But she couldn't take it seriously. It seemed silly she'd once been so wrapped up in throwing a ball. After she'd started high school, and especially after she'd met Esa, she stopped thinking about the game. Now, with the baby, she had no need for anything else.

Despite what Ruth thought, Esa Lewis had been her first and only boyfriend. She knew her mother didn't believe her. She had looked Kelly up and down and called her a slut.

It was true Kelly really had been interested in sex. She might have slept with any boy who paid her some attention, but she'd met Esa first, at the beginning of her freshman year. He was older and already out of school.

One day at the Dairy Queen, she waited for a girlfriend to get off work, and she started a conversation with him. She didn't know why. She was usually too shy to start talking to boys, especially older, good-looking ones like Esa. But he was sitting alone, and he seemed like someone who wouldn't give a smart-ass answer to a girl.

"I love the root beer floats," she'd said.

"Yeah, sometimes I just have to come in for one." He smiled a shy smile at her. "It doesn't matter what time of day it is. Even in winter, I get a craving for one. The fizz, I guess."

He began giving Kelly lifts home from school. Soon, their hours alone in the afternoons became all-consuming for her. It was what she daydreamed about during the long, boring classes at high school. She rocked back and forth on the metal stool in science class, getting slightly turned on from the pressure of the seat against her sex, and watched the clock, counting the hours until Esa came to the front of the school, driving his beat-up white Ford van. They usually went to the outskirts of town and found a place to park by the lake.

She spent the entire first semester of her freshman year in a dream of sex and Esa. She made up a whole other life to her family, things she did after school. She told her parents she had Future Nurses of America and Glee Club meetings. Her parents didn't get home from work until nearly six o'clock in the evening. As long as she set the table and started the meal, neither of them asked questions.

Kelly didn't know what sex was like with other boys, but when her few girlfriends talked about it, they made it sound fairly pointless. It was an excuse to be held, maybe, for a few moments. Most liked the kissing. Though, according to their reports, that didn't last long with the other boys, either. In general, the girls didn't seem to feel very much at all. They said their boyfriends clutched at their breasts, really kind of pawing, which hurt slightly.

"Why," several girls asked, "do boys think that pinching or pulling on nipples is a turn-on?"

The boys poked around down there with their penises and then clumsily stuck it in. After only a few rocking humps up and down, her girlfriend Melissa reported her boyfriend would get an agonized look on his face. He'd moan, he'd come, and it was over. It was messy, and none of the girls seemed to enjoy it.

That's why Kelly thought there was something wrong with her at first—she enjoyed it so much. She must be a slut, just as her mother thought. But, as the year went by, and more and more of the girls lost their virginity and talked about it, she realized that what she and Esa did was different.

"Esa. What kind of name is that?" Kelly asked. "I never heard it before."

"It's an Indian name. Something to do with wolves, my mom said. I don't know much about it. She said my father had a little bit of Indian in him."

He shrugged and didn't say anything else. He was terrible at talking. He flushed and mumbled when he had to answer questions, even from her. But he touched Kelly in ways that made her dizzy.

She loved him, she thought, as much as she could tell. She knew she was just a kid, but Esa was the only thing in her life that mattered. He made her feel pretty, too. Esa was good-looking, but completely the opposite of her. He was thin—not an ounce of extra flesh on him. His hair was dark and straight. Kelly traced his prominent cheekbones with her fingertips. Her own face was fleshy and full.

Esa spent a very long time marveling over her breasts that autumn. She thought they were heavy and cumbersome, and covered them in the big, old-lady bras she bought when shopping with her mom. When he took off her bra the first time one late October afternoon when the leaves were turning a beautiful orange, Esa stared at her breasts for a long time. He put his head down between them and rocked from side to side in the space between them. He inhaled and closed his eyes as if to concentrate on the smell of her. She felt his warm breath, and she began to dislike her breasts a little less. He began to kiss her there . . . soft, sweet kisses at first, and then using greater pressure, his tongue made circles around her nipples. His kisses raised goose bumps on her arms. He worried she was cold and tried to wrap his coat around her. But she shook it off, never wanting him to stop kissing her that way or to stop looking at her. She was glad neither of them smoked, glad she could smell his beautiful clean smell and not the acrid cigarette smell on so many of the boys at high school.

When they were driving home from the lake, she asked him about smoking. He said his dad had died of throat cancer. He'd been a Vietnam vet and had died when Esa was small. He'd promised his mother he would never smoke. He thought that was the least he could do. She asked so little of him, or of life, really.

For weeks, Esa seemed satisfied with loving her breasts and touching her arms, legs, neck, and belly. They got to know each other. While the last of the leaves dropped from the trees, Esa remained occupied with her breasts and softly touching her skin.

He shyly told her how he never tired of stroking her pale, white body. He loved the smoothness of it. She told him she was embarrassed by her fleshiness, how trim and firm he seemed compared to her. He seemed pained when she said that. He said all the women in his family were scrawny and skinny. They had nothing soft about them. He liked her softness best. He loved that she had flesh; he dreamed of it at night. He loved her large, deep-set hazel eyes, and her smooth, full cheeks. When he talked, it seemed possible to Kelly that she might not be ugly, and her bigness was not something to be ashamed of.

Finally, Kelly let him know it was okay to go further. He'd been perched over her, up on his knees, kissing her everywhere. They were in the back of his van, where he'd laid a big, clean piece of foam from the bike shop for her to lie on. She could see the bump in his jeans, the round fullness, and it was driving her crazy. She couldn't stand another second not to touch him there and she reached for his roundness. He looked into her eyes. Then she slowly unzipped his jeans. In a little while, he unzipped hers, slowly as well. She liked how he mirrored her actions exactly.

Esa was like that . . . everything slow and deliberate. He thought about each movement he made and everything he said. He was a little like her own father—a quiet man who considered every word. She'd always thought it was because her mother cut him off and spoke for her husband before he said what was on his mind. Kelly wished she could hear her father's voice more. Growing up, she thought about the absence of his voice in their house. There was so much he left unsaid. She vowed she'd wait for Esa to speak; she'd never cut him off as her mother did her father.

As winter started up in Madison and the temperature dropped, they continued to have sex in the van. Esa still came by for her after school and they still drove out to the lake. It was getting dark earlier, though, and their afternoons felt compressed as they lay together in the van. He brought a red wool blanket. It was scratchy, but she liked the feel of it when Esa pulled it over them. Esa always worried about his hands being too cold and spent a lot of time rubbing and blowing on them, so that he wouldn't shock her with their chill.

She wasn't sure how she got pregnant the first time because Esa always used protection. Sometimes, she was so impatient for him to enter her, she'd try to guide him toward her before he got the condom on, but he'd stop and methodically put it on, no matter how excited he was. Kelly actually felt hurt by his carefulness, as if Esa wasn't as excited as she was, as if his thoughts and consciousness weren't overcome with passion, as hers were. He'd stop and reach for the condom, tearing the wrapper off and sliding it over his beautiful, narrow penis, when she herself was so blinded with desire for him she couldn't have stopped. But he was careful and never forgot. Still, all that carefulness failed them.

In April of her freshman year, just as the worst of winter was over and the afternoons were finally beginning to lengthen, Kelly found herself sick to her stomach. She'd throw up when she'd smell her lunch—even a simple ham sandwich. With shock, she realized her period was late. A girl at school actually had a pregnancy test kit in her locker. With shaking hands, she took it and went into a stall in the girls' bathroom. She read the directions and peed on the stick.

She was only fifteen, Esa nineteen. She wanted to tell him in person, so she could see his face. He was getting more work at the bike shop in Larchfield, though, so it was a few days before they saw each other.

As soon as she got settled in the van and he started the motor, she said it, to get it over with.

"I'm pregnant. I already did the test. It came up positive."

Her words hung there. It was starting to rain and the roads were slippery. He kept his eyes forward, and other than a little wince, a wrinkling of his forehead, he didn't answer until they were headed out of town on the county two-lane road they often took.

"Just my luck," he finally said.

She was stung. It sounded so bitter, the first harsh thing he'd ever said to her.

He turned to her. "Sorry. I don't mean it the way it sounds, Kelly. I mean that it's just my luck I messed up. I tried to be careful. But, of course, I messed up."

His eyes went back to the road, driving slowly and carefully as the rain came down harder. His thin shoulders were slumped over. Then he pounded the steering wheel with his fist. "I'm so, so sorry," he said, his jaw clenched tight. "This is going to be a mess for you. It'll be so much worse for you."

They didn't talk for a while. The windshield wipers were the only sound in the van. She stared at his closed fist.

After he'd parked the van, he asked, "What do you want to do? Do you need money to get rid of it?" He asked it so meekly, as if he had no say in the matter.

"No, Esa. I want to have it."

She had been undecided before. At the very beginning, she thought she wanted the baby, just to get back at her mother. Then, a day later, she thought she wasn't strong enough for the arguments, yelling, and pain. She hadn't wanted to make more trouble in the house because somehow she knew her mother would take out her anger on her father in addition to her.

But when she sat in the car watching the spring rain come down in sheets onto the lake, Kelly made up her mind. She knew she wanted to give Esa this baby, like a present. He was so sure that he, or anything belonging to him, was of no value. She saw the surprise on his face. He expected her to tell him she'd decided to get rid of the baby.

"It's ours. I want to have it," she said. She sounded more certain than she felt.

He studied her. The afternoon was warm, and the rain came down on the piles of gray snow, melting away the last remains of the harsh winter they'd had.

"Your mother will kill us. You. I know how hard she rides you."

She shrugged. "It doesn't matter. She can't make me get rid of it."

"I'm scared, Kelly. But if this is what you want, we'll make it work." He kissed her softly on the lips. "I'm happy we're going to have a baby together," he said.

The next day, they went to see Esa's mother. Esa lived with her in a run-down house, more of a shack, really, about seven miles out of town. Together, they told her that Kelly was pregnant. His mother surprised them. A shy little smile formed around her lips. She wasn't a woman who ordinarily smiled very much.

"You can come here, Kelly, you know. You and the baby can live here. I'll help you. I can help out with the baby."

Kelly glanced around at the messy kitchen. One side of the sink was stuffed up and eggshells floated in the dirty water. Esa's mother had served fried eggs for their supper. Only one of the four burners on the stove worked. There was a smell of escaping gas, mixed with the cheap wine his mother drank. On the dish drain were two empty bottles.

Esa's and Kelly's eyes met. Esa had been to the DeGrasse's nice condo many times. He'd seen the spotless kitchen with its modern appliances. He had smelled the Pine Sol as soon as he entered the front door.

Kelly knew she couldn't raise her baby in Esa's mother's house.

"I'd better stay at home," Kelly answered the woman softly.

Esa's mother got a little teary and said, "Oh, Esa. My first grandchild." Her son put his arm loosely around his mother and shut off the gas.

"Are you going to be okay?" Esa's mother asked him.

"We'll be fine, Mom," Esa said.

Telling Ruth later that week was even worse than Kelly expected. She waited until after her father had already gone to work in the morning. She didn't want him to protect her. She knew he wouldn't be able to. When she finally got the words out, Ruth slapped her—a loud, forceful slap across her cheek. Her mom hadn't hit Kelly in several years, and the slap caught her off guard, leaving a large pink mark on her face. When she looked over at the mirror in the hall, Kelly thought she could actually see the outline of fingers on her cheek. The words Ruth shouted at Kelly had been predictable, though.

"You are a slut. And a whore!"

She also called Esa a fool. Then her mother took a breath and lowered her voice.

"Anyway, you're positive it's Esa's? That scrawny boy doesn't look man enough to father anyone's baby. Who else were you with? You might as well admit it. I know you're gone every afternoon. You're not in any glee club. You can't sing a note. Where do you go? Who the hell else have you been sleeping with?"

Throughout it all, Kelly did not defend herself. She'd made up her mind to let her mother rant and rave until her anger was spent and then tell her she was going to keep the baby. But to Kelly's surprise, her mother never brought up getting rid of the baby. Ruth went on and on about Kelly's stupidity, but she never mentioned abortion.

Instead, she yelled, "Do you know how hard it's going to be to raise the little bastard? We can't kick you out. You're a minor and that's probably against the law. But we're finished raising kids. Don't expect a thing from us."

Ruth grabbed her coat and keys and slammed the front door. Kelly heard her mother start her car and pull into the street.

Ruth worked at one of the mail-order firms that employed many women in town. Her mother answered the phone and helped people make selections from a catalog that offered goose-down clothing and comforters. She encouraged customers to add on to their orders, perhaps select from one of the daily shoppers' specials.

When Kelly was much younger, she had sometimes gone to work with her mother. She couldn't believe how pleasant her mother could make her voice sound on the phone to strangers. Kelly and her older brother, who was away in the service, used to laugh at how their mother had two voices: one for the family and another for the rest of the world.

Now, Kelly sat at the kitchen table after her mother left, not moving. Finally, she got up, automatically gathering up the cereal bowls. She wiped away the crumbs on the table. Then she stood at the sink and put her hand over her belly. The yelling had meant nothing. A lot of noise. What was shocking to her was her mother's apparent acceptance that Kelly would have this baby.

Kelly walked out the door, picking up her backpack on the way. The bruise on her cheek was darkening, but she didn't even think about it. She floated as she walked the six short blocks to school, aware of the secret inside her. She felt like she'd gotten away with something. This baby was hers to keep.

For months after she gave birth, it had been so precious, she and the baby and, occasionally, Esa. She thought of little else besides Sean. She left Esa to worry about the money. He assured her he was saving up his salary from the bike shop and soon they'd have enough to get a place of their own, just the three of them. They'd have to wait only a few more months. Kelly got good at ignoring most of her mother's unpleasantness. All she had to do was keep Sean relatively quiet, get the chores done so that her mother came home to a tidy house, and the dream state she was in continued.

Esa came as often as he could to visit the baby and Kelly. But every time Esa visited, he seemed to slink, not walk, through the front door. Her mother always reached the door before Kelly. She would let the boy in, but then barely say a word to him. Esa wiped his feet on the mat over and over, seemingly terrified to dirty the pale beige carpets in the DeGrasse house. Kelly's mom stood at the door, watching him wipe his feet, her arms crossed. If the baby was asleep, Kelly and Esa would pack him up and go for a ride. Sometimes they had sex in the van, on the same piece of foam that Esa always kept in the back, but it was quick and furtive, not the joy it had been when they'd first met. They were both aware every time Sean stirred in the basket they'd placed beside them.

If Esa arrived when Sean was awake and fussy, they usually stayed home. Even when Esa tried to help with Sean, holding him and trying to soothe his crying, Ruth watched and gave him unfriendly stares. Once they tried to go up to Kelly's room to be alone with the baby, but her mother gave them such a hard look when they came down, they felt like they had done something wrong. After that, they stayed downstairs in the living room.

Esa brought presents for Sean and handed them to Kelly proudly. Once he bought the baby some cute Green Bay Packers pajamas.

"Everybody likes the Packers," he said to Kelly.

But Ruth picked up the pajamas and narrowed her lips.

"My mom picked it out at Walmart," Esa said, turning to Kelly for help. "She said they'd keep Sean real warm."

"Hey, they're really nice and soft," Kelly said, and held the pajamas to her cheek. "He'll look so cute in these. Won't he look cute in these, Mom?"

"Looks like he'll outgrow them before too long, though, big as he is," her mother said, and pulled her glasses up from the chain around her neck so she could read the label. "They'll shrink up, too. You ought to save your money, Esa."

The boy's shoulders slumped.

When Sean was four months old, Esa told Kelly he thought

they'd finally be able to move in together. There was an apartment in back of the bike store where Esa worked in Larchfield, and the owner said he could have it the first of next month. Esa thought he'd have enough money saved for the deposit by then.

Just before they were to sign the lease, though, they had some bad luck. There was a robbery at the bike store. Even though there was no hard evidence, and he was never charged with anything, Esa lost his job. The accusation seemed to leave a stink on him at all the other bike shops in the area. Esa had never broken the law before, and Kelly was ready to swear he'd had nothing at all to do with the robbery. But the owners suspected him anyway. After all, they'd given Esa a key to close up the shop, and there'd been no forced entry on the night of the thefts. Although there was no proof, they assumed he had something to do with it.

Esa was a wizard at fixing bicycles, but he had trouble speaking up for himself. He had a terribly sad, hangdog expression whenever anyone asked him a question, as if he were, indeed, guilty of something.

"Come on, Esa." Kelly said. "Tell your boss where you were that night. Tell him you weren't even in Larchfield. Your friends would vouch for you."

But Esa was hopeless. He crumpled around people in authority, and though he tried, he couldn't find another job. Soon, the money he'd saved for the apartment was eaten up. And, at around that same time, Kelly found out she was going to have another baby.

Her second pregnancy was nearly half over when she discovered it. In her own voice, as well as her mother's, she heard herself say, *I must be the dumbest girl in all of Wisconsin.* She envisioned her mother scornfully narrowing her eyes, assessing before her the lump of stupidity she had for a daughter, then asking, "Haven't you figured out where they come from yet?"

Sean was eight months old, alert and eager to observe the

world. He was no longer as interested in the breast. She'd gone to Planned Parenthood because she thought she ought to start on the pill. The nurse at Planned Parenthood told her she needed to get a pregnancy test and an examination before she started taking the birth control medicine. It was a formality. After the examination, Kelly was taken in to see the counselor. They'd already been at the clinic for two hours. Sean was tired and leaned up against her, sucking on his pacifier.

The woman read the file on her desk, then studied the girl in front of her. She sighed.

"You're only sixteen, Kelly? Is that correct?"

"Yes," Kelly said, hoping not to hear another lecture.

"You're pregnant, my dear. Well into your second trimester."

Kelly stared at her in disbelief. "I can't be. The nurse said breast-feeding would keep me safe. I've been nursing all this time. I can't be pregnant. Sean never even had one bottle."

The counselor just watched her tiredly.

Kelly looked down at Sean and kissed the top of his head, her tears running into his ashy brown hair. The counselor must be wrong. The nurse in the hospital had assured her they'd be safe. Kelly had told Esa they didn't need to worry. He hadn't used rubbers or anything. But once again, they'd had bad luck. She and Esa seemed to have both bad luck and a talent for making babies.

As she held Sean tightly to her, she asked the counselor about her options. The thought of telling everyone—Esa, her mother, her father—made her so sick she wanted to throw up.

"It's too late for the simpler methods of abortion," the counselor said. "After eighteen weeks, we don't do them at this clinic. You have to go down to Milwaukee, where the clinic is more of a medical facility. You'll need to stay overnight, too, in a hotel. Do you have someone to stay with you and take you home? Maybe your parents?" the woman suggested hopefully.

Kelly slid down into her seat, still hanging on tightly to Sean, who had finally fallen asleep.

The counselor explained the procedure in Milwaukee, which involved a saline drip. This would induce labor and Kelly would give birth to the fetus. There could be complications. Of course, many of these second-term abortions were done every month. But because it was a more complicated medical procedure and because the baby was more fully formed, Kelly needed to think long and hard about it. She recommended the girl go home and consider things. But not for very long. She was going to have to make a decision soon.

Kelly contemplated this other baby, this almost formed one, inside her. She watched Sean sleeping so peacefully in her arms. *Poor thing*, she thought. *You don't even get to be my baby anymore.*

"You really didn't know?" the woman asked, examining Kelly's face.

Kelly shook her head miserably, then got up to leave. She supposed the woman wasn't being intentionally mean. She was tired. She probably saw a lot of girls like her every day.

Kelly had not had a bit of nausea. She had been tired, but Sean kept her up at night. He had colic, and he cried every few hours, night and day. She felt so sorry for him when he brought his little feet up to his chest and writhed in pain. Kelly gently rubbed his belly, trying to soothe him. She tried everything she could to keep him from waking her parents.

Her mother reminded her how *some people* had to get up in the morning. Once in a while, in the night, her father knocked softly on her door. He sleepily offered to help her, saying he could sit and rock Sean or walk with him. But his offers made her feel guilty, so she kept herself hypervigilant at night, never really sinking into a deep sleep. She woke with the baby's first whimper.

Her body hadn't revealed this second pregnancy at all, either. She had none of her mother's small-boned delicacy. She was large and square like her father. Her stomach was still loose and flabby from Sean, and her breasts were large from feeding him. She didn't feel pregnant. She clutched Sean tighter to her. She loved her baby so much, but, as usual, she and Esa had messed up.

At home, Kelly realized that, with this second pregnancy, the quiet, peaceful time of her life with Sean was over. There had been other changes lately, too, but she had tried not to think too much about them. Sex with Esa was no longer the comfort it had been. It had lost the magic of the winter of their first year together. They still went out to the lake in the van. But they made love quickly, as if to remind themselves they were still a couple. And they were afraid Sean might wake up.

In the last few months, Esa had started appearing with pills.

"What exactly are these, Esa?" she asked, when he offered some to her.

"Stuff some of the guys at the bike shop gave me," he said. "They're harmless. Everyone at work takes them," he said. "You'll like them. They'll help you relax."

She had liked them. Exhausted all the time from anticipating Sean's cries, sometimes she'd swallow one of Esa's tablets and have a little nap with the baby in the back of the van, curled up together. Those were comfortable afternoons. It was so nice to be out of her parents' house. And maybe because she was so relaxed on the afternoons after she'd taken something, she noticed Sean was quieter, too. He rarely woke on those nights, and so she herself was peaceful again, sleeping in a bit later the next day.

This second pregnancy changed everything. She didn't tell anyone after she found out, not for a while. She decided she really was a bad girl, someone who did foolish, irresponsible things. Now everyone would be hurt, even her beautiful baby. Esa was already worried about money, and her parents, even her father, were tired of her and Sean living with them. But if she moved out, she didn't know how she'd take care of Sean and another child. She couldn't come up with any answers and tried to put it out of her mind for a little longer. The pills from Esa helped her not think frightening thoughts. She figured if she was going to get rid of the baby, it didn't matter what she took. Esa said they weren't bad, either. They weren't addictive, just something to help her relax.

One day, she drove down to Hartland with Esa. He wanted to talk with his buddies at the shop to see if they had heard about a job. It was a nice afternoon, so she pushed Sean in his stroller, heading uphill toward Hartland's little park. She still hadn't told anyone, not even Esa, that she was pregnant again, but even her old floppy sweatshirts were getting tight. She was getting big. While she waited for Esa to be finished, she picked up a newspaper lying on a bench, glancing through the ads and the pictures. She turned the page, and there it was: the little advertisement that could solve everything. It had a thick, bold border, so her eye went right to it. She read and reread it. Then she carefully folded the paper and put it in the back of Sean's stroller.

During the next week, Kelly found other little papers like the *Hartland Weekly Sentinel*. She picked up one in Larchfield, another in New Berlin, and several more in Madison. All of them had advertisements from people who wanted a baby to adopt. The people sounded rich and offered nice things to get an infant. It was surprising to her how many people couldn't have babies and wanted one. She kept going back to the one in the Hartland paper, though, the ad from the California people. They sounded like a smart couple, educated people. It was finally getting warm in Wisconsin, and she thought about how nice it would be for her baby never to have winter. She thought of California like permanent spring. She decided it wouldn't hurt to make some calls. She'd phone the people in California and maybe a few others, too. If things worked out, she could tell Esa and her parents she was pregnant, but was doing a very mature thing. Even though she would be having a second baby, there was really nothing for them to worry about. It was all arranged. Nobody had to worry about this new baby because she had a plan.

Chapter 4

THE INTERSTATE COMPACT

August 1990

The only thing keeping Eleanor from returning to California with her beautiful baby boy was the Interstate Compact. He'd been born six days earlier. But without this document, transporting Joshua across state lines was a federal offense. Jean had asked several times how long she had to remain in Los Altos. Ron's mother asked this gently, but she sounded tired and said she had things to attend to back home in Denver. Ron was getting calls from the hospital. They were understaffed. He was needed back at work. So, with the temperature and humidity outside hovering around one hundred, Eleanor put the baby into his car seat and took Ron to the small Madison airport. She drove the rental car back to the Madison Residence Inn alone with the baby. There, she continued her wait. She poured cans of formula into bottles for Joshua, heating them in the microwave, then carefully shaking the bottle to avoid hot spots. She herself ate takeout.

She phoned Hal Mozart every day, asking when they could leave.

"Dealing with government agencies is slow and frustrating. Give me some time," he said. "I'm doing the best I can, Eleanor."

And every evening, after Joshua had been fed and his pale lids had fluttered closed, she called Ron.

"I miss you so much. How are the kids?" she asked on Tuesday. "I called earlier. Max said your mother made chicken soup and left it in the fridge for you."

"Yeah, it's terrible soup. Too much pepper. But we tried to be enthusiastic when we spoke to her. You know what kind of a cook she is."

"I wish I could come home. I miss you."

"I know, hon. But Eleanor, there is something you have to do for me. You've got to start arranging for Joshua's *bris*," he said. "The baby's nearly a week old."

"You're kidding. Here? Can't it wait until we get home?" she asked.

"No. He's supposed to be circumcised on the eighth day," Ron said. "'On the eighth day, the flesh of his foreskin shall be circumcised,'" Ron intoned. "Leviticus 12. That's the law."

"The *law*?" she asked incredulously.

"Jewish law," he said. "I want everything to be kosher with him."

Laws. She was sick of this nonsense with laws. First the Interstate Compact, and now Ron quoting the Bible to her. She just wanted to take precious Joshua from the damn motel to his home in California and enjoy him.

"I'm not sure you'll find a *moyel* there," he went on. "You might need to get someone from Milwaukee or even Chicago to come up and do the circumcision. You've got to start arranging it."

"Ron, a moyel didn't do Max's circumcision. Our pediatrician, Dr. Rabitz, did it. Our Jewish pediatrician. When I get back, we'll take Joshua to the pediatrician. He'll say the prayer and it'll be done. Clean, nice, and antiseptic. I don't want some old guy with his breakfast still in his beard touching Joshua."

"No," Ron replied slowly. "I don't think Dr. Rabitz will do in this case."

Eleanor recognized the tone. When Ron made up his mind, he couldn't be moved.

"Why not? What do you mean by 'this case'?" she asked, trying to stay calm, so that Joshua wouldn't feel her tension and start fussing. In her experience, babies could feel tension in the room and they reacted, even if they were asleep.

"Because you, Eleanor, gave birth to Max. Jewish law being matrilineal, Max is automatically considered a Jew. But Joshua was not born of a Jewish mother. So, we have to officially convert him. And the first step toward religious conversion is a religious circumcision. With a moyel saying the prayers and performing it."

"Ron, who will care? He's going to be our son. Who will ever know the difference? We'll raise him as a Jew. He'll be a Jew in everyone's eyes. He'll have a bar mitzvah."

"There might be a question someday. Like if he wants to marry a religious Jewish girl. Or if he wants to live in Israel. Or if he himself chooses to be religious. Orthodox. Then there'd have to be a ritual circumcision by a moyel, and blood would have to be drawn. You don't want him to go through that as an adult, do you? I've been thinking about this."

She imagined Ron stubbornly tightening his lips.

"We have to make sure he is Jewish by any standard, including the Orthodox one. He needs a paper from the moyel and then needs to be officially converted by a tribunal of three rabbis. We'll go to the ritual baths up in San Francisco for that, the *mikvah*, and dip him in the water there. But don't worry, that's not for a few months."

Eleanor was more relaxed about Judaism than Ron was. Yet this conversation was increasingly surprising her. A bris hadn't even occurred to her. It all seemed meaningless. But she knew

Ron had more firm ideas about being an observant Jew than she did, and even though it was probably useless arguing with him about religious matters, she tried one last time—taking a different approach.

"I thought we needed a *minyon*," she said. "Ten Jewish people. Men, right? A real Orthodox ceremony has to have a minyon of ten Jewish males present. I certainly don't know ten Jewish men in Wisconsin."

He paused and thought about what she said. "Doctors! There'll be ten Jewish doctors at the hospital. Go back to University Children's and call a Code Blue. When the doctors show up, you'll have *at least* ten Jewish men!" He laughed, proud of his little joke.

She groaned. "I'm sure this is all theoretical. I'll get the call about the Interstate Compact any day. But I do know that under certain hardship situations, and not just the baby's health, you're allowed to defer the circumcision. Please, Ron. Call a rabbi. Check it out. Get special permission, and we'll do it at home. I promise, we'll find a moyel." She shuddered. She'd been to a religious bris once and noticed the moyel had dirty fingernails.

Ron finally agreed to the delay, if necessary. But there had to be a moyel. On that point he remained adamant.

On the eighth day, there was still no Interstate Compact. She called Hal at home as soon as she awoke. It was seven o'clock in Wisconsin.

"Eleanor, it's five in the morning."

"What's the holdup?" she asked. "Ron's almost ready to make me do the bris here."

Hal told her it was out of his control. The home study was required for an Interstate Compact. A social worker was required to visit the adoptive family's home and do a thorough investigation of their fitness as parents. The Russell adoption had happened so quickly, they hadn't yet been scheduled for the home study.

"How can we do a home study if I'm not at home? I'm in Madison, Wisconsin. Remember?" She was shrieking.

"Of course I remember. I'm working several options. I'm trying to get this fast-tracked. There's a huge backlog of cases. I'm working on getting special permission for you to bring your baby back home, stating you'll have the home study when you return. Believe me, it's complicated. The Department of Social Services is not sympathetic. If you need to leave, they're recommending you place the baby in a foster home in Madison until we get this sorted out."

The mention of a foster home shut her up. She was not going to leave her baby in foster care. She must be gentler with Hal Mozart. Besides being a friend of theirs, she desperately needed him to get this paperwork completed. She softened her voice.

"I'm sorry, I Ial. I can't wait until you see Joshua. I can't wait to get him home. It's hard waiting here alone with him. But he's beautiful. Perfect. Thank you for all you've done."

She began working on the questionnaire for the Department of Social Services. It was in preparation for the home study and was over fifty pages long. The State wanted to know about everyone on both sides of their family. They asked personal questions about the Russells' marriage. How often did they fight? How did they resolve conflict? The State even wanted to know about each of their sexual experiences. Had either of them ever had counseling? She knew Ron would resent this invasion of their privacy. The questionnaire was yet another thing he was going through for her. She had better back off the circumcision issue. There was so much Ron was doing to make this adoption happen.

She used the canvas carrier she'd bought for Joshua and they went out into the heat for takeout and to buy the few other things they needed. When they made a trips into the hot, sticky world outside their room, she'd slip his little plump baby legs through the carrier's openings, then lift him toward her chest. She became adept at fastening the buckles by herself and tightening the shoulder harnesses and waist strap around her. She did it so skillfully that even if he was asleep, Joshua didn't awaken. Every time they went from the motel, her heart beat in fear of meeting Kelly or someone from the DeGrasse family. Madison was not a big town. Summers were quiet and sleepy without the students from the university. She worried she'd run into Kelly at the Kmart or at a fast-food restaurant.

On the tenth day of being alone in Madison with the baby, Hal finally called.

"Okay! We've got you sprung. An emergency exception was granted. You have permission to bring your baby home. The Department of Social Services has agreed to perform the home study next week, after you're back."

"Thank God," Eleanor said, aching to return to Los Altos with her son.

She packed the baby's things, amazed at how much they'd accumulated in such a brief time. On the plane, the flight attendants repeated the same compliments she'd given Kelly earlier.

"Look at you. So soon after giving birth, and you look great! You fit into your jeans already."

She felt undeserving of the compliments. And for the first time of thousands more to come, she heard comments about her baby's fair skin and hair.

"Where does he get that hair from?" the passenger in the seat next to Eleanor asked.

"From his grandfather," she answered. It was a kind of truth.

She flew over middle America, glad to be putting miles between Wisconsin and their new life in California.

"You'll get to meet everyone now," she whispered to the baby she held. "All your new family and friends." She kissed him softly on his forehead. Joshua was being a wonderful traveler. She thought about the big party awaiting him. As soon as her husband heard they were allowed to leave Wisconsin, he'd arranged for the bris. Next Sunday, the moyel would come from Berkeley to do the circumcision.

The bris went well. The moyel Ron hired had a neatly trimmed beard and immaculate fingernails. Joshua cried during the procedure, of course, but the tradition of letting him suck on a clean piece of cotton dipped in sweet kosher wine worked as it was meant to. Afterwards, over the trays of cold cuts and warmed *kugels* and cakes generously brought by friends and family, Eleanor was asked the same question again and again.

"Does it feel different this time?"

"No," Eleanor said, as she looked down at the sleeping baby in her arms. "The same smell. I remember it from Lara and Max. The top of a baby's head is the best smell in the world."

"Do you feel he's yours?' her neighbor Lila asked.

"It's shocking how much I love him already," she answered.

This same neighbor, a good friend, but someone who often spoke without thinking, turned to Ron. "And you, do you feel like you're a father yet?"

"Well, I never had a baby before," Ron said. "But yes, I do feel like he's mine. I feel like I'd kill for him. Is that what a father feels?" he asked.

Eleanor smiled at the thought of mild Ron ever hurting anyone.

A few weeks after the bris, Eleanor sent for a copy of the *Hartland Weekly Sentinel* from the date when their ad had originally appeared. When it arrived, she hurriedly turned its pages, searching through the classifieds to find the ad that brought them Joshua. She found it between a notice for a new feed and grain store and one for used tractor tires: the ad that had brought Kelly and her baby to them. She found it easily, because for a small extra charge, she'd had a dark, thick border placed around it. She cut out the whole page, planning to keep it for Joshua's album.

Pregnant? Let us help. Loving California couple with beautiful home and lots of room to play seek a healthy newborn to complete our family. Dad is a physician, Mom a college professor. Two older children will help us give your baby love, attention, and all available resources.

She waited also for the blanket Kelly said she was making for the baby. Unfortunately, it never arrived. For years, Eleanor wondered about that blanket. How much she wanted Joshua to have it. She imagined it—crocheted of a soft yarn with smooth satin edging. Blue, of course, as Kelly had always been sure the baby was a boy.

Chapter 5

KELLY MOVES ON

1990 and 1991

In December, Kelly received a holiday card from Ron and Eleanor. In it were photographs of the baby, nearly four months old. Eleanor had dressed him in a red velour Santa suit and propped him up in a white rocking chair with red cushions. He looked so precious, kind of mischievous, with a big, toothless grin. His big brother, Sean, had that very same grin. She imagined his baby giggles, the same wild giggles Sean made when he was particularly happy or when he was being tickled. The outfit included a wide, shiny, black patent belt, just like on a real Santa suit. The Russells had perched a floppy Santa hat on the baby's head, and Kelly saw bits of his silky, reddish-blond hair peeking from the cap. She knew in time his hair would turn blonder. Sean, too, had been born with the same color hair. Her mom called this hair color strawberry blond. As Sean had gotten older, his hair no longer had a reddish cast. It became lighter until now it was the palest of blonds.

Eleanor had also sent a picture of the baby with his older brother and sister, Max and Lara. They sat together on a soft-looking rose-colored couch. Kelly scanned every detail in the pictures. If she'd had a magnifying glass, she would have examined the pictures even more closely. Lara, the girl, was very pretty. But she seemed stuck up, something about the way she held her head like she was in a magazine and the way her long, dark hair was arranged so perfectly. The boy, Max, held the baby on his lap. He was looking down at him, making a funny face, his tongue stuck out and his eyes wide, like he was trying to make the baby laugh. Kelly liked Max, she decided. He wore a plain T-shirt and baggy shorts. That face he was making meant he must have a good sense of humor. The baby (even in her thoughts, she couldn't bring herself to call him Joshua, but felt it was wrong, somehow, to call him Chris) seemed healthy. This made her happy, of course. He was pink-cheeked, a really pretty baby. Perfect, even. Although the pictures caused her pain, she still felt pride at how her baby was so beautiful and seemed so healthy. Her thoughts returned to the baby's resemblance to Sean. She found a picture her dad had taken of Sean at his first birthday. She held them next to the baby Santa picture. It could have been the same child with the pictures taken at different ages.

She and Esa had twice produced the exact same model of baby. The boys clearly favored her more than their father, with their round, wide faces so like her own, and their deep, wide-set eyes under high, almost surprised brows. There appeared to be very little of Esa in either child. She wondered if that made Esa feel less connected to his boys.

Kelly hadn't finished biology—she'd dropped out of school before she'd even completed the second semester—but she thought children were supposed to have both their parents' characteristics. Even in middle school science class, they'd drawn that square, divided into four, showing how the genes mixed. But she herself looked much more like her dad, nothing at all like her slender and compact mom, and both her sons looked like she did. Maybe if the babies looked more like Esa, darker and slimmer, he'd have felt more connected to them.

She thought about the mischief she'd detected in the new

baby. She'd like to be invisible and watch him while he was playing around the house with Ron, Eleanor, and the older kids. She'd like to see if he did the silly unexpected things Sean did. If he did, Ron and Eleanor were in for it, and the thought made her laugh a little.

Sean kept her busy, that was for sure. He did everything early: sitting, crawling, walking, and climbing. She was proud of all the things he could do. The doctor said he was advanced for his age. She wondered how Eleanor would keep up with the new baby, since she was pretty old. She'd like to see Eleanor chasing after a baby in her big house in California. She looked more like the baby's grandmother than his mother. And proper, uptight Ron—she would also like to see Ron running after the baby, wearing his stiff corduroy jacket. But maybe the new baby didn't do the same things Sean did and was a quiet baby.

A few weeks earlier, in what people called Indian summer, Sean, who was not yet fourteen months old, had quietly turned the knob on the front door and left the house. A neighbor six doors down found him toddling around the neighborhood, naked. Sean slept in Kelly's room, but she hadn't heard him leave. She didn't even know Sean was capable of climbing over the railing of his crib, like a mountain goat. He must have pulled himself over the side railings (which might have, she was not certain, still been lowered from when she'd gotten up to quiet him in the night) and dropped silently down onto the carpet. He was gone before Kelly woke. He must have ripped off his clothes near the front door. Sean hated having wet diapers, and he loved being naked.

When the doorbell rang before seven that morning, Kelly sat up in bed. Her eyes went to Sean's crib and she immediately realized he was not in it. Ruth was already in the kitchen, drinking the first of the many cups of coffee she drank in a day. She got to the door before Kelly could get downstairs. A neighbor stood on the front stoop holding onto Sean's little hand. Sean looked past Ruth and pointed up the stairs.

"Mama," he said, with the same grin Kelly later saw in the photo of the baby in the Santa suit.

The neighbor said, "Missing anyone?" She was laughing.

Ruth grabbed Sean's hand out of the neighbor's and said, "Oh my goodness, thank you. Thank you so very much." The neighbor stayed in the doorway, a smile on her face.

As Kelly ran down the stairs and past her mother, her mom made sure to turn and give her one of her darkest looks. Ruth didn't need to say a word. She just tightened her lips. Once again, her daughter had messed up. Kelly bent to her naked little boy and hugged him. She then held him away so she could check to see if he was hurt in any way. She and her mom thanked the lady profusely and when the neighbor left and closed the door behind her, there was silence for a few seconds.

Then Ruth said, "It wasn't enough you let Frankie out into the street to get run over, was it? That poor little dog." Ruth gave one of her long sniffs, and she pointed to Sean. "You going to let the same thing happen to this one, too? I don't know how God allows people like you to have babies." Ruth stomped off to the kitchen.

Kelly gasped. She felt as if she'd been punched. It was the cruelest thing her mother had ever said to her, and it hurt her the most. She ran upstairs with Sean, hating her mother with such force that when she squeezed the baby to her chest, his smile became an angry cry. Kelly had loved Frankie, her first and only dog. She'd played with him for hours. Sometimes he felt like her best friend. Her older brother wasn't ever around after school, and he'd claimed he wasn't a dog person. Frankie was all hers, a fluffy white poodle mix. She and her mother kept Frankie spotlessly clean. Every day, he bounded to the door to welcome Kelly home from school.

One day, however, after Kelly unlocked the front door with

the key she kept tied around her neck and wore under her school blouses, she bent down and as usual, Frankie began licking her face to say hello. But suddenly he stopped and streaked past her and into the street, curious about some kids he spotted playing ball across the way. At that moment, a big raised truck belonging to some teenager from the neighborhood passed. The boy driving didn't even see the fluffy little dog.

At the time, Ruth hadn't really said it was Kelly's fault. She'd consoled her daughter, holding her for a bit when she came home from work and said Kelly couldn't really be blamed. Frankie just loved children too much and he had a bad habit of running out the door if it was left open too long. Ruth even wiped her own eyes. Kelly thought it might be the only time she'd seen her mother tear up.

Kelly missed Frankie. She missed how excitedly he greeted her after school and missed his sweet head on her lap. Now, six years later, Ruth had saved her poison for when it was liable to cause the most hurt.

Kelly shuddered. The image of poor Frankie squashed and bloodied on the street made her sick to her stomach, even now. She carried naked little Sean back to their room and put him on the foam pad on top of the dresser that she used for a changing pad. She vowed someday she'd get them out of this house. Esa or no Esa. She couldn't wait for him; she had to figure out some kind of a life for herself and her son.

She became desperate for money. The month before Christmas, she found a part-time job at the mall in Madison. There was a kiosk in the middle of the shopping center, which sold scarves, bags, and hippie things with beads and mirrors. They needed someone for the early afternoon shift. She worked only a few hours a day and found an elderly lady near her parents' development who would watch Sean. The lady ran a small day care, watching two or three children. Her house smelled like stale food, but at least she seemed kind, and her price was reasonable. Kelly's entire salary wasn't eaten up with paying for childcare, and she was able to put aside at least thirty or forty dollars each week, even more when she got extended hours as it got closer to Christmas. Occasionally, if she didn't ask too often, her mom agreed to pick up Sean at day care. Kelly knew her mother put Sean in front of the television as soon as they got home, and that he'd probably already watched too much television at the sitter's house, but she didn't see how she could tell her mother what to do with Sean when she was watching him as a favor.

When the Santa picture and card had arrived from the Russells, Kelly fervently wished she could show them to someone. She couldn't share the pictures with her own parents, except maybe her dad. Kelly's mother thought the best philosophy with the new baby was, "out of sight, out of mind." The idea that what they had, an open adoption, where both families were supposed to be able to communicate back and forth, seemed ridiculous to Ruth. It seemed like asking for trouble. She repeated this opinion to Kelly many times.

Kelly really wanted to show the pictures to Esa. She decided she would make a copy of the picture of the baby in his Santa suit for Esa and his mother. She would frame it nicely and wrap it up as a Christmas gift for them.

Ever since she'd been in the hospital giving birth to the second baby, when they'd met Eleanor and Ron, and then, the next day when the lawyer had pushed all the paperwork at them, Esa had been pulling away from her. He signed the papers for the adoption, but then wouldn't even look at her. He knew he had to sign; they'd talked and talked about it. But he acted like it was her fault they were giving up the baby. Esa said he realized there was no other option, but his hand had shaken when the lawyer handed him the pen. Kelly knew that giving up his son shamed Esa. It was further proof of his failure to do anything right.

The lawyer, Mike Lustig, smiled at Kelly and Esa, but she hadn't believed his smiles. He had been pushy about getting both their signatures down on the adoption forms. When Esa hesitated before putting his pen to the paper, the lawyer's face got a tight expression. He stopped smiling so nicely. He needed both their signatures. After a few tense minutes, Esa finally signed where he was supposed to sign, and the lawyer's friendly demeanor returned. But afterward, it felt like Mr. Lustig couldn't wait to get rid of them. Once he received the signatures he needed, there was no further small talk.

"A smart Jew lawyer," her mother pronounced after Mr. Lustig left and there was a cavernous silence in the hospital room. "You know those people taking Sean are Jews, right, Kelly?"

"I know, Mom," Kelly answered tiredly. "Eleanor told me they were Jewish right away on the phone. But they seem like good people. She's sweet. And Ron seems like he'll be a good dad, don't you think?" Kelly turned to her own father.

"Sure, honey. He does. He has a kind face. Looks you straight in the eye. And smart. They both seem real smart."

Kelly had dressed the baby in a cute, powder-blue onesie. It had been Sean's when he was a newborn, but Sean had grown so quickly, he'd hadn't worn it more than once or twice. Handing over her new baby to the fake-smiling lawyer had been worse than awful. It didn't make it any easier that this was her second. She ached with the worst pain she'd ever felt. The lawyer made a lame joke about how his girlfriend was waiting in the car in front of the hospital and how much she was wanting a baby. He said this was going to be making him a father before very long. He'd have Kelly to thank for his firstborn. He wanted to send her the bills for his kid's college. No one smiled or laughed. There was only silence. He clicked his briefcase shut. Holding it with one hand, all the papers carefully placed inside, he stood and watched Kelly. She realized she was supposed to hand the baby over to this terrible man. It was time. She lifted up her baby, clean and beautiful in his powder-blue onesie, and gave him to the lawyer.

Kelly's breasts were aching and leaking. She couldn't stand the sight of the lawyer walking out the door clutching her baby in one arm with his briefcase in the other. It would be the last time she'd see her new little boy. So she went out into the hall and called to him loudly, so that he couldn't ignore her.

"Mr. Lustig. Mr. Lustig, could you come back here, please?"

He was about to get on the elevator, but he turned and walked back to her, seeming annoyed.

"I want Eleanor and Ron to bring the baby to my parents' place before they leave for California."

She wanted to make sure the baby was okay and had gotten to the Russells safely. She didn't know where she got the courage to talk to the lawyer and order him around, but somehow she sensed if she didn't stand up for what she wanted then, when her signature was fresh and the baby still in his arms, she'd never be able to ask for anything again.

The lawyer appeared unhappy at first and said, "Kelly, you're not getting cold feet, are you? That would not be good. You don't want to lose such a good family for your baby after all the arrangements have been made."

Kelly shook her head and stood up straighter. "No, I'm not changing my mind. I just want to see my baby one last time. Tell them they can't leave until I see the baby with them tomorrow."

The lawyer nodded. He lowered his voice and made it sound a little more kind. "Okay, okay, I'll tell them. No problem. I'll arrange it. You just calm down and take care of yourself. Promise me that, Kelly. Okay?" Then he gave her one of his fake smiles.

Kelly wiped the tears streaming down her cheeks. Her mother had come after her and listened to the conversation. As soon as they were back in the hospital room, she berated Kelly.

"What do you want those people coming to the house for?" she asked. "How are we going to have people in the house right after you come home from the hospital? What will we do with Sean? He'll be running around like a wild Indian. Did you think of that, Kelly DeGrasse?"

Kelly got a Kleenex from the bedside table and blew her nose. She turned to Esa, who sat quietly in the corner and stared at her with his sad, dark eyes. "Esa, will you watch Sean tomorrow?" Kelly asked. "You don't have to work, do you? Will you come pick him up for a while?"

"Sure, I'll come. Have him ready around ten. I'll take him to my mom's. She's been asking to see him." He perked up a little and took a deep breath. He was probably glad to have something to do, particularly something that would annoy Ruth.

Ruth gave Kelly one of her storm-cloud looks, but Kelly started packing up the small turquoise train case she'd brought with her to the hospital. She had just a few things to put into the case, but she made the packing last as long as she possibly could.

Esa came for Sean at ten the next morning, just as he was supposed to. For once, he was prompt. And he returned Sean, not quite a year old at the time, back to the condominium a few hours after the Russells had gone. Kelly was sitting on the living room couch, watching out the window for his white van. But after that day, he came around less frequently, and when he did, he always seemed to have somewhere else to be. Maybe it was hard for him to see little Sean. Perhaps Sean reminded him of the shadow of the baby who wasn't there. Or maybe Kelly's mother got to Esa too much. Kelly couldn't blame him not wanting to face that stern woman at the door, frowning at him before she let him in to see his own child.

Esa seemed to feel his failure as a provider even worse after the new baby was taken away. He wasn't the same quiet, reserved boy who had lived for Kelly and their afternoons together, back when they'd first met. He was changing, Kelly saw. He had different friends now, people Kelly didn't know. Lately, Kelly smelled pot on him, sometimes beer, when he came to visit.

Kelly tried not to show Esa how hard it was at home for her. She tried to keep up the smiles and give him encouragement. She knew Esa was doing the best he could, and that it was hard for him to find work. But it got harder to be cheerful around him and to smile happily when she was with him. She anticipated his visits. However, if she was honest, it wasn't just Esa she waited for. She'd come to associate something else with his visits. It was getting so that she waited for the pills he gave her, and the little boost in energy she felt when she took them. Sometimes, when she didn't see Esa for several days, she wondered if she missed Esa or the pills more.

Sean was no longer an infant, so they couldn't tuck him away in the back of the van and have wordless, pleasure-giving sex, as they had once done. Their sex had been such a gift for Kelly. But it happened between them less frequently. Sean hardly napped at all anymore. He wanted to go all the time. When the three of them went out together, it was for fast food or to a park. At these times, they seemed like any other young family out for a few happy hours together. Except afterward, Esa drove Kelly and Sean back to her parents' condominium, and the tension of her loneliness began to build up again. She glanced at the vial of birth control pills she kept in her nightstand. She didn't need them anymore.

She missed Esa's touch. Sometimes she got scared, thinking maybe he had found somebody else. She tried to focus on other stuff that would keep him away. He was sad, scared, and guilty. His new friends were just a distraction from those bad feelings. In time, she was sure, the hurt would lessen and they'd be together again, be real parents to Sean. Esa would get more work and maybe, someday, they'd go to California.

She remembered their dreams of California from when she was

pregnant with Sean. Esa told her he wanted to see the Pacific Ocean more than anything in the world. Not the Atlantic, which was cold and gray. He wanted to go to the Pacific and feel the warm sand between his toes. She told him she'd always wanted to feel the warm California sun, too. She hated the Wisconsin weather. It was either miserably cold or miserably hot. Esa wanted to learn to surf. It was his dream. Kelly loved listening to Esa talk about it. She loved the happiness in his voice. Lately, she tried reminding him of his dream, and how someday they would all take a trip out to California, and he could try surfing. But he no longer seemed interested in talking about it.

On Christmas Eve, she gave Esa the picture of the baby in his Santa outfit. She'd placed it in a red enamel frame she'd purchased at the mall where she worked. Esa unwrapped the package and studied the baby's photograph a long time, then he shoved it back at her.

"Why would I want a picture of the baby we gave away?" His face was hard and mean in a way she hadn't seen before, his lips pursed angrily.

"But your mom. She might like to see the baby. He's so cute in the picture," Kelly insisted, still holding it out.

"My mom won't even let me mention him. She says it makes her sick that she has a grandchild being raised in some stranger's house, thousands of miles away. She says you didn't even ask her if she'd take the baby before you gave him away to strangers."

"I thought it was a sweet picture, and that you'd want it. Like a keepsake," she said miserably.

"I don't," he said and pushed his long, dark hair out of his eyes. "Get it away from me before I smash it on the ground."

By spring, Kelly had saved up some money. It wasn't a lot, but enough, barely, to move from her parents' condominium. She'd also found a new job. It was at the same place her mother worked, and it would pay more than the mall. Her mom had been surprisingly helpful about getting her in for an interview, and Kelly was grateful to her. She'd be working in a different department, which Kelly thought was a good thing. First, she would have to go through a few weeks of training. She was scared of the phone selling, but she was determined to learn. The woman who hired her said she had a good voice for direct sales. Kelly sounded sincere, the woman said, and was very encouraging.

She found a small apartment in downtown Hartland. It was above a hardware store. She had walked past the building many times, not realizing there was an apartment up there, until one day, she saw a sign in the window advertising a rental. The owner of the building was a man named Al Harney, and he worked in his store on the ground floor. When Kelly walked in, Mr. Harney was helping a customer in the electrical section. When he smiled at her, she asked about the rental. He told her to wait a minute until he was free and then he'd get the key to the flat. Sean pulled at her fingers while she waited, trying to break free and run through the aisles.

"Here's the key. You can go up and check it out. But you be careful with that baby—those stairs are steep," he said.

She hiked slowly up the rickety stairs at the back of the building, holding on to Sean as he took one step at a time. She saw with relief that the apartment was clean and bright. When she went into the bathroom, she noted with pleasure that there was a decent tub. She imagined soaking peacefully in the tub after she got Sean down to sleep.

"Thanks, Mr. Harney. I like it a lot," she said when she came back into the shop, this time holding Sean in her arms.

"That's good. Here you go, buster." Mr. Harney offered Sean a lollypop from a jar at the cash register.

She had to hold Sean tightly on her lap while she signed the lease. There were so many things in the hardware store Sean would like to mess with. He got his lollypop tangled in her long hair and it was awkward holding the boy while she tried to read all six pages of the lease, but she got through it and tried to act like she'd understood it all.

"You don't look old enough to have a baby, young lady. I thought you might be the babysitter." Mr. Harney took the papers from her and smiled down at her, still sitting in the chair next to the front counter.

She nodded. "No. He's mine. It'll be just the two of us."

He watched her, seeming to decide, then said, "I guess it'll be okay. I haven't had any kids up there before, but we'll give it a try. You're welcome to any of the furniture that's still up in the apartment from the last tenant. Just keep the place nice and tidy and we'll be fine. And you be careful on those stairs," he added.

"I'll be grateful for anything that's up there," she said. The rent was cheaper than other places she'd seen, and more importantly, Mr. Harney didn't ask for references. Kelly didn't know what she'd have done if he had asked for them.

Later that same day, after signing the lease, she found a day care center in Hartland. It was right on the bus line to Madison, so she could get to work after she dropped Sean off in the morning. It wasn't a bad ride, only about a half hour long. She rode the bus back to Madison that afternoon, with Sean asleep on her lap. Her boy was so beautiful as he slept. He'd really been very good all day, not causing trouble at all. She closed her eyes, rested her head on her son's, and went to sleep for a moment.

It had been a good day. She came home exhausted but very pleased with herself. As soon as she came in the front door, she told her parents about the apartment and the day care and the ease with which she'd taken the bus.

Her father seemed a little sad. "I'll miss you, Kelly. You and

Sean. But I think this is for the best. I'll go get a pizza to celebrate. You did good today, honey."

Her mother, however, started to bring up all the problems she could see with Kelly living on her own.

"What about furniture?" she asked.

"Mr. Harney said I could use the stuff that's up there. It's not much, but I think it will get me started."

"Did you check out the references for the day care? Do you know if this place has any complaints against it? You'll be working so far away."

She fired questions faster than Kelly could answer them.

"How are you going to afford groceries? What will you do in the winter when the buses tend to run late?"

This was just what her mom always did, Kelly thought. She wanted to get rid of them, but at the same time, she would try to scare Kelly and take away her confidence.

For once, her dad managed to distract his wife. He held up his hand. "So what kind of pizza should I get? Pineapple, like you like, Ruth? What do you think? Large or extra-large?"

When she told him the next day, Esa seemed happy for her. She hoped to hear him say he'd move in with her and help with Sean and the rent, but he didn't. His mother was doing badly. She could barely get out of bed some days. Kelly decided it would be best if she'd just stay patient with Esa a little longer. Perhaps they'd be able to live together soon, but she wouldn't pressure him.

Esa had recently found a new job. It was in an auto body shop. He'd been bringing her a little money in an envelope for a few weeks. Not much, but she made a big deal out of the envelope. On one of her more lucid afternoons, Esa's mother had also helped them figure out how Kelly could get welfare and food stamps. She would be receiving a small salary from the mail-order company, but the real money was going to be in commissions based on her sales.

It would take a while until she got proficient at taking orders on the phone and could earn some decent commissions.

Kelly felt hopeful, more than she had since before she'd found out she was pregnant with the second baby. She decided to write to the Russells. She had never before written them, but she wanted to answer their Christmas card and thank them for the pictures. She also wanted to give them her new address. Kelly was proud of her handwriting. Her teachers had always complimented her on its clarity, how nice and round her letters were when she wrote in cursive. She discovered some pale-blue stationary in her mother's desk.

"Dear Eleanor, Ron, and family," she wrote, wondering if she should say, "Dear Mr. and Mrs. Russell," but decided it made her sound too much like a kid. *"Thank you so much for the Christmas card and pictures. I'm sorry I didn't write sooner, but I've been busy moving and starting a new job. I hope the little guy is well. He looks exactly like Sean in the pictures. Everything is great here. I miss the baby, but I guess that is to be expected. Well, this is just a short note to say hi and thanks for the card and pictures. Here is my new address."*

She was glad she could write about her move and new job. She thought she sounded mature in the letter, less like the loser they'd seen right after the baby was born. She was a busy person now. She had a job, and she'd moved to her own apartment. She added a P.S. to the letter. In it, she told Eleanor and Ron that when she'd shown Sean the Santa photos, he had kissed the baby's picture. And then, he'd pointed to the big kids, Lara and Max, and said, "buddies."

Kelly wondered where he got the word from. He was such a smart little boy, not even two years old and already pronouncing his words clearly. The other little boy at the day care in Hartland was already two, but he never said words anyone could understand. He just pointed and made goofy noises. She wondered if the new baby would also speak clearly, the way Sean did. She thought it was important not to use baby talk with babies, so they'd speak better.

She hoped Eleanor didn't use baby talk with Sean's little brother. She guessed not. She couldn't really imagine Eleanor speaking baby talk.

Of course, Kelly's new life did not continue as she hoped. Within a few months of her big move to Hartland, everything got more chaotic. Her salary didn't go as far as she imagined, so she didn't always pay her rent on time. Sean became prone to ear infections, and sometimes she had to miss work. Whenever Esa did come to visit, he was in the company of his new friends from the auto body shop. One night he showed up after ten. She was tired and had to get up early the next morning to catch the bus for work.

"Esa, it's late. What are you doing here?" she asked from the door. He and his friend Bruce had come clumping up to the apartment, their heavy work boots loud on the wooden stairs.

"Can't I come over and see my own son?" Esa said. She smelled beer on him. His eyes were bloodshot.

By this time, Sean had awoken and was standing up in his crib, reaching out his chubby arms to be picked up by his father.

"Daddy," Sean squealed.

"See what you did, Esa? Now I'll have a miserable time getting him back to sleep. You'll get him all hyper."

"Hey, Kelly, that's no way to treat me. I just came over to see if you needed some help."

"Help? It's late," she said.

Bruce had a smirk on his face.

"Why don't you ever come over at a normal time? Or do something with us on the weekend? You guys probably just want to come up here and party. Well, you can't. Not now." She started to close the door.

"I brought you some money. For you and Sean," Esa said and took an envelope from his jacket and waved it at her.

She sighed and let him in. She guessed he felt it was okay to come over at any time because he gave her a little bit of money in an envelope every few weeks. But the money was never enough, and his friends tended to party too loudly, especially when everyone got stoned. Esa was quiet, but some of his friends created problems. A couple of times, the police had shown up. They weren't arrested, but she had some scares.

After four months, Mr. Harney asked Kelly to leave the flat. He had been kind to her, but she was behind on her rent. And he had been pissed off when he was informed by his policeman buddies that they'd had to visit the upstairs flat two weekends in a row. Kelly was embarrassed. She left the apartment in the middle of the night, carrying Sean, still sleeping, down the stairs. She also took some of Mr. Harney's furniture with her, stuff she didn't think he'd miss. Esa helped her using a friend's truck.

She moved in with Esa's friend Bruce Mendez, one of the guys who had most often partied at her place. She wasn't pleased with having to live with a guy whose apartment was such a decrepit shithole, but it was in Hartland and she didn't know what else to do. Esa and his mother lived so far out in the country, she wouldn't be able to get to work from their place, not that Esa asked her to move in with them. And she couldn't go home . . . not again.

No more letters from Eleanor ever reached her. She supposed she should have left a forwarding address with Mr. Harney, but she was embarrassed at how she'd treated the nice man, sneaking off in the middle of the night. She always meant to send Eleanor and Ron her new addresses. But she moved frequently in those days. And somewhere along the way, with the many moves, she even lost the piece of paper on which she'd copied the Russells' address, as well as the envelope from their letter. She always kept the picture of her baby in his Santa suit with her, though. She kept it in her wallet, or in her purse, and she never lost it.

When she was alone and had nothing to do, she wrote imaginary letters to California. On good days, she'd compose bright, breezy letters to her boy.

"Hi Son," she'd say, "your family here in Wisconsin sends lots of love. Do you like school? Do you like reading? I sure hope so. Reading is important. Do you get to the beach very often? Your dad always wanted to surf, you know? You should learn to surf."

But on bad days, in the bleakest times, she'd compose a different kind of letter. She went to jail for the first time when she was nineteen. It was for shoplifting. Sean was with her when she was arrested.

From jail she wrote, "Dear Son, Well, it's a good thing you got yourself another family because your mother here is a real screwup." She added, "I sure am glad you aren't here to see your mom get herself in trouble. Again. Your grandma has it correct, I suppose. I just can't do anything right." Thankfully, she never sent that letter.

Chapter 6

THE BUDDHA IN HIM

1996, 1995, 2002

When Joshua was six years old, he entered his Chinese phase. It began with their visit one Saturday to the Asian Art Museum in San Francisco's Golden Gate Park. The stone warriors from Xi'an, China, were on display. The walls of the exhibit were covered by massive photographs of marching figures, row after row of walking warriors, warriors on horseback, and warriors with bows drawn. Each soldier, and there were more than Eleanor could count, had a different pose. She read that centuries before, the whole army had been buried underground by a mad emperor of China. This emperor believed the warriors gave him eternal life or at least protection in eternity. A few of the life-sized stone warriors had been transported from the actual site in Xi'an to San Francisco. Joshua circled the statues slowly, intently studying each one's features. His silky hair was sun bleached almost white that summer. Eleanor watched Joshua, wondering what he was thinking and what about the massive figures appealed to her young son.

Everything at the exhibit was displayed beautifully, but it was not designed for a six-year-old. The dim light gave the illusion of being inside the dank caves in China. Joshua loved it anyway, patiently making his way through the exhibit. Afterward, they went to the gift shop. She'd always done this with the children after museum trips—given them a reward for good behavior. Joshua went to a stack of green brocade boxes. Inside each was a replica of one of the stone men. There were four different warriors to choose from. Joshua spent an inordinate amount of time choosing; Eleanor paced with impatience. She browsed through the jewelry at the front of the shop, picked up and then decided against a pretty green brooch, bought ten postcards, and still, Joshua was examining those warriors.

"Come on, honey, pick one. They're all nice."

The statues were not inexpensive, so she'd told him he had to select only one. Later, in hindsight and the parental self-doubt which came often to Eleanor, she wished she'd allowed him to get all four. He had been so enraptured with them.

"You really liked those guys, didn't you?" she asked, as they went down the steps into the San Francisco fog and chill.

After nearly half an hour of deliberation, Joshua had finally selected a replica of one of the soldiers: an upright one, wearing a tunic and stern expression.

"Yep," he said. "Someday I'm going to go to China and see them. All of them." He held tightly to the bag containing his treasure.

"Maybe we'll go together one day," she said, and took his hand as they crossed the street in front of the museum.

He adored his stone figure. He took it out and played with it carefully, then replaced it onto the box's soft satin lining. She'd bought Joshua, all three of her children, really, so many toys that sat unused and disregarded. Transformers and Star Wars figures cluttered their rooms. Useless pieces of junk. However, the stone warrior from Xi'an would become important to Joshua, staying on his shelf in a place of honor throughout his boyhood and adolescence.

After the stone warriors, he began in earnest to collect Asian items. When they strolled in Chinatown, he asked for a Buddha.

He made his interest in Buddhas known to their friends and family, and, within a year, figures lined his window ledge. They came in many poses, but Joshua preferred the sitting, laughing Buddhas. He happily placed a cheap pink plastic Buddha next to a delicately carved green jade one, not attaching any value to the individual figures. They were all part of his precious collection. He arranged and rearranged them, as children do.

Another time that same year, Eleanor took Joshua to a street fair where an old Chinese man was selling chops, carved small squares etched with Chinese characters, which could be inked. Chops, the man explained, could be used as a man's signature in Shanghai, where he was from. He helped Joshua pick out a chop that resembled the sounds Jo-shu-a. He showed the boy how to carefully ink it so the impression came out crisp and clear. After that, Joshua used the chop for his name at the top of all his homework. His first grade teacher, Mrs. Mollin, was an angel who understood the passions of children his age. She never said anything when Joshua turned in his homework with no name on it, just the Chinese chop at the top of the page. Mrs. Mollin knew who it belonged to.

Soon after, Eleanor took her son with her to a doctor's appointment. She had a sore shoulder. The orthopedic surgeon had recently returned from a medical mission to the Himalayas. He'd placed a large Tibetan prayer flag on his wall, as well as framed pictures of villagers in Nepal, whom he had operated on. The pictures showed smiling children and beautiful, dark-eyed men and women with chiseled cheekbones. Even the ones with terrible disfigurements, club feet, or twisted bodies, smiled into the doctor's camera. In the background were soaring mountains, sweeping vistas of the Himalayas. Joshua was enthralled. All through his mother's lengthy examination by the doctor, Joshua sat quietly cross-legged on the floor, studying the photographs.

"Dr. Ingram has been to the top of the world," Eleanor said.

"Really?" Joshua asked, and turned to the doctor with wonder. "The top of the world?"

"Not quite the top, son," the white-haired man replied. "I couldn't get that far. I'm too old. But we trekked very far up into the mountains. We had helpers, Sherpas they're called, to carry our supplies, and we did go into villages very high in the Himalayas." He stooped down to speak to Joshua. "The people were always kind to us, even when they were sick or injured. I don't think I'll ever forget them. They were the most generous, patient people I've ever met."

"Me neither," Joshua said solemnly. "I'll never forget them either." And he turned back to the pictures.

"That boy," Dr. Ingram said, "has the Buddha in him."

Eleanor knew exactly what the doctor meant. She had just never phrased it that way.

There was something quiet and good about Joshua. And there was something in him that felt the pain of others so acutely, she worried for him. He listened quietly, his perfect features seeming to understand everything, his straight golden hair bouncing up and down when he nodded. And when he smiled, it was impossible not to smile with him.

She wondered what connection there was between his Asian phase and the pain of the past year.

A year earlier, when Joshua was five years old, he'd waited on the carpeted bottom step of the big stairway of their house for his father to arrive home from the hospital. His eyes were fixed on the front door. Ron had promised Joshua he would leave the hospital early that day and come home to help him learn to ride his bike. The boy had received a two-wheeler for Hanukkah and insisted he was ready for the training wheels to be removed.

Joshua adored his father. He'd been waiting for the sound of his car since he had arrived home from school. The afternoon together was to be a treat for them both. Joshua jumped up when he heard the car door slam. He sped to the kitchen and tugged at Eleanor's shirt.

"He's here, Dad's here." Then he ran back to the living room and grabbed his father around his legs as soon as the door opened.

"Hold on, buddy, let me put my stuff down. Then we'll go."

Ron planned to take Joshua to the park and run beside him, holding on to the rear of the bike's seat. Joshua was such a coordinated child, both Ron and Eleanor predicted it wouldn't be very long until their little boy would take off by himself. However, not even a half hour later, as Eleanor was dicing vegetables for dinner, she heard the Volvo return up the driveway.

"That was fast," Eleanor said as she heard the front door open. Then she saw Ron's face. He was ashen and sweating.

"What's wrong?" She was about to ask if Joshua was okay, then she saw the boy hanging back behind his dad's long legs.

"Daddy's sick."

"I don't know what's wrong," Ron said. There was sweat on his forehead. "I suddenly felt so tired, I couldn't even run with the bike." He stared down at his son. "I'm sorry, buddy. Let me take a little rest now. Maybe we can try again after dinner. Or on the weekend, for sure. Your old dad just needs to take a nap right now."

Eleanor followed him upstairs and shut the bedroom door behind her. "You look terrible, Ron. What's going on? Bad day today? You've been working so hard." She smoothed his wavy brown hair.

"I don't know. I feel exhausted. Maybe the long nights this month are catching up with me. Let me take a little nap. I'll be down for dinner."

His tiredness didn't go away; it got worse. He came home from work early the next day, Tuesday, and lay down for a two-hour nap, something she could not remember him doing before. Joshua sat dejectedly at the bottom of the stairs, hoping his dad would wake up soon and take him to the park again. He wouldn't even watch television, a treat Eleanor rarely offered on school days.

That night, while Ron lay in bed studying the view of the city lights he loved so much, Eleanor made a suggestion. "Do you think you're depressed, hon?"

Eleanor rarely gave credence to problems of the body. It was the emotional that was real to her. She would listen empathetically to her children talk about small slights in the classroom but tell them to "shake it off" when they got hit broadside by a baseball. She thought now how aggravated Ron was about the whole wave of managed care in medicine. He was taking the changes personally, upset he was having to modify the quality of care he gave patients. She truly believed he might be so frustrated by the pressures and compromises at work, it might have made him sick. His work meant so much to him. The explanations were always psychological for Eleanor. Ron was depressed, but he just didn't know it.

"Fatigue is a symptom of depression, right, Ron?" she asked.

From bed, Ron watched her as she walked around the bedroom, tidying up and pronouncing her theories. Finally he spoke.

"I know what depression feels like. This is *not* depression. I'm so tired, I can't move. It started suddenly, but it's really catching up with me. I'm going to see Goldman tomorrow. I haven't had a checkup in a while. It won't hurt to get this checked out."

Suddenly she was scared; her psychological jargon now sounding foolish, even to herself. She nodded and got into the bed and held Ron's hand.

The next day, Wednesday, Ron went to see his internist, Arnie Goldman. Again, he came home early, going directly upstairs to rest after the appointment. Eleanor put on running shoes and took Joshua to the park herself. But both she and the boy were so distracted with worry about Ron at home, the bike riding lesson wasn't successful. She ran beside Joshua until she was out of breath, and still the boy didn't coast on his own. He'd wobble for a few seconds, then fall over into the bushes. She knew he was capable of riding without training wheels. He just seemed to have lost his will for the project.

"You don't run fast enough. I think we should put the little wheels back on."

The next morning, a Thursday, she and Ron were in the kitchen. She had no classes on Thursdays, and astonishingly, he'd taken the whole day off. She'd made them each a cup of tea. He sat at the counter staring into his. She opened the refrigerator, searching for some milk, when the phone rang. Ron picked it up. It was Arnie Goldman, and she stiffened.

"I see. Okay."

She stared into the refrigerator, listening to Ron's end of the conversation.

"Sure. I can come in tomorrow. We'll definitely get it checked out. Sure, and thanks, Arnie. Thanks for getting this moving so quickly. I appreciate it."

So polite. Her husband was always polite. "What is it?" She shut the refrigerator door and turned to look at Ron.

He sat with his head in his hands, still staring down into his teacup, soaking up the steam. "The liver enzymes are quite elevated. Way above normal," he said.

"What does that mean?" she asked.

"Well, it could be hepatitis."

"How would you have gotten hepatitis? You've had all the shots, haven't you?"

"It's not impossible. Sometimes we're bathed in blood in the operating room. I've had the shots for the more typical forms of hepatitis. But it could, I suppose, be some weird variant. Patients come to us from all over the world. Hepatitis would explain the fatigue and the elevated liver enzymes."

She knew he wasn't saying everything. She knew he was playing The Cat on the Roof. When Ron didn't want to tell a patient all the bad news at once, he played this game. He couldn't just tell someone their cat had fallen off the roof, as he had explained to her. He couldn't say their beloved cat was dead on the ground. He prepared people for bad news by first telling them the cat was on the roof, then continued with saying the cat slipped. It hung with one foot off the roof. Then, finally, he reluctantly told them both feet had slipped and the cat fell. Eventually, the cat was on the ground. Dead. Gone.

"What else, Ron? If it's not some weird hepatitis, what else could elevated liver enzymes mean?"

There was silence in the kitchen. "It could be cancer," he finally said. "But we're a long way from deciding that. There needs to be a biopsy, and then they'll scan the liver." He brought the cup of tea to his lips and took a sip.

He kept referring to his body parts as "the" and "it" and not "my." He was being a doctor, even to himself, depersonalizing whatever was happening to him. She supposed it was his way of coping, but she hated how calm and rational he was being. It was the same as after the earthquake, when she was fundamentally rattled and couldn't sleep soundly for months. Every time she heard a truck's rumble or thought she felt the house shaking when it was just someone bouncing their knee under the table, she became terrified all over again. But her husband, even after he'd come home from Atlanta and seen the front of their house collapsed and the piano on the front lawn, acted like he was a building inspector surveying someone else's destruction.

Ron's timing was off; they were *not* a long way from a cancer diagnosis. The very next day, Friday, she accompanied Ron to the hospital—his hospital. They took the elevator to the basement and went into the door labeled Nuclear Medicine. Because she was Ron's wife and he was on the staff, an exception was made and she was allowed inside. Ron was put on a gurney and prepared to go through the long MRI tube so that cross sections of his liver and spleen could be viewed. The radiologist sat behind thick glass, speaking through a microphone, telling Ron when to lie still, when to get ready for the next picture. Although usually so calm, Ron couldn't relax. He twitched and moved. Eleanor saw his hands trembling.

"Ron, why don't I start sedation?" asked the radiologist, a colleague Ron had worked with many times. "It'll make the MRI go smoother. The procedure is going to take a while."

"Sure, Andy. Not a bad idea. I want you to get a good look."

Eleanor crossed her arms, staring at her husband, his voice amplified by the microphone in the examining room. She watched as the doctor went to her husband and gave him medicine to make him sleep through the procedure. She thought not only did the radiologist want Ron to lie still, he also wanted Ron unconscious. Andy didn't want to face his friend and answer his questions.

Slowly, the radiologist pushed the buttons so that inch by inch Ron slid into the tube. She watched as Andy pushed more buttons, taking pictures of her husband's vital organs. The noise from the machines was deafening. There was a constant thumping and whirring. She had no idea an MRI was so loud. As her husband disappeared into the noisy tube, she wished she could have been with him on the other side of the glass, holding his hand, instead of watching him disappear into the dark tunnel.

The examination took a very long time. The radiologist was being thorough. About halfway through the procedure, another of Ron's good friends, a surgeon from his group at the hospital, joined them behind the glass. The surgeon and the radiologist glanced at each other as images appeared before them. Eleanor didn't know what the images meant, but she recognized the alarm she saw on the two doctors' faces. When the MRI was finally complete, a technician wheeled Ron out of the imaging room and into a darkened hallway. She followed behind. Ron was still unconscious.

Eleanor faced the doctors. "What's going on?"

The radiologist took a deep breath. "There are multiple tumors in both lobes of the liver."

Oh God, Eleanor thought. *Someone forgot to explain The Cat on the Roof to this guy.*

"How bad is that?" she asked.

"It's not good, Eleanor," Ron's surgeon friend answered. "We saw a lot of tumors. It's most likely metastatic. I suspect that a biopsy of the liver will detect cancer cells from somewhere else, indicating the cancer has already migrated. There are too many small tumors in the liver for it to be the primary. We don't know where the primary is yet, we'll still need to find it, but it's not good that his liver is so full of tumors."

Both men turned away, the radiologist toward his machines and dials, the surgeon friend examining the papers in his hands. She tried to get them to make eye contact with her. She wanted these men to tell her it was going to be okay. There needed to be more tests. Surely, it couldn't be decided already. Metastatic cancer was as bad as it got. Anyone who watched doctor shows on television knew that. Her husband hadn't been sick at all. This was happening too suddenly. He was a relatively young man. A healthy, fit man. But the two doctors had nothing else to add. Her world was collapsing. She had a five-year-old son coming home from kindergarten in a few hours, and yet both these men seemed as if they had somewhere more important to go to.

"Who's going to tell Ron?" she finally asked.

The radiologist seemed painfully uncomfortable. "You know, I think you should tell him. At least, the basics. He'll sleep another half hour, most likely. When he wakes up, I think you should talk to him. Or call me. Phone me this afternoon when you get home." The radiologist's mouth twisted in a way she supposed was meant to be well meaning, but was really a grimace. He retreated to his office, closing the door quietly.

Ron's surgeon friend studied his watch. "I've got to get upstairs. We've got a patient already under anesthesia waiting for me to start." He shrugged helplessly, then leaned over and quickly tapped her shoulder. "We'll be here for you, Eleanor," he said, and walked toward the elevators.

No you won't, you asshole, she thought. *You won't be here for me. You're not here for me now. You're going upstairs to work on your next patient unconscious in the operating room. I'm here now alone with my husband who is going to wake up and I have to tell him what I don't even understand. I don't have the words for this. And then, I have to go pick up my son from kindergarten.*

She went into the ladies' room and was relieved that she could lock the door. There, in the ladies' room of the imaging department, was one of the few times during Ron's illness that Eleanor lost control. She twisted the taps to full force and cried and sobbed and hit the walls with her fists until she stopped from the pain. She remembered Joshua's expectant expression when he waited up for Ron each night. Everything she had believed about their lives became suspect in the bathroom that day. *We are lucky people. We are a lucky couple. We just have to be smart and careful. We'll work hard and be success-ful. We can have it all. Lies, all lies.* She stayed in the bathroom only ten minutes more, because she knew she had to get back outside. Her husband would be awakening. And because she was a sensible woman, she also knew she had to call someone. This was no time to be alone.

She washed her face and stared into the mirror, wiping mascara from under her eyes. She did not reapply her makeup but unlocked the door and quickly located a phone. In her mind she went through the list of friends she could call, debating who was home, who could get to the hospital quickly, and who she wanted to be there with her. Her good friend Lila, her neighbor, answered the call and arrived just before Ron began stirring.

"Are you kidding?" Lila asked, holding her friend around the waist. "They want *you* to tell him that he has cancer? What kind of sadists are they?"

Eleanor shrugged. "That's what they said. I think that's what they said. Maybe I should wait and have the doctors talk to him."

"Of course you should. This is nuts. A wife shouldn't have to do this."

Just then Ron woke up. His eyes opened fully, and he stared at Eleanor. She tried to meet his eyes, but couldn't. He turned to Lila.

"She called you?" His lips twitched a bit, but there was no surprise on his face. He was going to be stoic, she saw, just as she would have predicted.

"It's cancer, isn't it?" he asked.

Lila held Eleanor's right hand and gently Eleanor put the back of her other hand on Ron's cheek.

They helped him dress, and Lila stayed with him while Eleanor drove the car to the front of the hospital. Lila said she'd collect Joshua from school and take him to the park. On the way home, even though Ron was groggy, he still commented on Eleanor's poor driving.

"I've got to teach you to drive better. You just cut that guy off. Can't you pay more attention to other cars when you merge onto the freeway? Look around you, for Christ's sake." For once, she didn't argue but just nodded.

That afternoon, in the chilly imaging center of Ron's hospital, Eleanor boarded what she came to call the Cancer Train. All of their lives were soon concentrated on the train. Max and Lara were on the train, too, but a few cars back. They were twenty and twenty-three, busy with lives just beginning. Max was in college in Arizona in flight school. Lara had her first job as a production assistant for a television show in Hollywood. Eleanor called them and told them about Ron.

"Ron's very sick," she said to Lara. "It's cancer."

"I thought it was hepatitis. You told me it was hepatitis," Lara said.

"We were wrong," Eleanor said. "We were hoping."

"It's cancer," she said to Max. "Come home when you can. Joshua is going to need you."

"I'll be there. Just tell me what to do."

And Max and Lara were sad, truly sad, and wanted to help. But Ron was their stepfather. Their own dad, Art, was very much alive. They had great regard for Ron, but the front cars of the train were reserved for Ron, Eleanor, and Joshua.

Eleanor made appointments over the next few days. She was the type of person who needed to talk to professionals and specialists in the particular crisis she faced. She spoke to the cancer doctor first. Ron quickly had found an oncologist he liked and respected. He'd known Dr. Podowsky since his own residency. Eleanor liked him as well; she thought he found the right balance between treating Ron as a patient and as a colleague.

Ron still acted as if the patient was someone other than himself, saying things like, "Well, in cases like this, what are the options we should consider as far as chemotherapy?"

Dr. Podowsky didn't shatter that professional veneer but explained all the treatments to Ron in explicit technical detail: Leucovorin, clinical trials, and granulocyte-microphage colonies. He spoke directly to Ron, glancing only briefly at Eleanor. Eleanor sat quietly and listened, but she focused on family photos Dr. Podowsky had on his spacious desk. He had a lovely blond wife—Scandinavian, she thought—and three attractive daughters. Eleanor wanted to sweep the family photos to the ground and hear the glass shatter. She was already jealous of happy, unscathed families.

Later, Eleanor called and made an appointment with Dr. Podowsky for herself.

"I have no idea what the hell you and Ron are talking about," she said. "I didn't want to cut in and make you explain everything. I know Ron needs to get the medical information straight from you, but I need to know what's going on, too. And I don't want Ron to have to explain it."

The oncologist stood up from behind his desk and came and sat in the chair next to her. This gesture meant a great deal to her.

"Of course. Ask me anything you want. I'll explain it to you. You can come by any time."

Eleanor learned her husband had a primary cancer in his stomach, very high, up near his esophagus. Though it had started as a tiny tumor, it had traveled to his internal organs. The oncologist said Ron's liver was so diseased, he was close to dying of liver failure. That's why Dr. Podowsky suggested chemotherapy should be started immediately. He gave Eleanor pamphlets. The chemo wouldn't be pretty, but it would give them time.

"Can't you just cut it out? Remove the cancer. Give him a liver transplant. Surely, you can do that," she said desperately, knowing before he answered that, of course, surgery had been considered and it wouldn't work. The doctor explained that anti-rejection drugs given for a transplant would cause the cancer to spread faster. So she asked the single question she'd really come to ask.

"How long does he have?"

"Ah," Dr. Podowsky said, "that is always a mystery with this disease. The statistics are in his favor," the doctor continued. "He's only forty-seven. He's been in good health."

"Tell me," Eleanor persisted. "I need to know. We have a five-year-old. I need to know."

"The studies say somewhere between six months and two years. We'll start the chemotherapy tomorrow. The tumors will shrink almost immediately, and he'll feel less sick. You'll have some good time together. He'll begin to feel better, I'm sure of it. But the chemo can only do so much. The cells will come back, and eventually the chemo will stop working. The tumors will take over the liver again. Or some other vital organ. It's a very aggressive cancer."

She left the oncologist's office and went to her next appointment, a therapist, Joyce Olberg. This was the same woman she'd gone to years before, after the earthquake. She thought she ought to talk to someone, get some help dealing with this, especially with Joshua. She woodenly recited the information about Ron to Joyce. But when Eleanor started speaking about five-year-old Joshua, the therapist's face became horrified, and she stopped Eleanor.

"Five years old? You said Joshua's only five? And Ron's cancer is metastatic?"

"Yes. But he's this very centered kid. People can't believe Joshua is only five when they meet him. He has this way about him." Eleanor felt she needed to give comfort to the therapist.

Joyce couldn't speak. She reached for a tissue, dabbed her own eyes, and passed the box to Eleanor. "Oh, Eleanor. This is terrible news. I'm so sorry." She searched through her desk and found a card for the local hospice organization. She told Eleanor there were grief groups for kids.

She went to see Joshua's kindergarten teacher.

"Everyone loves Joshua," the teacher said. "I'll make sure the other staff members know." She hugged Eleanor. "We'll help him," she promised.

Eleanor even went to see her own doctor. At a recent appointment he had scolded her about her weight, which had been climbing through the years. He'd warned her about her cholesterol and diabetes, and he'd recommended a diet. He called it the cave-man diet; it included only unprocessed foods.

Now, her doctor listened intently as she spoke about Ron. Then he sighed and said, "Well, you won't have to worry about your weight, Eleanor. We can cross that off the list of concerns."

She stared at him, confused.

"It's called the cancer diet," he said. "The only other diet that runs a close second to it is the divorce diet. Losing weight is the least of your problems now. Believe me, the pounds will fall off. I predict soon you'll be worrying about losing too much weight."

Be careful what you wish, she told herself grimly.

Then she visited Joshua's pediatrician. Joshua had been such a healthy little boy, they'd had few reasons in the five years since he'd been born to visit Dr. Rabitz, other than well-child checks. For the fourth time that day, Eleanor laid out the facts of Ron's illness. The pediatrician was a kind, older man Eleanor had known for many years, the same doctor who'd taken care of Lara and Max.

"How will this affect Joshua?" she asked him. "Will being adopted make the loss more traumatic?"

"I don't know, Eleanor. Kids are all so different. They have differences in resilience," Dr. Rabitz said, and reached in his filing cabinet to get yet another pamphlet for Eleanor. "When a Loved One Dies. A Family Guide to Helping Children Cope," the cover of the brochure read. He also pressed into Eleanor's hands a videotape of Mr. Rogers's show on helping kids understand death. Eleanor took the book and the video and thanked Dr. Rabitz. She added them to the growing pile on the front seat of information she'd accumulated, then drove home.

A few days later, Eleanor sat with Joshua at the kitchen counter. Joshua had a glass of milk and graham crackers in front of him, his favorite after-school treat. Eleanor cradled a cup of tea, and craved a cigarette, even though she'd stopped smoking fifteen years before. All that morning, while he'd been at kindergarten, she'd rehearsed. She used phrases from both the pediatrician's booklet and Mr. Rogers. Joshua listened to his mother and then reacted like a textbook case of a child hearing that his father was very ill. He blamed himself. All the books said kids blamed themselves.

Joshua said, "It's because I made him run with me on the bike. Isn't it?"

She would wonder if this conversation in the kitchen was the moment when the damage first happened to Joshua.

"No, Joshua. It did not happen that day at the park. The bad cells inside Daddy began growing months ago. The doctor said the cancer was there for a while. We just didn't know it was there. When he got sick, he got sick quickly."

"He isn't going to die, is he?" Joshua asked, tears beginning to run down his cheeks.

"I don't know, honey. The doctors say Daddy is very, very sick."

"I think when he was running with me at the park, he shook the cancer loose," Joshua whispered.

She closed her eyes and sighed. "No, Joshua, that's not what caused it. Running with you had nothing to do with it."

He stared at his glass of milk.

"But now," she said, "we can love each other and try to enjoy our time together. Dad told me he very much wants to take you on a special trip this summer. The medicine that the doctors are giving him will make him feel better."

Joshua's greenish-gray eyes remained fixed on her face. She had never known a child who could stay still so long, his long eyelashes blinking infrequently. She braced herself for what he would say next.

"I think that if I am very, very good and I never touch Max and Lara's stuff and I never make you so mad that you yell at me, then

Dad'll get fixed." He shifted his gaze to the refrigerator, where she displayed family pictures, as well as some of Joshua's school drawings. Each was attached with a colorful magnet. Joshua collected magnets back then, from wherever they went.

She was so tired, she didn't follow him when he walked into his room and shut the door.

One afternoon, years later, when athletic Joshua was already in middle school, he phoned. He sounded frantic. Eleanor was at the dining room table grading midterms.

"Mom, I have a soccer game after school, and I only have one shin guard. Can you find the other and bring it to me?"

Eleanor hung up and searched the chaos in Joshua's room. She felt under his bed and found the missing shin guard. While she was still kneeling on the ground, she noticed the stone warrior from Xi'an. It was on the boy's bedside table, left over from his Asian phase and behind the detritus of his twelve-year-old life. With sudden clarity, she thought she finally understood the Chinese emperor who, hundreds of years before, buried his army of terra cotta soldiers. He'd hoped to cheat death. Perhaps that was why Joshua kept his own Xi'an warrior all these years.

Chapter 7

THE CANCER TRAIN

1995

Eleanor, exceptionally good at the business of living, knew she lacked the skills needed during the time of Ron's dying. She chastised herself, wishing she could be a better model for Joshua. Throughout those months of Ron's illness, Eleanor remained a dry socket: no moisture to bathe and cleanse her wounds. She was unable to cry, unable to experience how tears gave relief. Fortunately, Joshua seemed to know better than she how to cope. Joshua possessed some gene that allowed him to openly express sorrow. He wept freely when she spoke to him about his father getting sicker and sicker. Eleanor cared for Ron, Joshua, and the house with remarkable efficiency, but felt herself getting hard and brittle inside.

She spoke frequently to Max and Lara, giving them bullets of information, reciting medical updates like a zombie. However, she could not speak about her sadness, not even to her children or dearest friends. She realized Jean, her mother-in-law, was the same. Until Ron's illness, she had seen little resemblance between herself and Jean. She thought her mother-in-law cold, the reason, she'd assumed, Ron himself was so inhibited. Eleanor felt as if the struggle of their marriage had been her trying to draw Ron out—sexually, emotionally—and she'd blamed and resented Jean for it.

Ron's father, long gone, had been the expressive one. But his expressiveness had tended toward yelling and bullying. In this way, he ruled the family, really his whole extended clan. Ron's father had been a physician, too. The oldest child in a family of immigrants, he had overcome great hardship in order to attend medical school. The entire family sacrificed for his education. He was the success story of the Russells—both admired and feared by his brothers, sisters, even his widowed mother. When Ron's father Anglicized the family name from Rubinowitz to Russell, in order to more easily beat the Jewish quotas for medical school admission, the Rubinowitz clan followed suit. They were all Russells now.

During Ron's illness, Eleanor grew more charitable toward Jean. She saw how containing her emotions was a form of survival for the older woman. Jean also never cried. She never even spoke about the severity of her son's illness. According to Jean, Ron had a "growth." Toward the end, she called it a tumor, not once uttering the dreaded "C" word. Many people commented on Jean's strength and how she never broke down. Eleanor knew exactly what that strength was costing.

Eleanor went on leave from the university. With Ron's disability insurance, they had the money and Joshua had become clingy. The books she read said a certain amount of regression was normal. But when he began soiling his pants again, after being toilet trained for over two years, she didn't know what to do.

The first time it happened, she was in the kitchen writing in her journal. The journal had become something she could do just for herself, without having to leave the house. When Joshua came into the kitchen, she noticed the odor. It was a day when she felt more overwhelmed than usual. She had given Ron his medicines, prepared Joshua's meals, and washed laundry. Now Joshua had dirty underwear.

"Joshua, did you poop in your pants?" she asked wearily.

He answered her with complete innocence. "No," he said.

"Joshua, don't fib to me. I smell your pants." She put down her pen and closed the journal, perhaps a bit more firmly than she needed to. "Come on, let's go to the bathroom and change."

"I didn't have an accident," he said and in the face of all the evidence, began to cry and shout, "I didn't poop. I already went to the bathroom."

She silently took him to the bathroom, washed and toweled him off, and for good measure, sprinkled baby powder on his backside, trying to improve the smell of the room. She washed her own hands with perfumed lilac soap and went back to the kitchen and her journal.

The journal was divided into three sections, with a colored tab at the beginning of each. The first section was for medical information about Ron. She entered the new words into the book: adenocarcinoma, helicobacter pylori, fluorouracil, and cisplatin, the names of all the chemicals desperately being dripped into her husband to try and prolong his life. She wrote down these words so she could look them up later or ask Dr. Podowsky about them. She considered causation, as well. Ron just shrugged, said it was bad luck, but she couldn't help asking why.

Did Ron's cancer come from an environmental source? Many members of Ron's family had had cancer. Most of them had vacationed on Long Island in the '60s. Perhaps there was something near the hotel at the shore that caused cancer. What about bacteria? Some of the latest evidence, and she found the journals and reprinted the articles, pointed to a bacterial cause to ulcers. Weren't ulcers somehow carcinogenic? Most awful of all, she thought that she herself might be the cause. Her nagging, carping, and willfulness. This stuffing inside of his emotions must have been a factor in Ron's cancer. She was as bad as Jean. In their own ways, they'd both caused Ron to repress his feelings. She never spoke this last theory out loud, yet wondered how she could have made her husband happier.

In the second section, Eleanor entered the names of all the people—parents at Joshua's school, neighbors, and friends—who were helping them survive the ordeal of Ron's cancer. Eleanor was a meticulous note writer. At first, she tried to write thank-you notes every time someone brought over a meal or ran an errand for her. But soon the list of favors became too long, and Eleanor gave up. Still, she recorded everything.

"Zena Ruben—homemade brisket with potatoes and mushroom." ("Ask Zena how she makes it," she added in her notes. "How does she get the meat so tender?")

"Gary Spizer—sent over dinner and wine from Le Mouton Noir."

Ron had been too sick to eat it and Joshua wouldn't touch fancy sauces, so she ate the entire dinner by herself. Dinner for three from Le Mouton Noir. It must have cost hundreds. She ate every bit, then threw it up.

"Mark McNeil—picked up Joshua and took him to T-ball tryouts."

The lists showed how she, Ron, and the whole family had been loved. It was also evidence of how sweetly good people were. Reading the lists of gifts—brisket, chocolate chip cookies, and sour cream chocolate cake—brought a small smile to her face. The cancer rocked everyone they knew. Ron was so young. He had none of the obvious risk factors—a doctor who (rather hypochondriacally, Eleanor used to think) went in for every screening offered by their health care plan. He was trim, a nondrinking, nonsmoking man, with a runner's body. Still, the random hand of death reached down to squeeze the life out of him at forty-seven. Forty-seven, with a darling five-year-old son, two lovely stepkids, and a nice house on a hill with a view. No one could believe it. All people could do was offer plates of food and volunteer to take Eleanor's carpools.

In the third section of the book, Eleanor entered quotes she wanted to remember from people during that time. The majority came from Joshua. Joshua sounded like the books on death and dying. Denial. Bargaining. Anger. Depression. He did not reach acceptance.

"I think the doctors are wrong. Daddy doesn't have cancer; he just missed his supper too much when he stayed late at the hospital," Joshua said. Denial.

In the midst of playing on the floor with his Legos, he'd get up and come over to where she was reading.

"I don't want allowance this week, Mommy. You save the money and give it to the doctor so he can find a way to fix Daddy." Bargaining.

"Joshua, you keep your allowance. Dad has a great doctor. He's working really hard to help him. We have enough money to pay him, don't worry."

Mostly his comments were of the angry variety.

"It's not fair," he'd say, and smash his trucks into each other head-on.

And it wasn't. She hadn't the words to refute this. It wasn't fair that her little boy, who adored his father, and who had already been relinquished by his birth parents, was going to lose his dad.

Finally came depression. She'd overheard him sorrowfully telling a friend that he loved his dad more than his mom. She knew this was true. She wished she hadn't overheard it, but she recorded what he said.

One morning Joshua came out of his bedroom and into the kitchen. He was still sleepy and held Boo, the scruffy stuffed raccoon that he slept with, by the tail. Ron was upstairs in bed, and Eleanor was brewing tea her aunt Wendy from Los Angeles had sent. Kombucha elixir was made from a mushroom found in Manchuria. Her aunt claimed the tea was being tested by the National

Cancer Institute, but Eleanor had absolutely no faith in what she was doing. She brewed the tea so she could appear hopeful for Ron, and she could tell her well-meaning aunt they'd tried it.

It was late May. Ron was on a three-week cycle of chemotherapy. The first week after the treatment, he was overcome with nausea and vomiting and felt too sick to spend much time with Joshua or anyone. The second week, he felt great, almost normal. He tried desperately to do things with the family during that window, because by the third week following a treatment, the tumors began to grow again. They always came back, and he became sick and weak again. She was fighting a major assault on Ron's internal organs with vile-smelling mushroom tea, an intifada against a nuclear war. This particular morning, during the middle of the third week, Ron was so weak he could barely get up.

"Mom, I don't want to go to school," Joshua said. "I had a bad dream."

"About what?" Eleanor asked.

"That daddy wasn't here when I got back from school."

"He'll be here when you come home from school." Eleanor poured boiling water into the pot. "I promise." She stopped pouring and watched him.

"But what if he isn't?"

"When he's that sick, Joshua, I'll let you stay home. If we're ever so worried that he might die during the day, I'll let you stay home with him."

"Oh," Joshua said, and took a small sip of orange juice.

Eleanor had never used the word "die" with Joshua before. It hung in the air. The child played with his cereal, not bringing the spoon to his mouth. He sat a moment or two longer, then slid off the stool and bent to pick up his backpack. He squared his shoulders and said, "Okay, let's go."

Eleanor nearly wept at the strength of this small, blond child whose world was collapsing around him.

The chemotherapy did its job in the beginning, giving small windows of health and even hope for a future. They thought there would be more time together. People with Ron's diagnosis lived two, three, even four years. Eleanor and Ron talked about how to use the time they had left. They were calm when they had these discussions. They spoke logically and pleasantly, rarely giving in to the horror of what they both knew was before them. Ron said he wanted to take three trips that summer, the summer that turned out to be his last. He planned them meticulously, as he had done everything in his life. They would take one vacation each month, and would travel during the second week of the month, the week Ron felt strongest.

The first trip they took as a couple was in June. It would be a romantic trip for just the two of them. They asked Joshua's former preschool teacher, Marcy, to babysit. Joshua loved Marcy, and he seemed happy with the plan. Ron picked Santa Fe, somewhere neither had been before. Ron's skin, after the first month of chemotherapy, had developed an unhealthy pallor, and his hair, though it had not yet fallen out, had thinned considerably over the past six weeks. Yet on the trip to New Mexico, Ron moved with alacrity. Eleanor was astounded when he insisted on walking the streets of Santa Fe, going into every gallery. They held hands and looked at endless paintings and fingered the polished black pottery made by the Navajos. He wanted to buy her a turquoise bracelet, and they went to shop after shop on Canyon Road searching for the perfect turquoise stone. She assumed he must be pushing himself for her, trying to give her happy vacation memories.

It was when they went outside Santa Fe to visit Bandolero State

Park and Ron insisted on climbing into the caves, exploring every inch of where the ancient cave dwellers lived, that she knew he was not only pushing himself for her. He was grasping at life. In her own sorrow at losing Ron, she sometimes forgot what Ron himself was losing. On the trip to Santa Fe, she saw how desperate he was to feel, see, and taste experiences. To live.

On the flight home, they remembered they had not bought anything for Joshua. He would be waiting for them at the San Francisco airport with Marcy and would surely be expecting something. Fortunately, they had to change planes in Phoenix. They were the first ones out of the plane. It was only a short layover before they had to board the second plane, yet Eleanor walked slowly, holding herself back. She usually had a fast stride and Ron never kept up—even before he was sick. Now, he walked even slower, carrying himself carefully. They found a gift store in the airport advertising Native American items. Eleanor went over to the moccasin display, thinking she would quickly find beaded slippers for all three of the children. But Ron went to a display of wooden dolls, each dressed in an elaborate costume of soft deerskin and feathers. They were called kachina dolls, she read. They were meant to be deities of the Pueblo Indians. They had weird, scary heads, and though beautifully carved, she couldn't imagine Joshua would like one. They weren't a child's plaything. But Ron lifted one and was reading the description on the tag. It was particularly fierce, with a feathered mask and an ugly face.

"Ugh. It's terrible. Masks scare Joshua. That'll terrify him," she said.

"Yeah. You might be right. But I want to get it. See, look." And he lifted the savage painted mask that fitted over the doll's head. Under, was another face— a head of a man with a serene smile.

She gasped at the tag. "Did you see the price?" she asked. "That thing belongs in a museum."

"I know. But it's beautiful. I like it. We'll tell him to treat it carefully."

"Yeah, right. The feather mask thing will be gone within the week."

It was ridiculous to argue. They took the kachina doll to the counter and on the way also picked up a small carved drum for Joshua and beaded moccasins for Max and Lara. Realizing they had only a few minutes to get their plane, she panicked because she knew Ron couldn't run with her. This was the last flight back into Oakland that day. They lumbered back, Eleanor awkwardly carrying the parcels with the carefully wrapped kachina doll, moccasins, and drum. They barely made it to the plane before its doors closed. Ron was pale and his skin felt clammy as they took their seats.

In the car going back home, Joshua unwrapped his presents. The Indian figure was under layers and layers of paper. Eleanor told Joshua his dad had picked it out 'specially for him. The drum was from her. Of course, Joshua loved the kachina doll. He pounded on the drum for a few moments, then went back to the figure, sliding the feathered mask on and off its head. At home, he put it on his bedside table. He gave his dad a big hug, and Ron seemed exhausted, but happy.

In July, they went on their second trip. Ron wanted to take Joshua to Disneyland. Serious Ron surprisingly loved amusement parks. Lara, who was also fond of Disneyland, would take the day off work and meet them. She went on some of the rides and, at times, kept their place in line so Ron could rest on a bench where Eleanor, who hated rides, waited. As he and her oldest and youngest got off rides, Eleanor watched them.

It made Eleanor happy to see her daughter being part of the family. Lara held Joshua's hand as they walked. Ron now had a straw Panama hat to cover his increasing baldness. The hat was loose because he had lost so much hair. Suddenly a Santa Ana wind came up, scattering dust everywhere, and Ron's hat went flying. Lara, in her shorts and running shoes, chased after it. As they stood and watched, Lara followed the hat, which seemed to take off again each time she got close to it. Finally, she swooped down on it and put it on her own head, crushing her thick dark hair. She came loping back to where they were standing.

"Here you go, Ron," she said and presented the hat with a flourish.

"Thanks, Lara." He put it back on his head, embarrassed.

Joshua stared up at his half-sister with admiration.

On the second day, Lara had to return to work. Ron insisted he could handle the day alone with Joshua. They'd go slow, if need be. She could stay by the pool and read. Eleanor saw how happy Joshua was with Ron and thought the two might like the day together. The utter cheer at Disneyland got on her nerves. Ron assured her he felt good—strong, even. So, after breakfast, she covered them both with sunscreen, kissed them goodbye, and went to the pool.

By nine that night, Joshua and Ron still hadn't returned. Eleanor was frantic. She thought about taking the monorail to the park to search for them but realized the futility of hunting for anyone at Disneyland on a busy night in July. Eventually she heard them laughing as they stepped from the elevator. Joshua held a half-eaten caramel apple and had a stuffed duck under his arm. Ron again appeared ashen, though, and was moving his body gingerly.

My God, she thought, *he looks like an old man*. He'd aged twenty-five years since the morning. It was just as she imagined he would look when he turned seventy. *But now*, she thought, *he will never be seventy*. Ron smiled at her as he walked into the hotel room and sank into a chair. His hat was low, fallen onto his forehead. His right eye, always weak, was drooping.

"We're fine," he said, seeing her worry. "It was a great day.

Perfect. We rode on every ride in Adventureland at least twice. You'd have hated it, hon. Especially Toon Town. That was particularly tacky."

She handed him a glass of water so he could take his pills and then helped Joshua into his pajamas. As she undressed him, he chattered happily about how many Disney characters' signatures he'd gotten for his autograph book.

After she'd gotten Joshua asleep on his cot, Eleanor went into the suite's bedroom. Ron was already in bed. She sat awake in the dark listening to his raspy snoring. Finally, she went to the bathroom and took a sleeping pill. Before she went to bed, she once more checked on Joshua, curled up on his narrow bed. She pulled the comforter up around him; the air-conditioning vent was on his side of the room. She cursed Ron for the coming grief. The child loved his father with unbounded, extravagant love.

Why does Joshua have to have such pain?

For the last trip of the summer, Ron wanted to go to Canada.

"Canada?" She frowned. It sounded cold and far away.

But he had it all planned. When he'd been a boy, his parents had taken him on a train trip across the Canadian Rockies. They had gone to Banff and then to the rodeo at Calgary.

"It was the best trip of my childhood," he said. "I want to take you there."

He had his parents' old super-eight movies from that trip converted to videotapes, so he could show them to Joshua.

"Look, that's Daddy when I was your age! I rode a pony for the first time," Ron said, when they watched the tapes.

Lara and Max were visiting, and they sat together on the family room floor, eating popcorn. Joshua laughed and loved it, swiveling his head back and forth between the child riding a pony on the television and his almost bald father sitting behind him on the couch.

He was trying to resolve these two images, trying to see the boy in the man and the man in the boy.

Max pointed to the screen, making fun of the '50s clothes and styles. "Wow, look at Grandma Jean." He whistled. "That blond hair and those red lips. Quite the babe."

Lara laughed and then said, "Ron—those shoes! They look positively orthopedic."

Ron took great pains planning this last trip of the summer. The three of them would fly to Vancouver in early August and travel by train across the Rockies from west to east, reversing the direction Ron had gone as a boy with his parents.

The Canadian Pacific no longer ran sleeping cars, and so, after a day of unbelievably beautiful scenery, the train deposited them in Kamloops, a small town in British Columbia made up almost entirely of strip malls. Everyone filed off the train and lined up to board buses with pictures of antelope or long-horned sheep printed across their sides. Hundreds got off in Kamloops—all to be driven to a hotel at the base of the mountain.

There, in the modern lobby, they waited in line again with people from the train: Germans, many other Americans, and then the largest group of all, several hundred Japanese tourists. Everyone was to stay at this enormous hotel and then, in the morning, be taken back to the train to continue their journey to Banff. It wasn't the same as when Ron had traveled with his family as a little boy. Sleeping on the train then had been part of the magic. But this was the best they could do, and to Joshua, it was still a grand adventure.

In the lobby, Joshua scampered off to play with a small Japanese boy who had a Transformer toy. Eleanor leaned over to whisper in Ron's ear.

"His birthday. Tomorrow. I saw a supermarket a few blocks from here. We could get him a cake." She tilted her chin toward

Joshua. "We could celebrate on the train. It'll be too late at night when we get to Banff."

Ron nodded. "I'll go. Which direction?"

Getting on and off the bus had taken all his energy. His skin had that ashen look again and his eye was drooping, the sure sign of Ron's fatigue.

"No, hon," she said. "It's better if you stay here and watch Joshua. Get us checked in. I'll go to the supermarket and then see if I can find a fridge here to store the cake until tomorrow."

Ron nodded. She knew he was relieved. He desperately needed to lie down and rest. But he also wanted to pull his weight and help her. She found Joshua, sitting under a tree playing with the other little boy and his interesting new toy.

"Stay near Daddy," she told her son. "I'll meet you in the room. I have to go to the store. I'll be back in a few moments." Joshua nodded, then went back to the toy that changed shape. He was being such a good boy, even though tired.

The next day, back on the train and heading east, Eleanor went to the front of the car and spoke to the conductor. The conductor was also their naturalist guide on the trip through the Rockies. He pointed out sights as they passed them: birds, mountain animals, and the stark cliff formations. Eleanor whispered to the conductor that it was her son's birthday. She'd bought a cake.

"Can everyone sing 'Happy Birthday'? And can you help me cut the cake and pass it back to the others in the car?" she asked.

The conductor smiled. "Sure."

He made an announcement. "Today is Joshua's birthday. He is from California and is five today. Joshua, please stand up!"

Everyone clapped. Then, in a very nice tenor, the conductor led the train in singing "Happy Birthday." The Japanese people didn't know the words, but they applauded again at the end and made appreciative noises over the plates of cake as Eleanor and the conductor served them. Joshua was thrilled and embarrassed by all the attention. Ron hugged him and told him how he should never forget his birthday on the Canadian Pacific train. Afterward, Eleanor went up the aisle and collected the plates and plastic forks. She noticed several passengers, the Japanese tourists, were moving toward the back where Joshua sat with Ron's arm around him.

The Japanese people were giving Joshua money.

"For his birthday," one woman haltingly explained, when Eleanor wrinkled her forehead. Some tourists gave him Canadian money, coins or a bill, while others pressed Japanese money into the boy's little hands. There was quite a collection of currency already on the seat beside Joshua.

"No, you mustn't. It's not necessary," Eleanor said.

But the people were adamant. The little boy must take their money. It was their custom.

Late that night, they pulled into Banff. Eleanor was groggy with the motion of the train and she'd dozed, resting her head on Ron's thin shoulder. He woke her, and they gathered the toys and Joshua's things. They were taken to their hotel—a palatial structure, towering over the town.

Joshua's eyes widened in amazement when he looked up sleepily.

"Is this where we're staying? A castle?"

Eleanor was happy to see her son's reaction. She had wanted Joshua to exclaim, to tell Ron how wonderful it was. Eleanor knew how important it was to Ron for the boy to enjoy the trip, for it to be something Joshua never forgot, as it had been for him. This was more than a vacation to Ron—it was to be a memory—Joshua's last vacation with his father. Yet the heaviness of meaning attached to the trip was too much for a five-year-old to absorb.

After they'd been in Banff for a few days, Ron suggested to Eleanor they go out for dinner, just the two of them. The three had been eating their dinners in the coffee shop of the hotel. Ron ate very little, picking at his food, and Joshua got hungry early.

"Come on, you'll enjoy it," Ron said. "The dining room here is beautiful."

She gazed at her husband questioningly. He had been so tired. They still had another full day to go, and he'd been getting weaker. Each morning he sat at breakfast with Eleanor and Joshua and helped plan what they should see in and around Banff, which activities they must not miss. She would put a hat and sunscreen on Joshua, but when it was time to leave, Ron sighed and said they'd better go without him. He was too tired. He'd see them back at the hotel in the afternoon. They must take lots of pictures and tell him about every single thing they saw. Eleanor was beginning to worry about the flight home. Ron seemed frailer with each passing day.

"You want to go out for dinner?" she asked. "You're sure you want to stay up that late?"

"I do. Come on. Let's see if we can get a sitter to stay with Joshua. I want us to go out tonight. Just the two of us."

Eleanor still doubted Ron would be able to do it, but she found herself getting a little excited. She phoned the sitter recommended by the hotel and she felt a little thrill of anticipation. It could be like the vacations they used to take. Always, when they traveled, they took a night for themselves and went somewhere special for dinner and a walk. She had bought a pretty cream-colored dress to wear in Canada. It was still in its garment bag, the price tags attached.

They ordered room service for Joshua. The bellman delivered his dinner on a linen-covered table, with Joshua's hamburger and fries under a silver dome. Joshua loved it, saying the creamy hot chocolate was the best he'd ever tasted. Eleanor changed into her new dress. When she came out, Ron had already dressed. He was in an armchair waiting. She saw how the collar of his shirt gapped, and his navy suit sagged at the shoulders. His too-large clothes accentuated his illness. The sitter arrived, a pleasant, older woman who told them not to worry. Joshua would be fine. She'd brought some games: Chutes and Ladders, Candy Land. They kissed their son and went down the hall.

Eleanor examined herself in the mirrored elevator. To her surprise, she saw an attractive, thin woman. She was as thin as she'd been in college, even thinner than when she'd married Ron. Her doctor had been right about the cancer diet. She lost weight each week of Ron's illness, just as he did.

As they entered the large dining room, the sun was setting. There were the cool blues and grays of the mountains and the fiery reds and pinks of the sunset. All around them were spectacular views of the Canadian Rockies.

Ron took her hand as they waited to be seated. "You look nice, honey. Really pretty."

She smiled at him and saw how he collected himself, making a special effort. He straightened his shoulders, which in the past weeks had begun to hunch forward, as if he was cold. He led the way across the huge dining room, following the hostess. In their thirteen years of marriage, they had done this often—dined in fancy restaurants, talked to each other across tables set with crystal and silver, and unfolded thick linen napkins, anticipating the good meal to come. She had taken these evenings for granted. They were just another thing a successful doctor and his wife did on vacations. She'd taken so much about their lives for granted. They had been lucky, and she'd thought it wouldn't end. She lifted her enormous menu with its gold cord and tassel. It was the wife's menu, and had no prices.

The August trip to Banff and the Canadian Rockies was their last. Within days of returning to California, Ron became more ill. This time, he did not rally in the second week of the month.

When they next saw Dr. Podowsky, he spoke gently, but said

what had to be said. The tumors in Ron's liver were recurring. The treatments were no longer effective. It was time to consider hospice. Ron did not agree.

In September, there was a back-to-school tradition at Joshua's school. The children made mugs for their fathers and the dads were invited for pastries and to drink their morning coffee from the mugs. The new teachers and fathers would meet one another. Ron desperately wanted to go to the breakfast, but he was too weak. The principal phoned Eleanor when he heard Ron wouldn't be attending.

"We want to make this easy on Joshua, Eleanor. If you like, I could step in for Ron. You know how I feel about Joshua. I'd be glad to come and drink coffee with the dads and sit with Joshua. Or he could stay home that morning. It's your call," the principal said.

"I don't know. It doesn't seem quite right to have Joshua stay home. He's excited about making the mug," she said.

"Why don't you ask him who he'd like to have as his guest?" the principal suggested. "Remember, I'm available."

When Joshua came home, Eleanor asked him about the coffee event. "Dad is feeling too sick to go. Is there anyone else you'd like to invite?"

He thought for a second. "I know," Joshua said. "Let's have Max come. They're going to have chocolate croissants. Max loves chocolate croissants."

Eleanor gulped. Max had returned to school in Arizona only three weeks before. But this was an emergency. There was no other option. She would ask him to fly home for the fathers' coffee.

Max agreed to come. Eleanor picked her older son up at the airport on Thursday night. He threw his duffle bag into the back seat.

"Thanks for coming, Max. This is a big deal for Joshua. The school makes it a big deal."

"Glad to help, Mom," he said. "How's the little guy doing?"

"I don't know. He's moving a little stiff. I can't explain it, but he's holding his body differently than he used to." Then she added, "And he poops in his pants sometimes."

"Oh great," Max said.

"Don't worry," she said to Max and patted his knee. "The teachers know. They've got extra clothes at school. They'll handle it."

In the morning, Eleanor stood at the door of her older son's room watching as Joshua excitedly woke up his brother. Max tried to put a pillow over his head, but Joshua yanked it free.

"Okay, okay. I'm getting up," Max said. He joined them in the kitchen a few minutes later. "Ready to go to school now, buddy?" he asked, and messed Joshua's hair.

"That's what you're wearing?" Eleanor asked. Max had on baggy shorts that fell below his hips. He wore a black Rolling Stones T-shirt with an enormous red tongue at its front.

Max stared down at himself. "Yeah, why?"

"Most dads will be in suits. On their way to work."

"He looks fine, Eleanor. He looks great." Ron spoke from the hall. He was slowly making his way into the kitchen. He hadn't come downstairs in over a week.

"Hi, Ron," Max said. He seemed shocked when he saw Ron. In the three weeks he'd been gone, Ron had gotten much weaker and thinner. "How're you doing?"

"I'm okay. About as well as can be expected," Ron said. His voice was hoarse, getting a rusty quality to it.

Joshua's school was only a few minutes from the house. Eleanor could see the sorrow in Ron's eyes as her two sons walked out the door. She knew Ron would have done anything possible to be the one going with Joshua.

When Max returned, he greeted his mother with a hug. Ron was still in the kitchen, sitting in a large, comfortable chair in the corner. Max handed Ron the mug, a big, chunky piece of pottery made from coils of clay. The cup was glazed a bright yellow and the handle a shiny blue.

"This is yours, Ron. Be careful. It leaks a little between the coils. I poured orange juice in mine this morning, and it spilled all over me." He wiped at the front of his T-shirt with a sponge from the counter.

"How was it?" Eleanor asked.

"Great. The food was fantastic. I wish I could have taken a whole box of pastries with me, but I thought that might not be okay. They got the stuff from that fancy French bakery in town."

"No one would have minded," Eleanor said. "Everyone our age watches their cholesterol."

"And the other fathers? How was it with them?" Ron asked.

"Mom was right. A bunch of dudes in fancy suits and ties."

"I'll bet you were the coolest guy at the breakfast," Ron said. "I'm sure Joshua was thrilled to have you there. Thanks, Max."

There was now some help in the afternoons. She'd resisted this, until Ron's colleagues ignored her and sent Mitch. When she'd opened the front door and seen the huge man in green scrubs embroidered with the name of Ron's hospital, she said there must be a mistake.

He said to her, with his sweet, gap-toothed smile, "Mrs. Russell, your husband's partners are paying my bill, and frankly, they're paying me pretty good. I'm glad for the extra money, so I'd appreciate it if you wouldn't send me away."

She invited him in, and soon, the burly, dark-skinned practical nurse came to the house each afternoon when he finished his shift at the hospital. Eleanor couldn't imagine what she'd done before Mitch.

The oncologist again recommended hospice, but Ron refused. He was not giving up. Shockingly, it had been only five months since the first MRI showed tumors in his abdomen. Ron wanted

135

more time. There had to be something else to try, he insisted at his next doctor's appointment.

Dr. Podowsky hesitated, then told them about an experimental protocol being developed at UCLA. He spoke haltingly, the words sounding as if they were being pulled out of him.

"It was a very small study, mind you. Nothing definitive, but it does seem to extend things for people like yourself, younger people with metastatic gastric cancer."

"What are the side effects?" Ron asked.

"Bad," the oncologist replied. "That's why I'm not sure about suggesting it."

Eleanor watched Dr. Podowsky. The lined face and the blood-shot eyes. She knew he saw people like them every day: people desperate for time, grasping at every word he said.

"Tell me about it," Ron insisted.

"Well, we start a line and give you nonstop chemotherapy. Smaller doses, but pretty much around the clock." Dr. Podowsky stared at Ron intently. "It's a very potent cocktail they've concocted down there in Los Angeles."

"You know I don't want to go into the hospital." Ron spoke to Eleanor as well as the doctor. "Let's be clear: I don't want to be admitted at all."

"I understand," Dr. Podowsky said. "We can do everything at home. I'll start the line for you and nurses will come daily and check on it. You can watch the numbers yourself. You'll know if the line's blocked or if anything's not working right."

"And the side effects?" Eleanor asked. "You didn't say what those are. Specifically."

"The nausea and vomiting will be severe," the doctor answered. "And persistent. We'll give Ron something to help with that. He'll be getting the medicine all the time, so he'll feel quite sick. But for some people in the study, the tumors shrank."

"And it gave them time? It fought the growth?" Ron asked.

"It gave them time. But it's months we're talking about, Ron. Maybe a year. Not years."

Ron nodded grimly. He said he wanted to try it.

The next night, in late September, after he had seen his patients in his office, Dr. Podowsky came to their house. Eleanor let him in, and they walked past the room where Joshua was watching a video. The boy was so engrossed in the movie, he didn't turn away. Eleanor and the doctor climbed the stairs to the bedroom. It was already after eight o'clock. The man seemed exhausted. She knew he had come as a special courtesy to Ron. A nurse could have done the procedure.

The oncologist started the line and adjusted the machine that would deliver medicine day and night. After he finished, Ron and his doctor sat quietly and stared at the view from the large bedroom windows. They talked about the days when they had been residents together at Stanford. Ron seemed to enjoy the visit enormously. It was a pleasant change; he wasn't talking about his illness. By the time Dr. Podowsky left the room, Ron had relaxed and even seemed drowsy.

Eleanor walked back down the stairs with the oncologist.

"I've given him antinausea medicine along with the other drugs. It will make him sleepy. But you have to be prepared. He'll probably feel pretty awful from this stuff within a day or two."

She watched him. His hand was on the railing, and it was dim on the stairway. Joshua had fallen asleep on the couch. She would carry him to bed after the doctor left.

"I don't know how you do it," she said to the doctor. "Work with dying people all day, every day."

The doctor sighed. "I just want to help people. That's what I wanted when I became a doctor. To help." He turned away. "Not all of them are dying, you know."

Eleanor shook her head and led him out the door into the cool California evening. She looked up at the uncountable stars overhead and the lights of San Francisco in front of them. It was Ron's dream view. She watched the taillights of Dr. Podowsky's car as it disappeared down the driveway. Alone under the stars, she tried to imagine her life with Ron, in this house, coming to an end.

The experimental protocol was nightmarish in its side effects. Within a day, Ron began to gag, plagued with dry heaves. He could keep no food down. Eleanor held the emesis basin to his mouth and wiped cool cloths over his forehead. He struggled with the medicine, each day getting weaker.

One day, after two weeks on the nonstop chemotherapy, he fell back on the pillow, depleted after several moments of gagging. The bones of his face had gotten more pronounced, chiseled. His long nose was even more prominent than before, as well as his strong forehead, wide and intelligent. He was painfully thin, but had a regal handsomeness now. She forced herself to speak.

"How much longer are you going to put yourself through this?"

He didn't answer.

"Sweetheart, Joshua doesn't even want to come up here. He can't stand seeing how sick you are. You wanted more time with him, with all of us. But like this?"

"I know," he said. And a tear fell from the right eye, the one that drooped almost all the time now. "I know."

She called Dr. Podowsky from the phone beside Ron's bed. She mouthed to Ron, as she waited to be connected, "Do you want to speak to him?"

He shook his head.

When she heard the doctor's voice on the line, Eleanor told him they had decided to discontinue the treatment. It was making Ron too sick. The doctor agreed, of course.

Eleanor worried about her son's impending loss. She knew how alone and scared she felt; it must be even worse for Joshua. He was so young. She remembered back to what Joshua's pre-kindergarten teacher had written on his report card the winter before, well before they had known of Ron's diagnosis.

"I believe Joshua Russell is the happiest child I have ever encountered. He is a real light in the classroom," Mrs. Clayton had written back then.

What joy it had been to think that one's child is the happiest of children. Now with Ron's sickness, this was over. Eleanor wondered how she would keep Joshua from sinking into despair. Remembering Kelly and the promise to give her child a full, rich family, she felt even more sorrowful. Now there would only be one parent . . . herself, the less favored one.

Eleanor went downstairs after she made the call to the doctor. Joshua was watching a video again. Mitch had put it on before he left. It was *The Lion King,* Joshua's favorite. He'd watched it again and again since they'd purchased it. She sat on the couch and placed Joshua's head onto her lap, then stroked his silken hair until the movie finished. She knew Joshua liked her to stroke his head in a very particular way, using her nails to softly rake back the hair from his forehead.

"That's my favorite movie," he said, when it was over. "I like how the lion daddy watches from the stars."

"I know, Joshua. I like it a lot, too."

Chapter 8
THE YELLOW YARMULKE
1995

Ron died on the evening of November 9, only six months after his cancer was diagnosed. Hospice had coached her for nearly two weeks, advising her that once the end came, she should not panic. She should not call 911. If she did, the first responders might well use extraordinary measures to resuscitate Ron. And, if successful, they'd likely take him to the hospital. Ron had made it clear he did not want extreme measures to be used to prolong his life and didn't want to be admitted into the hospital. He did not want to die there.

The hospice nurse who came to their home, a saintly woman named Laurel, placed hospice's twenty-four-hour phone number on a blue Post-it next to each phone. The hospice team would come whenever needed, night or day. They would be there to help her. She listened carefully when Laurel explained what she must do in order to make Ron's death a peaceful one. The warnings never seemed real. She was told what to expect, yet it was like the Lamaze classes she'd conscientiously taken before Lara and Max were born. She was shown how to breathe, pant, and push. Still, her labors were chaotic, messy, and she was totally out of control. Her flesh ripped, and no one told her how the sewing up would feel. After Ron died, no one prepared her for the ripping she felt then, either.

Mitch would be arriving soon. Marilyn, mother of her son's friend Stuart, had invited Joshua to spend the night. She decided to say yes to this invitation and now carefully considered what to do with the afternoon. She hadn't been out of the house, other than taking Joshua to school, for days. She didn't want to talk or visit with anyone, hating the pity and sorrow she heard in friends' voices. It made her feel worse. She decided after Mitch arrived, she'd take Joshua to Marilyn's house and go to a mall. It would be nice to lose herself for an hour or two, lulled by the crowd.

When Joshua arrived home, he had his snack and Eleanor said, "I have a nice treat for you. I'm going to drop you off at Stuart's house. You can play with Stuart, and then there will be a very special surprise."

"What kind of surprise?" Joshua asked, suspiciously.

"Marilyn invited you to spend the night. She'll drive you and Stuart to school in the morning."

"An overnight?" He knew the rules and knew that a midweek sleepover was not allowed, ever.

"I know, Joshua. We don't usually do that. But Daddy's feeling really sick, and I'm pretty tired. Marilyn suggested I have a quiet evening tonight, just with Daddy. You and Stuart always have fun at overnights. Right?"

"Are you sure I shouldn't stay home?" he asked. He did not seem pleased.

"Don't worry, Joshua. Daddy will be here tomorrow," she said. "Go upstairs now. Give him a big hug. On the way to Marilyn's, let's stop at the Wooden Horse. You can get a special stuffed animal. We'll call it your guard animal. You can hold it tight all night."

She had no idea what made her suggest the visit to the toy store. Joshua stared at her for a moment.

"I'm too old for stuffed animals," he said, but went to his room and got ready.

Eleanor went after him, handing him a toothbrush, clean pajamas, and school clothes for the next day. She was relieved he wasn't making a fuss.

"Go see Daddy."

When Joshua came downstairs, Eleanor was waiting.

"Did you say goodbye?" she asked.

"Nope, he's sleeping."

Her heart lurched. "Are you positive?" Eleanor asked. "I could try waking him. He'd like seeing you. Come on, we'll go upstairs together and try again."

"Nope," Joshua said. "I checked. He's snoring. Real loud. Asleep."

Mitch rang the doorbell. He grabbed Joshua's baseball cap, twirled it around his finger, then put it back on the boy's head, backward. Joshua giggled with delight. He loved the big man who'd been coming to their house these past afternoons. Eleanor led Mitch upstairs. They went into the bathroom, and she showed Mitch the bottle of rock morphine. The doctor said it could be placed under Ron's tongue in case he seemed agitated. There hadn't really been pain so far, or at least Ron hadn't complained of any, but he'd seemed restless, rolling and thrashing around in bed. Dr. Podowsky said agitation was to be expected. She'd given Ron a first dose that morning, placing it under his tongue, scared, hoping she'd given the medicine to him correctly.

Mitch nodded. He understood. He knew what to do. They went into the bedroom where Ron was, indeed, snoring. Eleanor kissed her husband lightly on his forehead, but he didn't awaken.

She drove down the driveway with Joshua, then stopped at the Wooden Horse. To Eleanor's surprise, Joshua planted himself in front of the store's enormous wall of stuffed animals: dogs, cats, bunnies, monkeys, and elephants. As usual, Joshua chose slowly, considering each and every possibility. Finally, he settled on a large

143

black dog. He carefully returned the other animals to the shelves. Eleanor thought the black dog looked fierce, not at all cuddly and reassuring. It had bristly fur and a menacing expression.

"This is the one?" she asked.

"That one. He's my guardian angel."

She paid for the tough black dog and put him into Joshua's arms. She couldn't remember ever using the term "guardian angel."

She dropped Joshua at Marilyn's house, promising her son she'd call him twice—once at dinnertime and a second time before bed. She got back into the car and put her head down on the steering wheel. She was so tired she didn't want to move. But she thought she ought to use this hour or two that Mitch and Marilyn had given her. She would drive to the mall, then maybe just curl up on the seat and have a nap. But once she got to the shopping center and found a parking spot, she felt pulled inside. There was a purposeful energy from people walking in and out the doors. She began to walk along with the crowd, idly glancing in shops, her interest, as always, captured by pretty clothes and stylish shoes.

She stopped in front of a store she'd always liked. A mannequin wore a lovely, black, wool dress, the collar trimmed in black velvet. *This would be a good dress for Ron's funeral,* she thought. Then she gasped. Ron's funeral. Suddenly, she felt a pain in her throat, more of a sensation, that she'd never felt before. This pain, first felt in the shopping mall that day, would come and go for years, particularly when she was scared. It was a fluttering in her upper chest, a spasm that rose into her throat. She saw a bench a few feet away and sat down, putting her hand to her neck. It was hard to draw a breath, and she began to panic. She tried to slow her breathing, forcing herself to relax, inhale and exhale with deliberation. After about five minutes, the spasms lessened. She stayed on the bench, willing herself to breathe in and out regularly, until it felt as if her throat was open again.

She stood and headed toward the exit of the mall nearest to where she'd parked. Then she stopped. She would buy the black dress. She went back to the store where she'd seen it and found her size on the rack. Eight. It had been a long time since she had been a size eight. The saleswoman opened a dressing room for her.

"Is this for a special occasion?" the woman asked over her shoulder. "It just came in. I love the fabric. It drapes nicely. Part cashmere and part merino wool."

Eleanor didn't answer, relieved to close the dressing room door and be alone. She'd almost replied to the chatty saleswoman, "Why, yes, it's for my husband's funeral. Do you think it's right for that?" She was glad she hadn't said the words out loud.

She pulled the black dress over her head, gazed at herself in the mirror, then smoothed the fabric once quickly over her hips. It was a perfect fit, so she bought it, not even looking at the price tag. She'd wear it just the once. Afterward, she'd give it to Goodwill.

When she got home, she stuffed the bag in the hall closet and ran upstairs to Mitch and her husband. She kissed Ron on the cheek. This time he opened his eyes and gave her a small smile.

Mitch said, "Dr. Russell did fine, Mrs. Russell. Peaceful like now. No meds, no nothing." Mitch stood up and rolled his shoulders, stretching them, the way big men seem to do periodically. "And, Mrs. Russell," he went on, "I wanted you to know something. You, too, Doc. Everyone at the hospital sends their prayers. They think the world of Dr. Russell."

"I know. Thanks, though, Mitch. A nurse once told me that he was the only doctor in the operating room who didn't yell. Not once."

"That's true." Mitch chuckled. "You know, sometimes some of the staff call him Grannie. No disrespect, Dr. Russell," Mitch said, and dipped his chin toward Ron, who seemed as if he might be awake enough to be following the conversation.

"They call him Grannie 'cause he does his cases so slow. But a lot of us know why Dr. Russell doesn't ever rush. It's so that he can take the best care of people."

She nodded. Her husband had closed his eyes again.

The refrigerator was crammed with containers of food brought by friends and neighbors. She should have asked Mitch if he'd like anything to take home. She heated a plate of grilled vegetables and lemon chicken in the microwave, then took it upstairs to eat at the desk in the bedroom, watching Ron. She tried to give him some water, but it dribbled down his chin. He hadn't opened his eyes since Mitch left. She wished they could talk. They had talked a lot over the past months, yet there was much more to say. But Ron had grown too weak, and Eleanor already had regrets about words left unsaid.

When she finished her solitary dinner, she showered and put on a freshly ironed white nightgown. She liked the clean, fresh smell. In her chaste white gown, she lay down next to Ron. His breathing was slow, his face relaxed. As often happened, once she'd gotten into bed, she wasn't tired anymore. She felt wide awake. It was still early. She thought of putting on a video.

There were plenty of films, perhaps a hundred, in neat stacks on the shelf next to the television. When friends learned of the seriousness of Ron's illness, they'd called or written, asking if there was something they might send. Ron had no appetite for food. Instead, he told everyone he wanted to laugh. He pointed to studies in medical journals showing how laughter fought disease. He wanted to watch funny movies—old or new, clean or dirty, it didn't matter. Like a chain letter, his request for humorous videos went out into the world and multiplied.

Films arrived from friends and friends of friends. He loved the silly British comedies like *Black Adder* and *Are You Being Served?* He enjoyed watching videos of the old *Saturday Night Live* stars

John Belushi, Gilda Radner, and Bill Murray. But most of all, he enjoyed the Marx Brothers. Ron watched *Night at the Opera* over and over. Joshua loved lying on the bed next to his dad. Even though he didn't understand most of the movie, he cracked up at the fat lady singing. Ron grinned happily as Joshua doubled over with laughter on the bed.

Tonight, however, Eleanor didn't feel like a comedy. She'd never found the Marx Brothers particularly funny. Lately their antics seemed annoying. She wanted to watch the news of the O. J. Simpson trial, which dominated the media each day. When she could, in the kitchen or in the car, she listened to every sordid detail of the trial: the knife, barking dog, bloodstains, and the low-speed chase in the Bronco. She was gripped by the crime and didn't exactly know why, except, she supposed, for the obvious reason that it proved someone had it worse than she did. Schadenfreude.

Ron detested the O. J. coverage. He groaned if it came on the radio or television. He thought the nation's preoccupation with the trial was obscene and could not fathom why Eleanor cared about it. So, she didn't turn on the television, but lay next to Ron in the silence of the evening and read a magazine. She realized she hadn't called Joshua. It was too late. Marilyn would have certainly put the boys to bed, so she went back to her magazine.

At around ten fifteen, Ron's eyes snapped open. He turned his head to her.

"What is it, hon?" she asked.

He didn't answer but kept staring, his eyes widening even more.

She got scared. She got him water, but his mouth was clamped shut. Was it pain? Did he need morphine? She called Lila next door.

"Lila, it's me." She tried to keep her voice calm. "Ron wants something, but I don't know what he needs."

Don't panic, she heard the hospice nurse's voice repeating inside her head. *Do not panic and do not call 911.*

"I'll be right over," Lila said.

"Yeah. If you could," Eleanor said. She clutched her throat. *Don't start,* she warned the spasm. *Don't start. Not now.*

Eleanor put down the phone and sat on the bed. Ron was still staring at her, eyes wide. She felt as if she was failing a test. Mitch would have known what to do. Lila would know what to do. *Other people are capable in ways I'm not,* Eleanor thought.

Within a few moments, Eleanor heard the kitchen door open and close. She listened to her friend climb the stairs and come into the bedroom.

The two women stared wordlessly at one another, then both went to Ron's side of the bed. His eyes followed Eleanor.

Lila tried to smooth the sheets. She reached under Ron. He was so thin she easily pulled the bottom sheet straight. The room was warm. Ron was wearing only his boxers and a T-shirt.

Then Lila said, "He's peed a little. It's kind of wet. Should we change his boxers?"

Eleanor nodded and got a fresh pair of shorts from a drawer.

Lila efficiently tugged off Ron's damp boxers, and together, the two women gently pulled the new pair up over Ron's frail legs and hips. They lifted Ron's hips and placed a towel under him, even though the sheet was barely wet. Ron had drunk very little these past few days and had eaten almost nothing.

He had closed his eyes again, perhaps to spare himself this indignity of the two women undressing and dressing him, even though they tried to be gentle and did the job quickly.

Eleanor tucked the top sheet around her husband, and the two women stood over the bed. Eleanor's brow was deeply furrowed. She was still trying to think if there was something else she should be doing. All at once, she realized she hadn't heard Ron breathe in a long time. She leaned over, listening. She held her own breath and put her ear close to his mouth. Then she stood again and stared down at her husband. His eyes were closed, and he looked peaceful. She waited. She was sure that if she waited quietly, another would come. *He's just breathing slowly*, she thought.

"Is this it?" Lila finally asked in an incredulous whisper.

"No," Eleanor said. "It can't be." *We just need to wait*, she thought. *All evening he'd been breathing softly. Another breath will come.*

This was not the way she had imagined it. So quiet. She wasn't ready. Hospice said it would be a while longer. She strained to listen. She might miss it, his next breath. But there were no more. Ron was gone.

Lila took her hand. Then Eleanor thought of Joshua. Her stomach heaved and her supper rose in her throat. She was glad, though, that Joshua was not at home, glad he was at Marilyn's house. She could not imagine going downstairs and facing him or having the little boy wake in the night and having to tell him that his father was dead. The morning would come soon enough.

Eleanor and Lila sat with Ron's body for another twenty minutes without moving. Lila wept softly as she held Eleanor's hand. Eleanor could not. *A dry socket, once again,* she thought. Lila left to make the phone calls downstairs.

Eleanor stayed by the bed and continued to watch Ron. She thought about the long look he'd given her before she'd rushed to the phone, when it seemed he wanted to tell her something. She and Lila had assumed he was telling her he had to pee or that he'd wet himself. They'd hurried to change his clothes. Maybe he'd been trying to tell her he loved her. Perhaps his long, lingering look had been a message of love that he'd been too weak to speak. She thought if only she had just slowed down and stayed with him, not rushed to the phone, she might have understood his message.

As she stood by the bed and continued to watch Ron, she was pretty sure she saw something leave his body. She didn't know if this was his spirit, or if she even believed in a spirit. But, as she watched, she knew precisely the moment when he was no longer Ron anymore. Of that she was sure, and so she stood up and left the bedroom, closing the door behind her.

By the time she slowly came down the stairs, people had started to arrive—friends first, then Laurel from hospice, and finally, shortly after midnight, two men from the funeral home. They went upstairs to get Ron and carried him downstairs wrapped in a sheet. One friend tried to shield her from the sight of Ron's body being carried from the house. She swatted the woman's hands from her face.

"No," she said. "I want to see." She didn't want to imagine any of it differently from the way it was.

The next morning, Eleanor sat on a stool in the kitchen. Someone had placed a cup of steaming coffee in front of her. Joshua was on his way home. Eleanor had told Marilyn she wanted to be the one to tell Joshua, but that wasn't the way it happened. Marilyn had two children younger than Stuart. There was a nanny, Heather, who watched the younger children while Marilyn worked. The nanny was at the house early that morning and overheard what had happened. She'd gone into the boys' room to get Stuart ready for school, and Joshua ready to come home. The nanny assumed Joshua had been told already.

"Oh, sweetie," Heather said to Joshua, who had been playing with Legos on the carpeted floor of Stuart's room. "It's such a shame about your poor daddy. Such a fine man, too young to be taken."

Marilyn said she was across the hallway, changing her baby. She heard the nanny and rushed in, still carrying the baby, but the damage was done. Joshua sat on his knees on the floor, frozen, staring down at the toys.

Marilyn phoned Eleanor to tell her.

"I'm so sorry," she said. "People can be so insensitive. Heather isn't always the most aware. I'm so sorry. I'll bring him home right away."

Eleanor sighed. "How's he doing?"

"He didn't cry. He just sat still, then called Heather a fucking liar. He said his dad was *not* dead. He didn't believe her. He actually used 'fucking.' I'm just so sorry he was told that way, by a stranger, not you. Damn Heather."

When Marilyn arrived, she carried Joshua inside from the car. He was a big child, and she was awkward as she walked with him. Eleanor took her son from her friend, Marilyn trying again to apologize.

Eleanor held Joshua on her lap in the kitchen. He tucked his head into her neck. She felt his warn breath and she rocked him. She told him how much she loved him. He had tears rolling down his cheeks. Finally, he spoke.

"You didn't call me last night," he said. "You said you'd call."

"I'm so sorry, Joshua."

"Is it true about Daddy?" he asked.

"Yes, Joshua, it's true. I'm so sorry."

"Why didn't you call me when he died?" He was indignant.

"It was late, Joshua. I knew you'd be asleep. I wanted to tell you this morning."

"Is he still upstairs? In bed?" the boy asked.

She had to tell him he'd been taken to the funeral home. Because Jewish funerals happened quickly, they had to get his daddy ready soon. The funeral would be the day after tomorrow.

Joshua got really angry and jumped from her lap. He screamed at her. "That's not fair. That's really not fair." He grabbed her coffee cup and threw it to the ground, splattering hot coffee and pottery shards on her and the floor.

"I know, Joshua. I know it's not fair," she said. She tried to reach for him, but he ran off to his room and slammed the door behind him.

Marilyn was backed up against the dishwasher, watching them and clutching the black stuffed dog Joshua had brought to her house. She put it on the counter and went for a mop and broom to clean the floor.

"I'll stay here today," Marilyn said over her shoulder. "I know you have a lot to do. Arranging everything. I'll give him the dog. It's fierce looking, isn't it? But he seems to like it."

Eleanor shrugged her shoulders and went upstairs to dress.

Friends came with her to choose the casket and print the funeral program. They found a picture of Ron that Eleanor knew her husband would have liked. It wasn't a professional photo. His glasses glinted, obscuring his eyes, but he had a warm, understanding smile in it. He wore a ski sweater he'd liked. She remembered the vacation when the picture was taken. It was up in Lake Tahoe when Joshua was still a baby. Ron cross-country skied with him in a backpack. Ron's long, lanky legs never wavered as, slowly and deliberately, he sliced tracks into the fresh snow, Joshua's little head bobbing up and down.

She had a painting Joshua had recently done in kindergarten. She'd use it as the cover of the funeral program. It was a rainbow. But there was something about the way the paint dripped down from each color of the rainbow to the end of the paper. Joshua had meant to write "To Dad" at the top of the picture, but sometimes he reversed his letters, and so it read, "To Dab."

By evening, Joshua had become less angry. Many people came and went, all trying to spend time with Joshua, to speak with him about how much Ron had loved him. When Max arrived from Arizona, he took Joshua out for their favorite meal of pizza and vanilla milkshakes. Joshua seemed less stricken when Max was there. Max was big and a male, and his older half-brother gave Joshua comfort. Eleanor had to smile when she saw her gangly teenaged son in his drooping trousers and torn tennis shoes, trying to be responsible and help his little brother. She watched her two sons, the young one, adopted at birth, fair and round, with a halo of blond hair, and the other, her biological child, swarthy and angular, with curly dark hair. The two held hands as they walked toward Max's old pickup truck.

She awoke the Friday of the funeral wishing the day over before it started. She wanted to be alone and soak in the tub for hours until the water became cold. She'd refused offers for anyone to stay, even telling Max and Lara to spend the night at their father's house, so she could be alone with Joshua. They were surprised but did as she asked. Now, she regretted her decision, wishing someone were in the kitchen to fix Joshua his breakfast, so that she wouldn't have to do it. She dragged herself from bed.

After breakfast, they dressed, Eleanor in her new dress and good black heels. She put out a powder-blue polo shirt and dark slacks for Joshua. It was a warm, sunny day, warmer than it should be in November. They were to drive to the funeral in a limousine with Max, Lara, and Jean. When the big black car drove up the driveway, Joshua's eyes widened. He was impressed. The car was so long, it had trouble turning into the driveway. The others arrived and got in the car.

Joshua sat on Eleanor's lap on the way to the funeral. She was glad to be holding him. His warm body and fresh little-boy smell blocked out everything and everyone else. Jean sat across from them, riding backward, seeming shrunken and alone. It pained Eleanor to see her mother-in-law so reduced.

Lara said to Joshua, "Your daddy was so proud of you. He once told me he had everything he wanted—Mommy, a job he liked, stepkids he loved, and then, you, the little boy he dreamed of. We were too old when we met him, so he couldn't play with us. He really wanted a kid just like you."

"But not for long enough," said Jean, riding backwards in the seat across from them. "He didn't have everything he wanted for long enough."

At the chapel, Eleanor was led to the front pew, still holding Joshua's hand, the family around her. She was aware of the long room filling, the numbers of people filing past her to pay their respects, though she could not specifically remember what anyone said. She did remember the eulogies, however. She was surprised at how much the words meant to her. She was proud Ron had moved people to say such lovely words. One of Ron's partners spoke first, a gruff man she had never known to say more than a few sentences at any given time, but whom she'd asked to speak because he was her husband's closest friend.

He said how Ron's calm wisdom would be missed, how Ron was the glue that kept their group of strong-willed doctors, with their big egos, together. His voice broke. She watched this usually unemotional man as he worked to collect himself.

Ron's cousin, an English professor, read a spare elegy he'd written.

Sweet family man
Russian at your roots,
A Jew, a good Jew
by many acts of kindness.
Ever the peacemaker
Proud father, proud husband
generous brother, son,
grandson.
Sweet seed of generations
buried too soon.

The principal at Joshua's school spoke of Ron. He told a funny story of Ron bumbling with hammer and nails on parent workdays, awkward but always willing. Their rabbi, a somber woman of quiet emotions, spoke last. Rabbi Lorenz seemed to reach deep within herself and spoke movingly of Ron and how, during his illness, he took time with each of the family members, giving them his final words of advice. She mentioned details that surprised Eleanor for their specificity and rightness. When he was older, Joshua should know more about the man who had left him too soon. These eulogies would help. Eleanor would ask each of the speakers to give her a copy of their speech.

After the funeral, people filed out of the chapel, following the hearse in cars or on foot, to the burial. Max held one of Joshua's hands, Eleanor the other, as they went through the tall metal gates separating Home of Peace Jewish Cemetery from the main cemetery. Folding chairs were set up for the family near the open grave. Eleanor again pulled Joshua onto her lap. The other relatives—cousins, aunts, and uncles—sat in a row close behind the immediate family. The other mourners (Eleanor was surprised at the numbers) did a curious thing. Instead of bunching up in a crowd behind the chairs, as she'd seen done at other funerals, someone's instinct had been to form a circle. Men and women Eleanor and Ron had worked with, neighbors, Max's and Lara's friends, children and teachers from Joshua's school, and members of the synagogue formed an enormous circle. There were hundreds of people, so they made a second circle within that outer one. Many held hands. The family, along with Rabbi Lorenz, who was wearing an embroidered yellow yarmulke, was encircled. The noon sun was directly overhead, and when the rabbi rose to lead prayers, her yarmulke seemed equally bright.

Eleanor looked out at the circles and felt connections to so many parts of the life she and Ron had built. Lara and Jean had both been right: it was all good—his home, his family, his work—his whole life had been as good as it could be, but too brief.

After the ceremony, people came to the house. Someone more religious than she had set up a basin of water on a stool outside the front door so that, according to tradition, mourners could wash their hands when they returned from the cemetery. She reached down and trailed her fingertips through the water, then walked upstairs. More and more people arrived and filled the downstairs. She heard the increasing murmur of conversation and noises of forks scraping plates and smelled coffee percolating in the large, industrial-sized coffeepot she'd borrowed. Lila had helped make sure there was an abundance of Ron's favorites: corned beef and brisket, rye bread, dill pickles, coleslaw, chopped liver, and lots of chocolate. She knew many would arrive with some kind of offering—a plate or platter filled with more food. The custom was to bring food to the house of mourning, usually sweets. The longer she sat upstairs on the edge of her bed and listened to the clamor downstairs, the harder it became to stand and join the others. She knew people were waiting to see her and offer their condolences, but she couldn't move.

Finally, there was a knock at the door and Lara walked in. She had wild, long hair in those days, the darkest brown, but with electric-blue streaking. Eleanor had once commented it was not a color found in nature. Lara had not spoken to her for weeks. Now her daughter sat on the bed next to her. The two did not have the kind of relationship where one comforted the other. The divorce from Lara's father and its angry aftermath still kept them apart. Mother and daughter were prickly with one another.

"Is that a new dress, Mom?" the girl asked. "It's nice."

"Mmm," Eleanor said vaguely.

"You coming downstairs?"

"I will. Soon. Not yet. Where's Joshua?"

"About a hundred people are playing with him out back. They're lined up to push him on the swing set. All your friends are making plates of food for him to eat. The kid is gonna weigh two hundred pounds after this."

Eleanor nodded, relieved she wasn't absolutely needed at the moment.

"Can I get you anything? Something to drink?" Lara asked, softly.

Eleanor didn't think she had ever been offered food by Lara before. It was nice. She wished she could think of something Lara could bring her.

"No, but it's good that you're here. I'm glad you're with me." She put her arm around Lara and her head on her daughter's shoulder. She breathed in the unique smell of Lara: patchouli oil and sweet hair spray mixed together. Her eyes moved downward. Lara was wearing sandals and a long wraparound skirt. The skirt fell open at the side and Eleanor spotted a tattoo on her daughter's lower calf. It was a sun, a round circle with rays jutting out in all directions. When Lara realized her mother was staring at her calf, she crossed her legs.

"Oh, Lara," Eleanor said. "You know how I hate tattoos."

"Well then," her daughter answered, "I suppose you shouldn't get one."

Eleanor breathed deeply, and somehow had the restraint or perhaps the tiredness, to say no more. This was not the moment for an argument about a sunburst tattoo, although she wondered how long the girl had hid it from her. It didn't matter.

Chapter 9

THE BALLPLAYER

2006

Joshua was sixteen on the tenth anniversary of Ron's death, and already in trouble with thefts and drugs and running away. On the anniversary, Eleanor asked Joshua to visit Ron's grave with her. She explained that when his father had died, he'd been too young to recite the *kaddish,* the memorial prayer. Once he was thirteen, however, and had had his bar mitzvah, it was traditional for the son to take on that responsibility. In Judaism, that was what a son was called: the kaddish, the father's legacy. Since Max was the stepson; it fell to Joshua to recite kaddish for his father on the anniversary of his death.

"But I'm the adopted son. Does that count? I wasn't born Jewish." Joshua searched Eleanor's face.

"Oh, Joshua. Of course it counts." She found that his question annoyed her. "When you were born, your dad made sure you had a proper religious conversion. You're a real Jew and you *are* definitely your father's son."

Joshua hesitated, then agreed to come to the cemetery and say the prayer.

She parked outside the iron gates of Home of Peace. They walked together and found Ron's grave, Eleanor's heels sinking into the soft earth. She clutched a booklet printed with Jewish prayers said at the graveside: the mourner's kaddish and some psalms. The words were transliterated, the Hebrew written out phonetically. She wasn't sure how much Hebrew Joshua remembered from his own bar mitzvah. She knew she herself was rusty. She began reading:

Yis gadol v'yis kaddash
sh'mey rabbo,
b'ol'mo di'vro chir'oosey
v'yam lich mal' chu sey,
b'cha ye chon
u v'yo me chon u v'cha yey
d'chol bes yisroel, ba ago lo u vis man ko riv,
v'im roo, Omen.

Joshua joined her and they recited together. Eleanor was surprised that her son didn't once look down at the paper, but said the kaddish prayer flawlessly in his newly deep voice, looking off into the distance. She herself read the transliterated words from the paper, stumbling over some, especially the middle verses, until she got to the familiar concluding lines:

O seh sholom bim' ro mov,
Hu ya aseh sholom,
o'leynu v'al kol yisroel,
v'im'roo, Omen.

Just as it had been at Ron's funeral, it was an unseasonably warm November day, though now the cemetery was quiet. Ten years before, this section was newly opened. There had been gaps between the graves. Now, there were more headstones filling the area. Eleanor usually came to Ron's grave on the anniversary of his death. She supposed this section had gradually filled in, but she hadn't noticed until today. It startled her that although there were many graves all around Ron's, the plot immediately to the right of her late husband's was still empty. She had not reserved the plot for herself. She was only forty-seven at the time of Ron's death. She didn't want a cemetery plot. Were they keeping it open in case she changed her mind? Should she be thinking about it?

Joshua wiped away a few tears with the sleeve of his sweatshirt as he looked down and read the words on his father's grave. Eleanor reached into her pocket and handed him a small stone to place on the headstone, as Jews did when visiting the dead. She placed one, a pale rose quartz, and Joshua placed another. There were other stones on Ron's grave, left from earlier visits from friends and family. Joshua stooped and removed them all, one by one, then took a bandana from the pocket of his jeans. He wiped the headstone. He burnished the granite until it was shiny again, then polished each stone, carefully replacing them. Joshua and Eleanor sat down together on the grass. She leaned back on her arms, holding her face up to the warm sun.

"What do you remember about that day, the day of your dad's funeral?" she asked Joshua. It felt vivid to her still, particularly the circle of people around them as they lowered the casket into the ground. She lightly rested a hand on her son's shoulder.

"Not much." He shrugged. "A lot of food at the house." He was looking down at the grass, plucking at stray weeds around his father's headstone. Then he stood up, pulling up the hood of his sweatshirt, seeming suddenly anxious to go.

She supposed he wanted to get back to his friends, skateboard with them on such a beautiful day, not remain with her in the graveyard. But she persisted. "Do you remember all the people who were here at the funeral? All the people who were there for us?" She so wanted him to remember that circle.

He shook his head. He hesitated, then added, "I remember the rabbi was wearing a yellow yarmulke. I was afraid to stop looking at it."

Once again, Eleanor was surprised by her son, his response to her question.

If Joshua actually attended class that November, he would have been a junior at Los Altos High. Instead, Eleanor had him escorted to Mount Richmond Therapeutic Boarding School in central Oregon.

It had been excruciating to send him away, especially since Eleanor had to make the decision on her own, but Mount Richmond seemed the perfect fit for her son. Nearly 30 percent of its students were adopted. Through the years, she'd tried many times to talk to Joshua about his adoption, but perhaps she did it awkwardly. She found him therapists, but even in therapy, Joshua steadfastly refused to speak of his adoption. At Mount Richmond, the staff was trained to deal with issues many adopted teens had in common: fear of abandonment, attachment disorders, and addiction.

Eleanor read through the school's material. It described the sense of loss experienced by adoptees. Even if they were adopted as infants, this was common. One expert was quoted as saying adopted kids had a wound they carried with them their entire lives. At first, Eleanor resisted this idea. She had held him when he was only a few hours old. *How can he feel abandoned? What memory can he have of Kelly giving him up for adoption?* Eleanor was the only mother who'd ever held him, their family the only family he'd ever known. Yet research said children were still aware of this loss. There were primal memories: smell, touch, sight, and senses recognized as foreign.

Eleanor willed herself to understand. The people at Mount Richmond were experienced. They said many adopted kids had trouble with identity, which was true of Joshua. He didn't seem to know who he was. He floundered more each day. Max and Lara had suffered their share of teenaged angst and been rebellious. But there was a difference. She felt something missing in Joshua. Ego, the psychologists called it. He had no strong inner core. As Lara and Max were reaching adulthood and thriving, Joshua was defining himself as a gangster, an outlaw.

For many years, Eleanor believed she could fill this hole. She'd blithely believed there was nothing she couldn't fix with love. But lately, as Joshua got into repeated trouble, and the nature of this trouble became alarming, she was beginning to realize that no matter how many ways she expressed her love, she couldn't fill that emptiness. She'd underestimated Joshua's feelings of loss. She had been naive.

Of course, all adopted kids weren't the same. Some had more problems, some less. Joshua had been a relatively easy child. This was not what she heard from some of the other parents. Soon after her son arrived at the Oregon school, Eleanor attended her first parents support group. They met over brunch in a private room at a nice restaurant in a shopping center in San Jose. They might have been parents of kids who played on a sports team, not parents who had sent their troubled teens off to a therapeutic boarding school in Oregon. As she listened to the others, Eleanor was struck at how many described their kids as having been different from the very beginning. Even as toddlers, many parents said, their children seemed odd, off in some way. Most had observed behavioral problems quite early.

One woman she chatted with, an attractive gray-haired mother from Los Angeles, said life with her son had been a challenge even in preschool.

"He got kicked out of the first three nursery schools we sent him to," the woman said, staring into her coffee cup.

"Three *nursery* schools?" Eleanor asked incredulously.

"Personally, if I had been in charge of the preschool he eventually went to, I would have kicked him out of that one, too. He was such a pain in the ass. But they kept him the whole year. They kept trying to *understand* him. To *reach* him."

"What did he do to get expelled from preschools?" Eleanor asked.

The woman from LA sighed. "Mark was a biter from the time he was two. I can't tell you how many times I got called to school to look at a set of teeth marks he'd left on some poor child's forearm. He even broke the skin a few times. Kids had to get tetanus shots because of my son. My husband is a dentist; he said maybe we ought to pull all of Mark's teeth. Ha. I actually considered it for a second or two."

Another woman at the seminar, one with a southern accent, overheard them and chimed in.

"You had a biter, too? My Evan finally stopped biting, but then he began exposing himself. A therapist thought perhaps he'd been sexually abused. They tried to find evidence for it but couldn't. When our son saw he could get hysterical screams out of the little girls in first grade, he kept pulling down his pants. He loved the reaction he got. You can imagine how popular *that* made him with other parents. Wasn't invited to very many birthday parties."

Both mothers spoke with nonchalance. Eleanor shuddered and wondered if she had made a mistake sending Joshua to Mount Richmond. Joshua had never been given a diagnosis of any mental disorder. He hadn't been a biter, and he'd never exposed himself. Just the opposite. Until he was nearly fourteen, she'd not seen problems. She called him her "50 percent boy" because he hit all the developmental landmarks right on schedule—not earlier, nor later. Joshua was polite at home and at school, not at all confrontational. She thought back to Joshua's early years. All she could remember was his sunny, sweet nature.

"Mom," he wrote in one of his first letters from Mount Richmond, "these kids are all weirdos. You got to get me out of here."

There had been nothing at all weird about Joshua's early years. When he'd been two and a half, Eleanor and Ron enrolled him in the local Montessori school, the same one Max and Lara had attended. The school brought back magical memories for her. After the earthquake, when she had been filled with desire to have another child, she'd reminisced about going to that little red building in the woods, rustic and simple. It held some of the sweetest memories of being a parent.

Behind the school was a little creek. Parents, teachers, and children wore rubber galoshes and played in the shallow water for hours, bobbing simple fishing poles into the water, pretending to fish. The children piled up rocks, making small dams to divert the flow of the stream. Beautiful, golden-haired Joshua threw stones into the water, smiling and engrossed with the ripples. No one bothered him as he stood on the small footbridge throwing rocks into the water below. He wore an expression of pure joy during those mornings. Each day ended with a picnic the kids helped prepare. She remembered Joshua's favorite food: peanut butter spread over celery sticks with raisins dotting the top. The kids called this treat "bugs on a log." As she had for all three children, she kept a folder from those days, each labeled with the child's name. She filled the folder with observation sheets provided by the school so parents could make notes on their toddler's day.

Joshua's file was thick. She made herself tea, then sat outside in the spring sun to read about her little boy. Some observation sheets were written by Ron. His doctor's scrawl was usually hard to read, but he'd taken careful, methodical notes on the days he'd gone to the program with Joshua. Seeing her husband's handwriting gave her a pang. She reread one quote written in Ron's slanted scrawl.

"I have never met such a pleasant, easy-to-like child as Joshua."

This was written in Ron's typically formal style, but it was all true. As she reread the weekly notes, it was as if she were back there in that meadow by the stream, sitting on the low picnic bench watching her toddler, the unexpected child she had been gifted in middle age.

"I love you sooo much," Joshua said to her one day, and she had carefully transcribed it. "And I love Max sooo much. And Lara, too. I love my whole fambly."

He'd come up to her when the children were called out of the stream for snack time. He seemed to have a magnet for knowing exactly where she was, at all times, even when playing intently in the creek and not looking in her direction. She'd dry off his little hands and peel off his wet boots. She still remembered the green boots with a duck's face and yellow bill sticking up from the toe. Joshua loved his duck boots. He tried to squeeze his feet into them long after he'd outgrown them.

On the last day at preschool, there was a tradition of every parent writing a letter about their child and reading these letters aloud to one another. Often the moms got so choked up, they couldn't finish reading without tears streaming down their cheeks. Now, Eleanor reread her description of Joshua as he was at three: beautiful hazel eyes, lashes that curled upward, sturdy, well made. He was physically adept, completely in charge of his little body. She wrote of his hair so golden it glowed and about his perfect straight teeth and ever-constant smile. She described how he never failed to kiss everyone at home hello and goodbye, and how if one of the family left the house without saying goodbye and hugging him, he'd stand at the door afterward and wail inconsolably. At the end of her letter, she wrote Joshua had added so much to their family, how grateful she was that he'd given her a chance to experience all these precious childhood things again, activities she'd done years before with Max and Lara. He'd brought joy to them all. She'd saved the letter for him to read when he was older.

After the preschool letter reading ceremony, she remembered another mother came to her and asked if they could speak.

"I hope I'm not being intrusive," the woman said. "But you've had both: biological children and now, Joshua, adopted. Is it different in any way? I wonder because I've only had the one child. We're thinking about adoption, but worry how it would be after having one of our own."

Eleanor had replied without hesitation. "I feel he *is* my own. Completely. He came into our lives so quickly—like it was meant to be. When I hold him now and watch him, the feelings are the same as those I had for my older kids. I know he's the last, so I treasure every day with Joshua. I know how each phase flies by. At night, when I lie next to him and feel him relax and fall asleep beside me, I'm completely flooded with love. Just as if I'd given birth to him."

That mother hugged her before she walked away.

She put away Joshua's nursery school file. In those early years after his adoption, she'd been so innocent in her optimism. She acted as if Joshua's life began when she'd flown with him on the plane to California. Of course, it hadn't. Now she knew better. His life had begun in Wisconsin in Kelly's womb. Even before that, with DNA and generations of family she knew nothing of.

When Joshua was in Little League, she had glimmers of this original family. Joshua had a very sophisticated windup when he threw the ball, amazing aim, and an even better catch. His batting average was always the highest in the league. She knew she'd have many more years of bench time ahead of her. Coaches fought to get Joshua on their team. Max and Lara had nothing of the single-minded focus Joshua possessed in sports. She watched his graceful throw, wondering where this skill had come from.

Neither she nor Ron were particularly athletic. From early on, Joshua loved to play ball, any kind of ball, but especially baseball.

While still in diapers, he kept himself busy with a game of his own creation. He'd found an old tennis ball in a closet and would throw it in the air, then bat at it with Lara's hairbrush. Over and over, he threw the ball and swiped at it with the brush.

"Where's my damn hairbrush?" Lara would ask, slamming her drawers open and shut. "Did he take it again?"

"Check Joshua's room," Eleanor would answer. "I think he was playing with it earlier."

Eleanor remembered his climbing phase, too. He'd never call to them if he needed something too high to reach. Instead, he pulled a chair over to the kitchen counter, and if he still couldn't get what he wanted, piled books on the chair.

One day, Ron found him climbing a bookshelf in the family room. (They kept meaning to affix the bookshelves to the wall after the Loma Prieta earthquake but hadn't yet done it.) Joshua was already up to the third shelf, hanging on with one hand and busily tossing down books with the other, when Ron came into the room. Ron told her he had watched, horrified, as the shelf swayed away from the wall. With long strides, Ron raced to Joshua, snatching him to safety seconds before the shelf toppled.

Ron told Eleanor, "I'm attaching those shelves to the wall. Today."

It was a close one, she realized. But back then, she used to feel lucky, as if there were a glass shield that protected her children. All of them. Nothing seriously bad could happen. She used to think the whole family was safe. They were the chosen ones.

At not yet fourteen, Joshua stole Ron's old Volvo sedan. It had been handed down to Max, but now with Max away at school, it sat unused. No one suspected that Joshua, only in eighth grade, knew how to drive. Early one morning, he took the keys from the metal hook where they hung in the kitchen. Joshua and the Volvo were recovered a few hours later, over a hundred miles south in Santa Cruz County. Another boy was in the car, a kid Eleanor hadn't met, but who was in Joshua's class. She didn't press charges and with the help of a friend who was an assistant district attorney, the matter was dropped. It had shaken them all. Joshua claimed he'd done it to help his friend escape from his abusive father. He claimed he wanted to help the boy find his cousins down in Watsonville. It was true he was always wanting to help someone. Eleanor's friend, the DA, tried to impress on Joshua the seriousness of what he'd done. She couldn't understand his actions, so she chose to think of it as a strange anomaly.

A few months later, Joshua was picked up at midnight by the local police. They found him drinking with a group of older kids in an abandoned shack up in the hills. Joshua was drunk. Again, there was a police warning but no arrest. She knew the whiteness of his skin and the affluent town they lived in softened consequences for Joshua. Eleanor tried to think of the incident as experimentation. Many kids experimented with drinking, even binge drinking. A friend's rabbi told her about a wilderness camp. The camp focused on Jewish values and practices. Located in Utah, near Bryce National Park, it was rugged and had strict discipline. Besides spirituality, it was supposed to instill responsibility in boys with behavior problems. It was expensive, but the rabbi told her it had had a profound impact on some of the young men he knew who attended. Eleanor decided to send Joshua to the camp.

Her son excelled at all the outdoor activities: the ropes course, cooking over an open fire, and building shelters out of almost nothing. He was an outstanding camper and liked the camp. However, soon after he returned, another incident happened. A mother from Los Angeles called Eleanor. Joshua and her son had been together at the Utah wilderness camp. The mother reported Joshua and her son appeared to be trying to buy and sell guns on the internet. She had installed spyware on her son's computer and had recorded their disturbing conversation.

The woman must be mistaken, Eleanor thought. Why would Joshua want guns? He was fifteen years old. This made no sense.

The woman forwarded Eleanor a transcript of the recorded conversation. It was frightening. The other child called himself "Black is King." The transcript went like this:

Joshua Creative One: "Yo listen up." This came from Joshua's computer.

Black is King: "I'm listening."

Joshua Creative One: "Yeah, bro. I can get you a piece. I can get you any kind of gun you want. I got a big-ass connection who is doing shit on da east coast and he is my new biggest wep connection."

Black is King: "How many can you get? Me and my crew can sell them. I'll split the profits with you, okay?"

Joshua Creative One: "No problem. I got a good source, like I said. Just let me know what you want. And how many."

Black is King: "I want a handgun. Like a little .45 cal."

Joshua Creative One: "He can get me anything. How's ur crew makin money?"

Black is King: "MJ, and a hella lotta stolen goods."

Joshua Creative One: "How old r ur guys in ur crew?"

Black is King: "Same as us."

The other woman made it clear to Eleanor there was to be no more contact between Joshua and her son. Ever.

Always Joshua had explanations. He told her the gun selling was a joke.

"You don't believe it, do you?" He laughed. "We were just goofing off with each other."

Eleanor lectured him, explaining how much trouble he could get in for talking about guns on the internet. He promised her he'd never do such a thing again.

Whenever he did anything wrong, he always had a logical explanation. But she was beginning to have prickles of doubt.

There was the party at their home. Eleanor had an educational conference in San Francisco, and Joshua knew the house would be empty. He was supposed to be spending the night at a friend's house. It was at the beginning of the winter holidays and seventy or eighty kids showed up. The police busted the party after a neighbor complained about the noise.

When she returned the next morning, the police were waiting for her.

"It was like watching roaches stream out of a building being fumigated," a uniformed officer said. "Kids were running from every window and door of your house."

"He's very polite, your son," said another Los Altos policeman. "Good manners. I heard you're a widow. Joshua hasn't got a dad. Sorry about that. Boys can be a handful. But when we got in the house, he was starting to clean up. Sweeping the glass and trash. He told us he didn't even know most of the people at the party. They brought in the drugs and booze and he tried to get them out. Said he was actually relieved when we arrived."

There were eight large black trash bags piled by the garage, all filled with empty beer cans and liquor bottles. The house was actually clean; Joshua had done a good job putting things back together. The police told her it happened all the time in Los Altos: kids discovered whose parents were out of town, and that became the party house. Again, Joshua wasn't charged with anything; the police just warned Eleanor and Joshua to be careful.

Puzzlingly, he remained sweet at home, helping with chores. Neither she nor Ron had ever really been good at home repairs. Joshua knew how to fix things. He could unstick the garbage disposal, replace outdoor lights, or repair sprinkler heads. Eleanor never knew how he learned to do the things he did; he was just good at it. But though he never raised his voice or swore, or even directly disobeyed her, she began more frequently to doubt him.

Then, at sixteen, he began disappearing. She'd wake and feel it, even before she checked. He was gone from the house. He'd have slipped out during the night or early morning. Eleanor never knew what precipitated the running away, as they rarely fought. It might have been when he was about to receive a bad report card, caught in a complicated lie, or sometimes nothing at all. She began to live in fear of the mornings when she found his bed empty. He was getting very good at living on the street or finding people to shelter and feed him. Although he was gone only a day or two at a time, sometimes three, it was terrifying.

The weekend before the last time he took off, his lying had been laughable, if outrageous. It was early spring. Eleanor got a call on a Saturday night from Joshua.

"Mom, I'm going to stay overnight at Todd's. Okay?"

Eleanor didn't think she'd heard of Todd before. "Do I know Todd?"

"Yeah. You do. He lives just across El Camino. He's in my biology class. Remember? I've talked to you about him. A bunch of times. He's really smart. He's my partner for the plant ecosystem project. Remember, I had to buy all that stuff? The two-liter soda bottles and the swamp plants? Todd and me worked on it all afternoon and now we want to relax and hang out here at his house. His folks are home, don't worry."

Eleanor could not remember if he had mentioned doing the ecosystem project with Todd. Sometimes she wasn't as attentive as she should be. Sometimes her mind wandered when he was talking to her.

"How about if I speak to Todd's mother. Remember, after the party we agreed that I'm supposed to know the parents of the people you spend time with. Could you put Todd's mom on the phone?"

He paused, then said cheerfully, "Sure. I'll go get her." Eleanor heard muffled talking and assumed Joshua had placed his hand over the receiver.

"Hi," Eleanor heard a female voice. It was a very young woman's voice.

"This is Todd's mom?" Eleanor asked.

"Yes, it is. We rented the boys some movies, and they're just going to hang out here and have some pizza. Don't worry, my husband and I are staying home tonight. They're behaving themselves," the woman said. "Like perfect gentlemen."

Eleanor thought she heard a short burst of laughter in the background. She felt really stupid. The woman sounded completely self-assured. Yet something was off. She had a thought. "Okay, but can you give me your home phone number? This call came in from my son's cell phone."

There was silence at the other end of the conversation. Then the woman said, "You know, we just moved to this house. I really don't know the phone number yet."

Eleanor got pinpricks on her skin. "Well, could I have your address, then?"

"Uh, I'll have to check on that. I'll be back in a second. I can't remember the address. We just moved here." The woman giggled nervously.

"That's okay," Eleanor said, grim now. "Why don't you just put Joshua back on the phone?"

There was more muffled conversation, and then Joshua said, "Hi, Mom. What's up?"

"Joshua, that is no one's mom. You either get back here in ten minutes or tell me where to pick you up."

"That *was* Todd's mom. I swear to God it was. They really did just move to this house. I can't believe how you never trust me."

"Which is it? Do I pick you up or are you coming home? You've got ten minutes. And if that was Todd's mom, invite her in. I'd like to meet her."

Joshua ended the call without answering her, but he did arrive home a few minutes later. He was alone. Eleanor waited by the front door, shaking with anger.

"That *was* Todd's mother," Joshua said immediately. "I can't believe you didn't believe me. You made me look like a baby. They *did* just move to that house."

"If that was Todd's mother, and you can prove it to me, I'll get down on my knees and beg your forgiveness. A mother knows her own phone number and address." She fought to regain calm.

Joshua stomped down the stairs to his bedroom, slamming the door.

Sometimes she felt like she was going crazy with Joshua. She hated second-guessing herself.

Three days after the incident with the phone call, her son disappeared again. It was the fourth time that year. She went down to his bedroom to wake him for school, and he was gone. This time there was a note on his pillow.

"I can't live in a place where no one trusts me. Don't try to contact the police. That will make it worse. Leave me alone. I can take care of myself. I'm not coming home."

Eleanor immediately went to the police with the letter. They politely took down the information, seeming bored. She got shrill at the police station.

"My son is only sixteen. He could be picked up by some perverts. Aren't you going to look for him? You need to put out an Amber Alert."

"Ma'am, this boy is a runaway. He left you a note. You told us he's run away before."

"But this is different. His note sounds like he's really going far. He could be hitchhiking."

"This is not a kidnapping. It's not an Amber Alert type of situation," the policeman said with finality.

She went through many emotions. At first, she imagined they'd find him dead in a ditch somewhere. Maybe he wanted to find his birth family. She'd read how adopted teens often want to contact the family. But within a day or two, she had the first of many "Joshua sightings." People called, saying they'd seen him around town. She traipsed around Los Altos after dark, searching for him, showing people his picture. She learned he was still in town, sometimes sleeping in friends' cars.

She went back to the police station.

"Even if we picked him up, Mrs. Russell," one officer explained to her, not unkindly, "what would we do with him? We'd bring him back to you. Then, if he ran away again, we'd have to start all over. We're busy here. It's a small station. We've got a lot of work to do. We can't be chasing after your runaway son."

"But he's a minor. Isn't being out on the streets against the law?"

The policeman shrugged.

A female officer watched from her desk. She went to Eleanor and studied the collage of pictures Eleanor held. All the photos were of Joshua.

"I'm sorry, but he really hasn't broken any laws. You *could* get him declared unmanageable. Then he'd be sent to juvenile hall. But you don't want to do that. He'd have trouble at juvenile hall. There are some really bad kids there. Murderers and rapists."

Eleanor's lunch rose in her gut. She stumbled out of the Los Altos police station, wondering again how she'd gone from being a Little League mom to the woman who carried her runaway son's pictures around town.

Family and friends searched for Joshua. They called all the kids Eleanor had phone numbers for. Some were evasive, others genuinely puzzled. He wasn't going to school, but she roamed the campus during lunch hour, thinking he'd want to hang out with his friends. Kids reported he was still in town, and although she was relieved, she was deeply hurt he wouldn't return. She put up posters in his usual hangouts. Days went by.

Only his music teacher would speak to her when she traipsed around the school. The principal and teachers appeared uncomfortable. They'd see her walking on campus and turn away, making conversation with each other. Their school did not typically have this kind of problem.

He'd been gone six days, when this music teacher, Mr. McDormand, walked up to her during a lunch break. "Your boy is a good boy, ma'am. Really talented in music. And funny. He could be a stand-up comic. He's just a little confused."

"Do you know where he is?" she asked him. He seemed to be one of those young teachers who wanted to be friends with students. Perhaps Joshua had confided in him.

"No, I don't. But I did see him around here earlier in the week. Give me your cell number. I'll call you if I see him again. I'll try to keep him here with me. Sometimes he hangs out in back of the school. In Vietnam."

"Vietnam?" Eleanor looked at the young teacher, puzzled. "What are you talking about?"

"Vietnam is down there, toward the freeway. In the bushes." Mr. McDormand motioned behind him with his chin. "I haven't been there myself, but I know some of the kids go there and smoke weed. When I went to high school here, that's what kids called it. Even back then, ten, twelve years ago. That's where they went to get stoned."

This was a revelation to Eleanor. She scrutinized scruffy Mr. McDormand. She imagined he'd been one of those kids getting stoned back there when he was in high school. She'd have to ask Max and Lara about it. Mr. McDormand had probably graduated around the same time as Lara.

"Thanks," she said. She wrote her cell phone number on a piece of paper from the pad she carried. "Please call me if you see him."

After a week, Joshua was still gone. He'd never before stayed away this long. Some people recommended she let the situation take its course. Eventually, he'd commit a crime. If he got arrested, maybe that would be good. Tough love might be what he needed. Maybe he needed to be scared straight. Another friend, a usually very wise friend, said if Joshua wanted to be free, let him be free, until things got too miserable for him. This friend was sure Joshua would return home soon on his own. When he came home, she should let him drop out of high school and get a job. Working would teach Joshua a lot. As this friend saw it, Joshua needed to take control of his own life.

All of this was too frightening to Eleanor. He could be exploited by some sexual predator on the streets. He was such a beautiful child. He could overdose on drugs. He must be helped.

She found her way to Vietnam. She was shocked by the garbage and broken chairs strewn around the area. It was a homeless encampment of sorts. She sobbed as she remembered the idyllic little stream Joshua loved at the Montessori preschool. Here, in Vietnam, filthy sleeping bags and torn pillows were on the ground amidst broken bottles. Although she saw no needles or apparent drug paraphernalia, she was still terrified.

One of the stories she'd read on the internet said that ecstasy was the current drug of choice, the tablets especially popular with affluent teenagers. Parents might snoop through their rooms or ask to smell their breath. Tablets were an easier way to get high without leaving evidence.

She saw remnants of old bonfires and tin cans for cooking. She smelled urine. She tacked posters of Joshua to a tree in Vietnam, thinking about his comfortable room at home, the soft checkered comforter on his bed.

A day later, Eleanor called one of the therapists Joshua had seen. In between Eleanor's sobs, the therapist mentioned Mount Richmond Academy, a therapeutic boarding school in Oregon. It was painful for her to think of sending Joshua away. She would be sending away her beloved child, who had already been relinquished at birth. But she was desperate, and as she read Mount Richmond's literature, sending him there seemed the answer. Joshua had loved the wilderness camp in Utah he'd gone to. Of course, the school was expensive. But, if her child had cancer and needed a bone marrow transplant, she would find a way to help him. She would take out a second mortgage on her house, if she had to. She had several conversations with the school. She liked the admissions coordinator, Mindy. The woman thought Mount Richmond might be a good fit for Joshua.

"There's a problem, though, Mindy."

"What's that?"

"Joshua isn't here now. He's run away. We know he's close; he's been spotted nearby. As recently as yesterday."

Mindy was nonplussed. "It happens all the time," she told Eleanor. "Most kids refuse to come on their own. They're teenagers whose freedom is being threatened. Of course they resist. Some kids, like Joshua, are runaways. He isn't the first, Mrs. Russell."

"So what now?" Eleanor asked.

"We recommend a gentleman named Julius Wollinsky," Mindy said. "He runs an organization called Youth Recovery Services. He's worked with non-compliant teens for twenty years. Julius is very good at de-escalating difficult situations. I promise, he'll find your son and safely bring him to us in Oregon."

"I don't want him to hurt Joshua. He isn't going to use force, is he?" Eleanor asked frantically.

"Oh no. We've used Julius for a long time. He may look a little rough around the edges, but he's a miracle worker with the kids. At the end of the drive, they usually give him a hug."

Eleanor called Youth Recovery Services. When the beige car drove up the next day and she saw Julius Wollinsky with his assistant, she realized she was about to have her youngest child kidnapped by two men she ordinarily would not have shown into her living room. She felt a sense of disbelief as she escorted them inside, wondering again how this had happened.

Julius was a short, thickset fellow who said he'd been a cop for many years. (Eleanor didn't want to ask why he was no longer working as a policeman.) He was accompanied by his assistant, Auggie, a scary-looking skinhead with multiple tattoos on his arms and neck. Auggie was huge, over six and a half feet tall.

When Julius introduced Auggie to Eleanor, he mentioned that when asked to recover a female teenager, he brought his wife, Nancy, instead of Auggie. She was soft and motherly with the girls, Julius said, but she was also hefty and strong, almost as strong as Auggie, and she could be tough when necessary. Julius showed Eleanor information about his company, with statistics on their success in finding and delivering teenagers to programs. There were affidavits from parents testifying to the safety of Youth Recovery Services. The two men perched on her rose-colored velvet sofa, Auggie cracking his knuckles while Eleanor reviewed the paperwork.

"Okay, when did you last see him?" Julius asked Eleanor. He wore a Harley T-shirt that barely covered his large belly, but took out a notepad and began taking notes professionally. She wondered how he and Auggie were going to blend into trendy downtown Los Altos.

"He was at the pizza place last night," she said. "Kids skateboard behind there, on the parking lot where it's smooth. I've been showing his picture around town, and he was seen there."

"That's a start." Julius nodded. "Where else does he usually hang out?"

"It's a small town. He's on his skateboard, no car. He's been spotted on the side streets around the school. And behind the school. They call the area back there Vietnam. And Jack in the Box and the pizza place."

Julius took notes.

"Does he have a cell phone?" Auggie asked.

"Yes. But he's not returning my calls. Or anyone's calls. Not his big brother, Max, or his older sister, Lara. So I had it disconnected."

Julius nodded again. "Okay, what was he wearing when he was seen?"

"He always has on a black baseball cap. Jeans, of course. And who knows what T-shirt."

"Sounds like every kid on the planet. Let's have a look at those pictures. Give us a few to take with us. We'll get them back to you," Julius said kindly.

His kindness made her feel so needy. She brushed back tears. She was so worried about Joshua. He'd been gone from home a week. Friends had seen him around town, but he took off when spotted. She'd checked with everyone she knew, every possible place he might be sleeping. The few kids who would talk to her said he was dirty, but seemed okay. She took a breath.

"How exactly do you do this?" Her voice was a whisper. "How do you find kids that don't want to be found?"

"Well, in your son's case," Julius said, and put down his pen, "it sounds like he's still close to home. This is going to be an easy one. We'll have Joshua by evening. I'm sure of it."

She studied the two men doubtfully. Her son was young, fit, and incredibly fast. These middle-aged men with beer bellies would be no match for a healthy teenager on the run.

"You won't hurt him, will you?" she asked. "You're not going to use a weapon or anything?"

Auggie snorted.

"Of course not," Julius said, and gave Auggie a stern look. "We're not going to have to get rough with your boy. This is how it goes . . ." He reached in his back pocket and took out his wallet. "I show the kid this, my old badge, and I tell them I'm Agent Wollinsky. I'll flash it in front of him quickly. He'll take a fast look at the badge in my wallet and won't, of course, realize I'm not a cop anymore. He won't know what kind of agent I am. He'll be scared. Your son isn't a hardened criminal."

"Not yet," Eleanor said, grimly.

"He's not. Believe me, he'll be scared of me and Auggie. He's a sixteen-year-old kid. He'll come with no fuss. Don't you worry. We'll get him in the car and start driving to Oregon. We'll stop for a good meal. He's a growing boy. He's probably starving. We'll get him as many cheeseburgers as he wants, and we'll call you from the road."

"No," she said. "When you find him, stop by the house. Let me see him. Let me say goodbye."

"Ma'am," Auggie said. "Excuse me, but that's never a good idea. He'll be afraid of us. Once he sees you, he might try to take off again. He'll get his momentum back. Let us handle it our way. Trust me. We've had a lot of experience."

She felt sick but incapable of resisting these men who seemed so confident. Sadly, she'd lost all confidence in herself when it came to raising Joshua.

She nodded her head.

"Now, please, Mrs. Russell, stay put at home. I'm sure we'll find him. We'll call you as soon as we have him."

She stayed in the house all afternoon, restlessly cleaning counters and watching the clock. She called her friend Lila next door, asking her to keep an eye out for Joshua in town but not to stop him if she saw him. Just phone her. She called a few other friends, the ones who knew Joshua was missing. As it got later, she got more discouraged. Finally, soon after dark, the phone rang.

"Is he wearing black-checkered skater shoes? And does he have a big, wide belt with silver studs sticking out of it?" Auggie asked.

"Yes, yes," she said, excited. "And that red shirt."

"No red shirt. He got rid of that. But we can see him right now in back of the pizza place you told us about," Julius said. "He's on his skateboard with a group of his buddies."

"Call me when you have him," she said. Her heart was pounding uncontrollably. "But please be careful. Don't hurt him."

In less than fifteen minutes, they phoned her again. They were on the speakerphone.

"We got him," Auggie said.

"What happened? Did he try to run?" she asked.

"No, not at all. He's very well behaved. Got off his skateboard and came with us nicely. Very polite. We're going to stop for a good dinner in an hour or two. We'll call you from Oregon."

"Can I talk to him?" she asked, the tears beginning again.

"Sure," Julius said. "But I'd keep it short and sweet."

"Joshua, honey, are you okay? You couldn't stay on the streets. I had to get you off the streets. It wasn't safe."

He answered after a minute. "I knew you'd do something like this," he said. "I told everyone you'd do something like this."

"I had to, Joshua. I had no choice."

"Yeah. Right," her son said. "No choice. I knew you'd flip out. Why couldn't you just leave me alone, for once?"

"Okay, ma'am," Auggie said. "Why don't we wind it up for now? We'll take good care of your son. Don't worry. You get some rest. You'll hear from us or the school in the morning."

With Joshua on his way to Oregon, Eleanor felt enormous relief. Her shoulders loosened. Perhaps she'd even sleep that night.

At eleven the next morning, Mindy phoned her. Joshua had arrived safely at Mount Richmond. The kids were given a complete medical exam before they were admitted, and he seemed fine. Mindy would fax her the last of the papers she needed signed.

"It's going to be okay, Mrs. Russell. Joshua seems resigned to being here. Some of the other kids are much more furious, even combative when brought in. Joshua cooperated with all the admissions procedures and is actually very polite."

Eleanor relaxed a bit more.

"Mrs. Russell, everyone here at Mount Richmond understands kids like Joshua. Many of our students are adopted. Many have also suffered crushing losses, just like Joshua."

"He's not a bad kid, Mindy. He just needs to figure out who he is. He can be so sweet, sometimes. You have no idea."

"We see that. He's got a great smile. Don't worry; Joshua will get the help he needs. He'll be safe with us here."

He's not on the streets anymore, Eleanor thought with relief. She wouldn't have to go to Vietnam again to look for him.

Chapter 10

FAKE IT UNTIL YOU MAKE IT

Joshua (Nick) 2006

After a few hours in the truck from Wilcox, Nick was desperate to get rid of Noa. She stank of drink and puke and never shut up. But Jacob and the girl were joined at the hip. Nick knew he'd eventually be fine on his own without Noa or Jacob. He'd get himself back to California in the stolen Ford. Then, he'd meet up with the kid from East Palo Alto, the one who knew about making E. First, though, he needed to get somewhere safe; somewhere where he could rest for a few days, clean up, and get some supplies. And Jacob had a destination for them. Even though Nick didn't have a license, he'd known how to drive since he was fourteen. He could drive much better than Jacob. He'd taken the wheel from Jacob just out of Bend because he drove like somebody's grandmother—his foot on and off the gas pedal. The jerking movement had made Nick crazy and Noa carsick.

They stopped for lunch at a McDonald's. When they were inside ordering, Nick considered going back out to the truck and leaving the two behind, with Noa talking some movie-star gossip shit she read about on the cover of *Star Magazine*, and Jacob chewing his Big Mac with his mouth open, staring at Noa like a fool. But he calmed himself and told himself to stay cool. They were headed to Salem, Oregon, and he just had to be patient for a few days. It was the same as it had been at Mount Richmond.

Fake it until you make it. Just go along until you find a way out.

Jacob's aunt lived in Salem, and Jacob was positive she'd take them in. She didn't speak to the rest of the family anymore, so Jacob felt sure she didn't know about the runaway. Jacob claimed his aunt Maya had been upset when he'd been brought to Mount Richmond against his will. She'd written Jacob letters asking if he wanted her to file for custody and get him out. She said she had even called the school and trashed Jacob's parents to the administration, claiming they had always exaggerated his problems.

When his parents found out, they completely freaked out and told the school he wasn't allowed to send or receive any more communication from Maya. She was removed from his list of approved letters or phone calls. But Jacob warned Nick and Noa that even though Maya was way cool, they shouldn't say the truck was stolen. That would upset her. They should just say they were on a road trip. Maya was big on road trips. There was a school holiday, and they should tell Aunt Maya they'd done well last term and had been allowed the trip.

The promise of a warm bed and shower sounded appealing to Nick. With Jacob giving directions, Nick parked in front of a small gray bungalow near the center of Salem. Jacob got out first and walked up the path to a brightly painted red front door. A rainbow flag hung next to it.

In the truck, Jacob had described his aunt Maya as the hippy-dippy type. But she obviously had some dough. The house was nice, and there was a new Prius in the driveway. The car made Nick sick. It was for arrogant, rich people. Lots of his mother's friends drove a Prius. Apparently, Aunt Maya had once been married to a famous rock star, an old dude down in LA who Nick had never heard of. She'd come out of the divorce in good shape.

"Jacob, I am so glad to see you!" the woman said when she answered the door. She wore a long, flowered skirt, her hair tangled in a white girl's version of dreadlocks.

Maya was a tiny chick, tiny everywhere, except her enormous tits, just like Noa's, which Nick tried not to stare at.

"They finally let you out of that gulag they were holding you in! Thank God. I've been so worried about you, praying they didn't squash that beautiful spirit of yours."

There were tears in her eyes as she hugged her nephew. Nick thought it was creepy how long she held Jacob, her big breasts pressed up against the kid.

"Hey, Aunt Maya," Jacob said. "Great to see you. I was so bummed when they didn't let you write me anymore."

"What kind of school censors students' mail? I knew it wasn't your idea," Maya said.

"Are you kidding? I loved getting letters from you. I tried to write you back, but they wouldn't let me do that, either. They said you weren't supportive of the program," Jacob said.

"Jesus, what sane person could be supportive? They tell you who you can and cannot write? Does anyone at that school read the Constitution? Freedom of speech? They don't believe in that?"

"I know, I know. They're crazy strict. But, Aunt Maya, I hope you're okay with our showing up here. You're not going to call my folks, are you?" Jacob nervously ran his fingers through his wavy brown hair. "We kind of want to do this on our own. We're on a school break and taking a road trip. You know, like you told me you did when you were younger. To see the real world."

"Don't worry, sweetie. I'm not even speaking to your father after he locked you up," Maya answered. "Not that we were on such great terms before you got sent away. I did research on this Mount Richmond place. Do you know that there is a federal investigation of these so-called therapy schools? There is absolutely no regulation.

Don't worry about me busting you, my dear. I'm just glad you're okay." She stopped talking long enough to take in the other two kids who were standing and listening in front of the white extended-cab Ford.

"Who are your friends? Do you need somewhere to stay? Where are you going?"

"Seriously, Aunt Maya, you're not going to call my folks, are you?" Jacob asked.

"Of course not." She reached out and touched him gently on his shoulder. "If you only knew how angry I am at your father and mother for having you kidnapped. Grandma, the whole family back in Boston, they can't stop crying. Whatever you did, sweetie, we could have worked it out. Your father reacts like an angry child sometimes. We could have handled it as a family without sending you away. You could have lived with me. Now come in, sweetheart. All of you, come inside."

Nick breathed a sigh of relief. He and Noa picked up their back-packs and followed Jacob into the house. Noa still reeked from all the booze she'd consumed on the drive to Salem and the two stops on the side of the road to puke. He couldn't wait to dump her.

"Aunt Maya," Jacob said, "this is my girlfriend, Noa, and my buddy Joshua."

"Nick," Joshua said. "I told you a million times, call me Nick."

"Right. Sorry. This is Nick. Joshua's his other name. He changed it."

"Your girlfriend, Jacob? Wow, what a beauty. Look at that red hair. Natural, too, I bet." Maya patted Noa's springy curls, not reacting at all to the girl's smell. "And, Nick, you're welcome here, too. I'll remember to call you Nick, don't worry. I changed my name, too, once upon a time. Did Jacob tell you? I was born Lois. Do I look like a Lois? The name Maya came to me one night in a dream. It was so powerful. I've been Maya ever since. We have to have a name from the earth, not necessarily the name our parents give us before they've even met us. Right, my dear?"

She reached out for Nick, and he stepped back, terrified she'd envelop him in a big hug like she'd given Jacob. He sidestepped her, letting her hug Noa instead.

They spent the rest of the day at Maya's. She gave them fresh towels, soap, shampoo, and everything else they needed. She would occasionally mention Jacob's parents, wondering if she should make peace with them now that the hellhole school was giving him more freedom, but Jacob begged his aunt to hold off for a while. He said the three were determined to go on their road trip. They wanted to go all the way down to San Francisco. There was a music festival and a band they wanted to hook up with there.

"Aunt Maya, my parents know we're on a break, but they'd never approve of our stopping here and going on a road trip to SF."

"I know my brother. He's been trying to tell me what to do ever since I was born. He can't stand the way I live or where I live or anything else about my life. He's never once visited me here. So, I get it, Jacob. You want a little space from your folks right now. Fine by me. The best time I ever had was on road trips. And music festivals. Oh, I envy you. I haven't been to one of those in a long, long time." She smiled.

Nick got nervous, wondering if she would ask to come along. He got up and went to the refrigerator. He was joined by Jacob and Noa.

"Go ahead, kids. Take whatever you want. There's plenty to eat," Maya said.

The three went through Maya's refrigerator like locusts, consuming anything with sugar first. But they had little to choose from because Maya was a vegan, nothing processed or refined. Maya and Noa then holed up in Maya's room, talking some shit for hours. By evening, the boys were bored and wanted to get out of the house and get some real food. They were hungry for all the things they'd been deprived of: greasy burgers, alcohol, and drugs. The one trip to McDonald's and two six-packs hadn't satisfied them, and the little house in Salem was getting claustrophobic.

"Maya, okay if I go outside for a smoke?" Nick asked as the sun set. He picked up his pack of cigarettes.

"Sure, sweetie. Out back through the sliding doors. But you know those things will kill you." She wrinkled her nose.

Jacob immediately said, "I'll go with you, man. I need to stretch my legs."

When the boys were outside, Nick lit a cigarette and inhaled deeply. "Let's get out of here," he said. "What if the police show up? What if your father calls?"

"I think we're okay for now. Maya won't call the cops. She hates them. Let's just stay a day or so. Then we'll take off. Noa says she likes it here. My aunt is really digging her."

Noa again. Jacob couldn't make a move without Noa's approval.

"Listen, we're not going to stay here all night babysitting some old lady, are we? No disrespect, but your aunt Maya is kind of a weirdo. We got any money left? I can always sell this, I guess," Nick said, and patted his waist, where he'd stashed the gun he'd stolen from the house in Wilcox. "It must be worth a fucking fortune. I ought to see what I can get for it."

"Nick, please don't take the gun out. My aunt will freak. She's a pacifist. She hates guns. She'll kick your ass out in the street if she sees it." Jacob seemed genuinely scared.

Joshua sighed. He understood. His mother also hated guns. On the other hand, he loved guns. He'd felt an attraction to them ever since he was small. When he was at home, he checked the internet and researched all types of guns. He felt good with the gun tucked in his pants. He'd been patting it all afternoon, liking the heft of it. It was giving him a buzz.

"I'm not so sure where to go in Salem," Jacob added, tentatively. "I haven't been here since I was a little kid."

"Ask your aunt," Nick said. "Ask her where she gets her weed. She's cool with weed, right? *Organic* weed." He ground the cigarette out under his heel, then hesitated and picked up the stub, putting it in his jeans pocket, feeling the gun again.

Jacob went back into the kitchen. Nick followed, closing the sliding glass door behind him. Maya was pounding down a big lump of dough. Nick stood and watched as she punched, pounded, and worked the bread with both hands.

"Do you boys need anything?" she asked, glancing up.

Jacob went to Maya and slung his arm around her shoulder. Both her hands were in a huge crockery bowl, but she sidled up to him, smiling.

"Wow, that's pretty cool," Jacob said. "What're you making?"

Nick watched her as well, surprised at the muscles on the woman's upper arms. Big muscles for such a tiny woman. Big tits and big biceps.

"It's going to be the best bread you've ever tasted," Maya said. "I get flour stone ground from a local farmer. We'll have it for breakfast, with some of my homemade preserves. Have you ever eaten lingonberry preserve? Like heaven. Sweet and tart at the same time."

"Sounds great. Say, Aunt Maya, we were wondering, and I hope you don't think it's rude or anything, but we wanted to go out tonight. You know, check out the town. I told Nick I thought you'd know where to go. I mean, you're really cool and everything."

Maya's face fell and her shoulders drooped. Jacob moved his hand away.

"I thought we'd all hang out here tonight," she said. "Have dinner, watch some movies. I could get a pizza. Maybe get loaded," she added hopefully. "I've got some amazing pot right here."

"Yeah, that'd be great. We'll go to town later, after we hang with you at dinner. But Joshua and Noa want to go hear some music," and he motioned toward the others with his chin.

"Nick," the boy muttered. "Nick, for Christ's sake."

"Sure, hon," Maya said, and gave them both a big smile. "I get it. You don't have to draw me a map. Not much night life in Salem, but I'll tell you about what little there is."

"Aunt Maya, like I said, you're really cool. You're my favorite aunt." He looked over at the other two kids. "But these other guys are kind of hyper. You know?"

"Please, Jacob. You don't need to flatter me. It's okay."

They ate dinner with Maya, who'd ordered twice as much pizza as even three hungry kids could eat. Then, to Nick's surprise, Noa got up and started to clear the table.

"I'll do the dishes," Noa said. "Jacob, your aunt Maya has been great to me this afternoon."

"Noa," Maya said, "talking to you has meant a lot to me as well. It's an honor to have you share your story with me."

In all the time Nick had known the girl at Mount Richmond, as well as on the run, he had never heard her volunteer for a single job. Astounded, he watched as she efficiently stacked the dishes, brought them to the sink, and began to rinse them.

While Noa worked, Maya told the boys she and Noa spent the afternoon getting to know one another.

"They know, don't they? The boys here know you're adopted, right, honey?" Maya called into the kitchen to Noa.

"Oh, yeah. Everybody knows who's adopted at Mount Richmond. They have this lame group us adopted kids have to go to. Joshua—I mean Nick—is adopted, too. He's in the group."

Nick sighed and shook his head.

Maya gave him a long look. "I have some interest in this subject." She paused dramatically. "Jacob, you probably don't even know this. But when I was younger, I myself had a baby that I relinquished."

"No kidding?" Jacob said. "I never heard my parents or Grandma or Grandpa say anything about it."

Nick played with the saltshaker, lifting it up and sliding it down.

"It was not a good situation. I was like you, traveling. Then I got into some trouble. I got pregnant. I thought I could raise the baby on my own." She ran her fingers through her dark, curly hair. "But I realized that would be impossible. The baby, a boy, was a mixed-race child. His father was Puerto Rican and gorgeous. Quite dark-skinned. Your grandfather Morris, may he rest in peace, was a very kind man and believed in racial equality. But he believed it in the abstract. He belonged to all the liberal organizations. He was even an officer in the Boston Anti-Defamation League. But his little girl bringing home a half-Black Puerto Rican baby? He called the baby a *schvartze*." Her eyes went to her nephew, then turned to Nick. "You know what that means? It's not such a polite word."

Nick nodded yes and she went on.

"I didn't dare to argue with my father. I gave up the baby to a Jewish agency in New York." Maya looked down at the table. "I'm not proud of it." Then she reached up and touched Noa's hand, who had come back to the table to carry another stack of dishes to the sink. "I told all this to Noa, here. Beautiful redheaded Noa, who also has a mother somewhere who had to give her up." Two tears rolled down Maya's cheeks.

Jacob spoke. "No one ever said Grandpa Morris was a bigot. He was supposed to be a real liberal dude, not some secret redneck. Everyone always said great things about Grandpa."

"Oh, Jacob, he was a product of his times," Maya said. "He couldn't help himself," she said and shrugged her shoulders.

Nick was riveted as he listened to Maya's story. Yet he didn't want to appear too interested; it was bad enough Noa was practically falling all over herself for Maya. He'd never before met anyone who had given up her baby. Well, technically he'd met his birth mother, Kelly, but he couldn't remember her. She'd given him up when he was only a few days old. But Maya was a Jewish ex-hippie, like Eleanor, his own adopted mother. He stole glances at Maya.

"Anyway," Maya went on. "I belong to this organization. Adoptees Anonymous, it's called. We meet every other month in Portland. It's for adopted people and people who've given up a child for adoption. We support each other. We help each other search. For either the parents or the child we relinquished."

"What happens when you find the person?" Nick asked. He felt prickles on his skin. He had a ton of questions, but he tried to slow down his breathing to sound as if he were just making conversation. Off and on, for the past couple of years, he had thought about searching for his birth mother, but he had no idea how to begin. He thought someday, when he was older, he'd get the money together and go to Wisconsin to find her. He didn't know if she'd want to see him, but he'd at least like to know what she was like and what she was doing. Now, Jacob's aunt, this crazy bitch he had just stumbled into, was indirectly telling him he didn't have to wait.

"Sweetheart, sometimes it's just comforting to know more information about them. Whether they're alive or dead. Sometimes it stops there. You find out about the person you're searching for, you get information, and the knowledge is enough. Sometimes, though, you actually make contact. I've met people who made contact at all ages. A lady in my group, Linda, she's sixty-two years old. She was adopted as a newborn. She always thought she'd never discover who her parents were because, back in her day, all the records were sealed. But now, with a change in people's thinking about adoption, Linda was able to find her birth mother. She got her original birth certificate. You should have seen her when she actually held that paper in her hands the first time.

"Her bio mom is an old lady now—over eighty when they had

194

their reunion. But what a reunion they had. Linda met all her cousins and even found out she had two half-sisters. She found out all sorts of things about her family . . . what health issues they had, what their personalities were. And what they looked like. She said she understood so much more about herself after the reunion."

"What about you, Maya? Did you ever find your son?" Nick asked.

"No, darling, I haven't. So far, my own reunion eludes me. My son would be twenty-one years old now, and I haven't found him. But that doesn't mean I won't. It's just going to take more time. I'd love him to meet you, Jacob." She smiled across the table at her nephew. "You and all his other cousins. But you in particular, you're so special to me. Grandpa Morris is gone, but Grandma Fanya is still here. I'd like him to know her, too. This is a whole other time we live in."

Noa came back into the dining room, holding a soapy sponge. "So, tomorrow, Maya is going to help me look for *my* birth parents. She told me she has some of the websites her friends in the adoption club have shown her. And names of private detectives from where I was born. My birth mother had me in Vegas. Maya's going to help me find her."

Noa was cheerful and animated. Nick was excited, too. Something stirred inside him. He tried to keep his voice casual, though. "Do you think you could help me, too? I mean, I might be interested in finding out some stuff about my birth parents."

"Of course, my sweet *punim*." She touched Nick's chin and pulled him to her. "Punim means face. You have such a beautiful face. Your mother must have been a beautiful girl. Look at those eyelashes. People pay a lot of money for eyelashes like those. You deserve to know your real family."

Nick pulled back from Maya's grasp, resisting her touch. He was shaking. He did want to know where he'd gotten his blond hair and his face that everyone called handsome. He wondered about his small nose, which turned up at the end—an odd nose in a family where everyone else's was long and straight. He wanted to know about his height. He towered over everyone in his family. He wondered if anyone in his own birth family had died of cancer or if anyone else was good at art. Maya was offering him a chance to answer his questions.

"Do you know your family name?" she asked Nick. She stared at the boy. He lowered his eyes under their long lashes.

"I do, yeah. My other mother got one letter from my birth mom, like right after I was born. She was going to send me this blue blanket she made or something. My mom showed me that letter. I remember my birth mom's name."

"That will make everything easier. Did you ever get the blanket she made?"

"Nah. I think my birth mother got busy or something. She was poor, my mom said. She probably had to work all the time." Then he added, "Or maybe my mom kept it and wouldn't give it to me. I don't know."

Maya studied him, then picked up her water glass, sipped, and put it back down on the table carefully. "I do not understand why your or Noa's parents couldn't help you with this before. They should have helped you find your families. It's your right."

Nick answered slowly, his head down. "Yeah, well, actually my mom says I should. Someday. But she said to wait until I'm older."

"And your father? Can't you talk to him about this?" Maya asked.

Nick didn't answer.

Then Noa spoke up from the kitchen. "His dad is dead. That's what Nick said in our adoption group."

"Noa, why don't you mind your own fucking business? Is this anything to do with you? You're not supposed to talk about stuff

196

outside the group. 'What's said in group stays in group.' That's the rule. Don't you remember that?" Nick shouted at her.

"Nick, it's okay. I think she's trying to help. Is your dad really gone, honey?" Maya put her hand on his shoulder.

"Yeah." Nick stood up and pushed his chair toward the table. "My dad died when I was little. Ron. He's the dad who adopted me. And I think it would kill my mom if I looked for my birth mom. She's always saying I'm her *real* son. About every five minutes, she says she loves me. It's such bullshit. She's always saying how she loves me the same, how adoption doesn't change a thing. Well, maybe for her it doesn't change things."

"You just want to know, right? You're not rejecting her. It's natural to want to know about the person who gave birth to you. And, anyway, you're the kid. You're not supposed to be taking care of her feelings."

Nick nodded. "I know," he said and sighed. Then, almost in a whisper he added, "I just figured I'd find out on my own. I didn't want her involved."

Noa had been standing in the kitchen doorway. She looked at Nick. "I get it," she said. "My parents are always saying how much they love me. Even when I do crazy shit, they go way overboard about how much they love me. It makes me feel guilty, like they have to love me, even though I'm so fucking crazy. I'm sure lots of times they wished they could give me back. How *could* they love me after the stuff I do? I wish they'd just forget about me. I don't want them stuck with me."

The room got quiet. Then Maya began to cry and picked up a napkin to wipe her eyes.

"Let's get going, guys," Jacob said to Noa and Nick. "Aunt Maya gave me directions. Let's see what's happening in town. You can play detective tomorrow. Meanwhile, let's check out Salem."

They drove toward town. "She's always been such a drama

queen," Jacob said on the way. "She makes scenes like that at every family gathering. Sorry."

"You don't get it, Jacob," Noa said. "It *is* a big deal to be adopted." She nodded at Nick, who turned away. "Us adopted kids know that. Your aunt knows that."

At the bowling alley, they hooked up with some local kids. Noa and Jacob got loaded pretty quickly and ended up sitting in a dark corner, making out, putting their hands all over each other, staring up at the neon lights in the bowling alley, laughing and generally behaving like assholes. Nick smoked some weed, too. He asked around and got the phone number of someone who might be willing to buy his gun. He called the number. The guy said maybe and offered him a hundred and fifty dollars. Nick wasn't sure, but it didn't seem like enough. So, he put the paper with the number into his pocket, thinking he'd keep it. He knew he was supposed to want to get laid. He'd never had trouble finding girls, but he found he was not in the mood to turn on the charm for some stupid bitch in Salem, fucking Oregon. He kept going back to what Maya had said about helping him find his family, his real family. He thought maybe he was here for a reason . . . to find out about his family in Wisconsin.

His mom had always said he was her real son. She swore to him her love was no different for him than for Lara and Max. She said it often. Too often. He supposed he believed her. She'd told him how much his father had loved him and had been so proud of his little boy. She said his father was the happiest when with him. She had made a book of photos of him and his dad. There were pictures of them hitting golf balls at a driving range and riding on a train somewhere in Canada. He'd left the book back at Mount Richmond, thinking it was safer there. She acted like a mom, but sometimes he couldn't stop thinking about Kelly. He thought about the one letter she'd written to his mom. He could close his eyes, and still see her pretty, round handwriting on the pale-blue paper.

He knew one thing. Moms were not supposed to give up their kids. What had he done to get given away? He'd heard the story. His adopted mom had this ritual every year on his birthday. They'd get all comfy on the couch and then she'd read from this book she'd made when he was a baby. *All About Me: A Book for the Adopted Child.* In it, she'd pasted a picture from when they'd gotten him in Wisconsin. She'd say how pretty Kelly was, but how she was too young to raise him. Kelly had made a big sacrifice by giving him up. They did the same damn thing every year. Lara and Max didn't have one of those books. His mother didn't sit them down and tell them "their story" on their birthdays. They didn't have stories of how their parents "found" them. Other kids just had birthdays with a cake and candles.

He decided to blow off Jacob and Noa at the bowling alley. They'd find a way home. Or maybe he'd go back and get them later. He wanted to get information from Maya. Right now. He didn't want to screw around in the bowling alley anymore. He found his way back to the small gray house, even without Jacob's directions. The lights were still on. Maya answered the door wearing a kind of long Arab robe. His mom called these robes caftans and she wore them around the house, too. Behind Maya, he could see candles still flickering on the table where they'd eaten dinner.

"What, sweetheart? You're home so soon. Where are the others?" Maya asked.

"They're still at the bowling alley. I kept thinking about what you said about finding my birth mom. I couldn't get into partying. I'll go back and get Noa and Jacob later if they're stuck. But I wondered if we could start? What you were talking about at dinner tonight."

"You want to search for your parents tonight?"

"Yeah. I keep thinking about it. I don't think I could sleep tonight. Can we start to look now?" he asked. He looked right at Maya. He knew people liked it when he made eye contact with them.

She hesitated, then said, "Okay, hon. I don't know how far we can get. My computer is still on. I was checking email. We can do the basics, I suppose. Bring one of the dining room chairs over to the table. Sit down next to me, and I'll show you how to begin a search. I'm not great at this, but I know how to get started."

Nick wasn't much interested in computers himself. He was more interested in drawing, painting, and thinking about what others thought about him. Later, he realized that if he *had* been more into computers, he could have already possessed knowledge about his birth mother. It did not take very long for Maya to find Kelly and discover some facts about her.

"Okay, Nick, let's start with where you were born."

"In Wisconsin. At University Children's Hospital in Madison, Wisconsin."

"Okay." She typed, then asked, "Now tell me when your birthday is and the exact spelling of your last name. I'll show you how to get an original copy of your birth certificate, the one filed in the hospital."

"It's DeGrasse. I was born on August 12, 1990." He spelled out DeGrasse carefully, emphasizing where the capital and lowercase letters should be. Maya typed on the keyboard as he spoke.

"Okay. Here's baby DeGrasse. Sean DeGrasse. Wait, no, that's from 1989. All right, here you are, August 12, 1990. Good. Christopher DeGrasse." Maya entered the information for the Wisconsin Office of Vital Records. She helped Nick complete the application to obtain his original birth certificate, even putting the twelve dollars needed to obtain the papers onto her credit card. She asked him where she should have it sent.

Nick didn't know. He couldn't send it to Mount Richmond, so he told her his home address in Los Altos.

"Okay, now tell me your birth mother's first name."

"Kelly," he answered. "Is Kelly a nickname for something else, do you think?"

"I don't know. But let's do a search for Kelly DeGrasse. We'll see if anything helpful comes up."

And that was how Nick read an article from the *Madison Times* in 1985 and learned that when Kelly DeGrasse had been a young girl, she had won the award for outstanding pitcher in the Dane County Under-Thirteen Girls Softball League. He liked the picture accompanying the article very much. It showed Kelly holding an enormous trophy, almost as tall as she was. She was really pretty. He noticed her eyes, how wide apart they were set and how they had an extra fold above the lid, just as his own did. He wished he could see their color, but he saw how her nose tipped up, just as his did. He felt proud of her and wished he could show her all the baseball trophies still on a shelf in his room back in Los Altos.

"Nice," Maya said, as she read the article along with him.

Then Maya scrolled to another article from the same paper, also about Kelly DeGrasse. In it, it was reported she had been arrested for suspected theft. The article described how Kelly had been apprehended while pushing her toddler, trying to conceal the stolen items in the child's stroller. The article stated that this child, aged four, was removed by Child Protective Services. Her child. Aged four. He reread those words. He was not a fast reader, but he saw the year of the article. She'd been described as a young mother. He kept looking at that sentence. Kelly had another kid. His heart was pounding. She had a kid *before* he was born who she did *not* give away. One she kept. This Kelly bitch had kept another kid. And she was a thief. Maybe he'd inherited being a thief from her. He was seething. *She can go to hell.*

"Nick, honey. This is not healthy for you to read," Maya said in her nasal, whining voice. She reached to turn off the computer. Nick tried to push her hand away, but still the screen went dark. *Jacob sounds just like his aunt*, Nick thought. *A family of whiners.*

He held up his own hand, trying to silence her annoying voice.

He stood and his chair clattered to the ground. He didn't speak to Maya, who followed him and babbled some stupid shit. He was so much taller than she was, he stared straight past her, above her, to the front door. He went into the bedroom where he had been staying and grabbed his backpack. Maya had done laundry for the kids. Clean piles of clothes were folded on the bed. He pulled a sweatshirt, still warm, over his head and grabbed the keys to the truck.

"Take some food, sweetie. You should take some food." Maya ran into the kitchen and grabbed a banana, some grapes, and a few bottles of water. She tried shoving them into Nick's backpack. She got the banana and grapes inside before he roughly shut the pack and went out the door, slamming it behind him. She opened the door and stepped onto the porch into the evening. He saw her watching him as he gunned the truck's engine and the tires squealed.

Maya shouted, "Nick, wait! Are you going to pick up Noa and Jacob?"

Nick had no intention of going back to the bowling alley for Noa and Jacob. He was going to sell the gun and then find Highway 5. Head south. Back to California. He was going to find his buddies who sold ecstasy and get really fucked up. After that, he wasn't sure.

Chapter 11

THE CLEANUP CALL

2006

The call from Oregon came at six o'clock in the morning, jarring Eleanor out of a deep sleep. It was Mount Richmond's director, Mat.

"Three kids, including Joshua, are missing," he said. "They took off last night and are reportedly heading to the town of Wilcox. That's about thirty miles from Mount Richmond."

"How do you know that's where they're going?"

"Because that's where the kids always want to go. Where the closest convenience stores and fast-food restaurants are. But there is nothing between us and Wilcox except rough state forest land. Thick piney forests. The kids will never make it through that. Police are patrolling the highway now. Don't worry. They'll definitely be picked up."

"Who's he with?" she asked.

"The boy, Jacob, was admitted around the same time as your son. And Noa, the girl. She's been here a while longer."

"Are they dangerous kids? Who's the ringleader?"

Mat hesitated.

"What's wrong? What aren't you saying?" she asked, now fully awake. Eleanor knew Mat had worked with problem kids for over thirty years. Other parents said he looked tough, like a wrestler, but prided himself on loving every student in the program. He was said to dispense hugs to each kid before they left his office—whether having come for discipline or reward.

"There's no nice way of putting this. But it's your son we're most worried about. He's been agitating for a breakout almost since he got here. Other students are coming forward now and telling us Nick has been trying to get kids to join him in a runaway. Nick's definitely the leader. But we'll find them. We always do in a day or so."

"Nick? Who's Nick?" she asked in some confusion.

"Oh. Sorry. Nick is what we call Joshua. He asked to be called that, and we thought there was no harm in it. In group therapy he said he always hated the name Joshua."

"I see." She put her hands to her throat, hating the phone call, feeling the beginnings of the muscle spasms she now associated with Joshua and bad news.

The kids were not picked up that day, nor the next, as Mat predicted. After three more days, the school's corporate offices authorized a helicopter and search and rescue dogs. The kids most certainly could not have much water or food with them, and they were not on the road. The mountains were not easy to traverse. Eleanor got another lump in her throat when Mat told her the water in the mountains was thought to be contaminated with E. coli bacteria from cows grazing on the steep slopes. A search of this terrain was difficult, but the school was making it a priority.

Mat phoned again in a day and said that the girl, Noa, had been spotted coming from a cave. She'd seen the helicopters and seconds later disappeared back into the cave. She seemed healthy and in no distress. The helicopter hovered overhead, but then took off again when the kids didn't reappear. The helicopter pilot and county trackers told the school, with some disgust, that they were a search-and-rescue operation. They went into the mountains to look for lost or injured hikers, not to chase after crazy teenagers. The search team refused to go out anymore. They couldn't waste their resources. Obviously the kids were not hurt. They were running away from, not toward, rescue. The school could hire their own trackers.

The next day, Mat called Eleanor to say there'd been a break-in at a house on the outskirts of Wilcox. A pickup truck and money had been stolen.

"You think they stole a truck? Joshua doesn't have a driver's license."

Mat didn't respond, but told her there was more—a gun and ammunition were also taken.

"A gun?" Eleanor repeated in disbelief. "Why would they want a gun?"

"The kids here at the school are finally talking. It took them a while to come forward because they didn't want to rat on their friends."

"What are they saying?" Eleanor asked.

"Well," Mat continued, in his calm therapist's voice, "we've learned there were actually three additional kids who'd originally taken off with the missing three. But those three came back after the first night. The cold and the dark freaked them out. They told us the kids were definitely headed toward Wilcox. And they said Nick talked about guns. Apparently, he told them he was going to get a gun when he got away from the school. I think it frightened the kids. It may partially have been why those other three came back."

Eleanor thought back to the earlier time when the mother from Los Angeles had phoned her, the woman who had discovered Joshua and her son searching the internet for gun information.

"Come on, Mom," Joshua had laughingly told her then. "What would I do with a gun?" What naivete she'd had.

"Where are the kids now?" Eleanor asked. "If the robbery was right there in Wilcox, why haven't the police found them and the car?"

"Wilcox is a small town. There are only three sheriffs on duty at a time. Apparently, the robbery happened early in the day. When the owners came home from work, they discovered their truck was missing and their house burglarized. It took the police until now to put it together: the missing kids and then the theft."

Eleanor rolled her eyes. "So the kids had at least a twenty-four-hour lead on anyone looking for them. They could be anywhere. Right?"

"I'm afraid so. I can't seem to get the police to step up the search. They're looking, but as you said, the kids could be anywhere. And half the population of Oregon owns a white Ford pickup."

"What are we going to do?"

"Just sit tight. I know this is hard. But we'll find them. One of the kids has connections in Salem, Oregon. An aunt. The police are going to check that out."

She hung up. Then she took a breath. She was in this alone. There was no one else she could talk to about Joshua. Again, she cursed Ron for leaving her alone with this. Many, including Lara, Max, and even Jean, were appalled Eleanor had him kidnapped and brought to Mount Richmond. She questioned whether she should have allowed him to run on the streets longer. She had a friend, a successful therapist, who told her that he, too, had been wild like Joshua. He'd advised her to let him be. But she couldn't. She had been too frightened when he'd disappeared for so long. She wondered if she had caused this escalation of behavior by having him brought to the school. But she'd had to protect him. He was only sixteen.

Another day went by, and Mat called again. He told her Jacob and Noa had been picked up in Salem, Oregon. They were found with the boy's aunt. The aunt had not known the kids were runaways.

"Hadn't known they ran away? Is she nuts?"

"Well, she is somewhat eccentric. Anti-authority. She thought they needed protection. She doesn't approve of the school. Obviously, the kids didn't tell her what was going on."

"What now? Where's Joshua?"

"He took off with the truck the night before last and left the other two in Salem."

For some reason, in addition to all the other things she'd learned about Joshua, leaving two other kids behind made her the most sorrowful. It seemed cold and unfeeling. He had talked the other two into leaving the school with him, then, when it was convenient, ditched them.

"So where is he, Mat?" she asked wearily.

"I don't know. But he has the stolen truck. And possibly the gun. Where do *you* think he'd be going? Do you have any relatives between Northern California and Salem? Does he have any friends up here?"

"No. No family, no friends up there that I know of. He could be anywhere."

"The boy's aunt told us Nick was in a bad way when he left her house. She helped him with an internet search for his birth family. I guess they came up with upsetting news. Do you know anything about that?"

She sat down, the breath sucked out of her, thinking of Kelly, the sad sweet girl she'd met sixteen years before. Once Joshua was in their lives, she'd given little thought to his Wisconsin family.

"No. I haven't heard from his birth mother in a very long time."

"The aunt told us he left her place in Salem in an emotional state after he read newspaper articles about his birth mother."

"I don't know anything about her. We lost touch." She remembered Kelly as she was on the day they sat together in her parents' condominium in Madison. Eleanor suddenly felt such pain. She and Kelly were bound together forever through Joshua. Was this how a transplanted organ recipient would feel toward the donor?

"As you said, he could be anywhere. The other two are making statements to the Wilcox police right now. But as Nick has the stolen truck and the gun, of course, he's in more serious trouble," Mat said.

"Joshua. His name is not Nick."

"Right. Well, you decide what you want to do. My boss at corporate tells me there are people we can hire to look for him. It'll be expensive, but they're willing to step things up. Maybe search in Portland or Seattle."

"Couldn't we put a picture of him in the papers? He's a missing kid."

There was a long silence from Mat. "Maybe. But I think he's going to surface soon. We'll hear from him. I'm sure of it. Corporate asked me to try to get you to wait this out a little longer."

When she hung up with Mat, she made her own internet search to find out what Joshua read that had sent him running. With just a few clicks, she read accounts of Kelly. She read how the girl had been a star athlete, but was later arrested for theft while her young son was with her. Her young son. That would be Sean, of course.

She covered her eyes and the blood pulsed in her head. All these years she'd been waiting to tell Joshua he had a full biological brother. She'd never known the right time or way to do it. She had wanted to spare him the pain she imagined he'd feel when he discovered his birth mother had kept her first child but given him, her second, away.

Eleanor worked a few hours at the university that day and tried to get some papers graded. When she arrived home from work, she knew Joshua had been in the house. She thought she could smell him. She went downstairs to his room and saw the window he used to climb through when he was sneaking in and out of the house. It was ajar. The room looked the same, the bed still neatly made. But Joshua's expensive electric guitar, which had been propped up against the wall in its case, was missing. And his skateboard, probably his most prized possession, was not in the room, either. She couldn't tell if anything else was gone, but she felt scared. She kept thinking about the gun. Lately, she felt she knew Joshua so little. Her son, and yet she felt she didn't know what he was capable of. Terrible things happened in the world. Even violent criminals had once been someone's baby. She didn't know if she was being irrational, but he'd stolen a gun and a car. And he'd been in the house. She called the police.

"911."

"Someone broke into my house." She did not say it was her son who'd broken in. She couldn't utter those words.

"Is the house now secured, ma'am? Are you safe?"

Damn. The window was not secure. She kept forgetting to get Misha, the handyman who did all her home repairs, to come and fix it. Joshua, with his nocturnal comings and goings of the past few years, had bent the window from the frame. It no longer could be latched from the inside.

"I'm safe. No one's here now, but I need to speak to an officer. It's complicated. I know who broke in. Please."

The dispatcher promised her the police would come by soon and to go outside and wait for them if she felt at all unsafe.

First, she called Lila, even though they'd been less close in recent years. Lila was now happily remarried, living in the same house. Her life with her retired, older husband was full of travel, rounds of golf, and activities from the tennis club. They were fit and trim, forever planning their next vacation. Lila's own kids were happy and successful.

"Lila. Thank goodness you're home. Can you come over? Joshua is back in town. I think he's been here."

"What are you talking about? I thought he was up in Oregon. At the therapeutic boarding school."

Eleanor sighed. "Yeah, well, now I think he's here. In town. I'm pretty sure he's been in the house."

Eleanor heard the squeak as the back gate opened and closed. Her friend had recently had plastic surgery. The smoothness of the skin around her eyes and the tautness of her jawline was remarkable. Eleanor felt old.

Lila came to the porch. "What's happened? Where is he?"

"Somehow he got down here to Los Altos. Probably in the truck he stole."

Lila's eyes widened.

"He's been in the house. I know it. Some of his stuff is missing. But he's gone now. I called the police. They're on their way over. I just needed someone to wait with me. Can you?"

Lila walked up the two steps to the front porch. She pulled another chair over to where Eleanor sat. They sat together without speaking for a while.

"What are you going to do with him?" Lila asked. "When they find him?"

"I don't know. I loved the school in Oregon. I was so relieved. I thought it was a perfect fit."

"I guess Joshua didn't agree," Lila said.

"No, I guess not."

The police car arrived. When a tall female officer got out of her car, Eleanor stood. She described her son and the stolen vehicle from Oregon. She mentioned the gun.

"Is your son suicidal, ma'am? Or violent?" the officer asked, motioning for Eleanor to sit back down. The policewoman perched on the top step and wrote.

Eleanor was glad the policewoman sat. She was so tall, she towered over Eleanor.

"No. Well, he hasn't ever been. But I feel uneasy. I don't know how this has all happened. I can't imagine why he stole a gun." She lowered her head and covered her eyes. She realized she'd lost all pretense of dignity and respectability.

"He can be very sweet," Lila said. "I live next door," she added, when the policewoman turned to her. "I've known him his whole life. He's not a violent kid."

The officer said she'd call Oregon and find out the specifics of the burglary. Then, they'd put out a stolen vehicle report.

"Okay, let's look around the house," the woman said and stood up. She turned the page on her notepad. "You tell me what's missing."

When they got to Joshua's bedroom, they saw the open window. The tall officer went outside the bedroom window and pushed, while Eleanor and Lila pulled from inside. The three managed to bring the window back into the frame, and Eleanor shut the bolt. The room was secure. Joshua could no longer get in. Eleanor showed the officer a picture of Joshua. In it he appeared to be a nice, typical high school boy, not a desperate felon who'd stolen a car and gun.

The policewoman said, "We'll patrol the neighborhood and keep an eye out for Joshua. We'll make sure the house is safe, too."

Eleanor noticed how the officer kept glancing at the art on the walls and the elegant furniture. *Is she judging me, thinking Joshua is another indulged, rich kid from Los Altos?* Eleanor wanted to tell her, "You know, I'm a widow. I teach child development at the university. I've tried to be a good mother. I've done all I could. It wasn't easy by myself." But why should she care what this woman thought? The important thing was to find Joshua and get him off the streets.

When the police left, Eleanor stood in front of the family portrait she'd commissioned before Ron died, when he still had hair but was terribly thin. She needed to make Joshua real to herself. He was her son; she'd tucked him in bed every night of his childhood. He was not a gun-toting car thief. He wasn't going to hurt her. She needed to be reminded of the Joshua she had raised, the little boy with the golden hair, not this new, frightening Joshua.

Lila came up behind her and put a cup of freshly brewed tea in her hand.

"Is it time to stop? Maybe you need to stop chasing him and let this run its course," Lila said. "Let him face the consequences of his actions."

Eleanor took the cup from her friend's hand. No matter how well Lila knew Joshua, he was not her son. She couldn't know what it was like to have held him on her lap, read him story after story after his father died, when his tears never seemed to stop.

"Lila, he's sixteen. I'm responsible for him. I love him."

Days went by. Again there were Joshua sightings, just as there had been the other times he'd run away. Kids told her he was bragging about how he'd gotten out of the school in Oregon she'd forced him into. She put up a poster of Joshua at the local convenience store. She told kids she met she'd give them a reward if they brought Joshua home. The kind of kid she was talking to might spend reward money on drugs or alcohol, but she'd worry about that later.

She was frightened, not only of Joshua, but for him. She'd read about SBC, Suicide by Cop. People got shot by police when they showed a gun or didn't follow policemen's orders. She knew Joshua was not thinking clearly. He might do something really stupid if stopped by the police. She had trouble sleeping, listening for noises in the house. Misha secured the window, but still she thought she heard noises.

After a few days, the police called her to report the stolen truck had been found. It had been abandoned in the Santa Cruz Mountains. The truck was in good shape, although someone had made some clumsy efforts to burn the documents inside the glove box. The Los Altos police had been in touch with the Wilcox, Oregon police department and the vehicle identification numbers matched. She was relieved at that, though it answered no questions.

Then, one day, while she was in her office during office hours, she got a call on her mobile. It was a young girl with a scared voice.

"Mrs. Russell? This is Carolee Kraus. I don't know if you remember me, but I'm a friend of Joshua's. From school."

She did remember Carolee from Joshua's middle school. She'd been a sweet young pre-teen then. When she'd last seen her, however, she had morphed into a leggy and voluptuous girl-woman whose tiny, shredded cutoffs revealed thong underpants when she bent over.

"One moment, Carolee. I'll be right with you." She muted the phone and spoke to the student sitting in the chair beside her. "I'm so sorry, Raheel. I have a family emergency. Can you possibly come back later?"

A flash of annoyance went across the student's face. He'd been arguing for a higher grade on his take-home midterm, but then his natural politeness took over, and he stood and gathered his books.

After the student shut the door behind him, she spoke into the phone again. "What is it, Carolee? What do you know about Joshua?"

"Actually he's with me. He was hungry, so I took him to Taco Bell. He's like, inside now, ordering. I saw your note. So I called you. You were always nice to me when I was at your house."

Eleanor's heart lurched. "Which one? Which Taco Bell? Can you keep him there? I'll come now. I can leave work right now."

"On El Camino. But I think he's through now; he's coming outside. I'll call you back." The girl hung up.

Eleanor quickly pulled her things together and rushed out to her car. She headed north from the university to Los Altos. It was about a thirty-minute drive, and it was nearly rush hour. She pounded the steering wheel with frustration as traffic slowed. When she was quite close to El Camino, she got another call on her cell.

"Mrs. Russell? This is Carolee again."

"Where are you?" she practically shrieked to the girl. "I'm close, maybe ten or so minutes away. I'm driving as fast as I can."

"He's in the trunk, Mrs. Russell. I got him to go into the trunk."

"What are you talking about? Why is Joshua in your trunk?"

"I was afraid he'd get away. A couple of my friends are with me. We stopped at Safeway to get some, uh, beer. We persuaded him to get into the trunk. The Safeway on Arastradero. I told him if he was in the trunk, the police or you wouldn't see him. He knows you're looking for him. But I'm scared that I won't be able to keep him here."

"What kind of car do you have, Carolee?"

"A Honda Civic. It's red."

"I'm on my way. Just drive around town a little. Drive carefully, sweetie. You're doing a good thing. You're doing great. I'll be there soon. Go back to the Safeway. I'll meet you at the Safeway." She was shaking, her voice calm by sheer will. She had to stop this craziness before her son hurt himself or someone else.

Eleanor called the Los Altos police. By some good fortune, she reached the tall officer who'd been at the house earlier in the week. She asked the woman to meet her behind Safeway, practically begging the officer to come or send someone. She said Joshua was in the trunk of a red Civic belonging to a girl named Carolee. Without help from the police, Eleanor was afraid Joshua would run again.

"I know I'm being confusing, but please, can you help me now and meet me behind the supermarket?"

The officer said, "I know Carolee, Mrs. Russell. We all know Carolee. She's not exactly an innocent little thing, your girl Carolee. But I don't know what we can do. Oregon hasn't issued a warrant for his arrest yet. We checked. He's just considered a person of interest at this point. They probably don't want to pay to extradite him." The officer continued. "And he's not wanted for anything here, yet."

Eleanor pleaded. "Maybe if you and I spoke to Joshua, we can persuade him to go to Oregon and turn himself in." She didn't mention the gun.

She heard the woman sigh. "Okay. I'll see. I don't know if my captain will agree that officers can be spared for this. And Carolee. She's not known to tell the truth all the time. I heard you've been offering kids reward money to find your son. Don't give her any money until you see your kid."

"Please," Eleanor said, "she's got Joshua in her trunk. Maybe we can stop this. Will you meet me there? I'm close."

Eleanor swallowed as she drove toward the Safeway. Carolee had seemed so sincere on the phone, like she was really trying to help. But she was probably the same girl who had lied to her all those months ago, pretending to be someone's mother so Joshua could spend the night with her.

When she turned into the Safeway parking lot, Eleanor saw with relief that a police car was already there, its red light flashing. She drove up and there was Joshua, sitting in the back seat, scowling and staring straight ahead. She almost didn't recognize him. His hair was cut in a rough Mohawk, his face filthy. When she got out and leaned toward the open window, she smelled cigarettes, dirt, and grime.

"Joshua, are you okay?"

Joshua looked at her briefly, but then went back to staring straight ahead.

A policeman, one she didn't know, greeted her. "Carolee was telling the truth. Your son *was* inside her trunk. He came out nicely, though. No fighting." He squinted at Eleanor, then added, "We patted him down. No gun."

She let out a sigh of relief. Then she saw the girls gathered around the red Civic. They were watching her. She said to Joshua, "I'll be right back."

She recognized Carolee. Underneath her tight tank top and heavy eye makeup, she was still young and frightened.

"You did the right thing, Carolee. I owe you a reward. Thanks for calling me. I know this wasn't easy."

"Yeah, well. I like Joshua. He's always been a good guy to me. He's just gotten real messed up," Carolee said.

"Listen, I'll call you tomorrow. I have your cell number. We'll work something out."

"I didn't do it for the money," Carolee said.

Tomorrow she'd ask Lara for the name of a clothing store where she could buy Carolee a gift certificate. Perhaps Carolee wouldn't exchange it for drugs. Before Eleanor went back to the police cruiser, though, she had to ask one more question. She lowered her voice.

"I need to know something else. Did Joshua have a weapon with him?"

Carolee's eyes darted to her friends. "A weapon? What do you mean?"

"A gun, Carolee. Did Joshua show you a gun when you were with him?"

"No, Mrs. Russell." Carolee frowned and looked frightened again. "Why would Joshua have a gun?"

Eleanor saw then her son had bypassed his high school friends, including the beer-drinking, drug-using ones. Even Carolee was shocked.

"What are you going to do with him?" Eleanor asked the officer sitting behind the wheel when she returned to the flashing red lights.

"He's wanted for questioning in Oregon. For the car theft. And for breaking and entering, apparently. We've talked to the police in Oregon. We'd just as soon have them deal with the mess up there. Right now, we'll take him back to the police station and keep him locked up while we sort it out. But he's a minor and we can't really hold him for too long without charges."

Eleanor followed the cruiser to the police station. She kept her eyes on the metal divider between the officers and her son in the back seat. When they got to the station, she was allowed to speak to Joshua for a few minutes. He was wearing handcuffs. His eyes seemed too bright, and his mouth had a mean, surly expression.

"Joshua. I've been so worried. I love you. I want to get you help. You need help, honey. The other kids have already spoken to the police in Oregon. About the stolen truck and breaking into the house. The car was recovered, so that should work in your favor. You have to go back up there now and talk to the police."

"Why don't you just leave me alone?" Joshua said. "I can handle this. I got into this on my own. I don't need you to fix it for me. I'm not your little boy anymore." He turned away from her, shaking off her hug.

She didn't recognize her child. His bravado was frightening and heartbreaking at the same time.

Eleanor drove the short distance home. She went into action mode. First, she consulted with a lawyer who confirmed she should get her son to go back to Oregon voluntarily before an arrest warrant was issued. He was still a minor. If he confessed to what he did, things would go better for him. Also, if Eleanor could tell the authorities in Oregon that she was going to get treatment for her son, in a place he couldn't run from, perhaps the judge would be lenient. They might give him probation to be served in a treatment facility. There were no guarantees, as Joshua had committed felonies, but the lawyer was sure Oregon was not in a hurry to put a kid into the Oregon Youth Authority at the State's expense, especially if a parent was willing to pay for a private treatment center. Oregon was a poor state.

Eleanor began work to find a treatment facility for Joshua. She was frantically busy, so busy she hadn't time to think or feel. Working two phones at once, her cell phone and the home phone, she made calls to educational specialists. She got names of several facilities offering greater security than Mount Richmond. The prices were astronomical. She phoned Jean at the retirement community in Denver. She agreed to help.

Lila came in just as she was hanging up with the Villages, one of the recommended treatment centers. "It has a school and therapy. It even has vocational training. You know how Joshua likes building things, how good he is with his hands," she told her friend.

"Oh, Eleanor. Cut to the chase. Can he escape from this one?"

"No," Eleanor said, and bit her lip. "It's on a peninsula of the Tennessee River in the Smoky Mountains. Water on three sides. He can't walk, climb, or swim away."

"Sounds ideal," Lila said and began washing the cups in Eleanor's sink.

Later that afternoon, she spoke to Tracy, the sweet-sounding admissions coordinator at the Villages.

"Yes, ma'am, we do have space," Tracy said in her strong southern drawl. "Yes, ma'am, you are correct. Here at the Villages, we specialize in 'treatment-resistant youth.'"

Treatment-resistant youth. That seemed to be the code word for kids who ran away. Joshua's recent run from Mount Richmond School, as well as his legal trouble, didn't seem to faze Tracy.

She merely said, "Have his paperwork faxed immediately. It will be shown to our clinical director. Also, please have Mount Richmond send information to the Villages right away."

"Of course. I'll make it all happen." Eleanor had to get help. She shuddered when she thought of her sixteen-year-old son at the Oregon Youth Authority in Portland. If he was sent to Portland, he would be with boys who might be as old as twenty-five, kids who had committed violent crimes. The Villages, however, was well regarded, difficult to escape from, and they would accept her son. Step One was completed.

Step Two was to get her son back to Wilcox. She knew he wouldn't get on a plane with her willingly, and she doubted she'd be much good with him right now. She needed to hire a youth transport agency again, but not Julius and Auggie. She needed someone more professional. Mount Richmond suggested another agency and their corporate office even offered to help pay for the transport.

"We all want resolution," Mat said. "None of this is good for the school's image. The robbery is what Wilcox has always feared. This will require some serious public relations repair. Getting Joshua's mess resolved is almost as important to the school and corporate office as it is to you."

The new youth transport company was licensed and bonded. They'd get Joshua to Wilcox and then out of Oregon. She went back to the police station to wait.

Bill and Jeffrey Myerson flew from Seattle, arriving at the Los Altos police station only a few hours after Eleanor contacted them. They were brothers and both ex-cops, dressed in suits, with freshly shined shoes. They treated Eleanor with great courtesy. The men immediately got chummy with the Los Altos officers, getting buzzed into the inner office as soon as they arrived, while Eleanor was told to continue waiting in the chilly lobby. She felt both guilty and incompetent as she watched the men through a thick glass window. Bill and Jeffrey laughed with the local cops, at home and at ease. Yet when the brothers finally emerged and spoke to Eleanor, their faces had become serious.

"Okay, it's been agreed. The police here aren't going to charge your son with anything as long as we guarantee we'll get him up to Oregon," Bill said. "The crimes were not committed in California, so it's not a California matter." He was the taller of the two. His stylish suit fit tightly across his broad back. "You know he stole a gun?" Bill asked but didn't wait for her answer. "Joshua says he sold it up in Oregon. Definitely not a plus having another gun on the streets. We did some fast talking, though, and everyone here wants to get your kid out of here, not drag this out any longer. The officers here are going to let Oregon deal with the whole mess."

"What'll happen up there?" she asked, scared of these two men, yet relieved at their efficiency.

Bill shrugged. "They're bringing your son out now. Say your goodbyes. My brother and I will get him to Oregon for the hearing tomorrow. We'll fly out of San Jose on an early morning flight."

Jeffrey spoke then. "Don't worry, we'll stay in close touch with you all the way." He was, obviously, the good cop, the one who smiled and helped parents get through these nightmares. "We'll spend the night near the airport and get your boy cleaned up and ready so he can talk to the authorities tomorrow. We'll stop on the way and get him presentable clothes. The cops here say he's been on the streets a while."

When Joshua was escorted out, she tried to hug him again, but his hands were handcuffed in front of him. She patted his shoulders and stood on tiptoe trying to kiss his cheek. There was no softness left to his face. His cheekbones had become sharp and prominent.

"Bend down, son, and say goodbye to your mother," Bill Myerson said.

Joshua stiffly obeyed, stooping and offering his cheek. He glanced at her for a fraction of a second, then stared ahead once again. His smell—the cigarettes and filth—were foreign odors, smells she could not associate with her son. Instead, she remembered sweet little-boy smells from nights when she tucked the covers around him and put her nose to the top of his freshly shampooed, still-damp hair. When he bent, she noticed a hickey on his neck.

This time, she didn't beg the Myerson brothers to be gentle with her son, as she'd done when Julius transported him to Mount Rich-mond. Her son had aged these past months, at home in this police station and even in handcuffs. It was easier this time than the first.

Jeffrey Myerson held a plastic bag labeled with her son's name. He gave it to her. "This stuff was in his pockets. He won't be need-ing any of it. And don't worry, Mrs. Russell. He's going to cooperate and be fine. Right, Joshua?"

Joshua nodded, still staring ahead.

Eleanor took her son's few possessions.

At home she opened the bag. In it was further evidence the boy who'd been escorted away was someone she didn't know. Inside, besides a beaded friendship bracelet, the kind teenaged girls make, was a dirty bandanna, a switchblade, and two condoms in wrap-pers. She buried the bag deep in the garbage bin.

Jeffrey Myerson phoned the next morning. He said the evening had gone well. They were in Portland and about to change planes for the short flight to Redmond, the airport closest to Wilcox, where Joshua's hearing would be. They'd take him to the Wilcox police station first. There, they'd be given instructions. They said Joshua was polite. He'd said thank you for everything. He'd eaten two cheeseburgers and downed a milkshake and some pie. He'd been well behaved. On the plane to Portland, they'd even removed his handcuffs. Nothing had gone awry. They'd phone her again.

Eleanor waited at home. Friends and relatives called, and again, everyone had an opinion. A few suggested she let him accept the punishment for his crimes, and not send him to the expensive school in Tennessee. Most agreed with her decision, though; she couldn't let him go into the youth penal system. Ultimately, of course, she was alone.

While she waited for news from Wilcox, she spoke to Tracy, the well-mannered admissions worker from Tennessee. They'd received the paperwork and the clinical director thought the Villages would be an ideal setting for Joshua. They would plan on admission when his legal matters in Oregon were resolved. Eleanor sighed with relief. Then she realized how low the bar had gotten. Her son had been accepted to a locked rehabilitation facility, and she was as excited as if he'd received a thick envelope from Stanford.

"We've been here for over twenty years, and we have a 70 percent success rate for our youths staying out of further treatment centers and off drugs for five years after they are discharged. Most of our kids go onto college when they leave us."

"What percent go to jail?" Eleanor asked.

"I don't believe that statistic has been collected," Tracy answered politely.

Bill Myerson called a few hours later. He told her they were at the Wilcox police station, and the sergeant had finished questioning Joshua. The officer wanted to speak to her.

"This is Sergeant Trainer. I'm in charge of the case, the break-in, the car theft, et cetera. Your boy was very helpful and honest. He told us what happened, and we appreciate his honesty. He also told us he has quite a drug habit, which he wants to turn around. To his credit, he's taking responsibility for his part in the robbery."

"What happens now?"

"He's going into custody. We'll keep him here in our county jail until the hearing. Don't worry, he'll be okay with us. We'll feed him and keep a close eye on him. I'm going to let the escort gentlemen go. They can find a motel here in town and then stick around until after the hearing."

"When will that be?" she asked.

"We were lucky. We have a time scheduled in front of the judge for the preliminary tomorrow afternoon. Your boy will have what we call a juvenile advocate with him, and if you want, a public defender will be called in. The judge already agreed we can put you on speakerphone. You can listen in and speak during the hearing, if you like."

"Thanks. I appreciate what you're doing, making this all happen so quickly," she said.

"No one thinks your boy here is a hardened criminal. He's just a messed-up kid. The folks at Mount Richmond have told us Joshua has some real problems that he's been working on. You hired people to bring him to us; so you're obviously cooperating. Everyone at this end thinks we ought to get this resolved as soon as possible. The truck's been recovered and on its way back here to the rightful owners. I wish we had that gun. Joshua says he sold it. We're not happy about that. He'll have to make restitution. The other stolen goods are fairly minor in nature. Most were taken by the other kids."

"Okay," she said. The gun, out there on the street, was heinous to her. When Joshua was a child, she had tried to keep him away even from toy guns. She'd made him decline invitations to paint-gun parties, popular with some of the kids in middle school. Now, he had stolen an actual gun and had likely sold it to a criminal.

"You still there?" asked the sergeant.

"Yes. Sorry. Thank you. I appreciate what you're doing. And I've got a school lined up. I think they can help Joshua." She sensed the policeman wanted a simple solution and wanted to blame all this on the evils of drugs, so she added, "They're very successful in treating addiction."

"All right, that sounds like what's needed. You get some rest, and we'll talk tomorrow. The case is scheduled for one o'clock. You stay by your phone around that time. Meanwhile, your son is going off to jail." He lowered his voice. "Might be a good experience. We'll see."

As she lay awake that night, Eleanor thought, as she had so many times before, about cause. What was causing Joshua's problems? Although he was now speaking freely about drug use, she just didn't buy it. He told the Wilcox police, the transporters Jeffrey and

Bill, as well as the staff at Mount Richmond, that he was an addict. But she had never found evidence of drugs in his room, searching both before and after the runaways. Joshua ate normally, looked healthy, and slept regularly. He had relative equanimity of mood. He had even been drug tested when Julius brought him to Mount Richmond, and the tests had been negative.

What caused Joshua's erratic behavior? Even though her son claimed he was familiar with every kind of substance, she thought drugs were too easy an answer. The therapist at Mount Richmond, who saw teenagers on drugs all the time, said kids rarely lied about using when they had not. More frequently, they lied and said they had *not* been using or they minimized their usage. Eleanor was confused. If it wasn't drugs, did he have a mental illness? Did it have a name?

The next day, at the appointed hour, the court clerk phoned her and told her she was on speakerphone in the courtroom.

"This is Judge Carlton Harvey. I'm presiding over this initial hearing today. I've got your son here in front of me. Joshua, say hello to your mother."

"Hi, Mom." He was quiet yet sounded strangely peaceful. Sweet, even. She didn't understand why, unless he was happy with all the attention on him.

Eleanor tried to answer but found herself choked up. She imagined Joshua at a big, oak table in an old-fashioned courthouse. He needed her with him.

"Mrs. Russell, can you hear okay?" asked the clerk.

She swallowed and managed to say, "Yes. I can hear. I guess I'm nervous. I wish I was there."

The judge went on. "Nothing to be nervous about, ma'am. Your son is safe here. He's got a weird haircut, but he seems to be a nice, polite boy. Also, we've got our county juvenile advocate, Mr. Kiser. He's here to represent the best interests of your son. One of our public defenders was in the courtroom on another matter, so I asked her to stay, as well. Now, Josh, are you going to need the services of a public defender?"

"I don't know. Do I, Mom?"

"I can arrange—"

"I'm asking Joshua, here. Do we get Miss Albright to stay? In other words, are you a trust-fund baby, son? Can you afford your own private attorney?"

Joshua muttered something Eleanor couldn't hear.

"I didn't think so. Well, you're in luck, Mr. Russell. Miss Albright is the county's very best public defender. I'm going to ask her to represent you. Now, let's hear about what kind of trouble you've managed to get into, young man."

He was being kind, Eleanor realized. The judge was trying to help her with the expense of hiring an attorney. The police read the charges against her son, and pictures of the stolen Ford truck were shown to the judge.

Eleanor gripped the phone, wishing she could see Joshua's face.

The police officer then read a statement from the family who had been robbed. This was called "The Victims' Statement." The statement said the victims, besides losing various items stolen from inside their house, as well as the truck, which they used with great frequency, now also felt anxiety in their own home. The robbery had made them lose their sense of security in what had felt like a safe, protected community. They were scared and anxious. They remained particularly concerned about the stolen gun and ammunition and worried about how it would be used.

Again, Eleanor pictured the gun.

The judge addressed Joshua. "Mr. Russell, that's three felonies: breaking into the house, stealing the car, and stealing a fairly valuable firearm, among other things. You've heard how the victims feel. Now, of course, your youth is in your favor. You're under eighteen, and as far as we can tell, there are no prior charges against you. But these three felonies are not light matters. And if we try you as an adult, which this county has the discretion to do, you're looking at thirty to forty years in the Oregon Penitentiary. At least." He spoke slowly and repeated, "Thirty to forty years. Did you know that, young man?"

"No, I didn't, sir," Joshua answered softly. His voice had lost its bright edge.

Oh, please, Judge Harvey, Eleanor prayed. *May this be scare tactics you're using. Tell me you're trying to scare him straight. Thirty years?*

"Let's hear from the juvenile advocate now. Mr. Kiser, do you have some recommendations for me about this young man?"

"Yes, Judge, I do."

Mr. Kiser had a prepared response. "If it pleases the court, I will note that Joshua has given a complete statement to the Wilcox police. He admitted his part in this and provided more details than previously given by the other two youths. In addition, the boy's mother has found a treatment facility. She's faxed me information on a program willing to accept this young man for fifteen months of treatment, putting him at his eighteenth birthday. The boy's father is deceased. The mother states she will be responsible for transporting the boy to the facility in Tennessee as well as for his treatment. I believe he would benefit from this facility, which will address his not inconsiderable drug problems, as well as his schooling, and provide therapy. He will benefit more than he would from the Oregon Youth Authority or from prison. Of course, we need also to make provisions for victim restitution."

"And how about the mother?" asked the judge into his microphone. "Mrs. Russell, you're in agreement with what Mr. Kiser recommends? You can manage this program?"

"Yes, Judge. I'll work it out. He needs this chance. He's only sixteen."

Eleanor heard coughing and page turning in the court. She supposed the judge was reading the literature on the Villages, which she'd faxed.

"Well, I'm inclined to allow it. Portland doesn't need any more customers at the Youth Authority. I'm going to recommend you be placed on probation for fifteen months, to be served in the confines of this Villages place. You will be under their jurisdiction, Joshua. If you get itchy feet again, we'll bring you back here where no such fancy school will be in the equation. We're talking three felonies. With a firearm involved. Do you understand, young man?"

Joshua apparently nodded, and the judge went on.

"Now, Mr. Kiser recommended that fifteen-months' probation coincide with successful completion of the program your mother found. But, in addition, I'd like to add that I'm holding you responsible, financially, for one-third of restitution to the victims. Do you know what that means?"

"No, sir. I don't," Joshua replied softly.

Eleanor could barely hear him.

"That means you'll pay one-third of the costs of this break-in as well as court costs. You'll share that with your two buddies. But you alone will pay the expense of transporting the vehicle back to Oregon, as well as the actual cost of the stolen firearm. The gun was valued at five hundred and sixty dollars. You'll pay the costs I've outlined, Mr. Russell. Not your mother. You work this off and you repay back these people you stole from. Do you understand now?"

"Yes, sir."

"And community service. This court expects that, as well. Work it out, Miss Albright and Mr. Kiser. Have this all drawn up for the final hearing. We'll do that one by phone, while this young man is in Tennessee. Stay standing, young man. I'm not through yet. I'm telling you, right now, there won't be any more deals after this one. We're giving you every allowance we can because of your age and the lack of any prior history. But, if you are seen in my, or any other, court again, that won't be the case. Just remember, your offenses could have landed you thirty to forty years. Three felonies." The judge put great emphasis on the last two words.

"I understand, sir."

"Okay, next case."

She heard the judge bang his gavel, and Eleanor let out a breath. She put the phone back on the receiver. *This is good*, she thought. Joshua was given a firm, clear warning by the judge, but the Oregon court was going to allow him to get treatment. Things were going to get better for Joshua; she felt sure of it.

The Villages was not like Mount Richmond Academy. Eleanor flew to Knoxville, then drove into the mountains to sign the paperwork to formally admit Joshua. He had been escorted there earlier in the week.

When she went through the gates in her rented car, the rain was pelting down so furiously, she could barely see around her. She finally found the administration building, a dark, low block looking as if constructed of Lincoln Logs.

"Please wait." The receptionist barely lifted her eyes from the computer screen. "Your son is downstairs in the Boys Intake Unit."

Eleanor took off her raincoat and shook it. No one offered her a hot tea or coffee, even though she was shivering from the cold and rain. Finally, a young bearded man wearing a bright yellow slicker came through the doors.

"Mrs. Russell. Glad you made it. I'm Roscoe. One of your son's frontline staff. I've been helping him get oriented. He arrived just fine, and the escorts said he behaved himself."

"When can I see him?" she asked.

The place felt like a prison. And Roscoe, with his stubbly beard, thick neck, and drawl, looked and sounded like a prison guard.

"I'm sorry they didn't explain. But our kids need to earn the privilege of a visit. Joshua isn't at that level," Roscoe said.

"I've come from California," she said. "I've been on a plane all day."

"I am sorry. I know you came an awfully long way. But we need you to complete paperwork and view the Villages before Joshua is formally admitted."

"I can't even visit him for five minutes?" she asked.

"It's our rules. The kids have to earn their first visit. You can speak to our clinical director. Or anyone else you'd like to talk to. But in our experience, and the Villages has been here nearly twenty-eight years, it's better this way. He'll be a lot more appreciative of a visit in a little while. Right now, he's just gonna be angry."

"I can't see my own son?" she repeated.

"You can see him through an observation window, but not visit with him. We try to get the kids to lose some of their attitude. They've been running the show for quite a while. Once they start to take responsibility for the serious behaviors that got them here, we move them to the outdoor program and to the cabins. They have more freedom out there, but they work hard. Then, they can earn a visit."

The educational specialist she'd worked with said this was one of the most successful programs in the country. The staff at the Villages knew what they were doing. Even if Roscoe didn't inspire much confidence, she was fairly sure her son wasn't going to run off and swim across the Tennessee River. At least he'd be safe here under Roscoe's watchful eye and rippling biceps.

She eventually met the whole team: the clinical director, the therapist who'd be working with Joshua, the nurse, the addiction specialists, the psychiatrist, and the teachers. Everyone was pleasant. She supposed they were used to frantic and desperate parents bringing their children to the Villages as a last resort.

Roscoe asked for her patience. He knew the rules seemed harsh.

But it all took time. "We've seen that treatment here follows the 80/20 rule," he told her. "Eighty percent of the improvement is seen in the last 20 percent of the program."

The place seemed cold and institutional, but she signed the papers. She felt she didn't have a choice.

Before she left, Roscoe allowed her to watch Joshua through the camera on the unit. He was sitting on his bed. Other boys were in the room, perhaps eight or nine others, some on their beds, others working at desks. A staff member was walking around but not interacting with the boys. One boy tried to get the staff member's attention, but this staff member, a Black man in his thirties, dressed in University of Tennessee sweats, held up his hand and pointed to the clock.

"Why won't he talk to the boy?" Eleanor asked.

"Our kids are not used to delaying gratification. They're used to getting what they want, when they want it. We'll talk to them, but it'll be on our schedule, not theirs."

Suddenly, Joshua got up and stretched. His hair was still in the Mohawk but he was clean. He wore sweats and a bright yellow T-shirt over his sweatshirt. Another boy wore an identical yellow shirt. Joshua did some knee squats, then lay down on the bed again, still speaking to no one.

"What's with the yellow shirt?" she asked Roscoe.

"That means he's a runaway risk. We keep a close eye on all the kids, but we want the runaways, in particular, to know they have to earn our trust. They wear the yellow shirt for as long as that takes. And no laces in their shoes. You can't run too well without laces. Not that there's anywhere to run."

She left the Villages with a heavy heart. She wondered how different the Oregon Youth Authority would have been.

By the time of Joshua's final hearing with Judge Harvey in Oregon, he had moved to the outdoor program and was living with a group of ten boys in a cabin in the woods. The boys were called a clan, and Joshua's clan was the Bears.

At the hearing, when the judge asked him how he liked the Villages, Joshua spoke enthusiastically about chopping wood, building bonfires, and hiking. He told the judge he got paid a bit for this work.

"My clan replaced a dock near the river. I'm saving the money I earn in vocational training to pay back the people I stole from. And I'm going to school. I got some As in my classes. Mostly Bs."

The judge said, "I knew you had it in you, but I remind you that if you run away again, you'll have those three felonies to face."

Joshua said, "I remember, Judge. They still have me wearing a yellow shirt. And they haven't given me my shoelaces yet."

After a month in the outdoor program, Joshua's therapist told her it was time for the Cleanup Call. This call meant Joshua would be admitting the exact nature of what he'd done. It was considered an important step in therapy. Then he could progress to repairing his tattered relationships and trust. Eleanor did not sleep the night before the call. She was terribly frightened of what Joshua was going to say and more frightened of her response.

The Cleanup Call took place during their weekly therapy telephone conference. Eleanor had learned her role was to listen. Joshua rambled, talked, and sometimes put things together for himself in what was close to self-knowledge and insight. She was on speakerphone during the call, but knew she shouldn't argue with him. It was important for him to work things out himself.

"Joshua, you ready?" the therapist asked.

"Yup, I've got my list," Joshua said.

"And, Mrs. Russell, how are you doing? Ready?"

"I'm ready. I'll love you no matter what, Joshua." Then she lied. "I'm glad we're going to be honest with each other." Truthfully, she was not glad at all and wished she could be anywhere else than at the other end of this call.

"Okay," the therapist said with his usual confident good cheer. "Let's get this started."

Joshua began to read from the list, his voice in a monotone. "Okay, Mom. You probably know that when I ran away from Mount Richmond, I got into the house."

"Yes, Joshua. I knew you were in the house."

"I took the guitar Max gave me."

"Yes, I suspected that. I saw how you bent the window frame to get in. I had Misha repair it so I could lock the window."

"I took some other things from my room. I thought they were, technically speaking, my stuff. So it wasn't really stealing," he said.

"What else did you take?"

"You know the gold ring that belonged to Dad? The one he got from Grandpa?"

"Of course I know that ring." A hefty pinkie ring with a raised enameled *R* on it, it was the old-fashioned, bulky men's jewelry worn in the fifties. And it had been one of Joshua's prized possessions. He was proud that it had belonged to his father and grandfather before him and had been given to him. He kept it in his top drawer, in its original velvet jewelry box.

"You took that ring? Where is it now?"

"I pawned it," Joshua said.

"Where is the pawnshop? Can I buy it back?" she asked miserably. Eleanor had loved her father-in-law. He'd embraced her like a daughter. She always felt, had he been alive, he'd have provided some guidance to Joshua. Now there was no ring to remember him by.

"I pawned it in San Jose, Mom. There were a lot of pawnshops, I don't know the street or anything. I don't think I could find it now."

"What else, Joshua?" the therapist asked. "Let's get through your whole list. Mrs. Russell, I know it's difficult, but let's keep going, okay?"

"I also took Grandpa's—your dad's—watch. The one you gave me for my bar mitzvah. But the guy at the pawnshop said it wasn't solid gold, just gold-filled, so he didn't give me much for it."

This watch was one of the few things she had from her own father, an immigrant who'd bought himself few possessions, but who'd worn his shiny watch proudly. She hadn't noticed it was gone.

"What else?" she asked tiredly.

"I sometimes stole cash from your wallet. A lot last year. Tens and twenties. I did it when you had just gotten cash from the ATM. I knew you wouldn't notice. You don't usually count your money, Mom," he said, chastising her a bit.

"Right," she said. At least it explained why she was always short of cash.

"I got a girl in town really messed up with some drugs I sold her," Joshua then said, his voice not changing. "Her boyfriend found me and told me she overdosed. They had to rush her to the hospital. Her boyfriend said she nearly died. I was so messed up myself, I didn't even care. I asked the guy, 'What's it to me?' I thought maybe he wanted a refund, and I didn't want to give him any money back."

She moved from the kitchen barstool into the living room. She sat on the couch, pulling her knees under her. *Is Joshua sorry about all this? It sounds like he's reciting the list because it was an assignment.*

"Anything else?" the therapist added. "Any more on the list?"

"I went to Hebrew School on Wednesday nights last year just for the girls. I never paid any attention to what the rabbi said, but I acted like I was interested."

233

"Not many teenagers go to Hebrew High to listen to the rabbi. Everyone goes to meet girls or guys," Eleanor said.

The therapist laughed, and Eleanor hoped they could end this call right now. She said to Joshua, "You know, when I meet some of those kids from your Wednesday night Hebrew class, they always ask about you. I saw a couple of those girls at the gym this week, and they told me they missed you when you stopped coming."

"No kidding?" he said, sounding genuinely surprised. "But I'm not like those kids. I never fit in with those Hebrew School kids."

"You did, Joshua. They all like you."

"Anything else?" the therapist prodded again.

"I had sex with one of the girls at Mount Richmond. We sneaked off and did it. She was really young, fourteen, and messed up. I didn't use anything, either. I think you should call Mount Richmond and see if she's okay. Her name is Angela. Maybe she needs an AIDs test."

"Okay, Joshua," she replied softly. "I'll call them. No, maybe you should."

"Yeah," he said. "I'll ask them here if I can." There was silence. Then Joshua asked his therapist, "Do I get to have a visit now? Will I get to take off this stupid yellow T-shirt and get my shoelaces back?"

The therapist said, "We'll discuss it at the Treatment Team meeting this week. It's a team decision. Anything else you want to say to your son now, Mrs. Russell?"

"No, I guess not," she said, speaking evenly to the therapist. She knew she was supposed to be reassuring to Joshua, to tell him he'd done well, but she didn't have it in her.

A few hours later, after she'd had a cup of tea and taken a long, hot shower, she went into her bedroom. She'd wrapped herself in the blue terry cloth robe which had belonged to Ron. She slipped her feet into comfortable slippers. On her dresser was a picture of Joshua, taken when he was three or four. It was at the Montessori preschool, where he'd spent hours in the stream, pretending to fish with a stick and string. He wore the green and yellow ducky boots he'd loved so much.

She stood up and after a moment, brought her leg forward and kicked the wall as hard as she could, shattering the Sheetrock and leaving a round hole that went right through to the closet on the other side. She stared at the hole. She would have to call Misha to fix it. She might also have to make a trip to the emergency room and have her toe x-rayed.

Chapter 12

THE WIDOW WAKES UP

2007

She was too young to be a widow; the other single women her age were divorced. Divorced and searching. When Eleanor met people, they assumed she, too, was divorced. Being a widow was different, she stubbornly thought. She knew the difference. When Ron died, it had been out of her control. Marriage counseling, makeovers, bargains, unlike in a divorce, could not be made with a terminal cancer diagnosis.

As Joshua's troubles escalated, she vacillated between resentment and sorrow at her widowed state. There was not even an adversarial ex-husband to share memories of Joshua when he was young, before the trouble started. She remembered him as a beautiful toddler, taking Lara's hairbrush and slugging away at tennis balls. She watched videos of herself, Ron, and the kids: their trip to Hawaii when Ron flew down the water slide with Joshua on his lap, his beard sparkling with diamond droplets of water; and a cousin's wedding in Baltimore where long-legged Ron gracefully danced, the video shot from above, highlighting his thick, wavy, brown hair, never smooth no matter how much mousse or gel she bought him. Ron would never get older than forty-seven, never get a paunch or gray hair. Damn him.

There had been men, of course, in the years since Ron's death.

Eleanor hadn't been opposed to it, but the ones she'd met had been odd. She was in her fifties, but it felt like prom time at high school again. All of the eligible ones were already taken. Teaching at the university in San Jose, Eleanor's days were busy. But she'd come to dread evenings and the emptiness they brought. The darkness oppressed her and sometimes the burden of making conversation with her little boy, after a long day of lecturing, exhausted her. She wanted to be cheerful, not to let Joshua see her exhaustion. He'd sit at the counter, chattering while she fixed their dinner, simple suppers of macaroni and cheese, or frozen pizza. It wasn't the cooking that exhausted her; it was being everything to Joshua. She worried that there was something she was forgetting. Something he ought to bring to school the next day? Signing him up for Little League? Asking him how his spelling test had gone? There was no backup, no safety net. That's what exhausted her.

A year after Ron's death, she was introduced to a likable man by her friend Roslyn. Roslyn worked in the physics department at Stanford and he was a colleague. He was a good man, sweet and considerate. She was hopeful. But after four perfectly pleasant dates, which had ended with no kiss, no hand holding, no touch at all, she bluntly asked him whether he disliked physical contact.

"I'm just not used to it." She saw how his cheerful mood had faded. "I don't know how to get it started." He looked so dejected.

"You've never had intimacy with a woman? Or a man?"

"It just hasn't happened." He became red with embarrassment and looked hopefully at Eleanor. "But I think it can. I was hoping you'd help me."

This was hard work. She had never missed Ron more. The Virgin became shorthand for all the men she met in the years after Ron died and Joshua was growing up. The Virgin. The Pathological Liar. The Man Who Only Liked Threesomes. The Man Who Rejected Monogamy. The Cheapskate. The Angry Israeli. The Angry

Divorced Man. The Angry Alcoholic. All had something seriously broken within, and she hadn't the energy to try to fix it. There were professional men and blue-collar men. There were divorced men and widowed men. Every time she developed a theory on what would be best in a new partner, the theory proved wrong and still, she was alone.

When Joshua was young, they'd gone on trips together. They explored Mayan ruins in Guatemala, swam at beaches in Hawaii, skied at Lake Tahoe. They even went to China, years after his Asian phase. With a group, they visited, among other sights, the terra cotta warriors at Xi'an. After a while, though, Joshua became disinterested in her company. He wanted only to be with his friends, and began to develop the secret life she'd never guessed at.

Now, with Joshua at the Villages for fifteen months, Eleanor realized she must make more of an effort toward building a life for herself. It had been over ten years since Ron had died. The older kids no longer needed her. Max was a pilot, living with a girl in Sausalito. Lara was married to a nice man in San Diego, expecting their first child.

One day, after a shower, she examined her reflection carefully in the mirror. She pulled back the skin on either side of her face with her index fingers. *Is this what a face-lift looks like?* Skin pulled taut, no lines beside her eyes or lips. It was interesting, but she questioned the effect as well as the expense. With her rosy, full cheeks, she would look like a kewpie doll. She pulled her breasts up as they might be without the pull of gravity. Her nipples pointed pertly upward. Ron had frequently spoke of elective surgery with disapproval. He'd seen surgical deaths from cosmetic surgery. She could still hear Ron's stern voice when he spoke about the women who'd had liposuction or breast enhancement, and then died accidentally on the table.

She released her breasts, allowing them to settle into their familiar place. Whoever it was who she found to love would have to be okay with wrinkles, some extra pounds, and sagging breasts. She studied herself, practicing the welcoming smile she'd give this phantom person, the interested expression she'd have as they exchanged life stories. She threw her shoulders back, pleased that her figure, although full, still had its hourglass shape.

It was her rabbi who introduced her to Oscar Padilla, a small, warmhearted man from Chile. Rabbi Lorenz served on a county social justice commission with Oscar. The rabbi phoned and asked Eleanor to join her for a cup of coffee. At the small table in the coffee shop, the rabbi explained that after a county meeting, she'd been approached by Oscar. He said he had a favor to ask of her.

"He's Latin American, a *goy*, but he wants to meet a Jewish woman," the rabbi told Eleanor, with a smile and shrug of her shoulders. "'A strong, Jewish woman.' Those were Oscar's exact words. 'I want to meet a strong, Jewish woman.'" As the rabbi repeated this to Eleanor, she spoke with a mangled Spanish accent and they laughed.

"Why a Jewish woman?" Eleanor asked.

"I asked him," the rabbi said. "He explained, 'You Jewish women want to change the world. You know what you want. At my age, I have no time for coyness. You are a rabbi,' he'd said. 'You must know of such a woman. A single woman.'"

Rabbi Lorenz said she knew of several strong Jewish women in her congregation, but there was one in particular she was thinking of.

Oscar had replied, "I only need one."

She told Oscar she'd get back to him.

"So, how about it?" asked the rabbi, sipping her coffee. "I like him. He's very charming. I think you'd like him as well."

"A Chilean non-Jew who asks a rabbi to introduce him to a Jewish woman? Hmm," Eleanor mused. "Okay. Why not? After all, I'm not doing that well at this on my own."

"Good," the rabbi said in her no-nonsense way, and put down her coffee cup. "I'll give him your number. After that, I'm out of this. Don't talk to me about it again. Unless he wants me to convert him." She stood up and buckled her well-worn trench coat. Rabbi Lorenz was always needed somewhere by someone. She leaned down and smiled conspiratorially at Eleanor. "You know, Jewish women have a reputation of being hot. Maybe that's it."

For several weeks, Eleanor and Oscar exchanged emails and spoke on the phone. The calls and emails created an intimacy. They spoke of favorite movies and books. Electronic conversations gave an illusion of closeness, but she knew they were never a substitute for meeting in person. She certainly had learned that from The Virgin. Yet she loved the sound of Oscar's deep, rich voice. He wooed her with charming Latin mispronunciations. He never used contractions, and she found this formal quality to his speech appealing.

"I am so happy to hear that," he'd say. "Let us plan to speak tomorrow at the same time."

They cleared their busy schedules to finally meet. Oscar, who traveled often for the biomedical company he worked for, was in town the coming weekend. Eleanor's body thrummed with anticipatory nerves.

Through the small, glass prism squares at the sides of her front door, she got her first look at Oscar. He was quite short, but she wasn't terribly tall herself. He had dark, wavy hair and wore a bright red scarf looped around his neck. The scarf was a dashing touch. She opened the door. His dark overcoat, a good wool, was long on him and flapped around the knees.

She regretted the heels she was wearing. But he leaned toward her, reached up, and gave her a brief kiss on the cheek. He held out a present to her. A volume of Pablo Neruda's poetry, *Twenty Love Poems and a Song of Despair: Veinte Poemas de Amor y Una Canción Desesperada*. They'd spoken of Neruda; he was one of the few

Chileans Eleanor was familiar with. And although Oscar didn't love poetry as passionately as Eleanor did, he'd thought to bring her this lovely, small volume. She was delighted and didn't bother to run back to her room and change her shoes.

They began to see one another, at first only on weekends, then more often. She enjoyed his company, but Eleanor still felt awkward about Oscar's small stature and his fine-boned body. She was so much bigger, but he seemed not to mind. In bed that first time, in the room where Ron had died, she wondered what Oscar thought when he saw her fleshy hips and thighs. She was embarrassed when Oscar took off his shirt and she saw his thin chest, no body fat at all. She dimmed the lights and lit a candle. Afterward, when they lay together, he stroked the sides of her body and stared at her with unveiled appreciation.

"I'm sure I'm much bigger than your ex-wife. These peasant, Jewish thighs," she said, and grabbed at her own flesh.

He looked down, then lay back and put his hands under his head.

"You are right," he said. "She is small like me. Delicate, even."

"No one has ever called me delicate," Eleanor said, and sighed. She reached for the sheet and covered herself with it.

"My ex-wife is delicate in many ways," he said, and under the sheet, ran his fingers lightly over her stomach. "She is afraid of life. She has never liked it in the United States, not since we moved here fifteen years ago. She misses our old life, the familiarity of Santiago. She is afraid of so many things here. She still won't drive on the freeways. She does not like to go out at night. I finally persuaded her to go on vacation last year, to visit somewhere besides Chile. It was, how do you say, a last-ditch effort."

"Where did you go?" She closed her eyes, feeling his fingertips moving in circles on her stomach. She touched him, and he was immediately erect again. Oscar was uncircumcised, the first man

242

she had ever been with who was uncircumcised. She decided she liked it.

"Hawaii. The Big Island. Nothing too exotic. But still, she did not want to leave the hotel room. She watched the same programs on television that she watched back in California. My daughter, too. She stayed inside the room with her mother. I could not get them to go out exploring with me." He spoke into her neck, his warm breath exciting her. "So I rented a car and went exploring by myself. I saw the black sand beaches and the still-active volcano."

"She's probably lovely," Eleanor said. She couldn't erase the word "delicate" from her mind.

"Yes, my dear, she probably is. But I never, ever had such a wonderful time in bed with my delicate wife. She accommodated me. You participate."

She opened her eyes, listening thoughtfully to his words. Still, she could not think of the two of them as a couple. First, his age: seven years her junior, he was too young for her. And too thin and fragile. She couldn't imagine people believing they were together.

Until one Monday morning, when she was in the department office at the college, and a colleague breezed in.

"I saw you and your honey walking together in Palo Alto on Saturday. You were deep in conversation. I didn't want to interrupt."

The department secretary lifted her fingers off the keyboard and raised her eyebrows mischievously at Eleanor.

Eleanor felt a blush creep up her neck into her cheeks, something that happened only rarely to her.

"Oh, yeah. Well, it's kind of a new thing," she said, and kept sorting through her mail.

"You go, girl," the secretary said, and resumed her typing.

Oscar had only one child, Andrea. He spoke about his family during late-night telephone calls with Eleanor. She listened to Oscar's hypnotic voice as she lay in bed with the phone tucked under her ear. Oscar said his ex-wife was entirely wrapped up in their daughter. The girl, a young teenager, was brilliant. She excelled at school, especially math, but she was timid, temperamentally like her mother. Oscar had separated from his wife less than a year earlier, when Andrea had begun high school. He and his wife hadn't slept together in years. He'd moved to a furnished apartment in Menlo Park which resembled a motel room, leaving his wife and daughter in the family home. Oscar thought his ex-wife would continue caring for their daughter and keeping up with her large, extended family in Chile. Someday she might return to South America, perhaps when their daughter started university. But he'd seen how some immigrants had trouble going home, having gotten used to the conveniences of America. Oscar was hungry for everything new. He never wanted to return home.

On the phone one night, he spoke about his divorce.

"I suggested to my wife that we go to couples therapy. I know this is quite common in America. Everybody here goes to counseling. At home, therapy is still stigmatized. My wife was offended by the suggestion. She said she could never discuss our intimate problems with a stranger. I didn't know what else to do. So, I left. It was difficult. In the first few months, I cried a lot. I questioned whether I had tried hard enough."

Eleanor closed her eyes and pictured him as he spoke. She thought he might be crying right then, small tears on his lovely, carved cheeks.

Eleanor grew fonder and fonder of Oscar. Everything she suggested, he met with enthusiasm.

"Line dancing?"

"Sure, where can I buy a cowboy shirt? One with those pearlized snap buttons?"

"A trip to New York?"

"Ah, I have always wanted to see a Broadway show."

"A Passover seder?"

"Sounds good!" He joyfully embraced all the people she'd invited and all the traditions of the meal (with the exception of gefilte fish, which he declared was worse than food for animals). His good cheer was endless, his enthusiasm for new experiences, unlimited.

"Oscar, I'm the first woman you've dated after you left your marriage," she said. "Perhaps you should see other women. You might enjoy being a bachelor longer."

"Why? If I have found a good thing, why would I keep looking?"

She worried about Joshua's effect on their relationship. It was so easy now. Oscar came and went, staying the night frequently. They spent weekends as they chose, lounging in bed until midmorning. They traveled; they went where they liked. When Joshua came home, things would be different. She worried what respectable Oscar would think of her wayward son.

She pictured Joshua's great height and broad shoulders. He would tower over dark-skinned Oscar. The boy's blond good looks would again set him apart. She worried what Joshua would think about having a man at the head of the table, eating a meal she had prepared. What would he feel when he walked into the bedroom she had once shared with his father, and instead saw Oscar?

She spoke to Oscar of these fears while they lingered over the good Chilean wine he had brought. The candles flickered, and he complimented her on the hearty roast chicken with lemons she had prepared.

"I don't know if you fully realize what Joshua is like," she said, scraping breadcrumbs from the table. "How difficult he is."

"I was sure you would not have sent him away if the problems were minor," he said. "But tell me what you are worried about." He took a sip of the wine.

"He's always been my baby. Mine alone, without a father most of his life. He's so much younger than Max and Lara, I suppose I overcompensated. And the adoption, too. I worried and overprotected him."

"You do not have to defend how much you love your son," Oscar said.

"But he's done some terrible things. I'm just beginning to grasp how dark some of those things are." She pushed the breadcrumbs into her open palm, then shook the crumbs into her plate. "You'd be shocked by some of these things. He's a thief. He took drugs. He sold drugs. He lies. I never know when to believe him."

He winced but put his hand on her arm. "I want to tell you that I will help you. But truthfully I don't know what I will do if I sensed he was going to hurt you. Or me. Or our relationship. I might need you to choose, sometime."

"How can a mother not be there for her son?" she asked and stiffened. "I have to be there for him. Always."

"Do you?" he asked. "Finding love is very precious, too, Eleanor. I will fight to protect what we have. Your son will soon be a man and living his own life. He'll leave. I want you and I to have each other after that happens." He said this very quietly, but firmly.

Eleanor took a deep breath. "I hope I never have to choose. I don't know if I'll be strong enough."

She began mentioning Oscar in her letters to Joshua and in their weekly phone calls with the family therapist. She'd casually say, "I went to the new James Bond movie with my friend Oscar."

Or, "Oscar and I took a hike in the Santa Cruz Mountains today."

Finally, in February, halfway through Joshua's fifteen-month stay at the Villages, Eleanor knew it was time to speak to Joshua about two important matters: his birth mother, Kelly, and Oscar.

THE WIDOW WAKES UP

She visited him in Tennessee and rented a car. Joshua had an eight-hour pass, the first since he had been relieved of the yellow T-shirt. He could officially go off-campus with her. She planned a drive into the Smoky Mountains, a hike, then dinner in a restaurant that advertised hearty southern home cooking.

She signed him out at the log cabin administration building. "I thought you'd stopped growing, Joshua. But you've gotten even taller since you've been here. Look, I barely come to your shoulder."

"Yeah," he said. "I'm the tallest in the Bear clan."

He was also more lean, his features more defined. When they got in the car, she glanced down at his calloused hands.

"We work hard here," he said, when he saw her staring at his hands. "We split logs every day after breakfast. The wood-burning stove is our only source of heat in the cabins. It gets cold here in the mountains."

Joshua said this proudly. "Sometimes I have to push the new boys to do their chores. The new kids can be real slackers. I like the work though."

She smiled at him. "You've always been a hard worker."

"I can make a fire easily now. No matches, even. I learned how in the wilderness camp in Utah you sent me to. It's called a bow drill fire. I showed the other boys."

"Show me how you do it," she said, and parked the car at a trailhead.

As he and Eleanor went for a hike, he demonstrated, picking up a stick and bending it like a bow. He explained that he attached a piece of twine to the bow, then wrapped the other end around a cedar spindle. He would work the stick back and forth, pushing hard with the bow until he saw smoke and knew he'd gotten a glowing coal from the friction. Then he would carefully transfer the red coal to a pile of moss. He knelt, right there on the path they were walking along, and demonstrated how he blew, gently and consistently, until he saw a flame. The important thing, he told her, was to not rush it, to do each step in order and thoroughly. She watched him as he recited the precise instructions. He sounded so reasonable, so mature. She nodded seriously, as if learning to make a bow drill fire might indeed come in handy at home in downtown Los Altos.

They got back into the car and Eleanor continued toward the mountain restaurant where they were to have dinner. As they went around the steeply banking roads, he spoke to her about the school.

"I think I can graduate from the Villages School before I get discharged next summer," he said. "I'm making up credits from subjects I failed last year at Los Altos High. They let us work individually to get the units we need for a diploma in California."

At dinner, Joshua looked out the window. "I'm actually getting mostly As, Mom. The highest grades I've had since I was a little kid." He seemed embarrassed.

Their window table overlooked a creek. It was a clear winter day. She was eating the best cornbread and fried chicken she had ever tasted. She wanted to let out a whoop of delight when he told her about his grades, but instead quietly leaned over and covered his hand with hers. "I knew you could do it, Joshua. You're a smart kid. I'm really proud of you."

They ate in contented silence for a while. She hated to change the mood, but they had only this afternoon together. "Joshua, I need to talk to you about a few things."

"What things?" he asked, suspicious.

"First, your birth mom. I think you found out things about Kelly when you were in Oregon."

"I know she got in trouble." He picked up a muffin and tore it apart as he spoke. "She stole things. Like me."

"What else upset you?"

There was a long silence. "I know she had another kid. A kid she kept." He said this bitterly. "You knew that, didn't you, Mom?"

"I did. I knew it from the beginning. Kelly told me she had another son when we spoke even before you were born. I kept waiting for the right time to tell you about it. I suspected it would be upsetting."

"I have a brother, and you didn't tell me? You don't think I have a right to know about my own brother?"

"You do. I should have told you about him sooner. I apologize for that."

Joshua began to cry very softly. "You said she was young. And couldn't take care of me. But all that time she was taking care of another kid. A kid she wanted. But she didn't want me." He wiped his eyes with a paper napkin he pulled from the dispenser on the table.

"Joshua, that's the big reason she relinquished you. She couldn't take care of you. She could barely take care of him. Or herself. She was really struggling."

"What's his name?"

"Sean. She told me you two resembled each other when you were born."

Joshua stared at her across the table.

"Whenever you're ready, you can search for her and the rest of your birth family. I'll help you any way I can. I hope you can meet your brother. He's just a little older than you."

Joshua squared his shoulders and picked at the pecan pie the waitress had set in front of him. "No, I don't want to meet her now. Maybe later, when I'm not in a place like the Villages."

"Okay, you tell me when you think it's right. But there's something else I want to talk about with you. Happy news. I've met someone really special."

He took a forkful of pie. "Yeah, you already told me about him. You go to movies and stuff with him."

"His name is Oscar Padilla."

"That's a weird name."

"He's from Chile."

"Where's that?"

"Come on, you've studied geography. It's in South America. The Andes."

Joshua shrugged. "Okay. What about him?"

"I like him a lot. I would say I love him." She swallowed because it was the first time she had said this aloud to anyone besides Oscar. "He asked me to marry him. He gave me a ring, but I've been keeping it in my purse, until you and I could talk." She pulled out the ring and put it on her finger, then showed it to Joshua.

Her son whistled. "Nice rock. Is he loaded?"

"No, not loaded. But he wanted to give me a nice ring. I hope you can meet soon. He's really sweet. He reminds me a little of your dad. Very kind, gentle."

"What kind of car does he have?"

"Oh, Joshua. Please."

"Yeah, well. I was just wondering."

"How do you feel about it? If we got married? He'd live with us in our house. His ex-wife has their old house."

"Mom, I'm almost eighteen. If you're happy, that's cool with me. I don't even know where I'll live after I get out of here."

She was stung by this information. "Where else would you live? You'll have to go to school or work or something. You always have a home with me. With us. My marrying Oscar doesn't change that."

"No, I'm glad for you. I mean it. I don't want you to be alone. But I'm not sure what I'll do when I get out of here. I'll be eighteen. I can make my own decisions then."

Her face muscles tightened, ready to argue. Earlier, the therapist had warned her to avoid arguments when she and Joshua went out together on a pass. They needed to relax with each other. She practiced her newly found self-restraint and said, "Okay. You've got time to look at your options. Whatever you decide, I'll try to support. I'm really glad you're doing well at school. That you'll graduate."

They drove back to the Villages and Joshua fiddled with the satellite radio in the rental car. He found a station of oldies. She appreciated this as the peacemaking gesture it was meant to be, finding a station they could both tolerate, not the heavy metal music they used to argue over.

On her next visit to the Villages, Oscar came with her. It was the annual Family Activity Day, held every April. Joshua ambled up to them and put an arm around both her and Oscar's shoulders, humorously introducing them as "my little mother and my little father-to-be." He showed them around his cabin and the vegetable gardens. He seemed delighted when Oscar proved himself a good athlete and represented the family well in the relay races and games. Despite Oscar's small stature, he was very fast and athletic. He and Joshua raced in the pool, and Joshua had to exert himself to beat him. When Eleanor and Oscar left at the end of Family Day, they were happy, feeling the visit had been a success.

"He's great, your son. I had a lot of fun with him," Oscar said as they found their seats for the return flight to California.

"It's a good thing you like sports; that was important today. I'd have disgraced him if I was the one doing those relay races," Eleanor said, smiling.

"My daughter, Andrea, hates sports," he said. "She has never played on any teams. I tried to get her interested—tennis, volley-ball, even golf. But she prefers staying indoors. So, I missed all that. Little League and soccer. Does Joshua by chance play soccer? I am crazy about soccer."

She held Oscar's hand as the plane took off. They'd marry late that summer, when Joshua came home from the Villages. They'd be a family. Joshua had always felt the loss of his father, but now Oscar would be a loving male presence in Joshua's life. She admired the sparkling ring on her finger and felt hopeful.

Chapter 13

JOSHUA COMES HOME

2008-2013

Before a student was released from the program, the Villages required a discharge planning conference. This happened in August, shortly after Joshua's eighteenth birthday. Oscar wanted to be present when Joshua was discharged, and so they again flew to Tennessee. The plan was for the three of them to return home to Los Altos afterwards, so Joshua could be at Oscar's and Eleanor's wedding.

The discharge conference was formal. Everyone who had worked with Joshua during his stay at the Villages sat around the long table, a manila folder in front of each, pens poised to take notes. Eleanor and Oscar were the last to arrive because Eleanor had insisted on finding a Starbucks on the way, a surprise for Joshua. She carried a sweating cup of Joshua's favorite—a sticky, sweet, caramel coffee drink. Immediately she saw her error. She couldn't pass him a cup of caramel topped with a swirl of whipped cream at such a serious event. She'd save it and put it under her chair. She waved to her son, sitting at the far end of the table, and blew him a kiss. He gave her a small nod.

The clinical director asked everyone to introduce themselves. They went around the table, each saying their name and title. Eleanor began and then Oscar charmingly introduced himself as "the soon-to-be stepfather." The introductions ended with Joshua. "I'm

Joshua. The kid." Then, he ducked his head and stared down at the table.

"Okay," the clinical director said. "Let's begin. We'll get a report from everyone who worked with Joshua for the past fifteen months and then work on recommendations for discharge. You interrupt with any questions, Mrs. Russell. You, too, Mr., ah, Padilla."

Miss Eckert, the nurse, began. "He's been well the whole time he's been with us. Most of the boys like to visit me, even if it's to get out of work, or break the monotony. But he's never come to see me. I've seen Joshua only for checkups. Or drug tests. Perhaps, Mrs. Russell, get him to a dentist when he returns to California. Other than that, he seems healthy."

The substance abuse counselor, George, also said Joshua never visited him voluntarily. He always had the correct answers in discussions, but seemed remote when he talked about his own problems—instead he'd give advice to the other boys. "I strongly recommend you find an AA or NA group when he returns home. Sometimes it takes a while for people to connect to twelve-step programs," George concluded.

Roscoe, the thick-necked, bearded Bear Clan leader, said he probably knew Joshua the best. "I've worked with him the entire time he's been here. Every day for fifteen months. Moved with him from the intake unit to the outdoor program. Here's the thing: he's never got close to anyone during the whole time he's been here. I worry whether he's taking away much from the program. He's kind of coasted through."

His psychologist echoed Roscoe. "Yeah, he's a moving target, always talking to new staff members. He tells them a canned, rehearsed-sounding version of his story: the adoption, his father's death, his mother's control. He recites his story, using the same words each time, but then moves on to another person. It never goes any further."

The only person with an encouraging report was Thomas, the vocational supervisor. "He's a hard worker, that Joshua. And careful, too. I never find fault with his gardening or with the construction jobs. He can name every tool we've used. He should easily be able to find a job when he returns home."

Listening to Thomas was the only time Joshua lifted his head and gave a small smile.

People at the table wondered whether the program had permeated Joshua, whether he had gained in self-knowledge. The staff spoke about Joshua in generalities. He didn't know himself, they said. It didn't sound to Eleanor as if they knew him either. There was no heart in what they said about her son.

As each person around that large table spoke, Eleanor listened, at first fascinated, then becoming disheartened. The Villages staff spoke about someone she barely recognized. None of these well-meaning professionals captured her boy. The reports didn't reflect his sweet tenderness that time when he'd re-run laps of the race at day camp, staying with an awkward kid who'd lagged far behind. He gave up winning, just so the gawky boy wouldn't finish alone. No one had seen the small, vulnerable scar at the back of his head, almost, but not quite hidden by his blond hair, that he'd gotten when he crashed into a porta-potty at the park and fell backwards off his bicycle, crying from embarrassment more than pain. The boy they described was obedient, had broken no rules at the Villages. But he wasn't the Joshua she knew. Or the Joshua she remembered.

She had flown across country, holding Oscar's hand on the flight, answering "No" when he asked if she was nervous. She hadn't been until now, when person after person around the table spoke in a way that she could only describe as muted. She had expected something different. In the newsletter from the Villages, and in the video she'd received when Joshua first enrolled, parents described this discharge conference as full of emotion, everyone in tears as the troubled youth that had been admitted had evolved into the healthier young person now going home. She expected Joshua's discharge to be filled with sentimental goodbyes and happy wishes for the future. She had placed tissues in her purse in preparation.

But everyone at the table remained dry-eyed. No one spoke about changes they had seen in Joshua. The staff sounded more puzzled than euphoric. They reported that, yes, he'd completed the program. He had just turned eighteen and, as agreed, he was done. There had been few problems; Joshua was not a troublemaker. But neither did she hear glowing reviews. Did she detect warning in their voices? Had he faked it until he made it? There was a guardedness, an obvious reluctance to giving encouraging predictions. *Damn*, she thought. All this money, all this time away from home. Couldn't they give her *some* good news? Besides how well he grew vegetables? She felt a growing apprehension.

At the end of the conference, they stood. Eleanor said goodbye to these people whose southern accents had become almost familiar. She even hugged Roscoe. She went to her son, who was shaking hands with staff members, and handed him his Starbucks cup, no longer steaming.

"Thanks, Mom. What time is our plane? Do we go to the airport right now?" he asked, taking a big sip of the sweet coffee.

"Well, sure we can. But I thought you'd have more packing, and you'd want to say more to the Bear clan," she said. She started to lean over to wipe away the foam mustache on his upper lip but stopped herself.

"Nope. Clothes get trashed here, since we work outdoors so much. I threw a lot of it away. The guys wanted some of my other stuff, so I gave it to them. I don't want to take much home. I just have the one bag. It's outside."

She bristled, thinking of the warm clothes she'd carefully

purchased and the steel-toed work boots she'd hunted for all over town to find in his size. She had stood in line at the post office, express-mailing them when he said he needed the things right away for vocational training.

"Nothing else? No one you want to say goodbye to?"

"No, I'm good. Let's just get going. I haven't seen California in over a year," he said, and rubbed his hands together. "I am so ready to leave Tennessee."

"It's okay. We can go to the airport now. This way we'll have time to get something to eat before we board," Oscar said.

Oscar was already the peacemaker, Eleanor thought. It was going to work out. He was going to help her with Joshua. He'd help her to relax more with her son.

Joshua swung the bag he'd left in the hall over his shoulder, and they got into their rental car.

The wedding preparations kept everyone busy in those first few weeks. Joshua was wonderfully helpful. He got his driver's license on his first try and helped them run errands. He picked up vases for floral arrangements and brought the *chuppah* home from the synagogue after a nice talk with Rabbi Lorenz. She knew he had community service hours to complete, and she suggested he volunteer on Sundays, helping out with the little kids at Sunday School.

Max flew in the night before the wedding, handsome in his pilot's uniform, and though he was tired and had a day-old stubble, he had a hearty greeting for Joshua. Her sons clasped each other in genuine fondness, and along with their secret handshake, there were many rounds of "Hey, bro!"

Before long, Max had his brother in a headlock, but this time, Joshua flipped Max around and the elder brother was on the ground at his younger brother's mercy. They went out that night to see one of the disgustingly violent movies Eleanor hated, first asking Oscar if he'd like to join them.

Her future husband seriously considered the invitation, but then declined and said, "I would love to see the movie with you, but I think your mother might cancel the nuptials tomorrow if I didn't stay home tonight and help her get things ready. But please, ask me again, because these are the kind of movies I will never get to see with my future bride."

They all laughed. Eleanor watched her two sons leave, Joshua whistling appreciatively at his brother's flashy red rental car. One of them dialed up the fancy sound system, and as they drove away, she heard the thumping heavy metal they loved. It was the happiest she'd seen Joshua in a very long time.

The next morning, she admired her two good-looking sons, one dark and compact, the other blond and lanky, when they came into the kitchen in their wedding suits and crisp white shirts. Despite their big age difference of thirteen years, the two seemed like peers. Max had always been young-looking. She wondered how people boarding the airplane viewed the boyish pilot in the cockpit. She herself could hardly believe he was allowed behind the controls of a commercial jet. Joshua looked like the older brother. His broad shoulders and muscular arms were part of this. But his older appearance had more to do with the toughness in his expression. When he knew he was being watched, Joshua's face lit up with his sweet smile. But, in the last few years, he'd acquired a surly scowl. The angry squint around his eyes puzzled and disturbed her.

Joshua rode to the wedding in Max's car. They followed behind Eleanor and Oscar. She turned around and saw them bobbing their heads up and down to the music. She was glad both her sons were going to be at the wedding and she put away her anxious thoughts, placing her hand on her soon-to-be husband's arm as he drove.

It was a beautiful fall day, crisp, but clear. Lara and her husband and their baby had gone ahead to the resort. Lara was good at details, and Eleanor had given her a list. Her capable daughter would take care of everything on it. The caterers had better have everything correctly prepared; Lara was not one to be ignored when she had a job to do.

The wedding was perfect. Her three children and Oscar's daughter, Andrea, each held one corner of the chuppah. Oscar smashed the glass under his foot with great gusto, and Rabbi Lorenz recited her stock line.

"That will undoubtedly be the last time you'll put your foot down to your wife."

Oscar had invited Chilean friends to play Latin music at the reception. They even did a salsa-inspired *hora*. Joshua answered everyone's questions with a poise Eleanor didn't realize he'd acquired.

"Yes, I finished high school at the program in Tennessee. I graduated with over a 3.0 average," he said to his mother's friends, who cared about such things.

"I was pretty scared by that judge in Oregon. He said I could have gotten thirty to forty years. I got three felonies! Man, I never want to go through that again." He shook his head, explaining to close friends and family who knew where he'd been during the last year and a half.

She watched Joshua all afternoon, the invisible thread that bound him to her still strong. Though more elastic, it never broke, even during her vows to Oscar. Always aware of Joshua, she watched to see how he was handling his new freedom as well as his mother's marriage. She tried not to sniff at the clear liquid in his glass or to wonder where he went when he left the room. Mostly, she was successful at enjoying her wedding.

After the reception, Eleanor and Oscar went on a brief trip to Big Sur, staying at a luxurious inn, and despite their ages, feeling like newlyweds. She laughingly told everyone they met they were on their honeymoon and enjoyed the surprised faces they received. They held hands and took long walks and had breakfasts in bed.

Lara invited Joshua to come to Southern California with her after the wedding. He could get to know his new nephew, Kent. Eleanor was immeasurably relieved he would be in the company of his older sister and brother-in-law. She enjoyed the honeymoon even more because she wasn't worrying about Joshua.

When she and Oscar returned from their trip to Big Sur, Eleanor noticed how little her son was doing with himself. They'd given him Oscar's old pick-up truck, but he had absolutely no structure to his day. He mentioned no plans for the future, nothing beyond his mandated daily attendance at Narcotics Anonymous meetings and almost daily trips to the video store.

After a week, with Joshua sleeping late every morning, she requested a family meeting.

"Joshua," she began as they sat in front of the fire Oscar had built. "We're wondering what you have in mind for yourself?"

"You're starting in on me again. What should I have in mind? I'm going to NA, right? My sobriety is supposed to be my number one priority. I'm doing chores you want done around here, right? I worked hard at the Villages. I need a break. There was no downtime there, ever."

"I know, sweetie. And I think you're doing great. I'm really proud of you. But I worry that you're getting bored. Or lonely."

"Sure, I'd like to see some friends," he said. "People my own age. But everyone my age is getting loaded. I can't see them. They don't support me in my program."

"Everyone?" Oscar asked. "Everyone is getting loaded?" He was still kneeling in front of the fire, slowly adding kindling in his neat, methodical way. "Maybe some of them are not. Maybe you could join a club. A team. I see signs at the gym for teams forming. Volleyball or soccer."

"You have no idea what it's like," Joshua said. "You don't know anything about being an addict. The only people I feel comfortable with are people in NA. And I can't bring any of them home."

"Your friends are welcome here," Eleanor said.

Oscar turned from the fire and raised his eyebrows.

The next afternoon, Eleanor returned from her classes to find Joshua sprawled on the couch in the living room, flanked by two of the seediest men she had ever seen in Los Altos. One was around forty-five and had no teeth. The other was a bit younger, but his face was rough and red. He appeared to have been exposed to the elements every moment of his life. Both men had tattoos going up their forearms and emerging on their necks—the younger one even had tattoos on his face. Joshua and these two men sat playing video games in the living room, each using his own controller to propel cars racing along narrow city streets. She smelled the fetid odor of unwashed bodies.

"Hi, Mom. This is Stan and this is Bryce. They're in my home group. At NA. We're going to the six o'clock meeting in a little while."

"Hi," she said and shook their hands, hoping she didn't show how appalled she was.

When Joshua came home after his meeting, she said they needed a family discussion again.

"You can't invite strangers into the house. And those men are so much older than you. Who are they?"

"I thought you said my friends are always welcome." Joshua gave her a sarcastic smile. "Which friends did you mean?"

"Oh, Joshua," she said tiredly.

"They support me in my program, but I know you only judge people by appearances. I could bring home some very clean-cut guys. You'd probably be happy with them, but they'd be stoners and you wouldn't even know."

"You might be right. But you need to be doing something con-structive during the day. Not playing video games with middle-aged men. That's the rules."

Oscar finally spoke up. He'd been concentrating on his dinner. "You must get a job. If you choose not to go to school or go to work, we cannot support you. If you need help with finding a job, we'll help you. But you have to be working soon. It's been long enough. This is not negotiable."

"Don't you guys get it?" Joshua shouted. "The Villages said I'm supposed to focus on my sobriety. It's my main priority." Joshua got up from the table and put down his glass with a loud thud. "I can never satisfy you. You always want more."

"Joshua," Eleanor said, turning to Oscar for support. "We've decided we're not going to pay your cell phone bill or your car insur-ance after this week. It's part of being eighteen, of being an adult."

Joshua stomped out of the room, and Oscar and Eleanor faced each other across the table.

"What if he starts using again because we're pushing him too hard?" she said. "At least he's clean. At least we know where he is at night."

"My sweetheart," Oscar said, and got up and pushed the hair back from her eyes. "He is holding you hostage. You know this. You are a smart woman. What we are asking is very reasonable. You must start holding him accountable. He needs to be working. He needs a job."

"You don't understand," she said. "Maybe he first has to get stronger."

"I do understand, my dear. He's using us, and we're not helping him by allowing it."

To her surprise, Joshua came to her the next day and said he was ready to search for a job. That night, Oscar sat with him at the com-puter and showed him how he could turn his previous history of unemployment into a series of respectable sounding job experiences. His time in the vocational program at the Villages became experience with gardening, woodwork, construction, and even project management. In the end, Joshua had a resume that surprised all of them.

"Joshua, *I'd* hire you, if I had a job to give," she said as she read over the final pages he brought home from the copy center. "Now all you have to do is take these around town. Go into all the restaurants and shops that are interesting to you."

"And don't forget the internet," Oscar said. "You should look at all the job site listings and begin forwarding your resume. There are many of these sites. I can show them to you."

"Friends, too," Eleanor said. "I'll give you a list of friends and their addresses, people who have their own businesses. We've got lots of contacts. You need to network."

She glanced up at Joshua and saw him staring at the kitchen clock. He'd lost interest. She and Oscar were the ones who were excited and full of ideas, not Joshua. She stopped talking and handed her son the pile of resumes. *Back off,* she said to herself. *Let him do this by himself.*

Each night at dinner, he gave them reports of where he'd taken his resume, what applications he'd completed. Two more weeks went by, but still Joshua had no job.

In the privacy of their own room, Eleanor asked Oscar, "Why is that strong, capable boy having no success? I've mentioned his difficulty to several friends. I even asked if they know anyone hiring. If only he could find that first job, I know he'll do well. He'd have a sense of accomplishment."

She thought about his job search every day, wanting to make suggestions on his hair, wardrobe, and following up at the places where he'd left his resume, but she restrained herself from meddling.

Finally, one night, Joshua came to the dinner table and announced triumphantly, "I got a job! I start working tomorrow."

She and Oscar were giddy with excitement. They raised their water goblets in a toast. Eleanor gave Joshua a big hug.

"Tell us everything," she said.

"I followed up on a lead from Narcotics Anonymous. Another NA member told me about a new branch of Quality Tires opening in Los Altos and that they might be hiring. The manager is willing to give me a chance to learn how to change and repair and rotate tires. They'll try me out on an hourly basis."

"I do remember seeing that a tire store was opening on Santa Cruz Avenue. I saw the balloons and the Grand Opening sign just the other day," Eleanor said.

"This is great news, Joshua," Oscar said and passed him the plate of beef Stroganoff, one of Joshua's favorites.

"Yeah, I like the guys," he said, piling food onto his plate. "It's a good crew. Most of them are older, but everybody seems like they're willing to teach me stuff."

"You'll do great. I know you will. You learn really quickly," Eleanor said. "Remember how quickly you read the directions for putting in the new garbage disposal, and how you installed it, before Oscar even got home? You're amazing at putting stuff together."

She made sure she kept plenty of food in the refrigerator. Each morning, Joshua got up at seven on his own, and made himself a huge sandwich: turkey, cheddar, lettuce, and tomatoes piled on whole-wheat bread spread thickly with mayonnaise. He packed a bag of chips and a juice box. It was the same lunch he'd eaten all through school, but in the past, she'd made it for him.

He was grubby when he drove to work in Oscar's old pick-up, often unshaven and wearing clothes that appeared slept in, but she figured his wardrobe hardly mattered in a tire shop.

At night, Joshua chatted to them about the tire store, describing customers and the cars he worked on, even giving them small lectures on repairing punctures or explaining the different grades of tires. Sometimes he said his back hurt because there was a lot of bending involved, and he stood in the kitchen and did stretches.

Soon he began to go out at night. He mentioned people from his NA meetings, as well as coworkers. He said he played pool, went to the movies, or even to his favorite—a place offering both movies and bowling. One evening, he told them he had a date with a girl he'd known in high school, and he got dressed up. Eleanor could smell strong wafts of cologne on her son even before he came upstairs to say goodbye. She recognized the scent, the same cologne Max had used when he was still at home. Max had taught his younger brother his secret technique to applying cologne.

"Spray it into the air, and walk through the mist," Max instructed.

"Where are you taking her?" Oscar asked.

"Out to dinner. I think to the sushi place downtown."

"Do you have enough cash?" Oscar asked. "I don't approve of this custom of sharing the bill. If you ask a lady out, you must pay for her."

"Yup. I'm cool. I got it covered."

"And, Joshua, make sure your nails are clean," Eleanor said. "Girls can't stand dirty nails."

"Got it covered, Mom," Joshua said, a bit more testily.

"Got it covered" was the code phrase the family therapist at the Villages had encouraged Joshua to use when he felt his mother was interfering. It was meant to be a polite way of letting her know she was trying to manage his life too much.

"You look terrific, Joshua. I hope it's a great evening." She meant it, too. "Here, take this," she insisted, and pressed a twenty into his hand. "You've been doing so well. It's a little gift. The sushi place can get expensive."

"You know," Oscar said pensively, standing at the door watching as Joshua drove down the street, "it is surprising how clean his hands always are. I mean, they are very clean for someone working in a tire store."

Eleanor shrugged. "He's growing up. Noticing things girls care about."

She had expected Joshua to have a girlfriend ever since he'd arrived home. He was so handsome and charming. She thought, just like a job, a girlfriend might give her son a sense of purpose, a greater enthusiasm for life. Once he had a girlfriend, she thought he'd feel better about himself. But the date at the sushi restaurant led to no others. She heard no more about the girl and didn't pry.

The job at the tire store seemed to be going well, and there was peace in the house, with only one bump in this relatively calm period. Joshua appeared around nine o'clock one evening and sat down opposite the couch where she and Oscar were watching a movie. He was wearing a long-sleeved flannel shirt.

"I have a surprise for you guys," he said, and seemed positively joyous. "It's something I've wanted for a long, long time."

He unbuttoned his plaid flannel shirt and took it off, so that he was wearing only his white T-shirt. Then he held his arms out, palms up. Both forearms were decorated with tattoos. On the right arm was a swallow, colored only in black. The left forearm, however, was ablaze with color. There was a large rose, inked in a gaudy bright red, and underneath the rose were words in a twirling, fancy script that, at first, Eleanor was unable to read. She reached for her reading glasses and leaned forward.

"What do you think?" Joshua asked, so excited he could barely stay still.

"I can't quite read it," she said. "It's still red and swollen." But she knew there was something wrong and tried to sort out what it was. "Perscription for Creativity," she read aloud. "It's spelled wrong, Joshua. Prescription is spelled wrong."

"No it's not," he said, the smile still on his face.

She turned to Oscar.

"Don't ask me," he said, and raised both hands in the air. "I'm a foreigner. I cannot spell your crazy language."

"No, Joshua, it's spelled wrong. Prescription is spelled p-r-e-, not p-e-r."

"No, it's not," he said, but he was no longer smiling.

As with almost everything that happened with Joshua, she began to doubt herself. Maybe it *was* spelled right. However, the spelling wasn't the point, though going through life with a mis-spelled tattoo on your forearm was worse than going through life with just a tattoo on your forearm.

"But, Joshua, why did you do it in a place that shows? Don't you think that's going to affect you in the future? Believe me, people judge people differently when they have tattoos all over them."

"I don't care what people think. You care about what people think. I did it because I like it. I was really excited when I turned eighteen and could get it done. I've been planning and thinking about what I'd get the whole time you had me away. I saved the money, and I checked out a lot of tattoo artists around here until I found one I liked. This guy is really cool. And if I don't want peo-ple to see it, all I have to do is wear long sleeves. Like tonight. You wouldn't have even seen the tattoo if I hadn't shown it to you."

"But you can't wear long sleeves all the time. Not in summer," Eleanor said.

"Darling," Oscar said gently. "It appears to be done already. I don't believe there is anything more to decide."

She nodded, then looked over at Joshua and tried to smile.

He stood up, grabbed his shirt, and stomped down to his room.

She couldn't resist, though. She got up and went over to the bookshelves and opened the dictionary, thumbing through the "Ps." P-r-e-s-c-r-i-p-t-i-o-n. Of course. She brought the dictionary over to the couch where Oscar sat and silently pointed to the word.

Oscar examined the dictionary and shrugged. "Well, he certainly spelled it creatively," said her husband, and picked up the remote to start the movie again.

By morning, she'd resolved not to speak of the tattoo again. Joshua was eighteen. She'd looked on the internet and learned 36 percent of people under age twenty-five had at least one tattoo. One in three people. Even Lara had gotten her tattoo. *It's not the end of the world,* she told herself, *even if it is misspelled.*

Joshua was already in the kitchen making his usual sandwich, piling on the lunch meat and spreading the bread with mayonnaise. He was the only one in the family who liked mayonnaise, so she bought him large jars of it. She, herself, could not stand the stuff; its texture vaguely revolted her.

She started the kettle for her tea. "What's up for today, sweetie?"

"Same old, same old. Changing tires. Just watching the wheels go round."

She laughed, and came over and stood on tiptoe, giving him a kiss. It was good to have him home and good to have him in the kitchen in the morning. She tried not to look at his arms.

Two weeks later, after Joshua had been working nearly a month, she got a call. It was from a woman who worked in human resources at the City of Los Altos. Joshua had left an application for work. The city's hiring freeze was over, and they'd like to interview Joshua for the recreation department.

Eleanor hadn't even known he was applying for city jobs. She was impressed with her son's initiative.

"Sure," she said. "I'll get a message to him right away. That's great." She hung up and smiled. This was a great opportunity for Joshua. The tire store paid him by the hour. They had called it a temporary job and couldn't promise how long it would last. Here was something Joshua could really excel at, even use his God-given athletic abilities. She waited until the noon hour, then called him on his cell phone.

"Hi, Mom."

"Joshua. Good news. Great news."

"Oh yeah? What's that?" he asked.

"The City of Los Altos just called about your application. They want to interview you. I didn't even know you'd applied to them. Do you have a pencil so I can give you the number?"

"Mom, I already have a job. Remember?"

"Sweetie, I know. But this job pays more, and it's permanent. It might lead to other things. Why don't you just go for an interview? The city job would give you benefits. Our health insurance for you runs out in a few months."

Finally, he agreed to call, although Eleanor thought it was without enthusiasm. A few days later, when the interview was scheduled, he arrived home early from work and went to shower. When he came into the kitchen where she was preparing dinner, he was clean, his hair wet and plastered against his scalp, but he wore an old T-shirt that left his arms and new tattoos exposed.

"Oh, Joshua. Put on a shirt with sleeves. Please."

"Mom, this is my interview. Not yours."

"I know. I know. But I also know the first thing they are going to see are those tattoos. It'll distract them from what you say. Please trust me on this."

Finally, he agreed, angrily grabbing the wrinkled shirt that was on the back of a kitchen chair and stomping out.

That night he told them he'd been interviewed by a whole panel of City employees. The job was for assistant facilities manager for the recreation department. They'd asked him a lot of questions about what he would do in various situations involving setting up and preparing the community center and athletic fields. He said he'd told the panel that he'd look for safety hazards first, like standing water on the fields. He told the panel that at his school, in vocational training, he'd been taught that a safety check always is number one, before any activity begins. Apparently his answers impressed the panel, because he said they'd all nodded and smiled at him, and told him they'd get back with him in a day or two. Joshua seemed pleased with himself. Eleanor went to bed that night feeling they were turning a new page.

Over the next four days, Eleanor asked Joshua several times if he'd heard from the rec department, and he said he hadn't. He shrugged and said he supposed he didn't get the job. Eleanor felt upset. But Joshua seemed nonplussed by the rejection and continued getting up each day, making his sandwich, and going to the tire store.

A week after the interview, Eleanor answered another call for Joshua.

"Is Joshua Russell at home?" a woman's voice asked.

"No. He's at work. This is his mom. Can I help you?"

"Sorry to bother you, ma'am. I'm calling from the City of Los Altos Recreation Department. We're wondering if we have the correct information for him. We've been trying to reach his cell phone all week, and he hasn't returned our messages. This number was on his original application."

The woman checked the cell phone number with Eleanor. It was correct. She didn't understand why Joshua had told her he hadn't received any calls about the job.

"Thanks," she told the woman. "I'll let him know you want to speak with him. I'll try to reach him right away. I'll call him at work."

"That's the other thing. We'd like to offer him the position, so we're checking his references. But Quality Tires never heard of him. We need to speak with him about that."

The familiar feeling of fear returned, the muscles tightening in her throat.

"I wonder if you're calling the right branch," Eleanor said. "The one here in town just opened. Perhaps you're calling one of the other stores. This one is on Santa Cruz Avenue."

"No, ma'am. We called the branch here in Los Altos. We spelled his name out, and we talked to the manager. Your son even gave us the manager's name. Richard. But Richard said he never heard of Joshua Russell."

Eleanor hung up the phone and replayed the past month in her mind. *Where had Joshua been going every morning? What had he been using for money? How had he paid for gas and the evenings of bowling and movies?* He had described changing and balancing tires in such detail, she was sure she herself could now do it. *How did he know so much about this job? And how had he sat at the table each and every night, cheerfully telling them about his day at work?* He'd complained about his aches and pains as he stood at the kitchen sink, washing his hands. He'd say the bending over was hard on his neck and shoulders. Oscar had said Joshua's hands and finger-nails were not dirty. She heard Joshua's pleasant voice as he replied to her questions about his job, giving her exact, precise answers to the questions he knew she might ask. He never hesitated giving her names and describing the people he worked with. He knew her so well, he smoothly anticipated what she'd be curious about and pre-pared all his answers.

She called Quality Tires herself, hoping there was some mistake.

"Hello," a pleasant voice answered. "Quality Tires."

"Is this the new store in Los Altos? Is your manager Richard?"

"It sure is. Would you like to speak to him?"

When Eleanor asked Richard if he had ever met Joshua Rus-sell, he confirmed Joshua had never worked there, and told her that coincidentally, there had been another call at the store for a Joshua earlier in the week.

She brewed a cup of tea before she called Joshua on his cell phone. She wanted to make sure her voice was calm. She rehearsed what she would say before she dialed.

When he picked up, he sounded jovial. "Hi, Mom."

"Hi, Joshua. Where are you?"

"I'm on my lunch break now. With some of the guys from work."

"Where are you, specifically?" she asked.

"Just on El Camino. Near downtown. At the Happy Hound. Why? Do you need something?"

"You're on lunch break from Quality Tires?" she asked, speaking precisely.

"Yeah. What's up?" He'd stopped sounding so happy.

"Joshua, they never heard of you at Quality Tires. The manager, Richard, told me you didn't work there. The City was trying to check your references and they called me, asking about it."

There was silence on the phone. She waited a long time, and still he didn't answer. *He's run out of lies,* she thought. After so many, he's finally run out. She herself felt empty as well, hope gone like air in the tires Joshua was supposed to be changing.

"You need to come home," she said. "Bring back the truck and come home now."

Later that evening, she and Oscar were in their room, lying side by side on their bed, speaking glumly about the day, trying to decide what to do next. At around ten o'clock, the doorbell rang, two sharp bursts of sound. She threw a robe over her nightgown and ran to the front door, her heart pounding. She pulled open the door. The street was deserted. Something on the front mat caught her eye. It was an envelope. She picked it up and closed the door. Oscar came up behind her and put his arms around her. She opened the envelope and the keys to the truck fell out. Inside, also, was a folded-up sheet of school notebook paper.

On it was a note written in pencil.

"Mom, the truck is parked behind 7-Eleven. I'm getting the old feelings again, so I'm leaving. It's better this way. I'm okay. Don't worry about me. Please don't look for me. I'll be fine. I love you. Joshua."

That phone conversation was the last she had with Joshua for over five years. She replayed the conversation over and over, thinking about each syllable, wondering if she had changed something, anything, how the outcome might have been different. And, over the next five years, Eleanor cried all the tears that had been stored inside her. She remembered how, after Ron's death, Joshua had wept every night, when she could not. She'd called him her designated crier. Now she finally wept for the loss of them both, Ron and Joshua. She cried for the hole inside Joshua she could not fill, no matter how much she loved him.

During that time, she felt a strong need to reach out to Kelly DeGrasse. She had suggested this to her son through the years, but Joshua never agreed to search for his birth mother. She knew Joshua had discovered information about Kelly from the internet while on the run from the Oregon school. She'd even received Joshua's original birth certificate, on which his name was entered as Christopher. At some point he must have applied for it from the Wisconsin Children's Hospital. When she showed the birth certificate to her son, he seemed disinterested. "Keep it for me," he'd said.

She did her own search and discovered that Kelly DeGrasse was now Kelly Fulton. She'd married a few years after she had been arrested. She had two more children with her new husband—both girls. Kelly was on Facebook and some other social media sites, unlike Joshua who seemed to be taking pains to not be found. Kelly still lived in Wisconsin. She worked for a medical device company and appeared to be a settled mother and wife. There were no more incidents with the legal system, no more newspaper stories. By paying a few extra dollars for a deeper search, Eleanor even discovered Kelly's phone number.

She got a recording the first few times she called and she hung up. Then, one night, Kelly answered her phone.

"Kelly, this is Eleanor Russell. From California. I'm sorry to surprise you, calling so unexpectedly, but I need to talk."

There was a long pause. Kelly spoke softly. "Eleanor? Is my son okay? Is he there now?"

"That's why I'm calling. He's not here. To be honest, Joshua has had some tough years." As she spoke, she studied Kelly's Facebook picture. The woman appeared surprisingly the same—broad face, pretty smile. She could have been Joshua's sister, not his mother. They had the same hazel eyes, the same smile.

They spoke for nearly an hour. Kelly shed tears when Eleanor told her of Ron's death.

"I knew as soon as I met you both, you'd be good parents. It gave me peace. I'm so sorry to hear he died."

Kelly cried again when she heard Joshua had left home. She told Eleanor that she had heard nothing from him. Not a call or letter. She promised to phone if he did make contact.

"Eleanor, please give Joshua a message when you do find him. Tell him not a day has gone by that I haven't missed him. I think of him every single day. And I've told his big brother and little sisters about him. They know they have a brother in California, and they want to meet him someday. Tell him we all love him. Remind him he has family here, too."

EPILOGUE

Joshua 2008–2013

Shawnee gave him a hard time about how he had stopped communicating with his family. He knew it was hard for her to understand, hard for anyone to understand what being around his mother did to him. After they had the baby, though, Shawnee brought it up with greater frequency.

"Don't you want Chris to have grandparents?" she asked, as she spooned orange-colored puree mush from a jar into the baby's open mouth. What little family Shawnee had were far away, scattered in the Midwest. "And an aunt and uncle?"

"You can't imagine what it was like. She drove me crazy. I always felt guilty. After disappearing for all this time, it'll be even worse."

"All I know is that you have family forty-five miles down the road from us. You're acting like a kid who stole cookies from the cookie jar and can't own up to it."

She was right. Only it had been many cookie jars, and because his mother never forgot or forgave, she probably imagined him with his hand still inside those jars.

When Joshua ran away that last time, all he thought about was escaping the guilt. The feelings his mother made him feel were unbearable. She had no idea what a look from her, a downturned mouth, and her sigh did to him. Even running through the Oregon wilderness, when he had nothing but PowerBars to eat for days, it was still better than hearing her sigh. At the Villages, locked inside the shitty intake unit when all he had to read were the creepy spiritual books they handed out, and he had to sleep with the florescent lights above him still glowing, it was better than seeing his mother's lips pursed with disappointment. After he faked the job in the tire store and she found out, he imagined—no, he knew—the sad, martyred expression on her face.

He used to be able to make her laugh when he was small. After his dad died, it was just the two of them. He could make his mom happy when nobody else could. He'd loved it. Once, they'd gone deep-sea fishing on a boat out of the Santa Cruz harbor. The captain handed out long poles with a bunch of hooks on them. Six or seven hooks on each. He had put his pole into the water, and like magic, when he pulled it up, there was a fish on every hook. His mom laughed uncontrollably. It had been fantastic.

He caught his legal limit and the captain said, "No more, son, you're finished for today."

But his mom handed him her pole. "Go ahead, Joshua, you catch my limit for me. You've got the fisherman's luck today."

She loved those red snappers he caught. She had them all cleaned and filleted at the dock and invited the whole neighborhood over. Everyone ate red snappers until they couldn't eat any more. For years, she repeated the story about how he brought up his pole and on every hook, there was a fish.

When he'd won the Junior Lifeguard of the Year award from some dumb summer camp, she was so proud. But then, when he was no longer a little kid, all he did was disappoint her.

After she found out about the nonexistent job at the tire store, he couldn't go home. He couldn't face her. He had started using again, relapsing only a month after he'd returned to Los Altos from the Villages. When he'd told her he was working, he was usually hanging with his old friends. He never returned the call about the job from the City because they'd have discovered the tire store job wasn't real. They might even have given him a drug test.

He'd also stolen her credit card from her desk drawer. It had been easy to use. He could have bought some serious shit with the card because it got accepted everywhere. But he exercised restraint, and only used it for gas and junk food. Just basics. Of course, she found out about that, too, and it stopped working a day or two after he ran away. He did bring the truck home right away, though. He was thinking his mom and Oscar might report it stolen. That's what some of his friends said they'd do. Another stolen truck. He could still hear the judge in Oregon saying he could have gotten thirty or forty years for the felonies up there. He brought the keys back, but did it so he wouldn't have to see her or Oscar.

His mom probably didn't know it, but that week he'd sneaked into the house one last time to get some of his things. He didn't take anything that didn't belong to him. There had been birthday and graduation money when he returned to Los Altos. He used practically all that money for new clothes. Clothes he liked—skater clothes—not the stuff his mother bought him. He went back for those few things he'd bought himself. She had already fixed the bedroom window he used to sneak in and out of, so he found another way into the house through his bathroom window. He took a warm jacket, a hat and a hoodie, some shirts and shorts, and a pair of shoes, things he thought he'd need. He never went back to the house after that. And he never contacted any of them, not even Lara or Max. Sometimes he told himself it didn't matter. He was adopted, so they weren't his real family. But he knew he was kidding himself.

At first he had a pretty good time, doing the same things he'd been doing the month before, when he was faking the tire job. He hung out with friends, got stoned, and watched movies. But he didn't have his truck anymore. He stayed at a friend's house. Mark was a guy he'd known in high school. Now Mark went to Continuation School. Mark's mom was a lonely, divorced lady. She was always a little tipsy in the evenings and liked it when he hung out in the kitchen with her.

"Joshua, you're such a sweetheart. You have the best manners. I wish some of that would rub off on Mark," she said.

"Yeah, well," he'd answered. "I just appreciate that you took me in after my parents kicked me out. I'd have nowhere to go if it wasn't for you," he told her.

"A nice boy like you is a pleasure to have around. You be sure to tell me if you want anything when I go shopping. Tell me if there are any special things you like to eat. You need some motherly love—anybody can see that," Mark's mom said, reaching up to hug him.

There was always food in the house, and except on those nights when she'd had too much to drink, she left them alone. This was all good for months. Joshua floated through the days and sometimes didn't even know, exactly, what day of the week it was. Sometimes he got up early with Mark and went to school with him. He'd found his dealer and went back in business selling, only this time to the Continuation School kids. They didn't have as much cash as the kids from the regular high school, but they were always looking for stuff, and they complained less about the price.

After a while, though, Mark got on his nerves, too. It was time to move on. He was finished with high school kids and their scene. He'd met some guys who offered to teach him to DJ, which was a good time. He went to raves, big dance parties in warehouses in Berkeley and Oakland, only he wasn't just one of the kids, he sat in the DJ booth, spinning. He loved it, and they paid him after he learned. But soon he was getting into trouble again with E. There was F. everywhere. He had once tried to explain about ecstasy to George, the drug counselor at the Villages.

"What's your drug of choice?" George asked him. "Most of the other kids like to drink or smoke weed. You never mention that stuff. What's your deal?"

"No, I don't care that much about alcohol," he'd told the counselor. "And I can take or leave pot. Me, personally, I like ecstasy."

"What do you like so much about it?" George asked.

It was hard for Joshua to answer George. The feelings he got from E were so powerful, it was frightening to even talk about. When he did speak about it, he craved it, even after being clean for months at the Villages.

"It makes me happy like nothing else," Joshua finally said. "I forget why I woke up bummed, or guilty, or depressed. It makes me feel peaceful. But then, I want more of it." He took in a deep breath and then exhaled it slowly. Deep breathing was something the staff recommended when he felt cravings.

He loved the stuff, pure and simple. And E was everywhere at raves. He began to take it like he'd taken it in high school, increasing to wicked amounts, six or eight or ten tabs a day. For a long time, this worked okay. Sometimes he'd dip into cocaine, which made him feel pretty good, too. But then, when he'd turned up the volume on what he was consuming, he couldn't really spin any longer. He developed a bad reputation for not showing up for DJ jobs or for leaving before he was supposed to. Eventually no one offered him gigs anymore.

At one rave, he ran into a girl, Sarah, who'd gone to Los Altos High with him and was now at Berkeley. She'd always had a crush on him, and she invited him home with her. She shared an apartment near the campus with two other girls. Sarah was smart and good to him. She cared about him and said she would help him get clean. And for a few weeks, he *was* clean. He thought Sarah was the love of his life. He slept on her couch, went back into NA, and tried to do everything right.

He was hopeful and even thought about contacting his mother during that time, to ask her for another chance. Sarah encouraged him to do that. She said he needed his family. But then, something happened to screw everything up. Sarah's sister, Dana, came to visit the Berkeley apartment.

He'd also gone to high school with Dana, but she had never been a fan of his.

"What the hell are you doing here?" she asked, when they were alone in the apartment for the first time. "Sarah's roommates say they're sick of you hanging out here all the time. They say you don't buy food or do anything but sit around stoned all day. They think Sarah's out of her mind for putting up with you."

"Listen, Dana," he said, and began folding the blanket always draped over the couch. "Sarah's roommates enjoy talking smack about me. But your sister is an angel. I'm starting to get my act together. I'm not using anymore. Sarah's been helping me."

"You know what I think?" Dana said, and stood above where he was sitting on the couch. "I think you're a loser. You're like a locust eating up everything in this apartment but contributing nothing. And I also think my sister is an enabler."

"You taking psychology in college?" he asked. "You trying to sound like a shrink or something? Sarah is just a nice girl with a big heart."

Dana shook her head. "My father is going to be really pissed off to hear his daughter has a drug addict staying in her apartment in Berkeley. My dad pays good money for her to live in this place."

Dana went home and told her parents God-knows-what crap about him. All sorts of shit came down after that. Sarah apologetically told him he had to leave immediately. She caved right after her parents said they'd stop paying her way through school if she didn't get him out of the apartment. She never stuck up for him at all. So much for the great love of his life.

Then things really turned bad. He forgot a lot of what happened during that time. He crashed in all sorts of places and met more people than he could remember. The faces went by in a blur. But always there were girls—good-looking girls, older girls, and younger girls. They wanted to take care of him. He'd tell them the standard story, that he had nowhere to go. They'd give him whatever he wanted . . . sex, money, food, clothes.

After a couple of years, he began to feel really bad. His teeth, especially, began to bother him. He'd always had lousy teeth. His mom told him he had the prettiest, straightest teeth in the family, but what she saved in orthodontist bills, she spent on getting his cavities fixed. Now, there was no one to pay for a dentist, and he always had a toothache. One time he felt really low, and almost called his mother. He needed help badly. He had an infection in his gums, and it hurt so much, he couldn't eat. He got really skinny. But then somebody told him about this dental clinic in Oakland for homeless kids. The clinic dentist told him the drugs he had been doing made his teeth bad, and the bones to hold them in weren't strong anymore, so his teeth were getting loose. The hygienist tried to get him to go to rehab, but he just got the dental work done. He wasn't ready for rehab yet.

It was another girl who finally got him to straighten out. Or he got her to straighten out. They both got clean, but she had been doing heroin and she went the methadone route. She was older than he was, nearly twenty-five. She had a hard, sexy look he liked, her long, dark hair swinging from side to side as she walked. They had the same gray-green eyes. People commented on this, sometimes even asking if they were related. She had been born in Oklahoma, and her name was Shawnee. She was named that because she had some Shawnee Indian blood in her. She might have been lying, but he knew she really liked to tell people she was Native American, so he never pushed the issue.

After they'd been together for almost a year, the biggest thing changed. He came home one day, and Shawnee was in the kitchen, standing at the sink crying.

"I'm pregnant," she blurted out when she saw him. Her shoulders shook, and her nose ran.

"Whoa. I thought you couldn't have kids. You told me there was something wrong with your tubes and the doctors said you couldn't ever get pregnant."

From the beginning of their relationship, she had told him she was infertile. But this certainly proved to be untrue.

It was the one thing he'd thought he would never let happen. He wasn't going to repeat what his own birth parents had done. He'd always used condoms, taking big handfuls from the bowls they kept at the clinics. He wasn't going to bring a baby into the world until he could do right by a child. But Shawnee had convinced him he didn't need rubbers and, stupidly, he'd believed her.

She'd gone to the emergency room because she'd been feeling really bad. She thought she had food poisoning or maybe had overdosed. Shawnee cried and cried that night after she told Joshua she was pregnant. She'd been using pretty heavily and knew what that meant for the baby. But he wouldn't let her get an abortion. He was all mixed up about it, but he just wouldn't let her do it. He yelled at her so much, she got scared.

"We'll clean up!" he shouted. "We'll get help, and you'll have the baby. That's final. You're not getting rid of it." The fight was the worst they'd ever had. The shouting went on for hours.

He had this certainty the baby was going to be all right, and even though the fighting got pretty ugly, Shawnee finally agreed.

"I'll stop using and do what the clinic doctors want me to do so I can have this baby."

EPILOGUE

She had to stay on methadone because the doctors said if she went into withdrawal, the baby would, too. Doctors at San Francisco General Hospital had plenty of experience with drug-addicted mothers, and they said this was the safest thing to do for the baby, both before and, if she going to breastfeed, after it was born.

He didn't know why, but it was like he came out of a fog when he discovered Shawnee was pregnant. His mom knew a lot about babies. She was kind of a baby nut. But he kept imagining her disapproval when she discovered both he and Shawnee had been using when they conceived a kid. It was the guilt again. His mother and guilt. His mom always said she wasn't disappointed in him and that she loved him as he was. But her eyes said something different. They said he was the biggest disappointment of her life.

He didn't call his mother.

Once they told people they were serious about cleaning up, they got plenty of help from clinics, nurses, and doctors. He and Shawnee found an apartment in a sober-living complex for families. He also got help finding a job. It was kind of screwed up because he was twenty-two years old, and he hadn't ever held a real job. There were a lot of things he hadn't ever done. But then, there were plenty of things he had.

He thought it wasn't too bad living a straight life and watching Shawnee get bigger, knowing she had his baby growing inside of her. However, Shawnee was worried Social Services would take away their baby, like they did her first child. She'd been using back then, too, but in an even worse way. She didn't even know who the father was. Sometimes when she talked about losing her first child, a boy, he thought she'd jump off the Golden Gate Bridge.

"Shawnee, it's going to be okay. I'm going to be here," he said.

"I couldn't stand it if they took this one away, too."

"Nobody is taking this baby away." He stroked her long hair. "It's our baby." And he meant it.

While Shawnee was pregnant, she spent a lot of time going to the methadone clinic and attending relapse prevention groups. They both went to classes to teach them about taking care of the baby. They were determined they'd do it right.

Every day, Joshua got out of bed, put on some shitty shirt and jeans, laced up his work boots, and went off to work. He had a job with a government program to retrofit public buildings so they'd withstand earthquakes, even the big one. He had to get up early and be on the job site by seven. Once he was there, it wasn't too bad. He liked the guys he worked with, but he didn't want to think too much about his life. Every day was the same. Nothing was ever different. His life was boring. Somehow, he'd imagined his life would be different.

Shawnee had their son in October. Joshua was twenty-two years old and a father. On the day the baby was born, he thought more about his birth father than he'd done in all the years of his life. He'd thought about Kelly a lot, but not his father. He had a lot of questions. Mostly, though, he thought the guy was a fucker. His father had let Kelly down, and so she'd had to give up her baby twenty-two years before. He wondered if his old man helped take care of his older brother.

He thought about his dad, Ron, as well, but didn't know exactly what to think. Everyone said Ron was a great guy, a man he should be proud to call his father, but he was a shadowy haze to him, a place they visited in the cemetery. A place where he and his mother brought beautiful stones and said prayers in Hebrew. He wished he remembered more about his dad, but they'd had so few years together.

Shawnee's labor was long and not what he expected. She made low growling noises that sounded more like an animal than a person. He wanted to run out of the hospital and get high. But they had a nurse, a guy, who helped them through Shawnee's labor. He told them he'd been an addict, too. He seemed to sense whenever Joshua was getting really scared.

Their nurse would say something like, "Joshua, she needs some ice chips now. Why don't you get some more ice and refill that cup?"

Or, "Joshua, the moms say it feels really good if you push down like this in the small of the back," and he'd show Joshua how to do it.

Shawnee would moan her approval. Helping Shawnee with her labor made Joshua feel better, and the desire to bolt out of the room and Shawnee's life passed. He didn't know how he was going to get through the birth, then afterwards take care of Shawnee and the baby and get a handle on his life. But he was sure he would.

When the baby crowned, and he saw the little whirl of hair, he knew the worst was over. Shawnee screamed with each push to get the baby out, but the screaming was better than the inhuman growling. They named the baby Chris. When he'd come home from the Villages, his mother had showed him his original birth certificate, the one Maya had helped him send to Wisconsin for. He discovered then Kelly had named him Christopher.

They tested the baby and he tested good. They checked out Chris's lungs, his heart, his hearing, and his sight. All his responses were normal. Chris didn't have any of the terrible deformities that could happen when a mom did drugs. Joshua wasn't sure if he believed in God, even after all his years in twelve-step programs, but if he did, he would call it a miracle.

From the beginning, everyone said the baby resembled Joshua. Joshua had to agree. The shape of his eyes, the roundness of his head, the well-formed lips . . . his son did look just like him. But nothing prepared him for what he felt when he held Chris to his chest. Tears easily came to Joshua's eyes in those first few days, sometimes dropping onto the top of Chris's head.

The doctors had to slowly get the baby off methadone, so they kept Chris in the hospital for a while. Joshua and Shawnee took turns visiting and feeding him, and he seemed to be a healthy little guy, bigger than most of the other babies in the newborn intensive care nursery, where he stayed at San Francisco General.

The staff seemed really proud of the baby, like they were responsible for his good health, high fiving each other when some new milestone was reached. Joshua and Shawnee took Chris home after only three weeks. The hospital staff said his stay was shorter than anyone had predicted, and they had a little going-away party in the hospital lounge. They gave Joshua and Shawnee a lot of really useful presents for the baby: a car seat, backpack, and clothing. They marveled over what a blessing it was that Chris was healthy and showed no signs of problems. Shawnee got a little pissed off when the hospital staff kept repeating how lucky they were. She said they were trying to make her feel worse for being an addict. But Joshua thought the staff was being really nice, and he appreciated all the baby things they received.

One of the nurses pulled him aside before they were going home and said, "We're all really proud of you and the way you take care of your little one. You're an awesome father to that baby of yours."

Joshua was embarrassed. He wondered if they said that to all the dads or just the dads who were former addicts and screwups. But he just shrugged and said, "I really love the little guy. I'm just trying to give him the best I can."

"You're doing a great job."

And Joshua thought the nurse seemed like she meant it.

Their apartment in the Haight looked pretty decent by the time they brought Chris home. They'd covered a piece of foam with yellow checkered cloth and put this on top of the bureau to make a changing table. Joshua built shelves above it so they could store things they needed for the baby: the diapers, powder, wipes, and a bowl for pacifiers. He was astounded at how much one little eight-pound baby required.

A year later, soon before Chris was going to have his first birthday, Joshua woke up and knew with certainty that the time had finally come to visit his mother. It was a Saturday, and he pulled himself out of bed and went to the crib. He picked up his son, who had just begun to stir. Shawnee worked evenings in a restaurant. She left for work right after he got home from his construction job, and she was always tired. He decided he'd let Shawnee sleep in and try to get the baby dressed and fed without her waking.

"Here you go, little man. Let's get these pajamas off and change you."

He peeled off Chris's flannel pajamas printed with the San Francisco 49ers logo. The pajamas were warm and fleecy, so Chris shivered from the cold when he undressed him. Chris kicked and waved his arms around. Joshua talked softly to his son, hoping the boy would not yell and wake up Shawnee. He dressed him in blue jeans and a bright green sweatshirt with alligators on it. Then he slipped green socks and sneakers onto his feet. The baby had taken his first steps about a week before, and each day he walked farther and more confidently. Joshua was proud of how coordinated Chris seemed. He learned everything fast.

"Come on, buddy," he said, and ran a comb through the boy's straight, silky hair, the same reddish blond he remembered seeing in his own baby pictures. "We've got a big day ahead of us. We're going to go see Grandma today. And Grandma really likes babies. She's going to think you are pretty darn cute."

He put a brown corduroy jacket on Chris, holding down the cuffs of the sweatshirt so they didn't get caught up in the sleeves of the jacket, something he suddenly remembered his mother doing for him when he was a little boy. He got dressed himself, then he filled Shawnee's diaper bag with extra clothes and diapers. With the baby on his hip, he went into the kitchen and put a banana in the bag, along with a few juice boxes and a Tippee cup.

Joshua slung the diaper bag over one shoulder and carried his son over to the bed where Shawnee was still sleeping, her long straight hair falling over her face. Joshua slid her hair back and kissed her on the cheek. She opened her eyes.

"I'm going to take the baby out for a few hours. Guys' day out. I'll call you. Get some rest," he whispered into her ear.

She nodded sleepily. He lowered Chris so that Shawnee could kiss the baby goodbye, too, and then carried his son to the street. The car was parked on Hayes. He fastened the baby into his car seat and gave him a hard teething biscuit as well as his special stuffed animal to play with, a soft, gray elephant named Boo. There would be little traffic going south on 101 this time on a Saturday. He and Chris would easily be in Los Altos by breakfast.

The house in Los Altos looked much the same as it had when Joshua left five years earlier. In these past few years, Eleanor and Oscar had replaced the redwood deck off the kitchen and planted a few more fruit trees behind the house. Oscar liked gardening, though the deer were increasing in number and nothing seemed to discourage them from gnawing on the bark of the citrus trees.

Oscar came into the kitchen just as Eleanor was pouring their cups of tea.

"You know what today feels like?" she asked her husband, looking out the window and up at the sky.

"Don't say it." He laughed, and put his hand lightly over her mouth.

"No, really, hon. It feels like earthquake weather."

QUESTIONS FOR DISCUSSION

1. In what ways does Joshua manifest his sweetness, as exemplified in the Buddha Within Him chapter?

2. In what ways is Eleanor clear-eyed about her son, and in what ways do we see her kidding herself.

3. Try to describe what factors you see as nature in Joshua.

4. Try to describe what factors you see as nurture in Joshua.

5. How do you think Joshua might have been different had he had more time with Ron?

6. What advice would you give to Eleanor before she sends him to Mount Richmond? Are there other options she may not have considered?

7. Explain what the epigraph of this novel, taken from A.M. Homes, means to you. *"To be adopted is to be amputated and sewn back together. Whether or not you regain full function, there will always be scar tissue."* Why would there be scar tissue, if an adoption takes place at, or very close to birth?

8. How can adoptive parents be better prepared before and after they adopt?

9. How close have you come, in your personal experience, to any members of the adoption triangle: a birth mother who relinquished her child, an adopted child, or an adoptive mother?

10. Have your ideas about adoption changed in any way after reading *The Earthquake Child*? What advice have you for parents who are contemplating adoption?

ACKNOWLEDGMENTS

The subject and activity of parenting is one that has consumed most of my adult life. Because of the many years between my oldest and youngest child, I've spent more years collecting trick or treat candy than anyone I know. Thank you to those four children and one step-child who taught me and humbled me and made me proud. And sometimes shared their candy.

This book is just one picture of adoption. Each adoption is different. I hoped to get this picture as right as I could in tone and detail. I thank my early readers who looked at the manuscript in various stages and shared details of their own adoption journeys. These include Melissa Hochler Ross, Pamela Hawes, Judy Levin, Dr. Lisa Clement, Susan Fagin, my dear sister-in-law Joan Klasson and my cousin, Elaine Gordon—all amazing nurturers and mothers of adopted children. I give them my gratitude, but take full responsibility for any mistakes in describing the adoption experience.

Thanks to Brooke Warner, publisher of She Writes Press, as well as Lauren Wise, Associate Publisher and Project Manager, who shepherded this manuscript and turned it into a book. Brooke's dream to create an alternative path for women writers' voices to be heard, has allowed so many She Writes Sisters' dreams to come true. She is a force in life and in publishing and for her I have the utmost admiration.

My admiration is unbounded for Alexis Schoppe, who consistently fills the blanks in my knowledge of social media and gracefully brings me into the twenty-first century.

Thank you to friends near and far who have sustained me through the Earthquake Child's actual and literary journey. They include Eleanor Intrator (for everything), Jan Schwartz, Marie Rector and Rhonda Lappen—the Gang of Five. I also thank Katherine Koch and Ariadne Weaver for listening as I revised and edited. And Barbara Stark Nemon, She Writes Press sister, for her ear.

From the deepest place in my heart, I thank my Earthquake Child, who rocked and changed my world.

Finally, I thank Bill Klasson and David Wong. Both men believed in me and understood my passion to tell stories. They gave me love that filled my cup to overflowing. My sister once said many women are not as fortunate as me to have found such great and sustaining love. Lucky me, I found it twice.

ABOUT THE AUTHOR

Elayne Klasson grew up on Chicago's northside. She attended university and graduate school in the Midwest, Ohio State University and the University of Michigan, earning a Masters of Public Health and then a PhD in psychology. She lived and worked in Barbados, West Indies, for many years. Her professional career has been in academia at San Jose State University, with her research and clinical area of expertise being the severely mentally ill. A transplant to the Santa Ynez Valley in California, she is a popular lifestyle newspaper columnist there. She has also appeared on San Francisco public television as a restaurant critic. Elayne is the author of the National Jewish Book Award finalist and best sell ing *Love is a Rebellious Bird*. She and her husband, David, have five children between them, biological and adopted.

SELECTED TITLES FROM SHE WRITES PRESS

She Writes Press is an independent publishing company
founded to serve women writers everywhere.
Visit us at www.shewritespress.com.

Love is a Rebellious Bird by Elayne Klasson. $16.95, 978-1-63152-604-6.
From childhood all the way through to old age, Judith adores Elliot Pine—a
beautiful, charismatic and wildly successful man—bound to him by both
tragedy and friendship. He defines the terms of their relationship; he holds
the power. Until finally, in old age, the power shifts.

The End of Miracles by Monica Starkman. $16.95, 978-1-63152-054-9.
When a pregnancy following years of infertility ends in late miscarriage,
Margo Kerber sinks into a depression—one that leads her, when she
encounters a briefly unattended baby, to commit an unthinkable crime.

How to Grow an Addict by J.A. Wright. $16.95, 978-1-63152-991-7.
Raised by an abusive father, a detached mother, and a loving aunt and
uncle, Randall Grange is built for addiction. By twenty-three, she knows
that together, pills and booze have the power to cure just about any problem she could possibly have . . . right?

Profound and Perfect Things by Maribel Garcia. $16.95, 978-1-63152-
541-4. When Isa, a closeted lesbian with conservative Mexican parents,
has a one-night stand that results in an unwanted pregnancy, her sister,
Cristina adopts the baby—but twelve years later, Isa, who regrets giving
up her child, threatens to spill the secret of her daughter's true parentage.

The Trumpet Lesson by Dianne Romain. $16.95, 978-1-63152-598-8.
Fascinated by a young woman's performance of "The Lost Child" in
Guanajuato's central plaza, painfully shy expat Callie Quinn asks the
woman for a trumpet lesson—and ends up confronting her longing to
know her own lost child, the biracial daughter she gave up for adoption
more than thirty years ago.

Eden by Jeanne Blasberg. $16.95, 978-1-63152-188-1. As her children and
grandchildren assemble for Fourth of July weekend at Eden, the Meister
family's grand summer cottage on the Rhode Island shore, Becca decides
it's time to introduce the daughter she gave up for adoption fifty years ago.